7/18

THE
KHAKI MAFIA

THE KHAKI MAFIA

a novel by

ROBIN MOORE AND JUNE COLLINS

CROWN PUBLISHERS, INC · NEW YORK

Library of Congress Catalog Card Number: 79–168317

Printed in the United States of America

Published simultaneously in Canada by General Publishing Company Limited

Design by Nedda Balter

THE
KHAKI MAFIA

PART ONE

1

JUNE, 1967

Not far outside the main gate of Fort Benning, Georgia, stood a thirty-thousand-dollar house belonging to Master Sergeant Elroy James. For years, in recognition of his skills and proclivities, the sergeant had enjoyed the well-deserved sobriquet, Jesse James. In the summer of 1967 a meeting of far-reaching importance took place at the home of Sergeant James. In the course of one long night, the Vietnam Battle Plan to be put into operation by the most efficient criminal syndicate ever to get a stranglehold on the United States Army was laid out by experts in the field. It had required months of careful preparation to bring about this summit meeting of what was soon to become known as "the Khaki Mafia."

The plan was conceived by the one man capable of executing it— Thomas Cotsworth, Sergeant Major of the United States Army. Cotsworth had been at Fort Benning for several days, planning the meeting. At nine in the evening everyone who had been invited was seated in the basement recreation room of the James home. Although every man in the room with one exception was on active duty, all wore civilian clothes. Cotsworth, standing in front of an array of maps, photographs, a blackboard, and a white screen, presided.

"Men, this is the first and last meeting of its kind that will ever be held in this country." He had a mellifluous southern accent, but his words were sharp and precise. "So listen and watch carefully. But do not make notes."

Cotsworth nodded respectfully to a gray-haired, florid-complexioned man at the rear of the room. "Before going any further let me welcome our old boss from Germany, Major General, retired, Arjay Crowninshed, to this meeting. We are happy to have you here, sir."

11

"It's good to see all of you again, Cotsworth," Crowninshed acknowledged in a gruff, commanding voice.

"Now men," Cotsworth continued, "I know two of you have a midnight hop out of here. So I'll make this as short as I can. This briefing took some tight scheduling. I had to take over the KC-135 assigned to the Commanding General in Vietnam to get Gambino and me here. So let's get down to business." Cotsworth looked slowly from man to man until he had met the eyes of each of the sergeants sitting in front of him.

"We all made ourselves some money with the Twenty-seventh Division in Germany. It got plenty hairy a couple of times, but two separate investigations were defused thanks to General Crowninshed here. Then Willy Halaby got himself caught skimming the NCO Club slot machines." Cotsworth looked reproachfully at Halaby, who grinned sheepishly and studied the tips of his highly polished shoes.

"Red Fisher didn't destroy the records of the club system in time," Cotsworth continued, looking at Sergeant First Class William Fisher, whose face began to match the color of his flaming red hair. Unlike the other sergeants, Fisher was lean, almost cadaverous.

"Jesse," Fisher said, turning to his host, "it took some doing to cover up for you paying the labor to renovate this house with NCO club funds." Master Sergeant James shifted his bulk uneasily, his small eyes staring out of his fleshy face at Sergeant First Class Ben Bigley, a plump man whose heavy jowls always showed a black stubble of unshaven beard.

"Ben," Cotsworth continued, "when you fixed up the records of the clubs that make up the Fort Benning Open-Mess System last month, did you have to let that female auditor find out what you were doing?"

Bigley shook his head, his fat cheeks quivering. "I don't know how it happened, Tom, I swear. I've been fixing records for eight years, and this the first time I ever got caught."

"Well I had to get the Provost Marshal of the Army to squelch the CID on that one." Cotsworth said. He looked about the room. "Just because you're home doesn't mean you can get careless. And Pancho, damn it!" He looked squarely at the swarthy sergeant major, Hernandez O'Leary. "The Inspector General's office knew damn well you'd taken a hundred cases of liquor from the clubs. I had a hell of a time keeping them from getting a search warrant to go through your house." He shook his head. "Anyway, you'll be retired in a week and they won't bother with you no more."

Cotsworth paused. His brown eyes could look deceptively lethargic or could lance a man he meant to rebuke. He was clearly a strong, forceful leader. Even the retired general, his ex-boss, sat attentively when Cotsworth talked.

"But we're not here to rake up old goofs," Cotsworth said with an understanding smile. "We came out of all the investigations smelling like a rose. The CID records have been sanitized or destroyed, and we all profited right handsomely.

"But now to present business," he went on. "You've been here at Benning or some other stateside post for two years now and it's time to move on. All right, men, this is it. What we've done up to now is fun and games compared to what we're going to do. If every man in this room isn't a millionaire in the next three years it's his own fault. We've got to work together, cooperate, and we'll make it big. In the next few months we'll all be going to Vietnam. I've got it worked out at OPO. Once you hit your assigned divisions in Vietnam, the division sergeant majors will assign you straight into the club system."

The room stirred with excitement.

"Goddamnit," Cotsworth went on, "it's the biggest opportunity for a team like this in the history of the U.S. military. There should be about six hundred thousand troops in Vietnam by mid-sixty-eight, and if we work it right, the way I have things planned, we'll run every enlisted men's and NCO club in the Nam, the whole damn Open-Mess System. We thought we had something when we had the Twenty-seventh Division locked up?" He laughed. "Ten thousand men? With all the civilian competition on top? Man, that was Monopoly money compared to what's waiting for us. We can have it all!"

Cotsworth's words sent shivers of anticipatory greed down the backs of the men listening to him. "Now let me brief you on what's coming up in the Nam." He turned to a large map of the Republic of Vietnam and picked up a pointer.

"Okay. Here's Saigon. Right around it, here at Long Binh, we have the headquarters of USARV, United States Army Republic of Vietnam. It's about twenty miles south of Saigon. By the beginning of nineteen sixty-eight there'll be at least twenty thousand troops there."

He moved the pointer across the map and tapped again. "Now here's Bien Hoa, maybe twenty-five miles from Saigon; the Hundred and First Airborne is here. In the Bien Hoa, Long Binh, Saigon triangle we have the First Division, the Second Field Force, and the Hundred and Ninety-ninth Brigade. A little further out, at Cu Chi, is the Twenty-fifth Division. Begin to see the target?"

Cotsworth ran the pointer north and paused. "Here's Pleiku, three hundred miles north of Saigon. The Fourth Infantry Division is building up here. And further north, getting close to the DMZ"—the pointer tapped the map—"is Chu Lai where the American Division is headquartered."

The Sergeant Major of the United States Army grinned at his cohorts and ran the pointer back down the map south of Saigon. "This here is a swamp called Dong Tam. But the Army Engineers are filling it in and building a big new base for the Ninth Division. Dong Tam is going to be the

13

most important base we got in the Mekong Delta supporting the Viet-namese army or ARVN. We can expect the Ninth in Dong Tam early in sixty-eight."

Cotsworth put down his pointer. "Our first objective is to take over the clubs at each of these key points. At the Pentagon I'm pushing plans ahead so that each division goes on the open-mess system and the thirty or so club managers in each division will report to one of our experienced sergeants who I'll see gets in as custodian of all the enlisted men's and NCO clubs in each division. Right now every club manager runs his own club. Our first objective in Vietnam, then, is to take over every club in the country."

"Sounds golden, Tiger," Jesse James exclaimed. "Can you fix up the transfers?"

"I'll have it done before my time as Sergeant Major of the Army is up the end of this years. My next objective is assignment as command sergeant major of Military Assistance Command Vietnam."

General Crowninshed nodded approvingly. "As top NCO at MACV you can really help us, Tom."

"That's right, sir." He turned to the others. "The general's got him a fine civilian job as head of Orient Architecture and Engineering in Vietnam. OAE is the biggest construction complex in Asia. We'll be doing a lot of business with the boss."

"When do we start?" Red Fisher asked eagerly.

"Well, right now our friend Earl Picking is the custodian at Long Binh, one of the places already on the open-mess system. He's straight, but he'll help us move in. Jesse, I've set it for you to take over at Long Binh. I'll get the rest of you in one by one. By early sixty-eight we ought to have control. I'll be in Saigon before the end of January. Now, if you'll look at the screen, I'm going to flash a few pictures to familiarize you with some of the people we'll be dealing with."

Cotsworth walked to the back of the recreation room where a slide projector was set up. He pressed a button, and a color slide was projected on the screen. It showed a handsome man with a big toothy smile and black wavy hair, his arm around a petite blonde. Behind them was a sleek twin-engine executive jet.

"You're looking at Ronnie Jasper, head man at Jasper Promotions. He is one of the biggest bookers of military-club shows operating in Vietnam." Cotsworth paused a moment as the men stared at the screen. "Ronnie pays off the major in flight manifesting and flies around the country in a military VIP jet. His business is big, but it will be a lot bigger as more and more clubs open up."

Cotsworth looked away from the screen and spoke to a swarthy sergeant with black hair longer than that worn by most sergeants. "Tony, tell us about your meeting with Jasper in Nha Trang last week."

14

Sergeant Tony Gambino's grating voice filled the room. "Knowing that the Tiger here was getting me this special emergency leave to say good-bye to my dying mother," he began, a smirk on his face, "I set up a meet with Ronnie Jasper in Nha Trang, where I have a half-assed enlisted men's club on the beach. Jasper is ready to pay us fifty bucks on every show we book from him. He's not the only booking agent, there's about twenty, but he's about the biggest. Once he starts to pay, all the others will have to follow him. He has six or seven shows now, but he expects to have fifteen going by early sixty-eight. His shows usually put on one performance a night at two different clubs. This means our syndicate will take in about fifteen hundred dollars every night of the year from Jasper alone. The total take on shows should be ten times that." Gambino chuckled. "And that Ronnie, he has other benefits to offer. Dig that broad beside him? She's one of the singers he books."

Gambino leered at the other sergeants and turned to Cotsworth. "Give the guys a break and flash on the next slide, Tiger." A new picture filled the screen—a remarkably ample-bosomed girl with wide brown eyes and a pretty face around which blond hair cascaded. She was standing on a side-walk in front of a handsome balconied villa. Vietnamese men and women in the background established the location of the scene.

"I'm ready to go," Red Fisher said.

"Who dat, Tony?" a husky voice growled.

"You are looking at Jody T. Neale," Gambino replied. "The villa behind her is the private club she runs in Nha Trang. She also puts on strip shows. Jody T. is as smart as she is pretty. I figure when we get our operation going she can be real useful to us."

"I'm all for that," Ben Bigley guffawed. "Any more like her?"

"If there are, I don't know where," Gambino replied.

"Thanks, Tony," Cotsworth cut in, his voice businesslike. "We'll hear from you again later." He pressed the button and a new picture came on—a rather haggard-looking man standing by a swimming pool, a cane clutched in his right hand. He was attempting a smile, and it was evident that his eyes were slightly crossed. On either side of him stood a lovely, slender Vietnamese girl wearing the traditional *au dai*.

"There is the man we'll be doing a lot of business with," Cotsworth said. "His name is Joe Crust. He's one of the richest Americans in the Orient. His company is called Snead Electronics. Crust now controls the slot ma-chines in the club system, and he's figuring on expanding in a big way. He's both our competitor and our partner. We'll have to work with him for now, but as soon as we get set we'll give him a taste of what we can do, what we can buy, and who we can buy from. Crust is very close to General Robert Hare, who runs the support complex up in Vinh Duc, a couple of hundred miles north of Saigon."

On the screen flashed a picture of a stout officer of medium height with crew-cut gray hair and a seamed face. He appeared to be in his mid-fifties or older. "Just three weeks ago I found out that General Hare is going to be the Deputy Chief of Staff and G-1 at USARV, starting in September or October. That means that among other things he controls all personnel assignments in Vietnam." Cotsworth paused a moment, then said, "General Crowninshed, could you tell us something about General Hare?"

Crowninshed cleared his throat. "Well I've known General Hare for many years. Just last month I talked to him in Vietnam after Sergeant Major Cotsworth and I explored some of the possibilities available to this organization over there. General Hare is willing to cooperate. As a matter of fact, he is here at Fort Benning now between assignments. I will be speaking to him later tonight. From now on, I'll act as liaison between us and General Hare. Naturally he must act with caution, but he knows the value of working with this group."

"Thank you, sir," Cotsworth said. "Now let's get into the business of protection. At the moment we don't have any on the spot in Vietnam, it's all in the Pentagon. We do have Major General Trenton Walter, the Provost Marshal General, working with us closely. He was the man who stopped the CID investigation on our action in Germany."

"With a little help," Crowninshed guffawed.

"That's for sure, sir," Cotsworth agreed. "And I have some influence with the Chief of Staff." He looked about the room as the men chuckled. Cotsworth was the Chief's right-hand man. "Okay. Gambino goes back in a few days. Tony, until General Hare gets settled in at USARV in Long Binh, we can't fix anything in Vietnam. So you be careful. I don't want to expose General Walter any more than we have to."

"I'm being careful, Tom. We sure used him to get to this meeting on time," Gambino replied. "Nha Trang doesn't give me much scope to operate anyway."

"I hear you're logging a lot of Saigon time," Cotsworth commented with a laugh.

"I'll tell you all about that later, Tiger. But I have been setting up a nice little mob of hoods we can use when we need them. There's about a hundred American deserters living in Cholon, the Chinese section of Saigon. I've made contact with one of the leaders of this rat pack. We can hire them to do anything for us."

Cotsworth gave Gambino a pleased look. "Our advance man is doing a good job for us," he remarked, flashing another picture on the screen. There were a few low whistles at the voluptuous brunette standing by a tall, thin meek-looking man with a toothbrush moustache. "Give them a rundown on the broad, Tony," Cotsworth said.

"That's Lavinia Ferris and her husband, Norm. He looks like a dick head, but he's smart as they come. They have a company called L & N Supply. They deal in anything that's profitable. They call themselves interior

16

decorators, and they've been operating in Saigon about a year. I gave them the job of decorating my club in Nha Trang. They can build clubs, decorate them, and sell the furniture. They come through with ten percent of the budget as a kickback for whoever gives them the job. And that Lavinia—" Gambino winked lewdly and chuckled. "All I can say is you'll get total service when you deal with the Ferrises."

"Right," Cotsworth cut Gambino off. "There are a lot of salesmen operating in Saigon now. We're going to have to squeeze them out or make them work for us."

Cotsworth switched off the slide projector and walked to the front of the room. "We've got a lot more briefing to cover tonight, but before we get to that I want to mention in front of General Crowninshed that we've started a corporation. So far the stockholders are myself, Jesse James, Ben Bigley, and Red Fisher, but you'll all be invited to become stockholders. We call the company Vamalot."

Costworth grinned shyly. "We took the first letters of our wives' names —Valerie, Mary, Lorraine, and Theresa—and put them together. The lawyers said we would be best off with a corporation. Pancho O'Leary will be a civilian in a month; he'll be running the company out of Saigon. Vamalot is the sales corporation the clubs will be buying from next year.

"Sound way to do it," Crowninshed acknowledged.

"Glad you approve, sir," Cotsworth replied. "The way I figure it," he continued, "by early sixty-eight we should have most of the divisions in Vietnam on the open-mess system. Oh, there'll be some holdouts by division commanders who say that individual battalions can run their clubs. But eventually we will have every club in Vietnam on the open-mess system— our open-mess system."

Cotsworth paused for emphasis and then continued. "There will be clubs and facilities to be built, furniture to purchase, decorations to be put in, liquor to buy, shows to hire, and of course the slot machines. Then there are the concessions to be given out. Gift shops can be a big source of revenue. It will be our objective to standardize all purchases and expenditures, taking a cut of ten to fifteen percent of everything we buy from the salesmen. And of course I expect that the biggest-selling organization will be Vamalot. No salesman will refuse to pay the commission, since they can raise their prices to compensate. Now I expect that every custodian will in turn pay back to the syndicate one half of all the money he collects on kickbacks. This money will pay for his protection and other help from my level. We will be well protected, I can promise you."

Willy Halaby's voice rasped out. "All that sounds good to me, Tiger. Just one thing though. This Vamalot has things going both ways. It's running the syndicate, so it gets half of all the bread we custodians turn in, and on top of that it makes a hell of a profit as a selling organization."

Cotsworth threw the sergeant an aggrieved look. "Willy, Vamalot will have a lot of muscle, of course, but the syndicate and Vamalot are not the same body. Syndicate money goes to the people that make it possible for you custodians to put half of everything you can take into your own pockets." There was unbroken silence a moment as Cotsworth stared at Halaby, whose surly expression faded, and whose eyes finally turned from Cotsworth's.

"Willy, if you want to, you can buy into Vamalot. We'll talk about that later. Vamalot expects to be moving in on the PX business." Cotsworth looked about the room again. "In case you didn't know it, the Post Exchange stores do the second-largest merchandising business in the world. Only Sears, Roebuck does a bigger volume. We'll be turning over a lot of merchandise through the PXs in the Nam."

"I'd like to buy into that Vamalot action," Gambino said.

"We'd be happy to have you in, Tony," Cotsworth said graciously. "Now,"—he became businesslike again—"we have one more objective. We will have to set up a safe system for changing local currency and MPC—you know, military payment certificates, scrip—into green dollars. General Crowninshed will be the key to that operation."

"I reckon you boys are going to make a real killing," Crowninshed commented.

"Whatever we do, you'll be part of, sir. The way it's always been," Cotsworth said smoothly. "Men, you'll get to know OAE pretty well on your tour. The company has thousands of people—Americans, Koreans, Filipinos, and Vietnamese—on its payroll. It legitimately moves tremendous sums of currency all over Asia and out of the United States. When we all arrive in this country, we'll have to figure out how our currency operations will work. But for now," Cotsworth went on, "if there are no questions we'll adjourn the meeting. I'll be seeing you all soon in Vietnam."

18

2

APRIL, 1969

The Monday after Easter Week of 1969, Senator Michael Rothmann called his special assistant, Richard Townsend, into the private office. Senator Rothmann looked up at the strong features of his well-built young assistant. "Richard, I think we're on to something of great importance. Have you any idea what goes on behind the scenes in our support activities in the Vietnam war?"

Rick shrugged his shoulders. "The usual I suppose, supply and maintenance. I was never assigned to Vietnam. Germany, remember? Counterintelligence."

"In any case," Rothmann went on, "the committee staff is developing a file on fraud and corruption in the management of the military-club systems, and another on currency manipulation. The enormity of this situation is shocking. We've just started to scratch the surface. You'll be working with your friend O'Neill on this."

Rick smiled to himself. "How did O'Neill dig this one up?"

"An article in *Life* magazine caught his attention," Rothmann said. "It was about American carpetbaggers operating in Vietnam."

"I remember the story," Rick said. "It came out just before I went on vacation."

"A lot has developed since then. Go down and see O'Neill. Naturally he wants the committee to authorize a complete investigation. I'll be most interested in your reaction."

Kasimer O'Neill—anyone who hoped for his friendship never uttered his first name—was a stocky man of medium height. His countenance, though not really unfriendly, was as inscrutable as that of the wiliest Oriental merchant or politician or waiter. A man in his mid-forties, he wore his hair, black without a trace of gray, in a neat medium-length cut. O'Neill's blue eyes were always deceptively calm and never seemed to reflect what was going on inside, although he occasionally allowed himself to show excitement when he wanted to generate enthusiasm in others. He was, Rick Townsend had always thought, a formidable man, and one he would never completely understand. It was no wonder O'Neill was a confirmed bachelor.

"What's it all about, O'Neill?" Rick asked, as he entered O'Neill's office.

"Good morning, Rick," O'Neill gave him one of his quick, tight smiles.

"It could be the biggest thing the committee has taken on in the fifteen years I've been with the staff." He picked up a notebook from his desk. "Here's some information that came in over the transom. An American husband and wife interior-decorating team paying thousands of dollars in kickbacks for contracts to build and decorate enlisted men's and NCO clubs."

"The Army hires interior decorators?" Rick exclaimed.

O'Neill nodded. "Apparently hundreds of thousands of dollars are spent on construction and furnishings by the military-club system. But this is only a small part of what's going on over there. As much as a million and a half dollars a week goes out of Vietnam illegally to banks in Switzerland, Hong Kong, and the United States."

"The boss says you want to go all out on the investigation," Rick prompted.

"It's all there. Stolen PX goods on the black market, thousands of slot machines, kickbacks to club custodians by entertainers, black-market money exchange, generals getting paid. We're calling this ring of sergeants and civilians who have been diverting millions of dollars to their personal accounts the Khaki Mafia."

O'Neill shook his head. "The implications are more far-reaching than anything we've investigated before." His eyes shone with excitement.

"The operative word, Mr. Townsend," O'Neill's voice quivered with intensity, "is nonappropriated funds. The United States military business enterprises, operated for servicemen through funds generated by their own purchases, out of their own paychecks, does six billion dollars' worth of business a year. The worldwide PX system, the GI clubs, and the slot machines together make up one of the world's largest single commercial concerns."

Rick shook his head as he absorbed the information. "Who regulates this business? Some general? A civilian? A commission?"

O'Neill twitched a smile. "It is totally unregulated. Since no taxpayers' money is directly involved, the government has adopted a laissez-faire attitude towards this gigantic operation. However, a syndicate appears to be in existence that is systematically looting the nonappropriated funds to the tune of billions a year."

From under his desk blotter O'Neill pulled a sheet of paper on which he had penciled a diagram. "This is my idea of how the syndicate is structured," he said, sliding the paper across the table to Rick. "Purely educated conjecture, but I think I'm close. The syndicate is divided into two basic sections. One is protection, the other is operations. On the Pentagon level, here at the top of the chart, are two boxes."

Rick stared at the two boxes on the top of what looked like the organizational chart of a large corporation. On the protection side of the chart, the top box read, "Provost Marshal General." On the operations side, the box read "Assignments." Rick whistled. "You think the Provost Marshal General of the Army is in on this?"

"Either him or someone who has tremendous influence over General Walter," O'Neill replied.

"And who in assignments is part of the syndicate?"

"I don't know yet."

Rick looked down at the next box, which was in the middle of the chart straddling operations and protection on the Republic of South Vietnam level. This box was labeled "Capabilities." Rick read aloud.

"Vietnam assignments, control of Provost Marshal and CID at MACV level, control of PXs, muscle at USARV over the Long Binh post commander—a colonel." Rick looked up at O'Neill. "Does one officer have all those capabilities?"

O'Neill nodded. "General Robert Hare, G-One, that's the personnel officer of the U.S. Army Vietnam."

Rick continued to look down the chart. On the protection side was a box in which was written, "Provost Marshal and CID (Criminal Investigation Division) MACV." To the left, on the operations side, were three boxes in a row. The level was marked "Money Generators." The first box was marked "EM and NCO clubs, Open-Mess System." The second box was simply labeled "PXs"; the third, "Currency Manipulations." Under the "clubs" box were eight boxes in a row marked with the names of the divisions and large installations in Vietnam. Below the "currency" box were two boxes, one labeled "Indian Money Changers" and the other "Swiss, Hong Kong, and U.S. Bank Accounts."

On the next-lowest level, still on the operations side of the chart, was a box marked "Enforcers." Spread across the bottom of the chart was a large box marked "Sales Organizations."

"That's the picture as best I can project it from here," O'Neill said. "What we've got to do is fill in the names of the people that belong in these boxes and document their operations."

"What about the big boss, the brains, the top honcho of this syndicate?" Rick asked. "Where is he on the chart?"

"That I don't know. It could be a military man or a civilian. Where he fits I have no idea." The frosty smile momentarily cracked O'Neill's lips. "That's going to be the toughest part of our job. We may not find him. Maybe he doesn't exist. But someone has to keep this apparatus in motion.

My guess is that we'll find him, or as close as anyone comes to being him, in this big box marked 'Sales Organizations.' I'll bet he will be closely associated with the slot machines. That's where the biggest piece of this whole action comes from."

"Who are the enforcers?" Rick asked.

"I don't know, but after fifteen years of investigating organized crime I do know that without the killers there is no discipline in syndicate operations, and without hard discipline an organization like this ceases to exist."

"What's our schedule?" Rick asked, excitement in his voice.

"We should be able to start hearings in the fall if the committee decides to go ahead."

"The Senator told me to work with you."

"Then pack your kit. We're going to Bangkok, Saigon, Hong Kong, and wherever else this investigation leads us. You're going to see generals fall and maybe even a former top Sergeant Major of the U.S. Army court-martialed."

"I'm ready, O'Neill." The enthusiasm generated by the usually taciturn senior investigator was infectious.

"Sorry you can't bring a female investigator along." O'Neill turned his bleak smile on the younger man.

"Oh, come on, O'Neill. You know I never try to mix business and pleasure."

O'Neill ignored Rick's protest. "I'm afraid there's going to be more danger than pleasure on this trip. By the way, I could use some help building up the files on the sergeants and generals we already know are in this ring. Can you spend the afternoon over at the CID office at Fort Holabird?"

Rick stood up. "I expect so. I'll go back to the office and make sure the Senator is taking me off everything else."

"Do that, Rick. We're well into April now. If we're going to be ready to go to the hearings in October, we have a hell of a lot of work ahead of us."

The final week in May, O'Neill and Rick Townsend met in Saigon. O'Neill had come in from Hong Kong where he had spent two weeks of exhaustive research at the many banks handling Saigon accounts. Rick's last two weeks had been devoted to taking depositions from American businessmen and promoters who had worked all over Southeast Asia and were currently engaged in activities in Singapore and Thailand. The American expatriates who devoted their lives to hustling in the East were a colorful lot of adventurers, gunrunners, and edge players who shared one common concept—it is more rewarding spiritually and financially to make money illegally in the Orient than to earn an honest living at home. Most of them had been away from the United States for many years and had never paid a tax dollar in a lifetime of intrigue. All of these schemers knew each other and had formed alliances at one time or another. Invariably, circumstances had conspired to

22

cause most of them to have betrayed one another at some crucial point over the years, so that virulent hatreds ensued. Rick had been able to take advantage of several such feuds to gather valuable information about the individuals who engaged in fraudulent and corrupt activities in Vietnam.

In a way Rick almost envied these people. Each one seemed to have his own little fiefdom where he was undisputed lord of the manor and its surrounding properties. Some of them had hundreds of Orientals in thralldom. All had a base of operations in apparently legitimate landholdings and business: rubber plantations, ocean-front real estate, docks and shipping, air-charter services, or many of the other burgeoning business enterprises in the Orient. Although they made money out of the Vietnam war, few maintained their main base of operation in that war-torn country. The Philippines and Malaysia were the favorite home areas for these people. Even Thailand was beginning to appear a little risky, although some of the Caucasian robber barons of the Far East were too firmly entrenched in Siamese enterprises to extricate themselves. They lived like sheikhs, complete with harems of Oriental women, whom most of them preferred to white women. None of them had any desire ever to return to the United States.

All of these expatriates watched for opportunities to profit, legally or illegally, from the Vietnam war and maintained Saigon residences and offices. The civilian air-charter entrepreneurs made vast sums moving opium from Vietnam to processing factories in Thailand and Hong Kong. By 1968 the American operators, with the aid of the American military and civilian officials who now controlled the destiny of Vietnam and its people, had firmly wrested the lucrative opium trade from the former French and Corsican exploiters. Although many of the American expatriates Rick and O'Neill questioned were happy in their own territory, safely away from the war, few of them could resist the rich spoils available in Vietnam. The war couldn't go on forever, they realized mournfully. And so it was, back and forth, from the palatial holdings near such relatively peaceful cities as Kaula Lampur, Singapore, Bangkok, Hong Kong, Taipai, Manila, to Saigon, where the loot was being taken.

In the USAID (United States Agency for International Development) Building Number One in Saigon, an air-conditioned office was assigned to the Senate investigating team. Rick and O'Neill, traveling as GS-18s, the civilian rank equivalent to lieutenant general, found their facilities highly satisfactory. They drew fifty dollars a day in counterpart funds for expenses. These government funds, somewhat equivalent to blocked currency, could only be spent in the host country in which the local currency was issued.

O'Neill had been in Saigon several days when Rick arrived from Bangkok in the middle of the afternoon. They immediately began comparing notes. "All the old names from Germany are showing up here," O'Neill observed grimly. "Major General Arjay Crowninshed, ex-commander of the Twenty-seventh Division, has been a civilian here for more than two years now. He runs the Saigon office of Orient Architecture and Engineering. His old sergeant major, Cotsworth, is the most powerful enlisted man in Vietnam. Sergeant Elroy James is custodian of all the NCO clubs at Long Binh. He's got forty-one units under his control. Master Sergeant Ben Bigley has thirty-eight clubs. And of course Brigadier General Robert Hare, our old friend 'Rabbit,' is G-One at USARV. He really does exercise control over the Provost Marshal and the CID."

"I also found something interesting in the CID files here this morning," O'Neill said. "There was an Australian girl in Vietnam for almost three years. Her name is Jody T. Neale. She seems to have been around the country doing a lot of shows for the troops. She even did a magic show. Then she took to booking shows as an agent. She ran into the Khaki Mafia and, since she objected to paying off, they put her out of business."

"Follows," Rick commented.

"Well, she submitted a detailed statement to the CID giving one of the best descriptions of the way Cotsworth and his mob have sewed up the club system that I've ever read. I'd sure like to find her."

"Didn't they have her address?"

"Yes. But she wasn't there. It seems she's gone back to Australia."

"So we fly Down Under and find her," Rick declared.

"It might be worth the trip," O'Neill agreed.

"I wonder what she looks like," Rick mused.

"I wonder what she knows," O'Neill countered. "With three years experience in the American underworld over here, it should be plenty. The files say she hit Saigon the summer of sixty-six, just as the big troop buildup was cresting."

3

JUNE, 1966

In her five years in the Orient Jody T. Neale had never felt heat like the blast that hit her as she deplaned for the first time in Saigon in June of 1966. Hong Kong, just two and a half hours behind her, had been moderate by comparison. For a moment she was tempted to step back on the plane and make the return trip north. But a new adventure lay before her. She was determined to make a fortune in the upward spiraling war economy in Vietnam and return to her native Australia and open that club in Sydney she had been dreaming of for so many years.

She would be much happier if she could make her fortune with someone more attractive than the liquor salesman she had become acquainted with in Korea. The deal was that she would be selling jewelry at U.S. Army installations. Jody walked down the ramp and followed the crowd to the terminal of Saigon's Tan Son Nhut International Airport.

Jody had been brought up in Sydney by her mother's wealthy parents. She was driven in a chauffeured limousine to the best girls' school in Sydney, at which she was always at the top of her class. Her friends came from the city's finest families, and she went to the nicest parties. Then, at fifteen, her idyllic existence was shattered. Her mother married a romantic though indigent sheep-station hand. Jody's grandparents withdrew all support of their granddaughter and, when Jody was forced to leave Sydney for the squalor of the sheep station on which her stepfather labored, she found herself out from under the protection of the candy-striped umbrella her grandparents had always held over her.

From being one of the wealthiest girls at the top of her class in the best school in Sydney, she became one of the poorer girls in a third-rate country school and dropped to the lower section of her class. The experience indelibly impressed upon her the value of money.

When Jody was eighteen she went to a football match in Sydney and fell in love with the star of the team. She arranged to meet him secretly, despite the strict regimen her grandparents imposed upon her during her brief stays with them, and fell into her first love affair. Dick Connors was the scion of an immensely wealthy sheep-station family, but when they married the Connors parents made Dick start at the bottom as a common station hand and work his way up. After three years of marriage and two miscarriages, the life Jody was living—cooking on a wood stove, constant debts, and her husband's increasing dependency on alcohol—became intolerable.

At twenty-one Jody left her husband, returned to Sydney, and studied dancing. In three years she became the champion ballroom dancer of Australia and was the top instructress at the Fred Astaire dancing school. Her drive to make money was becoming stronger day by day; to earn extra money she performed exotic dancing shows in Sydney night clubs. But the money she could make was limited, and she was far from realizing her dream to open her own place in Sydney.

When she was offered an opportunity to perform in a Manila night club for twice what she was making in Australia she leaped at the opportunity. Well-proportioned blond Caucasian girls were in demand all over the Orient, and from Manila to Hong Kong, from Tokyo to Seoul, she was always in demand. She formed a liaison with a Hong Kong jeweler and put all her earnings into gems, whose value rose sharply as more and more Americans visited the Orient. She became an expert in jewelry and, after five years of exhausting dance performances, began to look for another way of making her fortune. It was then she and the liquor salesman, Bert Bannahan, formed what he had promised would be strictly a business relationship in Saigon. He would get a string of jewelry concessions in the Army PXs, and she would manage them.

Inside the terminal building the utter chaos of the immigration proceedings completely confused her. Never had she experienced such incompetence among immigration officials anywhere else in the world.

Over an hour after landing she emerged from the terminal, a sweating, bruised, exhausted wreck. To Jody's infinite relief, Bert Bannahan was waiting for her outside, a huge grin on his beefy face. A big baldish man, he wore a belt buckled under his protuberant belly as though to give it support and held a big cigar in his right hand, the little finger sporting a large diamond ring. A wide gold Rolex watch gleamed from his left wrist, his short-sleeved sports shirt was sweat soaked. Bert looked every inch the retired supply sergeant successfully making his way in penumbral civilian entrepreneurial activities.

"Hiya, gorgeous," he shouted in a raspy voice. He reached for her and placed both huge hands on her shoulders. "Jeezus. You're the sexiest broad ever walked through this dump." He planted a slobbery kiss on her lips, his breath heavy with cigar smoke and stale liquor.

"Come on with me, baby." Bert's voice seemed to tremble, and his hands shook slightly as he steered Jody onto the sidewalk. He motioned a Vietnamese porter to pick up her bags, and they headed down the street. The diminutive porter struggled desperately with the suitcases as Bert led Jody to the mini station wagon. Bert opened the back door and stepped aside as the suitcases were put inside, then tipped the scrawny sky cap and helped Jody into the front seat. He reached over her for the bouquet of flowers in the driver's seat.

"Welcome to old Saigon, the pearl of the Orient, doll." Jody took the flowers and weakly smiled her appreciation, a little overwhelmed by his exuberant welcome.

"Well, well, well. Now we really gotta celebrate, kid. You don't know how old Bert's been missing you. We're gonna have us some fun and make lots and lots of green together." Again he reached into the driver's seat and pulled out a bottle wrapped in a cold, wet towel.

"Champagne, sweetheart. To celebrate the new duet." Jody couldn't miss the anticipatory leer that crept across his lips as he twisted the cork off the bottle. With a pop it flew off, and champagne foamed from the neck of the bottle, spilling down his shirt front. Bert laughed and held the bottle to his lips, drinking greedily as the wine bubbled over his chin and down his neck. Then he handed the bottle to Jody.

"Drink up, Goldilocks. Better times coming. You pretty broke now?" Jody nodded. Gingerly raising the bottle to her lips, she began to swallow. It was cold enough and refreshing, but it would have been better from a glass.

Bert's beady eyes never left her. "Oh, baby, the way you take it from that bottle does something to me. Yeah!" He closed the door on Jody's side of the car and walked around and sat in the driver's seat. "One more belt and I'll get this heap out of here and get us into more pleasant surroundings."

Jody handed him the bottle. He swallowed deeply and handed it back to her, belching expansively and putting the cigar back between his teeth. He started up the little car, turned on its air-conditioning unit, and started off for Saigon. Jody had committed herself to a business relationship, but there could be no mistaking Bert's expectations of something a bit more intimate. She comforted herself by remembering that Bert had always been, within the limited scope of his breeding, a gentleman in Korea.

Where's your wife, Bert?" Jody asked. "I remember she left Korea with you to come here."

"She's gone back to the States. Didn't like it here. Just as well. We

27

weren't getting on too well anyway . . ." He took a hand from the wheel and placed it on Jody's thigh. "You and me's going to have a great old time in Saigon, girl. It's a great town when you get to know it."

Jody sighed and pulled herself toward her window, trying to free her leg from Bert's firm grip. "The Vietnamese women seem very pretty," she said, peering out the window. "So slender. They make me feel heavy."

"Skinny little broads," Bert growled. "I can't stand 'em."

Jody stared in amazement at the heavy concentration of motor bikes, bicycles, motor scooters, and automobiles ranging from the tiny Renault taxis up to the American military sedans, large trucks, and personnel carriers. She was thankful for the air conditioning, which kept out not only the heat but the bluish smog of exhaust that settled over the streets.

"I thought there was a war going on here," she remarked, looking at the stately villas and the apartment buildings near the center of town. "I expected to find big war-ravaged areas."

Bert laughed uproariously. "War? It's all out in the boondocks. We sure as hell aren't going near any war. Saigon's a good, safe city when you know how to take a few precautions and stay out of trouble."

Jody still carried Bert's last letter, describing the spacious villa he had rented for their living quarters and office space. When the car turned off Cong Ly into the quiet, tree-lined Rue Pasteur she asked, "Is our villa on a nice street like this?"

"Oh, you'll like it fine." Bert paused. "It isn't quite ready yet, so we'll have to stay a couple of days at the Caravelle Hotel."

A few minutes later Bert parked in front of the Caravelle. While a porter coped with the baggage, Bert, his wide face split by a yellow-toothed grin, led Jody up to the desk.

"Ah, hello Mrs. Bert," the desk clerk enthused to her.

"Them Viets can't pronounce my last name," Bert explained solicitously.

"We wait for you. We happy you here," the clerk went on. "Mr. Bert all time talk you come." The clerk was so happy to see Jody that he missed the frown that darkened her face.

"Just give them your passport number, doll, that's all they need," Bert urged. Jody took out her passport, copied the number on the registration form, and, with further obsequities of the hotel staff ringing in her ears, followed Bert and the porter to the elevator.

Jody's next shock occurred as the door to her room was opened—not only was she sharing a room with Bert, but the twin beds had been pushed together to make a double bed. Bert was quick to explain that this was the last room left in the hotel and they would have to share it. The situation was becoming abundantly clear, and Jody wanted no part of it. As Bert continued to apologize, even calling down to the desk to confirm there were no more rooms to be had, Jody called two housemaids in from the hall and had the beds pulled apart.

28

In an effort to smooth over troubled waters, Bert suggested that Jody take a shower, a nap, and get dressed up; he would show her Saigon by night. Meanwhile, he would leave her alone and go to his company offices for a sales meeting.

Bert returned from his office around seven in the evening and found Jody somewhat mollified, though the idea of sharing the room with him still annoyed her. He took her to one of Saigon's best restaurants, the Guillaume Tell. The French cuisine was perfect, and suddenly she realized how hungry she was. Although she stuck to wine, Bert never stopped drinking whisky, before, during, and after dinner. When the table had been cleared, he sat back and lit up one of his mammoth cigars and reached for Jody's hand, giving it a contented squeeze with his own clammy, hirsute paw.

Jody had noticed a big, gray-haired man at the bar who seemed to be known by everyone. He was a gregarious type, she thought. Shortly after their table was cleared, Bert beckoned the man to come to their table, whispering to Jody that he was Tony DeMarlo, a very close friend of Joe Crust, the most important businessman in Saigon.

After DeMarlo had seated himself opposite them, Bert made the introductions. Tony was the largest seller of books, magazines, and novelties to the military in Vietnam, and Jody quickly took a liking to him. Tony, like Jody, was an avid reader, and as Bert nodded and blinked, they discussed books they had both read and enjoyed. It was apparent that DeMarlo disliked Bannahan, and Jody tried to find out as much about Tony as she could without being obvious. When Bert suddenly became conscious of Jody's interest in Tony DeMarlo, he sat up a little straighter and consulted his Rolex. "Getting pretty late. We better go before curfew." He guffawed. "Wouldn't want to spend the night here." He unceremoniously heaved himself to his feet and pushed the table into DeMarlo's stomach. Tony stood up, said a gallant good evening to Jody, ignored Bert's gaffe, and promised to contact her very soon.

"Please do, Tony. Whenever you can." She held his hand a moment and then followed Bert from the restaurant.

Back in the hotel room, Bert smoked another cigar, sucked at his bottle, and amorously pawed at Jody.

He lurched at her and tried to maneuver her onto the near bed, but she fended him off and maneuvered his hulk onto the other. No sooner was he horizontal than he fell into a stupor, mouth agape, grating snores tearing from his bulbous nose.

It was a long, miserable night, and the excitement Jody had felt at this new adventure had already fled, leaving only concern and disgust. Although the air conditioning kept the room cool, it did nothing to dissipate the stale odor of cigar smoke that hung stratified in the air, making her eyes smart and irritating her nose and throat. Bert's snores sounded like a gas-driven chain saw in the small quarters. The only bright spot of the day had been meeting Tony DeMarlo, who she prayed would come to her rescue. She had no money, no return ticket, and no friends—she was completely dependent on Bert. To take her mind off her predicament, she began planning the decor of the club she would someday open in Sydney. But her thoughts kept returning to the present. Over and over again one question intruded on her consciousness: Was the club she wished to own worth it? It didn't seem so.

They stayed two more nights at the Caravelle Hotel. Fortunately Bert drank himself into insensibility by the middle of the afternoon and posed little threat to Jody at night. On the second day Jody saw DeMarlo again. This time he gave her his card, so she could reach him if, as he put it, she needed a fast bailout. Jody, however, was still interested in the jewelry concession and hoped that she could straighten things out with Bert and concentrate on business. On her third day in Saigon Bert moved them into the villa. It was not as comfortable as Jody had hoped it might be, but it was adequate. The major drawback, she quickly discovered, was that her bedroom had no key and the house had only one bathroom, which happened to adjoin her room. Bert could traipse in and out of her bedroom at will.

Jody's fears for her privacy were soon proved well founded. On their first night in the villa Bert remained relatively sober, and no sooner had Jody gone to bed than he noisily barged in.

"You bitch, you've been a tease for three nights. I'm not waiting another," he muttered. He draped his bearlike body over her and wrestled her into position. Finally exhausted, Jody decided it was easier to give in than to fight the animal off. The bed shook and creaked under them as he moved, his porcine eyes glinting, his face flushed. In a few apelike, spastic motions he expended himself, withdrew, fell on his back, and passed out, emitting the usual loud snores.

Jody got up, stumbled into the shower, and then found her way into the other room and lay down. Even after the shower she still felt dirty, and she resolved to find a way to earn her own money and get away from Bert immediately.

Jody was not to escape from Bannahans villa easily. She had no money, no means of support, and no place to stay. Tony DeMarlo came to her rescue. He saw her almost daily and realized how desperately she needed to get away from the fat, heavy drinking, abusive salesman. One day Tony introduced Jody to Ronnie Jasper, a self-appointed booking agent who had recently arrived in Saigon.

Ronnie took Jody to lunch at Cheap Charlie's and made a proposition to her. He was looking for talent to send to the American bases that were springing up all over Vietnam. He had plenty of Vietnamese shows, but the GIs were tired of Orientals and wanted to see some round-eyed girls.

"What kind of an act can you do, Jody?" Ronnie asked.

"I can sing, dance, and do some magic tricks I learned from a magician in Hong Kong."

30

"That's great, kid. All you have to do is stand up on the stage and show that white flesh and those—" He stopped himself and grinned. "Well you know what I mean."

"How much could I make?" Jody asked.

"We'd split about two hundred dollars a show."

"Split?" Jody's voice rose an octave. "I thought an agent took ten percent."

Ronnie shrugged. "Can you do it without me? Where are you going to get costumes, music, props, all those things? How are you going to get transportation? Who's going to schedule you into the clubs?"

After a long pause Jody agreed. She told herself that after a few months, when she knew her way around the country, she could do without him.

"Okay, Ronnie," she sighed. "We've got a deal. Fifty-fifty."

"That's the girl," Ronnie cheered. "Now we'll get you moved out of that old bugger-begotten boozer's villa and into my place."

For a moment Jody wondered whether she was leaving one lecher for another. She looked across the table at the booking agent. He was an attractive man, she thought, probably Italian. But he was slender, in his mid-thirties, and seemed to be a gentleman.

As though reading her mind Ronnie laughed and said, "With me you'll have your own room and bath. You can lock yourself in if you like. And you can choose your own—friends. Oh, I may have some ideas for you. To help you get bookings, you know . . ."

As it turned out, Ronnie Jasper had just begun in business himself, and Jody was his first western act. He worked hard with her, shaping an act in which she did magic tricks, danced, and told jokes. In a few weeks she had put together the slickest act in Vietnam and was breaking in at the various clubs around Tan Son Nhut air base. The base, the safest in Vietnam, was large and modern, the clubs air-conditioned and well furnished, and the audiences blasé and demanding. After a few shows, Jody was anxious to get out into the boondocks where the men who were really fighting the war appreciated entertainment more than any other audience in the world.

Although it was obvious that Jasper would have been glad to have Jody share his bed, he remained a gentleman. Jody was determined to keep the relationship businesslike. She was equally determined to break up the partnership with Ronnie Jasper as soon as possible and keep a hundred percent of what she earned. After the booking at Tan Son Nhut ended, Jasper had secured a series of bookings at camps up the South China coast. Ronnie and Jody went out to the airport the opening day of the tour, looking for a plane hop to the first stop. Jody was wearing what would become her trademark —GI fatigues cut down to her size, which served to emphasize her firm, protruding breasts, a billed cap, and combat boots. Aside from the other properties for her act—the magic knickknacks and the tape player for the musical background—she carried a little white rabbit named Felix, which she wrapped in a piece of cloth and shoved down her shirt front.

Once aboard the plane, which was full of GI's she stood up straight, took off her fatigue cap, and let her long, shimmering hair fall about her shoulders. The troopers whistled loudly as she sat down in the bucket seat. The engines started, the plane began to shake, and Felix started wriggling. As Ronnie watched from his seat across the fuselage Jody opened the top button of her shirt, pulled the rabbit out, and let him hop around on the floor of the airplane. When she looked up, a sergeant sitting next to her had bitten clean through his cigarette and was sputtering tobacco from his tongue. Jody laughed merrily, and the sergeant chuckled back. Well, Jody thought, she was off on a new adventure for sure now. Where it would take her, what she would do, how much money she would make, only time would tell. She was ready for anything.

4

JUNE, 1969

Rick Townsend and O'Neill waited patiently in the office at the USAID #1 for their first interview of the morning to arrive. After considerable research, they had discovered that one of Jody Neale's friends in Saigon had been Tony DeMarlo. Major Edwin Unger, the provost marshal officer assigned to aid them in their investigation, had been sent out to locate DeMarlo and bring him to the office for questioning.

"I don't expect to get much of substance out of DeMarlo," O'Neill confided. "But maybe at least he'll know how to reach Jody T. Neale in Australia."

"He probably won't even tell us that much." Rick paced the office, smacking one fist into the palm of his other hand. "Nobody we've talked to wants to tell us anything."

"Patience, Rick." O'Neill twitched a smile. "If we dig long enough it will all come out. Always has before, anyway."

"But over here, these people have no respect for the Senate."

"Or their government," O'Neill added. "That's why they stay out here. You couldn't drag them home to the States."

There was a knock at the door. "Come in," O'Neill called.

Major Unger pushed the door open and walked in. He was a tall, thin-faced, hawk-beaked individual. The hair on his head was cut close to the scalp, partially disguising the fact that he was balding. "Mr. O'Neill, I have Tony DeMarlo in the next office."

"Send him in, Major," O'Neill instructed. "Did he seem annoyed at being asked to come see us?"

"He's a cool one, sir," Unger replied. "He's been around the Far East a long time." The Major went out and returned with Tony DeMarlo.

Rick studied the large, florid-faced man who entered. He appeared to be in his mid-fifties. He wore his graying hair long, ducktailing behind his head.

O'Neill gestured at the armchair in front of the desk and DeMarlo sat down.

"We're sorry to interrupt your business day, Mr. DeMarlo," O'Neill began, "but there is a certain amount of information we need. We thought you could be of some help to us."

"Always happy to be of assistance to my government," DeMarlo replied affably. "Anything I know I'll be glad to tell you."

To Rick, DeMarlo looked like the typical sales executive, outwardly cooperative and pleasant.

For several minutes O'Neill made innocuous conversation with DeMarlo about Saigon and the war, before getting down to business. "Mr. DeMarlo," he began, "you knew Jody T. Neale quite well, didn't you?"

DeMarlo nodded. "I tried to be of help to her when she first came to Saigon three years ago. Matter of fact, I guess I was responsible for the first phase of her career here, entertaining the troops. I introduced her to Ronnie Jasper, and the two of them helped each other become successful."

"Jasper is the biggest talent booker in Vietnam now, I understand," O'Neill led on.

"That's what I hear."

"Isn't it true that all the successful purveyors of talent, or in your case, magazines, books, and newspapers, have a central alliance governed by one man?"

"That's an extraordinary observation," DeMarlo said. He appeared to be really surprised, and then he smiled slyly. "Oh, I know what you are getting at, Mr. O'Neill. The rumors do fly about Mr. Crust, don't they."

"Perhaps you could clarify some of these rumors."

DeMarlo shook his head. "I can only talk for myself. Mr. Crust and I exchange information. But businessmen and merchants cooperate for the betterment of everyone in any community."

"But Mr. Crust seems to have some sort of a hold over certain key military figures who help his business proliferate," Rick broke in. "He seems to suborn them for the benefit of his own enterprises, such as the slot machines and large sales to the PX system.

"Suborn is a rather strong word, Mr. Townsend. Mr. Crust has been one of the leading sales executives to the military, both in the Far East and Germany, for over twenty years. He has many close friends. They know him to be a man of his word, and they deal with him."

"Is it not true, Mr. DeMarlo, that Mr. Crust was able to be of material

34

aid to you in selling your books and magazines to the PX system?" O'Neill asked quietly.

"He gave me some good advice. He introduced me to the proper people."

"Doesn't Mr. Crust do some rather unusual favors for his friends?" Rick shot out.

"I wouldn't say unusual," DeMarlo replied, unperturbed.

"What about the villa that the chief PX officer in Vietnam lives in?" Rick pursued.

"Well, yes, it is true that Mr. Crust owns several villas in Saigon. He rents them to U.S. personnel at a sacrifice figure, but that is because he is patriotic and, unlike the Vietnamese owners, he does not try to make enormous profits on rentals to Americans. I think the U.S. government should be happy that one of its most prominent citizens out here is willing to lose money in an effort to help the Army find suitable quarters for its personnel."

"But from our investigations we find that of Mr. Crust's three large villas, one, complete with swimming pool, is being used by the top PX officers, a second by general officers with support commands when they visit Saigon, and a third is a sort of social club and hotel in Saigon for sergeants who happen to be running the club system at the various bases." Rick paused and continued his thrusts. "In fact, a lady, and I use the term loosely, named Lavinia Ferris, whose husband, Norman, specializes in sales of furnishings to the club system, is the hostess at the sergeants' villa."

"I don't know that much about Mr. Crust's housing arrangements," De Marlo replied dryly. "However, no matter how you may think things appear, the fact is that U.S. military personnel is being taken care of comfortably at a most nominal cost to the American taxpayer."

Rick allowed the mockery to go by unchallenged. "Isn't it true, Mr. DeMarlo, that you have known Joe Crust for many years, as far back as the Korean War?"

"I suppose I have known of him that long," DeMarlo replied cautiously.

"What can you tell us about his background?" O'Neill asked.

"Just what anybody else knows about him. He was born in Shanghai. His father was an American riverboat captain. Less is known about his mother, although he says she was also a Caucasian American. When he was about fifteen years old, he was taken by his father and mother to live in the States, in California, I believe." DeMarlo paused as though this was all he had to say.

"How did you meet him? It was in Korea wasn't it?" Rick probed.

DeMarlo nodded. "I was selling to the military. Crust arrived. He was working for a liquor outfit in Japan and was doing very well. He had a partner, a very young fellow at the time, I used to see. Name of Art Line, Art the Cork they call him because he was always opening the bottles for

35

Joe's friends. Up until recently he was still with Joe. Actually, I saw a lot more of Art than I did of Joe Crust."

"Wasn't Crust close to a lot of important military people then? The same way he is now in Vietnam?"

"As I said, Mr. Townsend, I'm not an authority on Joe Crust. If you want to know more about him, maybe you should have a little chat with Art the Cork, if you can find him. I understand there was a misunderstanding between Joe and him. But I can't tell you any more."

O'Neill, sensing that Rick's frustration might get the better of him, abruptly took over the questioning.

"Mr. DeMarlo, do you know why Jody T. Neale left Saigon so abruptly?"

DeMarlo shook his head. "No. After three years here she was more or less a permanent fixture. I understand she had some sort of a falling out with her boyfriend at the time, a sergeant."

"Do you know the sergeant's name?"

"No. I really don't. I was sorry to see Jody leave. She and I had talked of going into business together."

"When did you last see her?"

"I can't remember, really. Let's see. This is June of sixty-nine. I suppose it was about a month, maybe six weeks ago. She was quite friendly with Sergeant Major Cotsworth. Perhaps he could help you."

"We would like to contact her in Australia. Do you have a telephone number for her?"

"I think I can do better than that for you, Mr. O'Neill." DeMarlo smiled. "I received a letter from Jody just yesterday, saying she would be making a brief stop in Saigon on the way to Hong Kong. It seems she wants to take me up on sponsoring her in business."

"She's coming here?" Rick asked in surprise.

DeMarlo nodded. "She had sudden financial reverses in Australia." He cleared his throat. "She didn't specify the exact nature of these problems."

"Did she say when she was coming?" Rick asked.

"Not exactly. She just said she would contact me when she got here."

"Will you let us know when she arrives?"

"Mr. Townsend, I will certainly tell Jody you are anxious to see her."

"Thank you, Mr. DeMarlo," O'Neill said. "Now for a few moments can we get back to Mr. Crust and his operations with the PX system. We have discovered that the only beer and liquor in any quantity that is sold to Americans on their ration cards are products represented by Mr. Crust's organization."

"On that you will have to talk to Mr. Crust. My knowledge is only of my own business—magazines, books, newspapers, and novelties. As I said, while my sales agency cooperates with Mr. Crust to a certain extent, I am not directly associated with him."

"Now about this cooperation." O'Neill prepared to start penetrating

DeMarlo's facade of casual naïveté, and Rick hitched his chair forward, ready to jump into the questioning. Major Unger regarded the entire scene with undisguised hostility. He was of the school that anything that affected the Army should be taken care of by the Army and not by civilians.

5

AUGUST, 1966

By the time Jody and Ronnie Jasper arrived at the strategic Binh Duc logistical area, two hundred miles north of Saigon, she had put on shows at camps all up and down the coast. She was an experienced military entertainer now and had learned all the tricks of working an audience of enthusiastic, howling GIs.

At the Binh Duc airstrip Ronnie commandeered a truck to take them to the main officers' club where Jody would put on the first of a series of performances. After she was comfortably settled, Ronnie took her back to the officers' club. By now it was six in the afternoon, and Jody sipped a Coke while Ronnie drank Scotch. It hadn't taken them long to discover that officers and enlisted men alike cordially hated their commanding general.

"Jody,"—Ronnie seemed nervous to her—"I've been trying to open up this area for my shows the past two months, but that old bastard Brigadier General Robert Hare hasn't been cooperative. I think you can do the job, though."

"What do I have to do?"

Ronnie ran his long fingers through his shock of black hair and gave her a long, significant look. "Old Rabbit Hare does like his women." He paused to let his meaning be absorbed. "And there must be twenty to thirty camps and installations in the valley around Binh Duc that would pay two hundred dollars a show, maybe more. Hare could make it possible for not only you but my other shows to hit these posts."

"You want me to play up to General Hare, is that it?" she asked accusingly. "You said I could choose my boyfriends myself."

"Just play it by ear. But remember, Rabbit could be a lot of help to us if he wanted to."

"Why do they call him Rabbit?" Jody asked.

"He was one of Army's greatest halfbacks," Ronnie replied. "The sports writers said he scampered through the opposition like a rabbit, and that's what he's been called ever since."

The lieutenant in charge of the club came up to Ronnie and Jody. "We just received word that General Hare will be at the show tonight. I want it to start exactly at eight."

"No sweat," Jody replied.

But two hours later, dressed for the performance, her props all in place, Jody suddenly realized that Felix was missing. Ronnie Jasper and three GIs desperately searched backstage, then outdoors, as the clock ticked off the minutes. At five minutes after eight a sweating Ronnie Jasper rushed up to Jody, triumphantly handed her the white rabbit, and the show went on. The glowering brigadier general was sitting in the front row, staring angrily at his watch.

The show was about as exciting as a can of C rations. No matter how hard she tried, General Hare would neither smile nor applaud. The rest of the officers, watching him from the corners of their eyes, became inhibited and were unable to relax and enjoy the performance. To save the show, not just for that night but for an expected month of Ronnie Jasper's continuing bookings, Jody knew she had to do something to make the dour old brigadier general acknowledge her. She decided upon a drastic course of action.

Jody danced up to Hare, sat on his lap, and caressed his bristle-top head. He looked startled at first, but then lapsed into a sick smile. The rest of the men let go and laughed. The ice was broken.

After the show General Hare invited Jody, Ronnie, and a few officers back to his quarters. The general's quarters consisted of a two-story villa near the beach, surrounded by the MACV compound, the nurses' quarters, and other high-echelon living quarters. In the middle of the general's garden, tastefully planted with flowers and shrubbery, was a large, open pit. Hare saw Jody staring at it.

"Come back tomorrow afternoon for cocktails and you'll see what that hole is for," the general said. Jody couldn't help noticing that he was looking her over with obvious relish. After she had been served a gin and tonic by an orderly, she bestowed her warmest smile on Hare. They sat down together and began talking about the war.

"It's clear that the only true allies of America here are the Koreans," Hare said.

"Are you implying, General, that Australia is not a good ally?" Jody hotly replied.

"That is correct," he snapped. "What have you got here? Just a few thousand troops? The Koreans have got forty thousand."

Jody put up a spirited argument in defense of her countrymen. "For

God's sake, don't you know the size of our Army? We've only got about thirty thousand troops total and out of that six thousand are here. That's as many as Korea and the U.S., percentagewise."

"Well, I still don't think they're doing their share." He took a long pull on his drink.

Jody felt constrained to set this smug, complacent general straight, whether or not he could help her get the bookings she and Ronnie Jasper were seeking. "Australia and New Zealand are the only two allies you have who are paying all their own costs. Your government doesn't like to admit it to its own people, but the American taxpayer picks up all the costs for everything involved in transporting and maintaining your Asian allies, the Thais, Koreans, and Filipinos." She paused for a breath.

"I find that hard to believe," the general pronounced.

Jody decided she had gone far enough. Ronnie Jasper was glaring at her. She kept quiet with difficulty. It was surprising that even so knowledgeable a general as Robert Hare would not know what was common knowledge among military commanders—that Koreans were signing waiting lists for the privilege of a year's duty in Vietnam. In their native country a newly enlisted private earned two dollars a month, and a soldier was lucky to work up to six dollars. But in Vietnam, the U.S. government paid them the same wage that American soldiers earned. Even with the kickbacks the Korean soldiers were obliged to pay, all the way up the chain of command to representatives of their government in Seoul, they made the equivalent of twenty years' pay in one.

For lack of information Hare changed the subject.

The following day, Jody did a show at one of the camps in the valley. After the show was over and Jody had returned to Binh Duc, Captain Postle, the general's aide, arrived to walk her to the general's quarters. In the street just outside the general's garden, she saw a huge crane and what appeared to be a company of engineers.

"What's going on?" Jody asked.

"They're installing the general's tree, ma'am," Postle replied.

"What?" she asked incredulously.

"General said he needed a shade tree in his garden, ma'am. So he sent out the engineers to dig him a rubber tree and bring it back and plant it."

There was a large rubber tree suspended from the long arm of the crane. The tree hovered above the street.

"They're trying to swing the tree over the general's wall," Postle explained. Jody, keeping a wary eye on the suspended rubber tree, walked around the crane. As she was about to knock on the garden gate, General Hare came bursting out, shouting at the crane operator and an engineering officer who was directing the operation.

"Major, can't you get that tree over the wall?" Rabbit sputtered in rage. "You've had it hanging there for an hour."

"We can get it over the wall, sir, but the commo wires are stretched about fifteen feet above the wall, and we can't swing the tree under or over the wires."

"Goddamnit, Major," Rabbit shrieked, "what kind of an engineer are you? Cut the wires!"

"Yes, sir. We were going to cut the wires, but Signal Corps sent a man over to tell us that those wires are the only communication they have with the Air Cav who are in major contact with the enemy now."

Wild-eyed, Rabbit surveyed the chaotic situation, the tree swinging back and forth at the end of the crane, the pit in his garden, and the engineers and equipment parked outside his quarters.

"Cut those fuckin' wires," he shouted. "That's an order!"

The Signal Corps officer, a captain, started to protest but was withered by a blast of invective from the general. He shrugged and motioned to a sergeant wearing heavy gloves, who climbed up the arm of the crane and cut the wires. The crane swung the rubber tree over the wall and in short order had it firmly seated in its waiting hole. A squad of Vietnamese gardeners immediately began filling in soil around the tree roots and pouring water over it.

When the tree was in place, the general finally noticed Jody, who had been watching the activity in amazement. "Come on in, Jody. I must apologize for the state of the garden. The tree should have been in several hours ago. Why don't we go inside until the gardeners are finished?"

Jody followed the general into his living room, aware that she was the only guest, and accepted the gin and tonic he made for her. Then he sat down beside her. For the next hour he described the ways in which he could help her for as long as she wanted to stay at Binh Duc. There were several dozen camps in his logistical area, he explained, and he would see that she was booked into every one of them. As he talked, Rabbit's hands strayed to Jody's knees and brushed against her bosom. There was little question in her mind what the general expected in return for his help. Jody was wondering how to keep from being attacked, right then and there, when a bell tinkled somewhere beyond the room. "Yes, goddamnit!" Rabbit called.

Captain Postle crept into the room. "Sir, Mr. Crust is outside."

"Oh, that's right, dammit." He looked at Jody unhappily. "I'm sorry. I had hoped to be able to talk to you alone."

"Don't let me interrupt your business." Jody tried to conceal her relief.

"You're not interrupting anything, Jody." To his aide he said, "Show Mr. Crust in." Then turning back to Jody. "Wait awhile. I'll introduce you to Joe Crust. He could probably be a big help to you. Got his finger in every business in Vietnam."

A tall, gray-haired man wearing a white sport shirt and dark slacks shuffled in. As he moved, he leaned on a black cane with an ivory handle.

41

The almost obsequious attitude Rabbit Hare displayed toward the civilian surprised Jody. She had heard about CIA agents and their businessman cover stories and wondered if Crust was an important CIA agent, maybe even the top man in Vietnam. Crust regarded her with more than passing interest as they were introduced.

Hare proudly told his visitor that Jody would be in the area a month, and that he was going to be looking out for her interests. Crust extended an invitation to Jody to visit him in Saigon when next she was there and promised to further her career as an entertainer. His agents, he said, visited every club in Vietnam twice a month. He looked frail, leaning on his cane, but there was something frightening about him. His left eye seemed dead, as though it were glass, and his moustache gave a cruel cast to his down-turned mouth.

What sort of agents? she asked herself.

"How are we doing in the Binh Duc area, Joe?" the general asked.

"Excellent receipts in all the slots," he replied, looking over at Jody questioningly.

"Jody," Rabbit said, "I guess Joe and I do have some business to talk over. I'll have you escorted back to your quarters by Captain Postle. Perhaps you would like to join me for drinks after the show tonight?"

Jody politely declined the invitation. In Joe Crust's presence, Rabbit Hare seemed unwilling to press her. Instead, he called his aide and told Jody he would contact her the next day. As she said good-bye to Joe Crust, it was hard for her not to shudder. There was an aura of evil about the man, and yet he fascinated her; she knew she would be seeing more of him.

After her show at the enlisted men's club that night, Jody and Ronnie Jasper had a final conference before he left for Saigon. When Jody mentioned meeting Joe Crust, Ronnie nodded knowingly.

"Rabbit is a big friend of Joe's," he said. "He stays in Crust's guest villa in Saigon, complete with girls. It won't be long before I'm paying off and have a few generals and top sergeants in my hip pocket. Then you'll never have to worry about making top dollar in this country, Jody."

"And paying you half of what I make," Jody said dryly.

"Pretty soon we'll cut the commission down to a third," Ronnie said magnanimously.

Jody let the remark pass. "What does this Joe Crust do?" she asked.

"For openers he owns most of the slot machines in Vietnam. This support area is one of the most lucrative military complexes in the country; since the troops never go out to the field, they are in the clubs every night." Ronnie looked at her brightly. "Actually, Crust should be very happy with my operations. When we put on a show it drags the men into the clubs and they play the slots. I'll have to get to know Crust better. He could be a lot of help. Now look, Jody," he said, leaning toward her intently, "you'll be here a month. Try to be nice to Rabbit Hare. You're one of my first big acts.

Get him friendly to Jasper Promotions and I'll make it worth your while. You might even become junior partner in my operation, come in for a share of the overall profits, besides what you make with your act."

"Maybe I could come in as a full partner and give up my act," Jody suggested seriously. "I came here to make money in business, not as a performer."

"It's a possibility," Ronnie allowed. "Rabbit Hare's your first target, and if Joe Crust is around, try to get next to him too."

"But I'm still not going to be their girl friend," Jody insisted.

"There's a lot of money to be made with the right people, kid," Ronnie said admonishingly. "It's nineteen sixty-six. The way this war is going, in two years those of us in on the ground floor will be making fortunes. Joe Crust will always be the biggest. He has all the clout with the PXs, the clubs, construction work, currency changing. Anybody in with him is going to get seriously rich. So if the cockeyed old screw wants to give you a bang, let him. I'll show you how to make it pay off."

"Ronnie, I'm tired," Jody said. "Walk me back to the nurses' quarters?"

"Sure, kid. By the way, before I leave, you want to pay me the commission on the checks they've given you so far?"

"I haven't cashed them yet."

"Just write them over to me and I'll give you your half in cash, right now."

"Dollars?" Jody asked.

"Oh, come on, kid. We don't use green over here. I'll let you have it in piasters."

"That won't do me any good on post," Jody protested.

"Okay. I'll give it to you half in MPC and half in Ps." At Jody's questioning look he explained. "That's Military Payment Certificates. Scrip, they call it. It's supposed to keep green dollars off the black market. All GIs get paid in scrip. It's all they can spend on military posts."

Jody instinctively knew that Ronnie Jasper was getting the better of her, but she was too tired to care now. She'd figure it out later.

6

Every night Jody put on a show at one of the many camps in General Hare's logistical area. But what the unit commanders enjoyed most was having Jody at their clubs, tents, or trailers after the show for a party with the men. They would all tell jokes and talk about home. The men out in the field did as much for Jody's morale as she did for theirs.

The only problem was that Rabbit Hare's interest in Jody became increasingly evident. As Jody learned, he had an attractive Korean nurse who spent one night in the middle of the week with him at his villa. Almost every weekend a handsome French woman, and her twenty-year-old son (who had learned not to make a nuisance of himself), stayed with him. Furthermore, he was trying to make time with an adorable Vietnamese girl who acted as a bilingual secretary in the MACV compound. She was acting coy with him, and this served only to increase his ardor. After the pretty young Vietnamese girl left him in the evenings, his burning carnal desires unfulfilled, Rabbit would sink into a foul mood from which his minions attempted to flee. Often he sent his aide out to find Jody and bring her to him on such nights.

Trying to be helpful at all times, Jody frequently sat with Hare on his bad nights and usually succeeded in joking him into a better mood. One evening after her show, Jody found Captain Postle waiting to take her to the general's quarters.

"Is the general all up-tight again?" Jody asked.

"He's fine tonight," the aide replied happily. "The nurse from the Korean hospital is with him."

"Then what does he want me for?"

"He has an important civilian at the villa he wants you to meet. Mr. Line, Joseph Crust's personal representative."

"I hope he's in better condition than Joe Crust," Jody remarked.

44

"Oh, you'll enjoy his company," Postle assured her. "He's quite a genial fellow."

Rabbit Hare was delighted to see Jody, and after she and the Korean nurse had exchanged greetings he introduced her to a tall slender, man Jody judged to be in his middle to late thirties. Postle had been right, she thought. Just looking at his smiling countenance, his eyes crinkling into merry lines, made her feel cheerful. He had carefully parted, wavy brown hair, and he exuded warmth and goodwill, she thought, as he took her hand.

"Jody, meet Art Line," Hare said jovially. "He's one of our good friends here. You met his associate, Joe Crust, the other day."

Jody smiled and shook Art's hands.

"I was just about to open a bottle of the *Cordon Rouge* sixty-one champagne Joe sent up to General Hare," Art said. "Shall I pour you some?"

"I'd love it," Jody replied.

Jody sat down on the sofa as Art walked over to an ice bucket, took out a champagne bottle, and wrapped a towel around it. As they watched, he expertly loosened the cork, took a champagne glass in one hand, and tucking the bottle under his right arm, completed popping the cork and poured the bubbly liquid into the stem glass, which he presented to Jody.

"Tell us if it's all right, Jody," he said.

"They don't call him Art the Cork for nothing," Rabbit chuckled as Jody sipped from the glass.

"Ummm. It's delicious, Art."

Art filled three more glasses, gave one to the nurse and another to Hare, and sat down beside Jody.

"I told Art he ought to get to know you," Rabbit began. "He travels around the country a lot, knows all the clubs. When you've played all the places in this area, he might have some ideas for you."

The way Art the Cork was looking at her, she knew he had at least one idea very much in mind.

Rabbit quickly became absorbed with the lovely Korean nurse, leaving Jody and Art Line alone. She delicately questioned Art about Crust. Since Art had been drinking with Hare before Jody arrived, it didn't take much flattery to loosen his tongue.

"How did we meet?" He laughed. "It was nineteen fifty-two in Hong Kong. I was a kid, twenty-two. I was born in China, like Joe."

"But you're not Eurasian," Jody protested.

"Of course not, neither is Joe."

Jody gave him a sly look. "I know he's your business associate, but what's wrong with admitting you're Eurasian."

Art stared at her sternly. "Don't ever say or even think that Joe Crust is part Oriental. He's very sensitive about that. He'll tell you at least three times a day that his mother was an American, the daughter of missionaries in China."

"But I heard his father was a Yangtze riverboat pilot."

"That's right."

"Well you know what kind of renegades they were and what kind of women they took up with." She shook her head. "Besides, he looks a bit Eurasian."

"Look, Jody. You're new in Vietnam. I think you're going to make a lot of money here. In fact I can help you. But never forget one thing—Joe Crust was born of Caucasian parents."

Seeing that Art the Cork had suddenly turned serious, Jody realized she had stumbled onto a tender subject. She raised her glass. "Well, here's to Joe." As soon as they emptied their glasses, Art reached for the bottle. He filled the glasses again and turned to Rabbit, who was holding the Korean girl's hand in both of his.

"Shall I open another, Rabbit?"

Hare shook his head. "It's getting late, Art. I think it's about time to turn in." He grinned foolishly at the nurse, who smiled back.

"By the way, Jody," Hare said earnestly, "you know what a great debt of gratitude we owe our Korean allies for joining us in our fight here?" Jody said nothing. "I would appreciate it if you would put on a show at their hospital tomorrow morning. You could go over with Miss Pak." He patted the hand of the pretty Korean nurse. "I'm sending her in a chopper, and it will wait for you."

Jody was always willing to put on a free hospital show anyway, and knowing that Rabbit particularly admired the Koreans, she quickly agreed to the performance.

Art stood up, seeing that the general wanted to get to bed with the Korean girl. "Been a great evening, Rabbit. See you tomorrow." He turned to Jody. "Like to have a nightcap in my quarters? Rabbit has me fixed up nicely in the guest villa."

"Why don't you, Jody?" Hare urged. "You really should get to know Art. The two of you could have a lot of fun together." He winked lewdly and stood up, taking the nurse by the arm.

"I could use one more, Art," Jody agreed.

"Mind if I borrow a bottle of champagne?" Art asked the general.

"Go ahead" Hare said, as he led the Oriental girl from the living room, leaving Art and Jody to find their own way out.

In the villa assigned to him on the general's compound Art popped another cork, and he and Jody sat down to talk.

"You never got around to telling me how you and Joe Crust joined up," Jody pointed out.

Art laughed. "Okay, Jody. Like I said, I was a kid. Green as hell but ready to try anything. My father had been a businessman in Shanghai, and we had to get out when the Communists took over in 1949. I went to college in the States, but when it looked like I was going to get drafted I went back

46

to Hong Kong where Dad and Mom were living. My Dad said I should have gone into the Army, so I told him where to go and looked around for something to do. I knew about boats and airplanes, so I hung around down at the marina looking for work. Then, one day, I see this cockeyed guy with a cane limping out to the dock. So I just asked him if he needed a first mate, and he said he didn't have a boat but maybe he could use me in something else." Art paused reflectively. "He's got a two-hundred-thousand-dollar yacht now."

"And that's how you met Joe Crust?"

"Right. I didn't know it at the time, but he was almost broke himself. He'd made a lot of money in Shanghai, but he had to get out and leave most of his money there. Then he went to Germany, selling liquor to the occupation troops. He made a lot, and somehow lost most of it." He poured another glass of champagne and went on with his story.

"Joe has muscular dystrophy, which limits what he can do physically. Poor guy is almost always in pain, that's why he drinks so much. And he can only see out of one eye. But he sure has a brain. So he needed a strong young guy around him to take care of physical things. He let me move into his house. He also had a lovely Chinese girl living with him at the time."

"I hope she had a friend for you," Jody chuckled.

"She did," Art replied. "So we started living by our wits. As I said, he has always been a big drinker—one and a half, two bottles of Scotch a day. Naturally he was always trying to buy his supply cheap, and he stumbled onto something big. There was a big liquor importer in Hong Kong who had thousands of cases of Scotch in his warehouse that he couldn't get rid of. They had been brought in to be distributed in mainland China, but when the Commies took over, that market was killed.

"Well Joe made a deal with the liquor guy to let him take a couple of thousand cases of Scotch on consignment to Korea. He left me to find an airplane that would fly it over cheap, and he went to Korea to see if he could peddle it. How lucky could he be? He ran into Lieutenant Colonel Rabbit Hare, who was a supply officer in Seoul. He and Rabbit made some kind of a deal, and Rabbit got the Army club system to buy the whole load for about three times the price Joe had to pay back to the Hong Kong merchant. I found an old C-47 and a pilot, and we smuggled the load into Seoul. That was the beginning of Joe's new business."

Art laughed heartily.

"Before the end of the big boom in Korea, Joe had damned near every important American officer and civilian eating at his house, staying in his guest villa with the girls he got for them, and buying everything he was selling. It was in Korea that he got into the slot machines. Every military club in the country had them."

"You mean he bribed American officers?" Jody asked, wide eyed.

Art chuckled scornfully. "Bribe? Hell, no. It was just that the officers and sergeants who did well by Joe Crust won so goddamned much money in the poker games we ran. That was my job, one of them—to play poker and lose to the right guys. And always keep them drinking. That's where I got my nickname, from always opening a bottle."

"And now you're doing the same thing here?" Jody asked.

"Sure. But things are more sophisticated now. We bring in a lot of stuff to sell to the Army and the civilians here—air-conditioners, cars, you name it. The way we do it we don't pay any duty. One of my jobs is finding Army bases where we can store our stuff until it's sold, so the Viet customs officials don't find it. One of our best storage areas is right here in Binh Duc. Not only is everything safe, but it's close to the installations where we sell it."

"You've really got things going, don't you?" Jody said, wondering how she might be able to make money in the operation.

"You ought to come to Saigon, doll," Art suggested. "You'd have a ball. That's where the action is, and it's only beginning." He paused, a bitter expression fleeting across his face. "Of course, Joe hardly gives me a night a week there. I'm always on the move."

"There aren't enough clubs in Saigon to keep me busy," Jody replied. "Besides, I like getting out in the field and cheering up the men."

Art the Cork shrugged. "As I said, I spend most of my time out in the field. We have a thousand slot machines spread around. I visit them all. We have a maintenance contract at eight hundred dollars a month for each slot machine. That's eight hundred thousand a month right there. The way the troop buildup is going, by 1968 we'll have four times that many."

Jody was overwhelmed and confused by the mention of so much money. Art put his arm around her and, drawing her to him, said, "Baby, I'd like to have you with us. No reason you can't make some of this loot. Just last week Joe and I met the four civilians who are going to run the PX system out here. We put them in a villa that would ordinarily rent for two grand a month. Charged them a hundred dollars a month each." He laughed. "Already we have a million-dollar contract to supply the VRE, that's Vietnam Regional Exchange, with jukeboxes."

Jody finished her drink and put the glass down. "It's all too big for me to understand. I think I'll go to bed."

"So soon? I thought we might get to know each other better."

"Maybe we will, but I'm tired and I promised to do that show tomorrow."

Art concealed his disappointment manfully. "I've got to go up to Danang tomorrow. But when I come back can we get together?"

"I expect so. I'm usually back here after my show."

"I'll try to let you know next time I'm coming." Art Line walked her back to the nurses' quarters. "By the way, Jody," he cautioned, "what I was telling you just now is for your ears only. I guess I talked a little too much."

"Don't worry about me, Art. I'm known to be very closemouthed."

"That's my girl. We'll find some way to work together."

"Maybe." But after hearing Art's story, Jody had serious doubts about getting tied up in anything that seemed so near to being outright gangsterism. "See you soon, Art," she said at the entrance to the nurses' quarters.

"I'll try to schedule a quick return, Jody."

After the show, the Korean nurse thanked Jody profusely for the performance and asked her to give her love to General Hare. Jody detected a twinkle in the girl's eye. A bright nurse like this obviously knew that her lover didn't pine away between her Wednesday-night visits.

Three weeks later Jody left the Binh Duc support complex on the most cordial terms with Rabbit Hare, without ever succumbing to his lust for her. She felt she had scored a triumph. Neither Joe Crust nor Art the Cork had reappeared, so there was no question of having to pay with her favors for the goodwill in that quarter which Ronnie Jasper was so avidly seeking. Ronnie, who visited Binh Duc every two weeks and was now handling all the bookings for the installations in the area, had come to accompany Jody to her next series of engagements.

After farewells, Jody and Ronnie boarded a special VIP plane that Ronnie had arranged for and headed for Nha Trang, the headquarters of the Green Berets. Jody was looking forward to meeting them.

OCTOBER, 1966

By the time Jody arrived in Nha Trang, one of the most beautiful seacoast resort cities in Vietnam with its crescent-shaped, three-mile-long beach, she had managed to save fifteen hundred dollars. As soon as she arrived she established residence at the Hotel Nautique. It was just across the road from the beach, but that was its only asset. One had to be starving to eat there, since one had to compete with the flies that swarmed out of the foul-smelling toilets next to the kitchen. It was best not to visit the kitchen. The food was prepared by squatting women sitting on the floor in front of their bowls and hibachis while dogs wandered in and out, sniffing at everything.

The bedrooms of the Nautique were to be avoided except for sleeping and using the ancient flush toilets. The floors were unrelieved tile, and the windows were hung with limp, gritty curtains. The bed linen and towels, liberally sprinkled with cigarette burns, were a yellowish gray. Vietnamese cockroaches that would menace a cat entered from the shower drain. There was, of course, no hot water, and there were apparently no chemicals available to the housekeepers to remove the humiliating odor from the area of the toilet bowl.

Jody might have been driven to drink but for the sparkling, sandy beach with the light surf of the clear blue South China Sea washing in on it. She developed a rich suntan as she sat on the beach, plotting means to separate herself from the Ronnie Jasper management. He still insisted on taking half of what she earned, and she paid her own expenses. She was now beginning to get the feeling of the economic opportunities in Vietnam. Entertainers were earning more over here than ever before in their lives. It was not unusual to meet singers, dancers, even rodeo acts, pulling in up to two thousand dollars a week.

When Lee LaRue arrived in Nha Trang and checked into the Nautique, Jody realized that Vietnam was becoming open territory for the flotsam and jetsam of the Caucasian outcasts of Asia's entertainment netherworld. Lee was a tall, blond American woman in her middle thirties who had accumulated lines on her face and the form of a woman ten years older. Jody had known her in Korea where, for a number of reasons, she had become the most infamous round eye in Seoul.

A big girl, Lee had a bad habit of losing her temper with cabdrivers. She had frequently dragged Korean cabbies out of their seats, beating them over the head in the street. She had been deported by the Korean police when she lost her temper with the driver of a limousine which had been lent her by a Korean official upon whom she had lavished intimate favors. This particular chauffeur happened to be employed by a Korean government agency that was spying on the official with whom Lee had been sleeping.

Lee LaRue arrived in Vietnam just as the strip business was becoming profitable. The average price a girl could collect for forty-five minutes of salacious gyration was two hundred and fifty dollars. Considering that the only props involved were a G-string or two and a tape player, and adding the fact that it was easy to pick up two shows a day, it wasn't surprising that word of this bonanza spread to the entire female round-eye carpetbagger community of Asia. The result was that, although several professional strippers were working in Vietnam, a plethora of "female entertainers" inundated the country, prepared to give stripping a whirl. You don't have to be an economist to see that a traveling sporting girl would rather make five hundred dollars for a few hours in her altogether than work a night at more strenuous activity at the going rate of a hundred dollars a night.

Lee's fame spread like an epidemic of gonorrhea, and she was much in demand. That no one ever knew what to expect when she performed only increased the size of her audiences. She was normally drunk by the time she made it onto the stage, frequently with the help of GIs fortunate enough to have a front seat for the debacle. It was a rare exhibition when she maintained an upright position for the entire forty-five minutes. Sometimes she finished her act to enthusiastic shouts of "More!"; other times she fled the stage after being pelted with beer cans, cigar butts, and other objects.

Out of curiosity, Jody went to see Lee's act at the enlisted men's club at the Nha Trang 8th Field Hospital. She was in the middle of her act, standing drunk under the blazing lights, when Jody appeared. Her clothes lay in a heap on the floor as she stood, arms outstretched, stark naked. The tips of her sagging breasts rested wearily on her protruding belly, which was supported by her skinny legs. Dark stubble shadowed her shaven pubic area.

The music of her finale blared scratchily from her ancient tape player as she pulled three unprotesting young GIs from the audience. She pushed one of the boys onto his knees, spread her legs apart and held his head against the stubble. The GI kept his face pressed there long after she had taken her hands away to fasten the other two GIs against her. The curtain came down with the three youths feasting off her form, egged on by the shrill encouragement and lewd suggestions of their buddies.

One night when she did not have a show to do Jody decided to spend a few hours at the MACV officers' club, supposedly the most staid club in Nha Trang. When she arrived she found the place crowded. A friend of hers informed her that a show was about to start and invited Jody to sit with him. To Jody's surprise the main attraction was Lee LaRue. The stripper plunged right into her act, quickly divesting herself of her costume. With a little urging, she brought an American lieutenant and a Korean officer up on the stage to join her, picking both men for the amount of alcohol they had consumed. She commanded them to take off their clothes. They hastily threw themselves into the spirit of things, pulling off their uniforms. Their faces reflected anticipation of the orgy they were obviously expecting, and their fellow officers cheered them on from across the footlights. True to form, unpredictable Lee was getting out of hand, which is why so many officers had stormed the club that night.

After the two youthful officers had stripped, Lee leaned over to kiss the American, presenting her naked rear end to the Korean, who stared at it dumbly. Lee turned her head and called out in perfect Korean, "Kiss my ass!"

The group of relaxed, laughing Korean officers came to immediate attention at the quip. Their national pride wounded, the Koreans jumped to their feet and started for the stage. Lee fled with the Koreans in hot pursuit, chasing her furiously until she reached her dressing room and slammed the door shut.

The American lieutenant was severely reprimanded under Article 133 for behavior unbecoming an officer. As for the Korean, his behavior disgraced him, the Korean officer corps felt, and he was sent home, no doubt harboring a giant hang-up over American blondes.

Lee LaRue found it expedient to leave Nha Trang and its environs altogether after the scene with the Koreans. She went to Saigon to become a talent agent. The rumor was that she was going into partnership with the sergeant who was running the NCO clubs at a base near the capital. The thought that such an unsavory person as Lee was profiting from the hard work of girls like herself so disgusted Jody that she decided to terminate her arrangements with Ronnie Jasper. It was time to do what she had come to Vietnam to do; to get into a moneymaking business of her own.

She was happy in Nha Trang and began formulating a plan to open a nice club where the Americans could come to drink and talk in congenial surroundings without being cheated. To offer the really posh surroundings she envisioned would require considerably more capital than she had saved. She couldn't help but be aware that even faded and jaded strippers like Lee LaRue were making upwards of a thousand dollars a week. The answer to her financial problem was obvious. Jody T. decided that, temporarily at least, she would join the ranks of the take-em-off girls. She was determined that her club would be the fanciest in Vietnam outside of Saigon.

When her act was ready, Jody got in touch with some of the clubs she had worked previously. The response to her proposal was overwhelming, and she immediately began flying around the country doing shows, while maintaining her base of operations at the Nautique Hotel. Her first show was in Pleiku.

Pleiku is the chief city of the II Corps Tactical Zone, nearly two hundred miles northwest of Nha Trang, in the central highlands. The largest camp in Pleiku is Camp Holloway, an aviation center. It was an early installation, and instead of tents it had permanent buildings, makeshift structures of rough timber, wire, and corrugated roofing.

When Jody arrived at Camp Holloway in the late afternoon she found the club manager drunk. The sergeant was a mess, his eyes bloodshot, his face covered with a stubble of gray whiskers, his shirt buttons straining under the pressure of his bloated belly. Leaning back in his chair, feet up on his desk, he was gulping vodka straight from the bottle. As Jody came toward him, he put down the bottle and wiped his mouth with the back of his hand.

"Wotcha doin' here, girlie?" he slurred.

"You booked a show with me tonight, sergeant. Don't you remember?"

"Yeah. Guess it slipped my mind. No sweat though, happy to spend the money. I done got myself fired," he announced sourly.

"Why?" Jody asked. "You're showing good profits, aren't you?"

"Sure, but that goddamned son of a bitch who runs this camp doesn't appreciate all the work and sweat I put into this old dump. The dirty chicken-shit colonel, firing me because he says I drink too much and have one of the waitresses for a girl friend." He turned his head and belched loudly.

"Gee, that's a shame." Jody clucked her sympathy.

"The two-faced bastard! He's got himself a little dink girl. But he's a colonel, so it's all right for him." The sergeant swiped viciously at a fly.

"I heard most of the officers don't like him either," Jody said.

"Well, don't you worry none." The sergeant heaved his bulk out of the chair and tottered in a standing position, then started for the rear of the club. "Come on, girlie, I'll show you where you can stay."

He led her to a small plywood cubicle built inside the club. It was about six by eight feet, furnished with a tall, gray-painted steel wall locker and a narrow double-decker bunk up against the wall. She unpacked, threw her clothes on the top bunk, and with two hours to wait till supper, lay on the bottom bunk to rest before the exhausting evening show.

The big barnlike club was packed to capacity. The air was thick with cigarette smoke, and the air-conditioner was virtually impotent against the pungent smell of sweat mingling with the choking tobacco smoke. The troops were a sea of hollering, shouting, grinning, or melancholy and home-sick faces.

Her tape recorder playing a blues number at full volume, Jody glided onstage wearing a long, flowing gown. As the GIs stared, she twirled back and forth alternately smiling and pouting. During the second number she began seductively to remove the long gown. The troopers began to voice their approval as Jody slipped her gown down, trying her best not to let it catch over her shoulders. Then, as the guttural din rose, she turned side-ways, her formidable bosom silhouetted, and gave her audience a sultry smile. As the gown fell to the floor, a cry of excitement rose from the men.

In a one-piece, shimmering gold leotard, Jody gave her audience two straight dance numbers, the music up-tempo. She sensed their waning inter-est about halfway through the second number. They obviously wanted less dancing and more undressing. To humor them, Jody stopped dancing as the music blared out in a slow, grinding rhythm and shot a long sizzling stare out at the restive troops. Then, standing legs apart, gently swaying, she slowly reached for the zipper tab over her breasts and began to ease it down.

A lusty roar broke out. Then, halfway down, the zipper stuck; the damp air of Vietnam had rusted it. Jody smiled bravely, cursed under her breath, and tugged at the zipper, but nothing happened. The aroused spec-tators called out advice as Jody kept smiling and tugged some more. Then she turned her back to the troopers, grasped the zipper with the fingers of both hands, and tried to rip the track apart, but it held fast. "Son of a bitch," she spat, exasperated. Again facing the audience, worried that she would be out of timing with her tape player, she advanced to the first rank of spectators.

"Will someone kindly step forward with a knife?" she called out sweetly. In seconds, a pocketknife was produced, and Jody guided the trembling hand holding the knife to the zipper track. With one cut, the leotard fell open, and Jody was standing in the briefest of bikinis. A wild Watusi played on the tape machine, and Jody danced with some of the GIs near the dance floor. Each man, fresh and lively, wanted to outdance her, and she had to try to keep up with their efforts. It was the most strenu-ous part of the show.

After she had danced with several men, she decided to take one last partner. A big, grinning Negro youth sitting in the fourth row had been trying to attract her attention for several minutes. She looked over at him

54

and waved him onstage. He immediately leaped over the four rows of seats and landed in a split at her feet. Leaping up again in front of her, he jumped and wiggled like a human vibrator. Jody, tired as she was, struggled to keep up.

Suddenly with an exuberant cry, he shot high into the air, did a double spin, and again landed in a split. Not to be outdone, Jody took a deep breath and tried the same maneuver. Unfortunately, she was in no shape for acrobatics, and after one valiant lurch skyward she crashed back onto the boards. She lay stunned, her ankle twisted and aching. The black GI finished his dance spectacular before he noticed her lying there. Then he pulled her to her feet, gave the black-power sign to his buddies, and jumped from the stage grinning.

With her ankle throbbing and shooting pain up her leg, Jody hobbled on through the rest of the routine.

She called for another volunteer, this time a shy-looking lad, and asked for a can of beer, which was quickly produced. After telling the obedient GI to put his hands behind his back and keep them there, she placed the can of beer on her right breast. Her breasts were not only large but extraordinarily firm. No other stripper on the Vietnam circuit was capable of doing this particular stunt. Jody ordered the young trooper to drink the beer from the can until it was empty, keeping his hands behind his back. Accompanied by roars from the audience, the volunteer gulped the beer, tilting the can as the liquid slid down his gullet. Finally, with the last of the beer drained, Jody thanked the blushing youth with a big hug and a kiss and sent a new hero back to his peers.

Finally, with less than ten minutes left, the lights dimmed and a slow blues number oozed from the tape player. Giving the hushed, intent crowd a sultry look, she began slowly to undulate about the floor in a limping gait, her ankle still throbbing. The younger men were sitting wide-eyed on the edge of their seats or standing, agitated. The older men assumed a bored, once-you've-seen-one-you've-seen-'em-all attitude.

Jody flashed a hard look at the men and slowly slipped the bra straps down. Then, staring at the bobbling Adam's apples in the front row, she turned her back, wriggling her rear end, and slipped out of her bikini bottoms, letting them slide slowly down her legs. Only a brief G-string, unnoticeable from the rear, adorned her below the navel. Then she reached behind her back and unfastened the hooks on her bra and again turned to the front.

The troopers stared anxiously, but the unfastened bra did not fall from her breasts. Slowly, tantalizingly, she danced about as every eye in the place was riveted to the bra, waiting for it to fall. Then when she knew the troopers had been titillated long enough, she smiled and reached for her bra. In one deft motion it came off.

"If grandfather could see me now!" she thought, tossing the bra off-stage, unfastening the G-string, and striking a statuesque pose before bowing and painfully hobbling off.

The troops screamed their delight, banging their neighbors on the shoulders, whistling shrilly on their fingers and stamping their feet. This girl was for real. What a pair . . . what a motherloving pair.

It took Jody half an hour to recover from the performance. Then, her ankle still hurting, she called one of the masters-at-arms to come look at it.

"Jim, my ankle hurts."

Jim appeared to be no more than twenty. He knelt on the floor and gently touched Jody's swelling ankle. She let out a cry of pain.

"Looks like you've sprained it, Jody. I'll drive you down to the dispensary." He picked her up gingerly and carried her from the club to the jeep.

An hour later, her ankled bandaged up and the doctor's warning to keep off her feet still ringing in her ears, she was back in her room.

Jody looked in on the club sergeant on her way back from the dispensary, but there was no communicating with him. He was drunker than ever and mumbling incoherently to himself about the colonel. The MAs had cleared all the stragglers out of the club, and it was quiet when she lay down on her bunk in the hot little cubicle. The small fan standing on the chair beside her did little to cool the place, so Judy pulled off her clothes and threw herself exhausted on the bed.

She had been asleep only an hour when she was awakened by what seemed to be unusually heavy artillery. She had become accustomed to the sound of artillery, since at this time many camps in Vietnam defended their perimeters at night with artillery fire, but the constant booming sounded closer than usual. Jody listened awhile, then climbed off the bunk, threw on some clothes, and favoring the bandaged foot, went out to find the sergeant. The club manager was still in his office, drinking. She shook him and said, "What's all that noise outside?"

He gave her a bleary-eyed look and held up a shaking hand. "Doan worry. girlie," he answered thickly. "Thas' jus' our outgoin'."

"Are you sure?"

"Am I sure, for Chrissake?" he mumbled. "Eighteen years I'm in this goddamned man's Army. If I doan know, nobody knows."

The sergeant belched, hiccupped, and wobbled to his feet. He lunged toward a filing cabinet, caught himself from falling, and jerking open a drawer, extracted a fresh bottle of vodka.

"Now doan worry, girlie," he said gruffly. "You run along to bed."

For the second time that night Jody undressed, threw her clothes down, and fell on the bunk, reassured by the sergeant's casualness. She was just drifting off again when the building shook and an ear-shattering *whomp-whomp-whomp* rolled her out of her bunk. She jumped to her feet, heart pounding, and heard someone banging at her door. It flew back on its

56

hinges and two MAs were standing there. For a moment they feasted their eyes on her nude body.

"Quick, Jody, we're being attacked," Jim shouted, grabbing her hand as the other MA reached for the mattress on the bunk.

"Behind the bar," Jim cried. "That's the only shelter."

"Wait, wait!" Jody screamed, trying to pull back. "I've got to get some clothes."

"Clothes, hell! You wanna get killed?" The MA pulled her out of the room. There was another loud crash, and the concussion almost knocked her over. Terrified, Jody ran after the MAs, oblivious to her nudity and the pain in her ankle. When they reached the heavy masony bar, they caught a glimpse of the firelit sky through the window. The two MAs and Jody threw themselves on the floor behind the bar and pulled the mattress over their heads. As shrapnel whistled through the air and shredded the building, all three of them were too frightened to be conscious of Jody's naked body. For over an hour there was nothing but mortar shells screaming over the camp, machine-gun fire, and the cries of the wounded.

Finally, the attack ended. Jim covered Jody with a towel, and they went looking for the sergeant. He was in his office, lying flat on his back, totally unconcerned. Still clutching a bottle in his hand, he was loudly singing a song derogatory to all commissioned officers.

The following morning Jody learned that nine men had been killed in the attack, several times that number wounded, and the VC had overrun the airstrip, destroying several small planes and helicopters. Over two hundred and eighty mortar rounds had pounded the camp.

And so, night by night, strip show by strip show, Jody built up her treasury toward the day when she would find the right spot for her club in Nha Trang.

8

JUNE, 1969

After the two Senate investigators had completed their interrogation of Tony DeMarlo, O'Neill reviewed the notes he had made for the next interview, with a Sergeant First Class Earl Picking. Picking had been assigned custodian of the open-mess system of the First Division at Di An six months before. This was his second tour of duty as a custodian in Vietnam. Two years before, in 1967, he had been at USARV Headquarters at Long Binh. His first tour was just coming to a close at the time General Hare was reassigned to Long Binh from his previous post as commanding general of the Binh Duc support center.

While reviewing the CID records, O'Neill had come across charges that had been brought against Picking the previous month and then almost immediately quashed. It was alleged that the custodian had falsified records and stolen a large quantity of beer, which he sold to the custodian of a nearby unit.

This was the first potential bit of leverage he could use to pry some information out of one of the sergeants suspected of being involved in the syndicate. By having Picking brought into Saigon, O'Neill hoped to instill some measure of fear in Picking's mind. The sergeants had been immune to any legal action against them for so long that it never occurred to them that an investigation of any consequence could be launched.

Major Unger let Picking into the office. Now that O'Neill was interrogating Army personnel directly, Unger did not try to disguise his antipathy toward civilian usurpation of the traditional right of the CID and the Military Police to delve into wrongdoing in the Army. O'Neill understood Unger's attitude, but had been unable to change it. Perhaps, O'Neill thought,

58

if Unger could realize how serious things were, he might become more friendly.

"Major Unger, why don't you sit in on this one too?" O'Neill said. When both Unger and Picking were seated, O'Neill, with Rick beside him, began his questioning.

"Sergeant Picking, I was just reading these charges made against you by the CID last month relative to falsification of club records at the First Division." O'Neill's voice was pitched low as he started out.

"Then, sir, you must of seen they was dropped. Those ole CID boys just plumb made a mistake." Picking talked with a southern drawl. He was tall, and rather thin for a custodian—most of them had huge bellies—and his sandy hair looked like a pile of straw over his brown, somnolent eyes.

"The CID didn't make a mistake, Sergeant. Someone high up made them drop the case. But the facts are all here." He tapped the dossier in front of him. "These charges could be brought up all over again."

Of course a Senate investigator had no powers to bring charges, but the implication seemed to be playing in Picking's mind. A concerned expression replaced the sergeant's self-assured air.

"You could be a great deal of help to us if you so desired," O'Neill continued.

"I don't know what I can tell you, sir."

"Sergeant Picking, does the name Jerry Nason mean anything to you?" Rick suddenly shot at him.

Picking stared at the second inquisitor in surprise. After a moment he replied, "Yes, sir. Sergeant Nason was a friend of mine."

"What did you think when Nason was sentenced to a year at hard labor?"

"I thought he—" Picking cut himself off.

"He took a bum rap, Sergeant?" O'Neill took over from Rick.

"I don't know. That was a long time ago, Nineteen sixty-five, in Germany."

"You remember what happened?" O'Neill probed.

"I was only a staff sergeant at the time. Nobody told me nothing."

"If we had you subpoenaed before the Senate committee, and you testified under oath on your part in falsifying club records, and the CID followed up on the charges, as they would have to do, do you think in that case that the others in your syndicate would do any more to help you than they did to help Nason?"

"I didn't do nothing. The CID guys just made a mistake."

"When they dropped the charges," O'Neill added dryly. "You and your syndicate people may have been safe up until now, but a big change is coming. Your operations have attracted the attention of the Senate, and that's higher than anyone at the top of your Khaki Mafia. Now remember what happened to Nason?"

Picking swallowed and nodded. "His wife left him when he was sent to jail. After he got out he never could get a job."

"And you'd like to go through that experience?" O'Neill hammered on.

"No, sir," Picking answered in a low tone.

"Do you think you'd get any more help today than Nason got in nineteen sixty-five if you were brought up on charges?"

"No, sir."

"Oh, they promised him everything if he'd take the rap," O'Neill went on scornfully. "But what did they really do? Nothing." He stared at the sergeant a few moments. "Do you remember all the circumstances around Nason's arrest?"

"I think so."

"Why don't you sum them up for me."

There was a long pause, then Picking began haltingly. "Nason was accused of stealing from the slot machines of his club in the Twenty-seventh Division in Germany."

Picking paused but O'Neill said nothing, he simply continued to stare at the sergeant, who finally continued. "There was a CID investigator, Major Hardey. Major Hardey figured all the club managers in the Twenty-seventh were skimming the slot machines and turning the money over to a syndicate of sergeants. Hardey wanted to raid all the clubs simultaneously, but General Crowninshed kept him down to one. The CID hit Nason's club after he had made out the money count for the day's slot machine take. They found Nason had about six hundred dollars more cash than he had reported taking in."

"Didn't all the club managers in the Twenty-seventh follow the practice of skimming?"

"I suppose so." Picking looked at O'Neill defiantly. "I never did anything like that. I wasn't even a club manager. I was an assistant custodian."

"But you knew what was going on, didn't you?"

"I suppose so."

"How did you first find out what was happening?" O'Neill pursued.

"I guess the first time I figured something was wrong was when, right after I was assigned to the Twenty-seventh club System, I saw Fisher—"

"That's Sergeant First Class William Fisher, who is known as Red?"

"Yes, sir. I was only at the Twenty-seventh a few days. I was assigned there kind of by accident, when I saw Red walk out of the club he was managing. He was carrying a bucket of dimes and quarters in each hand. I remember staring at those two buckets. Must have been a few hundred dollars in them. He choggied right across the company area and put them in the trunk of his car. I remember I was surprised because he was driving a Cadillac. I asked him where he was going with all those coins. He was dressed in civilian clothes. He looked at me like I was crazy and asked me who the hell was I. I told him I was assistant custodian and he began laughing. 'Go back to Pancho O'Leary,' he said—Master Sergeant O'Leary was my boss then—'and tell him Red made the best count of the year today.' Then Red gets into his Caddy and drives away." Picking was pouring out the words now.

"I run for Master Sergeant O'Leary's office and tell him what I saw and give him the plate numbers on the Caddy. O'Leary laughs until he's almost crying, and then he tells me I've got a lot to learn. 'Red Fisher is Tom Cotsworth's boy,' O'Leary tells me. 'The Twenty-seventh Division is Cotsworth's, and don't never forget it. I don't know how you got transferred into here, but you got lucky and if you act smart you'd do right well.' "

Picking sat, eyes downcast, silent. After several moments O'Neill asked, "How much did the sergeants make in the Twenty-seventh off the slot machines?"

"I don't know exactly, sir. I was at a meeting—once they figured I'd get smart—where Cotsworth mentioned a figure of three hundred and fifty thousand dollars a year. It was a lot, anyway. I drove into Munich one night when Cotsworth, Fisher, and Bigby were entertaining a major who was supposed to be the officer adviser to the club system. They took a packet of twenty-dollar bills out of the main NCO safe and spent damn near a thousand dollars in one night. They all had beautiful young fräuleins all covered with nice jewelry."

"Now, Sergeant Picking," O'Neill probed, "this is all very interesting and not really new to me. What I want to know is, what happened after Nason was convicted?"

"They all stopped skimming the slots for a while. They had to make it look like the slots at all the other clubs weren't paying out any more." Picking laughed for the first time since he had entered the office. "For once the guys got a break. The sergeants fixed them to pay out a much higher percentage in jackpots, and they made it hard to play. You could never get any change at the clubs. They kept the winnings made by the machines way down, so it would look as though Nason had been the only one skimming.

"This Major Hardey kept trying to harass the club sergeants," Picking continued. "He knew they were getting a cut on everything. Of course each club manager was paying himself five or six hundred bucks a month over his Army pay, and on top of all that he was getting back his share from the syndicate every month. The syndicate owned the soft-drink concessions in the clubs, and all German civilian construction companies that did any repairs and maintenance kicked back up to fifty percent to the syndicate. This Major Hardey kept trying to get something on Cotsworth and O'Leary, until they finally put the muscle on him. His wife got dirty-talking phone calls, his life was threatened, even his kids. He finally asked to be transferred out of Germany."

"What finally happened, Picking?"

"Well, we didn't have no more investigations. When it came time for General Crowninshed to retire, he nominated Cotsworth to the Chief of Staff for the job of Sergeant Major of the United States Army."

"Did you stay in Germany after Cotsworth left?" O'Neill asked.

"No. Soon after he went to Washington in sixty-five the whole syndicate went on to Fort Benning and took over the club system there."

"Except for Nason," O'Neill amended.

Picking nodded. "Yeah, Nason finished his jail term in Germany."

"Sounds as though Nason took the rap for the whole syndicate," O'Neill remarked.

"Sure he did." Agitation crept into Picking's voice. "And he was the smallest frog in the pond. They promised to get him off if he kept his mouth shut and pleaded guilty. But they let him down in the end."

"And you're ready to do the same thing for them?"

"Sir, I didn't do nothing that isn't being done all the time over here."

"Except you got caught, even if the CID was fixed." O'Neill let Picking think about this a few moments. "It's true, isn't it, that you were the first member of the syndicate to come over to Vietnam?"

"Sir, I was never a member of any syndicate. When I was assigned as custodian of the clubs at Long Binh in early sixty-seven it was routine. And I ran the clubs honestly. I never took any kickbacks. I never skimmed the slots. I was just happy doing my job the way I was supposed to do it. I didn't have to steal, change records, or look the other way. It was the first time I felt right since the day I saw Red Fisher carrying those buckets of money out of the club back in Germany."

"But when you were reassigned to Vietnam this year you started in following the example of the others."

"It was the only way, sir. If you don't go along with Cotsworth's boys you can get into a lot of trouble. They would have transferred me to a line company and I'd get my ass shot off the first day in the field. I'm not a combat sergeant. If I didn't kick in my share from my clubs, they'd fix it so Charlie'd have me. You understand?"

"I'm beginning to, Picking."

"You wouldn't bring up those charges again, sir?"

"Not if you go along with me, with your government."

"I'll do the best I can, sir."

"Fine. Just stay in your job, keep your eyes open, and tell me what's going on. I'll expect you back here tomorrow morning."

"If they thought I was telling you all this they'd kill me before I even had a chance to be transferred to a rifle company."

"I'll be careful," O'Neill promised. "You can go now, Picking."

After the thoroughly cowed club sergeant had left, O'Neill flashed a wintry smile at Major Unger. "Are you beginning to see why we're pushing this investigation?"

Unger stood up and nodded slowly. "I'm getting the message, O'Neill."

"Good. I didn't want to push Picking too hard the first session. We'll get more tomorrow. And Unger, we are appreciative of your help."

"You'll get it," he said positively.

9

DECEMBER, 1966

After three months of strip shows and frugal living Jody had saved up the money she needed to start a club; she decided to name it The Waltzing Matilda. With the help of friends she searched Nha Trang for just the right building. Most of the villas she looked at were in deplorable condition, and the rentals charged to the American "allies" were exorbitant. But finally Jody located a villa under construction and leased it from a Vietnamese captain for eight hundred dollars a month. Most of the better villas in Vietnam were owned by either Vietnamese officers or bar girls.

The carpets, furnishings, and glassware were shipped air freight from San Francisco. Jody stinted on nothing. The Waltzing Matilda was going to be first class all the way.

Fortunately for Jody, one of her friends was Colonel Vu Van Tri, commander of the Nha Trang air base. The Vietnamese weren't eager to let a foreign girl get into a lucrative business. It was only because Tri and his close friend Mr. Troc, the chief of police in Nha Trang, used their influence that Jody could open her club at all.

Jody was also fortunate to find a young Eurasian girl named My Linh who worked as a cashier in a Nha Trang restaurant where Jody frequently went to eat. The two girls soon became friendly, and Jody noticed that the pretty Eurasian was quite pregnant. An American sergeant named Jack Talltree was the father, My Linh confided, but he was not giving her any help. Furthermore, he was married and had children at home.

Jody felt sorry for My Linh and offered her a job at four hundred dollars a month to help run The Waltzing Matilda. It was a high salary, but Jody never regretted paying it.

64

After elaborate and costly preparations, The Waltzing Matilda opened its doors in January, 1967, a profitable reality. Mr. Troc was an honest administrator who surprised Jody by not asking for a payoff.

Jody's club was incredibly plush and undisputably the finest in Vietnam outside the U.S. Embassy's International House in Saigon. The floors were covered with thick carpeting. Beautiful paintings on velvet of nudes hung on the walls. The corners of the rooms were illuminated by ornamental lamps. Elegant draperies and furnishings complemented every room in the club, and the drinks were served in gold-rimmed glasses. All this in a hot war zone.

Jody experienced two major problems in operating her club. Preventing the Vietnamese staff from stealing the club into the red was the most serious one. My Linh was adept at coping with thievery. She was an efficient manager and saved much more than her salary every month by keeping a sharp eye on the waitresses, who never missed an opportunity to steal from the club. The other problem was getting her money out of the country. Members always paid for their drinks and food with piasters or military scrip. This money could not be sent abroad and therefore had to be spent in Vietnam or used to buy American dollars illegally on the black market. Not only was this risky because of criminal charges, but worse, it cut profits in half, since green was sold at one dollar in cash for two dollars' worth of piasters or $1.60 in scrip. The only money Jody was able to send home were the checks in dollars she received for membership fees, twenty-five dollars a quarter year, which she mailed off to her bank in Australia.

She had only been in business a short time when she learned about the black market in American liquor. All the bars in cities like Nha Trang, cities with nearby American military installations, stocked black-market alcohol. A bar had to sell American liquor if it wanted to attract the GIs. But because of import restrictions liquor couldn't be purchased by civilians for less than two or three times the regular price in taxes. The most successful ruse employed by bar owners and black-market operators to obtain liquor was to become friendly with the young nineteen- and twenty-year-old GIs. As a favor they gave the boys marihuana to smoke. Handing it out free at first, they succeeded in building up an enormous demand among the youths, and then they began to exact payments. Rather than accept money for the pot, the bar owners asked for PX items such as liquor, watches, and cameras, which they could resell on the black market for two or three times what the GIs had paid for them.

In the bars of all the Vietnamese cities, a GI paid a dollar for a watered-down drink in a dirty glass, and almost that much for a thimbleful of cold tea for a bar girl if he wanted feminine companionship. A proficient bar girl averaged eight hundred dollars a month by sipping Saigon tea and encouraging the GIs to drink up. But it wasn't Jody's intention to sell members expensive drinks or make a profit on Saigon tea.

The Waltzing Matilda didn't have bar girls, because that would have been too competitive with the other bars in Nha Trang, all of which paid off the province chief, an ARVN lieutenant colonel, for the privilege of staying in business. Mr. Troc, the police chief, was Jody's defender when the province chief tried to close her down, but he made it clear to her that the less she antagonized the province chief and the bar owners who paid him off, the more secure her business would be. Actually, the members benefited from Jody's reluctance to employ bar girls. She hired twice as many waitresses as she really needed. They were exceptionally pretty and of a much higher class than the Saigon-tea drinkers. The waitresses were allowed to sit and talk with the customers. There was only one rule: If the girls wanted to let a customer buy them a drink, it had to be a real one.

At The Waltzing Matilda each member had his own bottle, tagged with his name and number, in the club's bar. The bartender made the drink, and the members paid fifty cents for the setups and the posh surroundings in which they consumed them. Thus, the hard-liquor problem was solved. But it was getting soft drinks, soda, and bar snacks that was even more difficult.

One evening in the club the bartender reported to Jody that they were running out of Coke and ginger ale. She was obliged to ask a member to buy the soda for her at the PX on his ration card. But even as she was asking the favor, a flash of inspiration hit her. The next day she went over to the Trident, an enlisted men's club that looked out over the beach, and found Sergeant First Class Tony Gambino, the club manager, in his office. After an hour of discussion, Jody and Gambino arrived at a deal of benefit to them both. In return for two strip shows a month, the club would provide her with all the soft drinks, peanuts, pretzels and other consumables she needed, plus some liquor as well.

Every day around noon Jody left The Waltzing Matilda to go down to the beach for a swim while My Linh bought fresh flowers and did the marketing. On the beach she generally joined Lieutenant Colonel Ed Dickson, the provost marshal, and Roy Johnson, the staff judge advocate in Nha Trang, familiarly known as the Judge. These two officers and some of their friends started working every morning at seven, so they could spend two hours in the middle of the day on the beach.

Two months after Jody had opened her club she was talking with the Judge and the Sheriff, as they called Dickson, on the beach—they were warning her of the coming Tet celebration, the Vietnamese New Year. They expected it to be noisy and uncontrolled. The South Vietnamese authorities had no intention of curbing their people's exuberance. Downtown Nha Trang would be off limits for the twenty-four hours of Tet. The Judge advised her to close her club over the Tet holidays.

After the swim Jody returned to the Waltzing Matilda and found that a small truck had driven into the garage; the doors were closed behind it.

My Linh was watching as two GIs lifted crates from the truck and placed them on the cement floor.

"The fruits of the striptease, My Linh," Jody said with a laugh.

"We have at least a two-weeks' supply of mixers here," My Linh said happily. "We would have run out tonight."

"When everything else was unloaded, one of the GIs took a cardboard case from the front seat and put it down at Jody's feet.

"Sergeant Gambino asked me to give you this personal, ma'am," the GI said.

There were twelve bottles of liquor and a note written on a slip from a memo pad. "Hope this is useful to you. See you tonight. Tony."

"Well he came through in style," Jody remarked.

"We are lucky," My Linh agreed.

"Thanks to Sergeant Gambino we're ready for business."

The Waltzing Matilda had been open an hour that night when Jody heard a loud commotion at the downstairs entrance to the club. She hurried down from the main floor and found that Jack Talltree the half-Indian father of My Linh's child, had forced his way into the club. He was not a member, and the Chinese doorman had refused to admit him.

"What's going on?" she asked.

"This chink slope-head wouldn't let me in. I've got to talk to my wife," he cried angrily.

"If you're talking about My Linh, she isn't your wife. You've done nothing to help her since you got her pregnant, and now you think she'll come back and be your girl friend. She doesn't want to see you anymore, and besides she's busy."

"I've got all night. I'll wait."

"You're not a member here."

"Yeah?" he said. "Well either I'm coming in or My Linh is coming out. We've got a son together we should do some talking about."

"Ha!" Jody laughed bitterly. "You talk about your son. Where were you when she needed you?" She gave him an angry glare. She didn't want him in the club, but she didn't think she could throw him out either. He was big, powerful, and mean, and there were no members upstairs who were a match for him in a fight. She decided to let him come up to the bar, trying to disregard the frightening glint in his eyes and his pupils that were like two small black points. She wondered if he was on some sort of drug.

"All right," Jody said reluctantly. "You can come up if you behave yourself. But make a fuss and I'll have you thrown out, even if I have to call the MPs."

Talltree sneered at Jody and walked upstairs. Jody turned to the Chinese doorman and berated him for letting people into the club before checking their membership cards. Then she went back upstairs, saw that Jack was sitting at the bar, and authorized the bartender to sell him drinks from a club-owned bottle. Jody found My Linh on one of the upper floors and told her about Jack's forced entrance. "See if you can persuade him to leave quietly," Jody asked.

Talltree made several attempts to engage My Linh in conversation. He stood by the bar, sullenly drinking, watching the members coming in and filling the place. My Linh walked among them, smiling, enchanging light banter, occasionally sitting at a table for a few moments, and always keeping an eye on the waitresses and the cashier. Talltree never took his eyes from her as he gulped down one drink after another.

Sergeant Gambino entered the club at about seven and found Jody.

"Jody," he said, "I have an important guest coming here to meet me. Do you have a private room where we could talk?"

"There are several on the third floor. When your guest comes you can have one. I'll ask one of the girls to take care of you." She noticed that Gambino was carrying an attaché case. "You're looking very businesslike, Tony," she said. He didn't reply.

Later in the evening as Jody wandered among the members, she noticed My Linh, a strained expression on her face, standing next to Jack Talltree at the bar. Talltree had a firm grip on My Linh's left wrist, and the girl was unobtrusively trying to wrest free of his grasp. Talltree was speaking to her intensively. His reddish-brown face was flushed. Jody sensed trouble ahead and quickly walked over to the bar.

"Jack," she said pleasantly, "do you mind if I take My Linh away. I need her just now."

"She's not going anywhere until we get ourselves straight." His eyes flashed dangerously as he turned back to My Linh. "Look, baby, you're the mother of my son, you come with me!" My Linh stifled a cry of pain as he wrenched her arm, pulling her away from the bar.

"You've been drinking too much, Jack." Jody tried to keep her voice calm. "Now walk out of here nicely and sober up."

"I'm not going without her," Talltree growled.

Jody looked around for help as Talltree hauled My Linh away from the bar and toward the steps to the ground floor. Since there had never been even a bit of trouble at The Waltzing Matilda, to a large extent because Jody was particular about the membership, the men and waitresses watched in shock as the tall, fierce-looking sergeant dragged My Linh, protesting, from the room.

Suddenly, up the stairs strode two Special Forces sergeants in uniform. They sensed the situation instantly and threw Jody a questioning look. She gave them a nod. At the top of the stairs Talltree confronted the two green berets. "Get the fuck out of my way," he muttered.

"Sure. No sweat," one of the sergeants said. "Just let go of the girl."

68

Talltree started to move between the sergeants. "She's coming with me."

The two sergeants looked at each other, shrugged, and stepped apart. As Talltree shoved his way by them, one stuck out his foot, and the other snapped a sharp chop at the back of his neck. Talltree's grip on My Linh loosened, she pulled free, and ran back into the club as he tripped, fell forward, and somersaulted down the steps, collapsing in a heap at the bottom. Very slowly he pulled himself into a crouching position and finally, rubbing the back of his neck, managed to get to his feet. The whole matter had been handled with such dispatch that only the members of the club in the immediate vicinity had noticed the disturbance.

With deliberation Talltree started up the stairs again, breathing heavily. His eyes were fixed on the sergeant who had given him the rabbit punch.

"Don't try it, fellow," the sergeant said softly. "Quit while you're ahead." Talltree continued up the stairs, and the two green berets joined shoulders to stop him. With a sudden motion Talltree reached into his back pocket and pulled out an ugly little snub-nose revolver.

Waving the revolver in front of him, he continued on up the stairs. The two Special Forces men edged away.

"Anybody gets in my way I'll kill 'em," Talltree cried. "I'm not leaving without my woman."

"She's nowhere you'll find her, Jack." Jody was standing beyond the two sergeants at the top of the stairs.

"Why don't you go back to your quarters before you get in trouble."

Talltree continued to advance up the steps. One of the Special Forces men stepped beside Jody and pushed her out of the line of fire.

The Sheriff and the Judge, standing at the bar, slowly became aware that something was wrong. They moved from the bar and saw Jody being steered around the corner from the top of the stairs by a Special Forces sergeant. The Sheriff strode to the head of the stairs just in time to confront Talltree, eyes blazing, his gun held before him. Colonel Dickson backed off as Talltree moved into the room.

"Tell that big-titted broad if she don't want her place shot up she better let my woman come to me!" he shouted, his eyeballs rolling.

"Sergeant," the Sheriff said in a commanding voice, "I'm Colonel Dickson, the provost marshal in Nha Trang. I advise you to put that gun down and walk out of here peacefully. If you do, nothing will happen to you."

Talltree answered by thumbing back the hammer that cocked the revolver. Of the seventy-five to a hundred men in the club none was armed. Suddenly, the nearest Green Beret made a move toward Talltree. The Indian whirled on him. "Make another move like that and I'll blast you, Sergeant!"

Then, in the tense hush that followed, My Linh reappeared and walked up to Talltree. "Come on, Jack. Let's go," she said.

He was breathing heavily, keeping the revolver moving in a controlled fan-shaped pattern, covering all those near him. "That's right, honey." His voice softened, and some of the wildness seemed to leave his eyes. "Let's get out of here and go home."

My Linh recognized the inherent danger in the situation. Standing beside Talltree, she said to the crowd, "Just let Jack and me go quiet." She laid a hand gently on his gun. "Ready, Jack?"

"Sure," he answered, his voice even. "You walk downstairs. I'll be right behind you, baby." My Linh started down the stairs, and Jack half turned, holding the banister with his left hand, his gun still pointing up the stairs as he sidled down.

Colonel Dickson shook his head. "Looks like the Sheriff has work to do tonight."

Outside The Waltzing Matilda Jack reholstered his revolver in the small of his back and led My Linh to a parked jeep. "I borrowed it for the night, baby. Let's go to my hooch downtown."

Many of the higher-ranking enlisted men kept rooms in town where they could spend the night with their Vietnamese girl friends. It was in this hooch that Jack had courted My Linh and conceived their child.

"No. Not tonight, Jack," she replied, her voice still shaking with fear. She was filled with remorse at being responsible for Talltree's forced entrance into the club. Somehow, she resolved, she would make up for it.

"It's been so long, baby," he said huskily. "We got to get back together."

"You like to see your son?" My Linh hedged.

"Sure. But your mother and aunt will be all over the place."

"Come. We see Andre," she insisted.

"Why did you give him some crazy frog name?" Talltree asked.

"That was my father's name," My Linh announced proudly.

Reluctantly, Jack headed his borrowed jeep toward My Linh's house. He drove down an alley and parked behind the house. "Now I've got two ways—front and back—out of here," he said. Inside, My Linh's mother was sitting beside the wicker basket in which the baby lay asleep. My Linh took Jack's hand and led him to his son. Talltree stood looking down at the sleeping infant in a prolonged gaze. The sight seemed to have a calming effect on him, My Linh noticed with relief. He put an arm around her, and they sat down on the settee near the baby.

"He a very good boy," My Linh said. "Quiet." She smiled at Jack. "Not like his father."

Talltree reached for her and kissed her gently. "I need to be with you, My Linh." For a moment she felt herself slipping back under the spell of the strangely handsome American.

"That's better," Jack whispered. "Can we send your mother to bed?"

"You go back to post tonight, Jack. There no trouble you go."

"I'm not going back there tonight. You're my woman. We must be close tonight."

70

"I your woman," she said scornfully. "When I needed help only Jody T. give me help. You listen, Jack. I still like you, maybe love you a little. So please go back. The Sheriff good friend to Jody T. Maybe she tell him not to hurt you this time."

"I'm not going back until I make love to you," Talltree answered stubbornly. He turned to My Linh's mother and pointed toward the back of the house. "*Di di*, you!" he said.

The old lady shook her head, and Jack, his eyes flashing once more, started to stand up. Instantly My Linh's mother jumped to her feet and scuttled out of the room.

"Now come on, honey. How about it? I love you." He began caressing her, kissing her neck and trying to put his lips to hers, though she turned away. "What's the matter?" he asked impatiently. "Used to be you couldn't wait for me to love you."

"Oh, Jack. Please. Not now. Not here!"

"Well, where? When?" His hands tightened on her arm as she tried to pull away from him.

"You hurting me, Jack," My Linh cried softly.

"Are we going to get a house together here?" he asked.

"We talk tomorrow. Go back before you in trouble."

There was a rattling of a vehicle and a squeal of brakes outside. "I'm already in trouble," he replied. He went to the window and looked out, then turned to My Linh. "Tell the MPs I haven't been here, I just dropped you off."

"Where are you going?"

"To the hooch downtown. It's early. Come meet me?" He was asking, begging now, the hard edge of possessiveness gone from his tone.

"Go back to the post, and I will see you tomorrow."

Talltree pushed through the strings of beads hanging in the doorframe leading to the rear of the house. He was out the back door and climbing into the jeep as the knocking sounded at My Linh's front door. Talltree drove down the alley at the rear of the house, and came out on another street, out of sight of the MPs.

In ten minutes he reached the small bar behind which he kept his room. Once more he hid the jeep in an alley and walked into the bar. A few soldiers in fatigues were drinking beer with their Vietnamese girl friends. Jack walked through to a back room. The old, whiskered papasan recognized him and greeted him with a toothless smile. One GI and a thin-shouldered girl were lying on a cot inhaling the pungent, musky smoke from a loosely rolled marihuana cigarette.

Jack slumped into a chair and snapped his fingers. The papasan handed him a joint, which Talltree lit and inhaled deeply. The resentment that had been buliding up in him seemed to dissipate as the joint shortened. A girl looked in from the bar and, seeing Jack, went over to him and sat in his lap.

He let her take a drag on the cigarette and then finished it off himself.

Once again Jack snapped his fingers and another hand-rolled cigarette was brought to him. The girl on his lap took a match from the old man and lit it. Jack and the girl took turns drawing on it. After a while, he asked her to come back to his hooch. "You buy me wikky Coke?" she asked.

"Sure." He reached in his pocket and brought out some bills. "You bring me two wikky-seven *nuc da*." The girl scrambled from his lap as he continued to draw on the joint. Soon she was back and handing Jack his double Seagrams Seven on ice, and sipping her own whiskey and Coke. "Thank you, My Linh," he said, looking at her through hooded eyes. The girl laughed when he called her by a name not her own, but put her face against his. Finally he set her on the floor and stood up.

"Come on, My Linh, we go hooch. Nobody going to get you away from me now." No protest was forthcoming, and they started for the back door of the bar. Then, just as they reached the door, there was a sudden shouting and the scraping of tables and chairs from the front bar.

"Okay, everyone on his feet," came the harsh cry.

Jack threw the rest of the drink down his throat and dropped the glass. "Less get out of here, My Linh. They not going to take you away from me again."

He grabbed the little prostitute by the wrist and started to duck out the back door when he heard a cry of "Halt! Stand where you are. Let's see your ID."

Jack turned to see an MP advancing toward him. The MP gestured for the girl to move away from Jack, but he held onto her. "She stays with me," he cried.

The MP walked toward them. A wild and crafty expression that flickered in Talltree's eyes should have warned the round-faced young MP. He let go of the terrified whore, and she backed away from him.

"Wait, My Linh. This won't take a minute." He looked straight at the MP. "Okay, I'll show you my ID. This is the third time you trying to get me away from my girl."

He reached toward his hip pocket with his right hand as the MP watched. A sardonic smile played across his lips as, reaching beyond the pocket, his fingers found the butt of the revolver and eased it out of its holster. Then with a deft motion he pulled the gun from behind his back and aimed it at the MP. "There's my ID, you bastard!" he snarled.

Before the MP could call out to his partner or reach for his own gun Talltree squeezed the trigger twice. The MP staggered backward into the front bar, turned, and pitched forward on his face. Then Jack made a lunge for the bar girl, who began screaming.

"Come on, My Linh," he called out thickly. "We'll go to Saigon. I know how to live there." Still shrieking, the girl ran for the bar, colliding with the other MP, who was advancing with his gun drawn. The force of the crash

72

swung the MP around as Talltree ran out the back of the bar and made for the jeep he had concealed in the alley.

Instead of pursuing him the unwounded MP went to his partner, who lay groaning on the barroom floor.

"He only had two weeks to rotation," the grief-stricken partner cried. "Two weeks and he'd of been on his way home." Talltree's shots had caught him in the stomach and the chest.

10

FEBRUARY, 1967

Two days after Tet of 1967 Jody woke up disgusted. The Vietnamese celebration of the Lunar New Year had been going on for two nights, and the
performance of the Viet troops was incredible. Were it not for men like
Colonel Tri, whom she had had the opportunity to know well, she would
have talked as disparagingly about them as the GIs did.

Jody had followed the Sheriff's advice and kept The Waltzing Matilda
securely locked during Tet. The mindless "celebrations" got underway
around seven o'clock in the evening when the ARVN troops took out their
U.S.-supplied carbines and welcomed in the Lunar New Year by shooting
up Nha Trang.

The Sheriff telephoned Jody several times to see if she was all right. He
estimated that the ARVNs had expended more ammunition in their orgiastic
shooting spree than they would have needed to fight off a major VC attack
on the city. Of course, all the ammo was paid for by the American taxpayers.

The ARVNs apparently decided that bullets were more effective for
frightening off the New Year devils than the firecrackers customarily lit off
at Tet. Anyone who sat near a window, much less ventured out into the
street, was in danger of losing his life. It was a long night of unremitting
machine-gun fire, and the sky was ablaze with crisscrossing tracer bullets.

Jody, alone in the club, crept onto her roof garden late in the night and
watched the random streaks of the tracers converge in the sky as an American helicopter flew over Nha Trang. The chopper pilot quickly turned out
his lights, but the tracers followed the low-flying aircraft anyway. The
Sheriff told Jody later that the chopper had made it back completely free of
Tet devils, a dozen holes in its fuselage attesting to the ARVN bullets that
had scared them away.

The windows of houses all over town, including those of The Waltzing

Matilda, were shattered by the aimless fire. Several Americans billeted in town, and even two Special Forces men out at their post, were wounded by stray rounds. But as usual the severe casualties occurred among innocent civilians. Thirty civilians were killed in Nha Trang, the wounded were in the hundreds.

Naturally the GIs were cursing the "gooks" and "slopeheads," but the top American command, concerned with the animosity between the GIs and the ARVN, issued an order that Americans must not speak badly of their Vietnamese brothers.

Several evenings later Jody decided to let the members of the club enjoy the evening without her. To raise their sagging spirits, she, the Judge, and the Sheriff went down to the beach. They took a bottle of Mateus wine with them and paid a waiter at one of the native kiosks to set them up at the water's edge with a table and three chairs. With the wavelets lapping at their feet, and the moon shimmering over the sea and the deserted beach, they soon became more cheerful.

"This was a great idea," the Judge said, leaning back in his chair contentedly. "Everything seems so peaceful out here."

Hardly had he finished these words than the waiter, who had just opened the bottle of wine and put it on the table, turned his back on them and, without moving away, opened his pants and urinated, splashing the Judge on his outstretched ankles.

"What in God's name are we doing in this country, anyway?" he asked rhetorically, pulling his legs back under the table. "I get the feeling they don't want us here."

Sergeant Gambino was fast becoming one of Jody's most frequent customers at the Waltzing Matilda, but her feelings toward him were ambivalent. She had an instinctive sense that his presence did not bode well for her club. Under ordinary circumstances she would never have invited him to become a member. Yet he was generous with the cocktail snacks, soft drinks, and liquor he traded to her for the biweekly strip shows.

About once a month Gambino would appear carrying a briefcase and ask for a private room. On these occasions a distinguished-looking older man with gray-white hair, a florid complexion, and military bearing arrived at the club asking for a Mr. Gambino. Carrying his own attaché case, he was shown to the room where Gambino was waiting. After a short meeting, the gentleman left without even having a drink. Jody noticed that a gleaming new civilian car picked him up outside the club entrance.

The greatest difficulty for Jody and My Linh in the early days of the club's existence was with the cashiers. Each one thought she was smarter than the club's owner and manageress. One night Jody and My Linh were overheard by Gambino bemoaning the fact that stealing from Caucasians appeared to be virtually a hereditary trait among the Vietnamese.

"Jody," the club sergeant said in a confidential, friendly tone of voice, "we've been good friends. I'd like to help you on this problem, and I think I can."

Jody stared at the stocky, swarthy sergeant. His glossy black hair, long for a military man, was parted in the middle. She couldn't explain to herself or others the instinctive antipathy she felt for him. After all, he had only tried to be cooperative with her.

"I've got me a real honest cashier down at the Trident Club. She's never stolen a dime. She's Chinese, not a Viet girl. Maybe that's the reason. Anyway, I'll send her to you if it would help. I just got a directive that I should train a GI for the job instead of hiring a local," he said, explaining away his generosity.

"I'd certainly be much obliged, Tony," Jody replied. "When can we talk to her?"

"I'll send her around to you tomorrow morning," Gambino promised.

"Thanks, Tony," Jody said warmly. "Can I buy you a drink?"

Over the following month the new cashier, Pearl Chin, turned out to be as honest as Gambino had promised. For the first time, My Linh and Jody could entertain the customers at the same time, without constantly having to watch the cash register.

The Sheriff and the Judge were still steady customers, but now the Sheriff had a serious problem—he was anxious to apprehend Sergeant Jack Talltree. He had witnesses to the shooting, but Talltree could not be found. It was vital to the morale of his military policemen to find Jack and bring him to court-martial.

Each night when the Sheriff entered the club he gave My Linh a questioning look, and she answered his unspoken question—she had heard nothing from Talltree. "He's obviously made it to Saigon and joined the deserters," Colonel Dickson was saying one night. "I have no jurisdiction in Saigon or I'd go down and pull Cholon apart until I found him."

"With all the people being killed in this war, all the confusion," asked My Linh, "why do you make so much trouble to find Jack?"

"He's a murderer," the Sheriff answered sharply. "It is your duty to help us find him. Someday he'll want to see his baby boy again. I'm sure of that. When he does, send word to us immediately."

"Yes. I do that," My Linh said without much enthusiasm.

"Don't you understand, My Linh?" the Judge interjected. "We may be at war, but we still have to live by the law."

"I understand," My Linh replied dubiously. Jody had grave doubts that My Linh would betray Jack Talltree if he got in touch with her. The baby was now living with her mother, and My Linh stayed at the club.

It was late in May, five months after Jody opened her place, that General Hare paid his first visit to the club.

"I'm going back to the States on leave, Jody," he told her, "but by the end of the year all personnel assignments at USARV Headquarters down at Long Binh will come under my direction."

"That's wonderful, Rabbit," Jody responded, not understanding how crucial a job General Hare would be assuming. "I hope you'll get up to Nha Trang and visit the club from time to time."

"It's a nice little resort. If I find any special reason for visiting here—" he cleared his throat and leered at her—"I just might."

He turned to the large, florid-faced man beside him. "Jody, have you met my friend General Crowninshed? He's retired and over here working as a civilian."

Jody recognized him immediately as the individual who frequently met with Gambino.

"General Crowninshed has been here before," Jody said, "though I've never had the pleasure of meeting him." She took the general's outstretched hand. "Welcome to The Waltzing Matilda."

"You have a fine club," the general complimented her. "I never miss an opportunity to look in when I come to Nha Trang."

"Anything I can do for you this evening?" Jody asked.

"As a matter of fact, Jody, there is," Hare answered for his friend. "I understand you have some private rooms. We have a little business to discuss."

"Of course," Jody said. "Please follow me."

The two followed Jody upstairs. She opened the door to a high-ceilinged, sparsely appointed room. "I'm sorry the place is a bit bare. I had planned to put a crap table in here, but I was told the CID would not look favorably on me if I did. Anyway, it is private."

"It will be just fine for us, Jody," Hare said.

"I'll send a girl up to take your drink orders," Jody offered.

"Thank you," Crowninshed said. "By the way, we are expecting two men to join us. If they should ask for us, send them up."

Jody nodded. "I'll see they find you." She went downstairs and asked one of the waitresses to go up and help the gentlemen in the private room.

Jody was standing at the crowded bar near the head of the stairs when she saw Sergeant Gambino coming up with another man she had never seen before. They were both wearing civilian clothes, but the tall, powerful-looking man who made Gambino seem shorter and paunchier than usual had a more military bearing than either of the two generals with whom she had just been talking. When Gambino saw Jody a wide grin crossed his face. He proudly presented his companion.

"Jody, meet Sergeant Major Tom Cotsworth. He's the top sergeant of the whole U.S. Army."

"This really is a pleasure," Jody said. "I've heard so much about Sergeant Major Cotsworth."

"He's up here for a visit, and I'm showing him around Nha Trang."

"And you showed me to the right place, Tony," Cotsworth said. Then to Jody, "I wish my visit would permit me more time here."

"Say, Jody," Gambino said, looking all about the bar area, "have you seen General Crowninshed here yet?"

"He's upstairs in the private room."

"Good, Tom and I will go ahead. We'll see you a little later." Jody watched the two sergeants walk up the stairs. She couldn't help wondering what was going on in the room upstairs.

As always, the evening passed rapidly. Shortly before curfew Jody noticed Rabbit Hare talking to her cashier; the familiar suggestive grin on his face indicated the nature of their discussion. Seeing Jody watching him, the general walked over to her. "Jody," he began, "they've assigned me a nice villa near the beach for quarters while I'm up here this week. Maybe you'd like to come over after the club's closed. My driver has a curfew pass, so he could bring you back later if you want. General Crowninshed will be staying with me."

Jody tactfully declined the invitation. Hare grinned at her. "Sorry about that. Say, that cashier of yours, Pearl is a pretty little thing."

"Well, she's a good cashier and she's honest," Jody agreed.

"I'm having a few officers and civilian friends over for a party tomorrow night, and I asked her to join us when she's finished here."

"What she does after hours is her business," Jody replied.

"I don't know what your business arrangements are with her, but she suggested a place in town where, for a price, girls would go out to parties in local villas."

Jody pursed her lips in concern but didn't reply. Hare continued: "I figured there were enough girls here that it wasn't necessary for your cashier to send business somewhere else."

Jody was angered at Hare's innuendo. Her girls were not prostitutes, but she was interested to hear more about the cashier Gambino had found for her. Uneasily she realized that Pearl Chin was too good to be true. "Where did Pearl suggest you go?" Jody asked.

"Naturally I would never go near a place that smacked of prostitution," Hare said self-righteously. "But Pearl did give me the address of a villa on the beach where some girls are living." He chuckled to himself.

"I'm glad to hear she's so full of information." The irony in Jody's tone was lost on Hare.

"Oh, she knows, all right, and tells your customers. Well, what you don't provide here at least you can steer a man to. This is a fine little club, Jody. You've come a long way since you were dancing and doing magic tricks.

"Ah, Jody,"—Hare cleared his throat as though a bit embarrassed—"one of the things they tell me makes your club so popular is that you are most discreet about discussing who meets with who on your premises."

78

"That's one thing you can be sure of, Rabbit."

"Yes, of course. It's something we all appreciate. Well, I'll go look for Crowninshed, and we'll be going back to quarters." Hare left her, stopped by the bar to say a few words to Sergeant Major Cotsworth, ignoring Gambino, who was standing beside him, and made his way through the crowd to the table at which General Crowninshed was sitting, talking frantically with one of the lissome waitresses. Instead of trying to pull him away, Hare sat down and bade another girl join them.

Gambino came up to Jody and asked her to walk over to the bar with him and talk to the sergeant major. "He has less than a year to go in Washington," Gambino confided. "He's hoping his next assignment will be here. He could be very helpful to you if you decided to expand your operations."

"I've got quite enough to occupy me with this place," Jody retorted. "But it will be a pleasure to get to know Sergeant Cotsworth better." She followed Gambino to where Cotsworth was standing.

"How much longer do you expect to be with us, Sergeant?" Jody asked. "I hope you've had a chance to enjoy our beautiful beach."

He smiled wistfully. "I'll be heading back to Washington in a few more days, Jody. As for beach time, I'm afraid I'm too busy this trip."

"The Sergeant Major will be back," Gambino interjected eagerly.

"I hope we'll see something of you then." Jody didn't try to disguise her personal interest in the strong-looking sergeant major. "I just wish I could get you out on the beach for a swim tomorrow."

Cotsworth's eyes seemed to visualize Jody in a bathing suit for a moment. "I'm afraid not, Jody," he said ruefully. "As a matter of fact, I was supposed to go back with the Chief of Staff in his plane several days ago, but I talked the old man into giving me a little more time in country."

"I'm going back with the Sergeant Major on business myself," Gambino said importantly. "But I'll only be gone two weeks."

Jody held her glass up. "Here's to a good flight."

That night, when the last of the members had left and the waitresses were going home, Jody called Pearl Chin into her office. "Pearl," Jody said, "are you arranging dates with prostitutes for members of this club?"

"Oh, no," Pearl replied.

"Don't lie to me," Jody snapped crossly. "I heard about the villa on the beach you recommended."

"Oh, yes. But that not make date. Just send men to Tony's place."

"Tony's place!" Jody exclaimed.

"Oh, yes. Tony get girl, get place. But men at his club no have money for number-one girl. So Tony tell me send rich American from this club to villa. Very nice girl. Young. Seventeen, eighteen. No girl more than twenty-one."

"Do you get money if you send a man from my club to this villa?"

"Oh, yes. Five percent. Very nice for your customer."

"Very nice!" Jody exploded. "I could get into trouble for procuring."

"No trouble." Pearl smiled sweetly. "Very nice girl. No trouble."

Jody sighed deeply. There was no way to argue with her. Pearl could afford to be honest if she was making a commission on every visitor to The Waltzing Matilda she sent to Tony's girls.

Later, Jody talked the situation over with My Linh. "I'm worried," she told her. "Tony Gambino has gotten a foothold into our club, and I'm afraid he's in the middle of a lot of illegal activity. What does he have in that attaché case when he comes here and takes a private room. Why would generals talk to Gambino?"

"I not know about that," My Linh replied. "You leave Pearl to me. She very good cashier. Maybe customers happy she find them girls. I tell her to be more careful."

"If the CID knew my club was directly responsible for finding prostitutes for guests, they could close me down. They've been looking for an excuse for a long time."

"You stop worrying, Jody," My Linh counseled. "I watch careful. Remember, we need Tony help."

Jody nodded. After all, almost every man who came into The Waltzing Matilda had as his ultimate goal getting a pretty young girl into bed. But Sergeant Major Cotsworth wouldn't let himself become involved with any Vietnamese whores, she told herself confidently.

JUNE, 1967

The day following the Chief of Staff's departure from Vietnam after his inspection trip with the Sergeant Major of the Army, Sergeant Cotsworth met with General Zachary Flint, the Commanding General of all U.S. Forces in country. The meeting took place in the general's office at MACV, the sprawling, heavily bunkered headquarters of U.S. high command at Tan Son Nhut airport.

"Has your visit with us been informative, Sergeant Major?" Flint asked in his gruff voice.

"Yes, sir, thank you, sir. May I express my appreciation for the consideration the command has extended me."

The general nodded. He was standing at the situation map of Vietnam which covered one wall of his office. "Another few months and we'll change the face of the war with our new installations. Did you see the job the Army Engineers are doing down at Dong Tam?" He pointed at the spot well into the Mekong Delta.

"Yes, sir. I was there."

There was a long pause between them as though both men wanted to say something, neither willing to be the first to broach the subject. The general stared at the impressive-looking sergeant major. Every inch the professional, he thought.

Finally Flint broke down and asked, "Sergeant Major, have you thought about what you are going to do when your present assignment is completed the end of the year?"

"Yes, I have, sir." He paused and the general waited for him to continue. "With your permission I would like to request assignment as command sergeant major of MACV."

Despite his dislike of any show of personal feelings, the general could not prevent an expression of pleased satisfaction from creeping across his face. He needed a top-flight command sergeant major, and who in the Army was better than Cotsworth? "I would approve such an assignment with the greatest pleasure, Sergeant Major," he replied.

The hint of a smile tugged at the corners of Cotsworth's mouth. "Then I'll put in the request, sir."

"And I shall be looking forward to your arrival, Cotsworth." The two men smiled openly at each other. Had they been civilians, they would have clasped hands warmly.

"Cotsworth," General Flint said, "I understand you are getting ready to go back to the States. It happens that in two days I'm sending the KC-135 assigned to this command over to pick up my new deputy commander and a dozen new staff officers. You are welcome to make the trip to the States in it."

"Sir, I appreciate your consideration," Cotsworth replied. "I had arranged to fly back with some senior sergeants, but under the circumstances —" He hesitated questioningly, and for a moment the oppressive silence of decision-making hung in the room.

"By all means, Cotsworth, invite your men to fly back with you in my jet. It will be making the eastbound flight empty. Give you a chance to take any gear you all have comfortably."

"Thank you, sir. I'll make all arrangements through your sergeant major."

There was a knock on the office door, and both men looked toward it. "Come in, Rich," the general called across the room. A three-star general walked in. "Sergeant Major Cotsworth, I believe you know General Richardson, my deputy."

"Yes, sir," Cotsworth replied.

General Richardson will be going home as soon as General Partley gets back here on that jet to relieve him."

"Very good for both of us then, General Richardson, that the KC-135 is on its way for your replacement," Cotsworth observed.

"I suggested to Sergeant Major Cotsworth that he ride back on the flight," General Flint explained.

"You should have a good flight, Cotsworth," Richardson said. "It's a comfortable plane, well appointed. Not quite what you came over on, of course," he chuckled. "But more than adequate."

"I'm very grateful. I did buy a lot of souvenirs for the boys at the Pentagon."

"You'll be delivered right to Fort Benning," Flint said.

Cotsworth thanked General Flint again for the flight home and then left the office to locate the sergeant major he would be replacing at the end of the year.

Sergeant First Class Anthony Gambino was the master of ceremonies at the party for Sergeant Major Cotsworth the night before the flight in General Flint's plane for the U.S. It was held in the senior NCO club in Long Binh with Sergeant Picking, custodian of the open-mess system, acting as host. All the custodians in Vietnam had obtained leave to come to the party, and most of the sergeant majors were there. Each custodian had brought his token of homage to the Sergeant Major of the Army in the form of several cases of liquor. The club custodians, from those in the northernmost Fourth Division below the DMZ to those from the cluster of installations surrounding Saigon, arrived bringing the booze appropriated from their club stores. Many toasts were made, and by the time the party was over, Cotsworth, Gambino, and the other sergeants who were flying out on the general's plane had to leave directly for the Bien Hoa airport, from which the military version of the Boeing 707 jet assigned to General Flint would depart.

There were a couple of dozen cases of Scotch, bourbon, gin, and brandy left as the party broke up, and Cotsworth directed that they be loaded aboard a truck and driven to Bien Hoa and transferred to the general's plane. Sergeant Cotsworth's group followed the liquor-laden truck straight to the loading door of the KC-135, and the crew chief ordered the mechanics giving a final preflight inspection to the jet to load the cases aboard and stow them in the rear.

The last item to be loaded aboard the plane was a large crate of weapons. Ten captured AK-47 Russian-made assault automatic rifles in perfect condition, complete with ammunition, were packed in with two dozen other assorted new American weapons. The sergeant majors from all over Vietnam had contributed to this weapons cache. All they knew was that the Tiger wanted them. They didn't ask why.

The general's plane had a luxurious forward section to which the sergeants repaired and sat back in the wide plush seats waiting for the Air Force pilots to take off. They were airborne at dawn, all of them snoring off the effects of the party the night before. They slept through the refueling stop at Clark Field in the Philippines and finally began to wake up as the jet started its descent for Guam eight hours later. There were glad to deplane and walk around, stretching their legs as the jet refueled. And then they were airborne once more. Six hours later, in the middle of the night, the Air Force pilots put down at Honolulu and pulled up to the military ramp. Stairs were rolled up to the door, and the four sergeants stepped out of the jet. The pilots, who had been alternating at the controls for over fourteen hours, decided to lay over and get some sleep.

Tony Gambino gave the others a broad wink and pulled a brown-leather address book from his pocket. "We've all been sleeping pretty good. Let me show you how to put this time to good use," he chortled. "Just let me make a couple of phone calls."

"You do what you want, Tony," Cotsworth said affably. "I have a little business with the sergeant major over at Schofield."

"Hey, Tiger," Gambino rasped, "you work too hard. Come out and have you a little fun."

Cotsworth shook his head. "We take off at seven hundred hours. I don't care what you do, but be back half an hour before then."

"What about Customs?" Sergeant Major Danforth asked.

"What about it?" Gambino asked.

"There's a lot of liquor on this plane. Customs will want duty paid on it."

"I don't believe Customs agents will search General Flint's airplane," Cotsworth replied easily. "I'll have a guard put on it while we're away. Now you fellows do what you want."

When Cotsworth arrived at the plane at six thirty in the morning he was surprised to find several U.S. Customs inspectors standing about the ramp at the foot of the steps which had been rolled up to the plane's front entrance. Talking to the Customs men was an Air Force sergeant and the command pilot of the jet.

"What's the problem, Major?" Cotsworth asked the pilot.

"Seems the Air Force gave the plane a preflight inspection a couple of hours ago, and Airman Menlo here found twenty-three cases of booze aboard which wasn't declared upon landing. He mentioned this discovery to Customs. Your MP guard is keeping the Customs inspectors off the plane, but now they want us to pay duty and penalties."

Cotsworth gave the Customs agents and the Air Force sergeant a withering look. "It's all official military-club supplies," he said forcibly. "You're interfering with the cargo in an aircraft assigned to the Commanding General of U.S. Forces in Vietnam," the sergeant major's voice whipped.

"As I see it, Sergeant," the chief Customs agent replied slowly, "there's a load of liquor on board, and no taxes or duty has been paid on it. Since you and the other sergeants are bringing it back from duty-free areas, you owe us a lot of money. I haven't calculated it exactly, but I'd guess somewhere around two and a half to three dollars a bottle." He turned to the Air Force NCO. "How many cases did you see aboard, Sergeant?"

"I counted twenty-three, sir."

"Well, then," the Customs agent drawled, "twenty-three cases, each with 12 bottles, makes 276 bottles. At two and a half dollars a bottle that would come to eight hundred and twenty-eight dollars. And of course there's the penalty for trying to avoid paying duty."

"That is the most idiotic position I ever heard a man take," Cotsworth blustered.

"Maybe," the agent replied nonchalantly. "But until we figure the duty and penalties, you will have to come with us and consider yourself under arrest."

"Arrest!" Cotsworth's voice shrilled an octave above its usual pitch. "You can't arrest me. I'm the Sergeant Major of the United States Army!"

"Maybe so, Sergeant. But you'd better come with us anyway."

"I'll go to one place. Army headquarters at this field."

"We'll be glad to take you by there on the way to Customs detention."

"Detention!" Cotsworth shouted.

"Better go with them, Sergeant," the pilot advised quietly. "I'm sure you'll be able to straighten everything out. We'll stay right here until things are squared away."

Angry and blustering, Cotsworth allowed himself to be led to the black sedan. Before stepping in he took a notebook and pencil from his shirt pocket. "Airman!" his voice cut through to the Air Force man who had discovered and reported the liquor, "I want your name and outfit."

In a firm voice the blue-uniformed airman gave Cotsworth the information he had demanded. Then the sergeant major stepped into the sedan between the two Customs agents. A third agent sat in the front. They drove to U.S. Army Headquarters at Hickam Field, and Sergeant Major Cotsworth followed a Customs man out of the car. He and the three agents walked into the headquarters and asked for the sergeant major. The NCOs came to their feet smartly when they recognized Cotsworth.

Sergeant Major Matterson won't be in until eight," a duty sergeant said.

"I want to use his office," Cotsworth said curtly. He glanced at his watch. It was seven in Honolulu; that would make it one p.m. in Washington.

"This way, Sergeant Major," an NCO said courteously.

"Now if you gentlemen will wait right here, I don't think this will take too long to work out," Cotsworth said smoothly.

He then followed the sergeant to Sergeant Major Matterson's office and identified the direct line to the Pentagon. He waved the NCO out and then picked up the red phone and put the call through. In moments he had the Pentagon switchboard on the line. "Extension two-four-three-four-five," he intoned. He looked up and saw Sergeant First Class Gambino come into the office.

"I tore ass over when I heard what had happened," Gambino said breathlessly.

"I'm calling Fort Fumble now." Cotsworth pointed to the chair beside the desk. He heard a familiar secretary's voice. "Cotsworth here, Emma. Can you put General Walter on. It's urgent."

Grinning and holding his hand over the phone, Cotsworth turned to Gambino. "When he hears about the contribution we're making to his gun collection he'll have anyone arrested he even thinks might keep those AKs from getting to his basement."

Gambino nodded in comprehension. "Now I get it. I wondered—"

"He's on!" Cotsworth took his hand off the mouthpiece. "Yes, sir," he called heartily. "Sergeant Major Cotsworth here."

Twenty minutes later Cotsworth and Gambino walked out of the Army headquarters and were driven to the Customs office. They had hardly entered before the chief of Customs in Honolulu walked in. He looked around and saw Cotsworth.

"Good morning, Sergeant. We just this moment received instructions to turn your case over to Army CID. This is out of the ordinary, as our jurisdiction in cases of deliberate avoidance of paying duty—smuggling," his tone became nasty, "to use the more common term, takes in the military as well as civilians. My advice would be for you to pay duties and penalties, and we will forgo any further action. I suppose the CID will take its own action."

A few minutes later a CID sedan arrived at the Customs office. Cotsworth turned to Gambino and said, "Danforth is carrying a lot of money, and so are you. Settle up with Customs, but don't pay any penalty. I'll have CID fix that. We'll be in the air again only half an hour later than our original ETD."

The Customs agents watched sourly as two CID men in civilian clothes identified themselves. Then, with much respect, they told Cotsworth they had a car and would drive him where he wanted to go. Cotsworth walked out, and Sergeant Gambino commenced financial negotiations.

Cotsworth arrived at the provost marshal's office at the same time as the head of CID in the Honolulu command. The local CID chief put through a call to the head of Customs. When it was over he turned to Cotsworth, smiled broadly, and the two of them had a genial chat. Then Cotsworth was driven back to General Flint's airplane. The pilots were standing on the ramp in the morning sunlight, squinting up at the sky and checking their watches. Moments after Cotsworth and the other sergeants had re-grouped at the foot of the steps up to the plane, a blue Air Force staff car screeched to a halt beside them and a blue-uniformed major, fuming mad, jumped out. He approached the command pilot of the plane and angrily let out a tirade. The pilot shrugged and pointed at Sergeant Major Cotsworth. His face contorted with rage, the sputtering Air Force major, followed by the chief pilot, marched briskly to the group of sergeants. None of the sergeants bothered to salute as the major halted and cried out, "Who is Cotsworth?" Languidly Cotsworth took a step back from the sputtering officer. "I'm Sergeant Major Cotsworth—sir." No other sergeant in the Army could have made the word *sir* sound as insulting as Cotsworth did. "What can I do for you?"

"What can you do?" he shrieked. "Airman Menlo was just arrested by the CID for tampering with an aircraft assigned to General Flint. You know goddamned good and well he was doing his duty when he reported the contraband liquor you were trying to smuggle into the United States."

"He did it for half the penalty, sir," Gambino threw in, approximating Cotsworth's skill at making the word of respect an insult. "That's the racket here, as I'm sure you know."

Cotsworth frowned at Gambino, immediately quieting him. Then turning to the major he asked mockingly, "Contraband? That liquor is the legitimate property of the NCO open-mess system. Your airman," he sneered the word, "had no right to tamper with it. He was supposed to be on board to give the plane a preflight inspection. That's why the MP guard let him on board."

"You won't get away with this, Sergeant!" the Air Force major cried.

"We're not trying to get away with anything, Major," Cotsworth said levelly. "We paid duty on the liquor in order not to delay our takeoff. Which is what you are doing now."

"You'll hear more about this, Sergeant."

"If I do, you can be sure every charge in the book will be pressed against your man Menlo. You'd better teach him a little procedure in handling KC-one-thirty-fives on special assignments."

Deflated, the major stood sputtering as the grinning sergeants, one by one, ascended the steps and entered the military jet.

"Next stop land of the long PX!" Tony Gambino cried exuberantly as they draped themselves into the contoured plush seats of the forward section.

"With almost eight hundred bucks less than we started with," Danforth grumbled.

"Shit, Danforth," Gambino deprecated, "even after paying duty on the stuff it's cheaper by a whole hell of a lot than buying it at home."

"It would have ran us up toward two thousand if we'd had to pay the penalties," Cotsworth added. "The CID colonel had to really kick ass and take names to get that Customs prick in line."

"I hope the CID keeps that little Air Force bastard in the lockup forever," Danforth spat.

"Young Menlo will have time to consider the merits of keeping his mouth shut at the right time," Cotsworth replied. He opened a copy of the *Army Times* and stared at a flattering picture of himself, and then began to read as the big jet taxied out onto the runway and prepared to take off for San Francisco.

The Waltzing Matilda flourished as the summer of 1967 progressed toward the autumn rainy season. Tony Gambino was missing from the scene for over two weeks and then, more enthusiastic and full of schemes than ever, he reappeared. He boasted to Jody that he had flown to the United States on board General Flint's own jet for a week of R and R. His great friend, Tom Cotsworth, had arranged the whole junket for him. Great things were going to happen to Vietnam, and he was personally going to see that Jody was included in the new order of business as the war heated up and became bigger.

Instead of getting excited, Jody's heart grew heavy, and she felt a sense of foreboding. No matter how hard she tried to keep her club removed from the stepped-up illegal activities in Vietnam, which seemed to escalate in direct proportion to the American casualties, now running an average of a hundred a week deaths and many times that number wounded, she could feel herself being sucked into the corruption. It was as though she had inadvertently wandered into a mire of quicksand.

Almost every week Jody walked through the wards of the 8th Field Hospital, talking to the wounded men, trying to cheer them with jokes and chatter, listening to them talk about their homes, and giving them what encouragement she could. The young men who had lost arms and legs particularly depressed her, but she always kept up a cheerful facade.

One day in September, when she made her regular visit, she arrived just as three litters were being carried out of the hospital, the wounded men on them groaning with the movement. As she watched, the men were placed in an ambulance. She turned to her doctor friend, Captain Thornton. "Where are they being taken?"

Thornton shrugged. "Maybe you didn't hear, but President Johnson is paying a surprise visit to Vietnam today. He landed in Cam Ranh Bay."

"I'm glad they picked a safe place to land the President," Jody remarked.

"He's safer in Cam Ranh than in Washington," Thornton agreed. "That's the trouble. He expressed a desire to pin a few Purple Hearts on some wounded. Well, you know there are no combat wounded in Cam Ranh Bay, so the commander sent us an urgent request for three reasonably seriously wounded men to be flown in to be cheered up and decorated by the President. A dust off is picking those men up at the pad, and they'll be decorated by the President before he takes off in the next couple of hours."

"They don't look overjoyed at the prospect," Jody commented.

"Seriously wounded men seldom look overjoyed at being moved around," Thornton replied. "Well, come on in. We just received twenty-seven new cases this morning. They'll be happy to see you."

In late September the beginning of the end for The Waltzing Matilda came about. Gambino walked into the club one evening carrying his attaché case and asked for the private room. Over the course of the next hour several men in civilian clothes entered the club as guests of Tony Gambino and went up to the private room to meet him. Then, without warning, three CID agents forced their way past the Chinese doorman and up the stairs to the main room of the club. Two of the men were obstreperous, but the third, who introduced himself to Jody as Chief Warrant Officer Alvin Bruce, was soft-spoken and managed to keep the other two from disturbing the guests.

"We're sorry to barge in on you like this, Miss Neale, but it's the only way to get our man with the evidence."

"What are you talking about?" Jody asked.

"Is Sergeant First Class Anthony Gambino on the premises?"

"Gee, I don't know. So many people are here," Jody hedged.

"We saw him come in. We've been watching him for quite a while, before and after his visit to the States."

"You can look around," Jody invited. "But try not to make a scene."

"The best way you can avoid any unpleasantness would be to tell us where Gambino is."

Feeling like a Judas, but wishing to preserve calm in the club, Jody bowed to the inevitable. "He's upstairs, first room on the right," she sighed.

The three CID agents proceeded up the stairs. Jody beckoned to My Linh. "Turn up the tape music, and tell all the girls to make a special effort to keep the members occupied," she ordered.

"What's the matter?"

"The CID is here to arrest Tony."

"Oh, no," My Linh gasped. "Why?"

"Any one of a number of reasons, I suppose. Though I expect it has something to do with illegal money changing. You get to the cash registers and quietly get rid of all our MPC. We have about one minute to make ourselves clean with nothing but piasters."

My Linh hurried off, and Jody turned to the stairs. As she started to go up she saw Bruce and the two other CID men coming out of the private room. Gambino was handcuffed to one of the agents, and another one was carrying his attaché case in one hand and was handcuffed to Gambino's most recent visitor by the other.

"Sorry to disrupt your place, Miss Neale," Bruce said. "We'll leave as quietly as we can."

Jody backed down the stairs and, as Gambino passed her, said, "I'm sorry, Tony. What happened?"

Gambino gave her a cocky grin. "Don't worry about me, Jody. These guys don't know what they're doing." Jody walked along beside them to the top of the stairs, her head held high, trying to make it seem as though she was merely saying good-night to some of her guests.

"I'll be calling you, Jody," Gambino said over his shoulder to her as he was hustled down the stairs. Chief Warrant Officer Bruce and one of the agents left the club with their prisoners while the third agent remained behind. He watched his fellow agents depart and then walked, swaggered, Jody thought, to the bar. He ordered a drink from the bartender, who looked questioningly at Jody. She walked over to the bar and said, "All the members have their own bottles, but since you're not a member we'll sell you a drink from my personal supply." The bartender made the drink, and the CID agent sipped it slowly. Jody walked about the club, hoping the Sheriff would be there. But Colonel Dickson was nowhere to be seen. She returned to the bar in time to see the CID agent try to pay for his drink with military payment certificates. It was illegal for any civilian or non-military establishment to accept or possess MPC, although this scrip was in fact used as extensively as piasters.

"I'm sorry, we don't accept MPC here," Jody said. "Only piasters."

"Don't give me that," the agent said gruffly. "We know that your customers spend MPC here."

The few customers at the bar watched the CID agent closely, and pulled out piasters from their pockets and slapped them on the bar.

"We don't accept MPC," Jody repeated.

"It's all I've got," the agent insisted.

"Well then, you may have this drink on the house."

"We know you operate on MPC," the agent growled. "We'll get you on it."

"Every bar, every store, every cyclo driver in Nha Trang accepts MPC," Jody said, her voice rising. "If you're so sure I use it, take a look in the cash register." She pointed across the bar. "Or look in the cashier's drawer," she said, pointing to where Pearl Chin was sitting taking checks and payment from the waitresses.

"Not now, Jody T. Neale." The agent gave her a shrewd look. "We've got our eyes on you. You're buying black-market liquor, you're hustling prostitutes, you're in black-market money. How long do you think you can get away with it?"

"I'm not trying to get away with anything. I run the only honest club in this town, and you have nothing better to do than harass me. All the Vietnamese bars do the things you unfairly accuse me of, as well as selling the GIs dope and operating premises that are filthy. Why do you bother me instead of them?"

The agent grinned at her, turned, and started to leave. Then he turned back. "Thanks for the drink. It will be interesting to find out where the bottle came from."

During the following weeks, the CID always had an agent stationed outside The Waltzing Matilda noting who came and went. Business slumped, since nobody wanted to risk getting into trouble. Even the Sheriff was powerless to stop the CID harassment. He had jurisdiction over military police but not the CID.

When Tony Gambino was arrested his thriving prostitution enterprise came to an end. Through the Sheriff, Jody heard that Gambino was acting as the Nha Trang link in a large money-changing enterprise. He was buying MPC and dollars when they were available for piasters and turning them over to someone much higher up. Jody and the Sheriff had been suspicious since the evening Gambino had met with General Arjay Crowninshed. "It definitely looks like Leavenworth for Tony," the Sheriff remarked.

The heat, so to speak, was full on Jody T. Her friends stayed away from the club, except to come in by day and surreptitiously remove government property they had loaned her. A three-and-a-half-kilowatt generator was retrieved by a company commander. A safe of the type issued to club sergeants which Jody had used for several months was taken back. The CID waged a ceaseless campaign of harassment for no reason Jody or anyone else could perceive. The Judge was furious, but he, like the Sheriff, was unable to discover the reason for the CID persecution of Jody, much less put a damper on it.

To further complicate matters, President Nguyen Cao Ky was supplanted by Nguyen Van Thieu as top man in the government's power structure. Mister Hinh, the chief of police, had been a strong Ky supporter and was notified by the province chief, a Thieu adherent whose position was considerably strengthened by the power shift in Saigon, that a new police chief would soon be brought in. Colonel Tri advised Jody that there was little he could do anymore to help her.

Jody always tried to do things with style, even going out of business. The last day of September she threw a farewell party for herself which rivaled any party that her guests had ever attended. To prepare the sumptuous feast for her forty guests required the combined operations of the Vietnamese Air Force, the U.S. Air Force, and the U.S. Army Special Forces. She bought lobsters in Nha Trang, lobster capital of the country. The Green Berets provided the tenderest filet mignons, no questions asked. Colonel Tri had dispatched a plane to Dalat, Vietnam's market-gardening center. The plane returned to Nha Trang laden with fresh vegetables, salad, and flowers. A U.S. Air Force commander in Saigon diverted a C-123 transport plane to Hong Kong, where it was loaded with cases of vintage French champagne and then made another unscheduled landing at Nha Trang.

To add to the gaiety of the occasion, Jody's invitations called for guests to come in costume. As the jeeps began arriving in front of The Waltzing Matilda, a motley assortment of Russian cossacks, beachcombers, doctors gowned for the operating theater, even a cannibal, invaded the club. The Judge's protégé, a young Jewish draftee, arrived resplendent in authentic Arab costume. A sign pinned to his chest read, SEND ALL JEWS HOME.

Jody's guests, who ranged from generals down to Green Beret sergeants, amazed and delighted their hostess with the ingenuity of their dress.

The party quickly moved into high gear. Everyone was having a fine time, guests and street spectators alike. The Vietnamese band Jody had hired was belting out rock numbers on the roof garden. As a crowd of Vietnamese gathered in the street outside the club watching the arrival of the caravan of jeeps with their strange-looking occupants, the Judge decided to stage a show just for their benefit.

Casting My Linh and his young "Arab" assistant in the roles of damsel in distress and would-be rescuer, he took the part of the villain himself. The three of them enacted a scene on the balcony overlooking the street. My Linh screamed at the Judge's advances on her, and much sword waving by the villain and hero ensued. The Vietnamese love this sort of entertainment, and soon the small crowd in front of the club had swelled into a cheering, dancing, shouting throng. They milled about the street and blocked traffic.

Carried away by the enthusiasm of his audience, the Judge renewed his villainous assaults on My Linh with untiring energy. The crowd grew larger and more unruly. Shrilling whistles and shrieking sirens split the air. Tires skidded, and eight jeeps screamed to a halt around the milling crowd. Leaping from the jeeps and racing angrily toward The Waltzing Matilda, roughing their way through the crowd, piled the law. They were all there: the U.S. MPs, the Vietnamese OCs, and the White Mice (Vietnamese National Police). Jody stared at disaster in the making. The guests had not even sat down to the feast yet. She quickly ran among her guests and found Colonel Tri, Mr. Hinh, and the Sheriff. The three looked at each other grimly a moment, took a deep breath, and headed for the stairs down to the front entrance. Halfway down they collided with the zealous young law officers who were charging up. The members of this joint police action were understandably shocked to be confronted by their respective top bosses, each dressed in outlandish garb. The front rank stopped so abruptly that those behind crowded forward into them. Recovering from their surprise they snappily came to attention, saluted briskly, and stood, mouths open, wondering what to do.

Mr. Hinh made a hopeless gesture as though to say, I'll be out tomorrow for sure, and the three commanders turned their men around and marched them outside the club, where order was quickly established and the crowd dispersed. The Sheriff returned to the club and, after lightly admonishing the Judge and Jody, ordered all the guests to keep off the balcony for the remainder of the night. The party resumed as merrily and boisterously as before. Soon the gourmet banquet was underway.

The party continued until curfew time when the guests reluctantly left. Characteristically, the Vietnamese band, the last to leave, stole all of Jody's going-away presents, which had been proudly displayed on a table in the center of the floor for everyone to admire.

The next day Jody gave Colonel Tri much of her best furniture; the rest she donated to one of the smaller enlisted men's clubs. The next day she hopped a flight for Saigon.

SEPTEMBER, 1967

The International House, or the I House, as the membership club run by Americans under the auspices of the U.S. Embassy was familiarly known, was the most lavish establishment of its kind in Vietnam. Food and liquor there, brought in duty free through the Embassy, were inexpensive. The I House had two floors. The second floor was a dining room and night-club operation. At the front door on the first floor an American civilian attached to the embassy checked membership cards. Behind him were a gift shop, a newsstand, and a raft of the ubiquitous slot machines. Behind the foyer was the coffee shop, and at the rear of the first floor was an intimate, dimly lit bar with rich red carpeting and comfortable oak and leather furnishings. A most ornate bar, with framed mirrors and nude paintings adorning the red-brocade walls, it resembled a movie set of the most expensive bordello in town.

In theory, membership in the I House was limited to U.S. Embassy personnel, State Department people, and a select group of military men. However, the hard-core cadre of regular customers who crowded into the back bar from ten o'clock in the morning until the club closed at curfew was made up of salesmen, show girls, pimps, prostitutes, swindlers, Army club sergeants, black-market specialists, and other assorted carpetbaggers who had obtained unauthorized membership cards through the club managers. The club managers, on contract to the Embassy, supplemented their income several hundred percent through dubious dealings with the back-bar bunch.

Confidence men sat at the International House back bar daily, their ears open as they dawdled over their drinks. Invariably a salesman or club sergeant would have too much to drink and give away some commercially usable piece of news which the con man, or woman, would squirrel away until it could be sold. If, for example, a club custodian was in the market for fifty thousand dollars' worth of furniture, this information would be given to a furniture salesman in return for a percentage of the sale.

The majority of the male regulars at the back bar called themselves salesmen. They all looked as if they had been poured in the same mold— an overweight, loud-mouthed, balding, cigar-chomping bunch. Their wrists were weighed down with gold Rolex watches, huge diamond rings adorned their pinkies, and none of them trusted any of the others. They were secretive about the leads they picked up, frequently "blundering" false information to confuse their competitors.

All in all it was a cozy arrangement at the I House back bar. And to this coterie of worthies, which included her erstwhile business associate, Bert Bannahan, came Jody T. Neale. She was far from impressed with the bar crowd, but it was the only daytime American hangout and she hoped to hear of job opportunities there.

The entire club had recently been redecorated by Norman and Lavinia Ferris, the most successful decorators in Vietnam. The upstairs dining room was beautifully done in shades of green and gold, featuring crystal chandeliers, sparkling silverware, snow-white linen tablecloths and napkins, and lush silk drapes, all paid for at inflated prices, which included numerous commissions and kickbacks, by the American taxpayer. During lunch and dinner, a quiet, sophisticated Filipino combo played softly in the background. The menu was superb. The downstairs-bar crowd seldom ventured upstairs, and the Embassy people seldom went downstairs. Jody, as always, went everywhere.

Perhaps the most valuable facility the International House offered the back-bar bunch was the jewelry counter of the gift shop, which sold Caribe diamonds. These fine diamonds, guaranteed to be Triple-A quality, were shipped to San Juan to be cut and then sold to the worldwide U.S. military market. The diamonds were sold for MPC at the low PX prices. Since the back-bar bunch had no government status in Vietnam, they were unauthorized to buy at the PX. MPs at every PX entrance checked authorizations carefully. However, unauthorized I House members could buy at the gift shop. All of them found themselves with considerable amounts of MPC, which had been created for the purpose of making it impossible or difficult, at least, for just such opportunists to make a profit in currency manipulations. They could not exchange MPC for green dollars except by risking a heavy fine and accepting loss of value on the black market. However, by buying Caribe diamonds, which could legally be sold at a profit for piasters in Vietnam, or in any country of the world for dollars or local currency, anyone who could get into I House was able to get rid of his black-market MPC legally and profitably. Many of the Vietnamese women who were brought to the I House as guests also exchanged their illegal MPC for Caribe diamonds.

Thus, on one small counter at the International House alone, the Caribe Diamond Company made a fortune unequaled by dozens of jewelry concessions in U.S. camps all over Vietnam. The Vietnamese ladies of Saigon wore a fortune in diamonds. More so than the ladies of most major cities of the world.

Not many days after Jody began frequenting the I House, she met an American with a furniture factory in the Philippines who offered her a job selling furniture to the military clubs, her income to be derived strictly from commissions. Jody diligently studied the furniture business. Her first requirement was transportation, so she rented a large green 1960 De Soto and hired a Vietnamese driver. Tien was a ragged-looking little Viet, unshaven and proudly displaying gold-covered, blackened teeth. He looked like a wily little character, but he drove carefully and had a pleasant disposition.

Loaded down with a briefcase full of catalogs, Jody joined the burgeoning company of Saigon salesmen who began hustling the clubs. There were enough Army installations within a twenty-five-mile radius of Saigon to keep Tien and the De Soto constantly rolling up and down the dusty, traffic-clogged, fume-blanketed roads from dawn to dusk. The biggest camp in the area was Long Binh, about an hour's drive from Saigon. At the time, toward the end of 1967, there were thirty-two clubs at Long Binh. The custodian of the clubs was Sergeant First Class Earl Picking. Picking was cold to Jody and her sales pitch at first, but she kept returning to see him. Finally, Picking began to show her a little courtesy.

"I'd like to buy your chairs, Jody," he drawled. "But to tell you the truth, I can buy them for half what you're asking."

"But Vietnamese made. They don't last," Jody argued.

"Maybe not, but what's delivery time on yours?"

"Two to three months."

"You see! I get these Viet chairs from Ferris the same week."

Jody could see there was no point in arguing. "Just in case you change your mind," she said standing up, "I'll continue stopping by."

Selling furniture was a serious loss of prestige for Jody after being the toast of Nha Trang and the owner of her own club, but she kept trying. After several discouraging weeks she finally arranged for a large furniture sale to a club custodian at a new NCO club under construction. Her commission on the sale would be six thousand dollars. In her excitement over making the sale she mentioned it to a fellow Australian, Marie Monahan. Marie had lived in the Orient for fifteen years, and at one time had been one of Asia's most famous call girls. In her mid-forties and inclined to overweight, she had snow-white hair and a face that looked as though it had been chiseled out of a granite cliff. She was loud of voice, quick of wit, and vicious of tongue. Jody was instantly sorry she had mentioned the furniture deal. Marie could be hilarious company, but she lied compulsively. She had no visible means of support and spent all her waking hours drinking at the I House.

Two days after Jody mentioned her furniture deal to Marie it was canceled. Somehow Norman and Lavinia Ferris had secured the order for their company and, at the same time, picked up the decorating contract. Marie, who Jody was convinced had sold the tip about her sale in the first place, confided that Norman Ferris had offered the custodian a ten percent kickback and Lavinia had offered her blowsy, overly voluptuous self. Both offers had been accepted.

Jody was shocked at the information. In 1967 kickbacks to club custodians were rare. The sergeants then were not the kind to ask for or accept personal considerations; a contribution to the unit "party fund," perhaps, but no outright payment.

Bitterly discouraged, Jody decided to look for another line of work, and once again took to sitting around the International House, pointedly snubbing the Ferrises, who were regulars in the back bar.

At three p.m. one afternoon every chair in the bar was taken. The air-conditioning was turned on high, and although it was over 110 degrees outside, Jody had goose bumps on her arms from the cold. As the liquor was consumed, deals were made, lies told, and gossip traded. Jody was sitting with Marie Monahan. She didn't blame the ex-white-whore-of-the-Orient so much as herself for the leak that caused her to lose the deal. Marie's girl friend, Rhonda, an exotic-looking Negro stripper, sat with them. Although a good performer, Rhonda was lazy and didn't like to work. Rhonda stayed in Saigon with Marie, always appearing to be on dope. The consensus in the back bar was that Marie was pimping for Rhonda.

Then Picking entered the bar. A few minutes later, Tony DeMarlo walked in, looked around, and joined Jody, Marie, and Rhonda. Jody was well aware of the rumor, fostered by Marie, that Tony had a particular yen for black girls and hungered for Rhonda more than for any of the other girls of all colors and nationalities who would have loved to accommodate him. It was well known that, besides his delightful home in Saigon, he had his own airplane and pilot. He kept a luxury yacht in the Philippines and, after Joe Crust, exercised more power in the field of military sales than any other man in Vietnam. He also paid Rhonda's rent and had given her the diamond bracelet she so casually wore. Still, Jody admired Tony since the night in Saigon when he had given her a small feeling of security.

As Jody sipped her drink and chatted with DeMarlo, Sergeant Picking stood up and came over to her. Lowering his head to her level he drawled, "Jody T., can you make it to Long Binh tomorrow? Got something I think will interest you."

"I'll be there, Earl. Have you decided to put some of my furniture into your clubs after all?"

97

"No. Something else. You been working real hard, and I just figured to give you a break."

Sensing that Marie was zeroing in on their conversation, Jody dropped the subject quickly. "Okay, Earl. See you tomorrow."

14

Late that afternoon, when the temperature outside the I House had dropped into the low nineties, Tony DeMarlo suggested they all go over to Joe Crust's place for supper. Jody rode in Tony's car with Marie and Rhonda.

Joe Crust lived in a palatial villa on the Saigon River separated from the road by a high wall. They rang the bell outside the gate, and a caretaker looked out through the grillwork and then swung it open. They drove down a white gravel driveway through manicured Japanese gardens toward the stately white house with a red-tiled roof. The car pulled up before the front door, and the girls piled out and waited for DeMarlo to park. They rang the doorbell, and a servant let them in and led them through a wide hallway to the other side of the house, which overlooked the polluted brown river. Set in the center of a flagstone terrace was a large, blue-shimmering swimming pool. Joe Crust shuffled across the patio toward them, leaning heavily on his fancy cane. His face looked as though two powerful thumbs had forced in the deep depressions that ran from the bridge of his nose, down under his slightly crossed eyes, and into his sallow cheeks. His gray-white hair was combed back from his forehead. He stared at Jody, something approaching a pleased expression on his dissipated face. Walking up behind Crust was General Hare. He gave Jody a hearty welcome and threw an arm over her shoulder.

"Joe, you remember meeting Jody T. Neale in Binh Duc."

"Of course," Joe Crust said, the firm voice belying his frail appearance. He extended his left hand, which Jody shook gingerly, almost afraid she might hurt him.

"Nice to see you again, Mr. Crust. It's been a long time."

"Too long, Jody. And call me Joe, won't you? I'm happy you found your way to my place."

"I intended to contact you, Joe. By the way, is Art Line around? He said he might have some business opportunities for me if I ever came to Saigon."

"The Cork is checking out the clubs up north," Joe replied affably. "But anything he had in mind for you I'm sure I can take care of." Joe's small moustache accentuated the twisted, lewd smile on his face; his one good eye burned brightly.

General Hare, perhaps planning a pitch of his own, spoke up loudly.

"Jody I heard you closed the club in Nha Trang and moved to Saigon. Why haven't you looked me up? I might be able to help you."

Jody had thought of seeking Hare's aid in her selling activities, but she had no desire to become obligated to him. "I've been planning to, Rabbit," Jody lied. "Are you G-1 at USARV now?"

"Just breaking in," Hare replied. "I got back from the States ten days ago. Here, let me introduce you around." As Joe Crust greeted other guests, Hare took Jody about the pool area. First she met a young Japanese couple. The girl looked young and had startling round eyes and incredible breasts for a Japanese woman. She and her husband bowed slightly to Jody. They were introduced as Yoko and Arki Yamamura.

"Arki handles Joe Crust's business in Japan," Hare explained. Jody said a few words in Japanese to them, and Yoko smiled and replied in Japanese. Suddenly a raucous shout of glee rang out, and Marie bounded across the patio to them. She and Yoko embraced. They seemed delighted to see each other. Each took a drink from a passing servant, and in un-Japanese fashion began chatting together. Jody was introduced to the rest of the guests, including a Vietnamese woman in her late twenties who had two obviously half-Caucasian children with her.

"I wish I'd brought my bikini," Jody said when the introductions were over and she was sipping a drink.

"Joe keeps a few handy in the bathroom closet," Marie said. "Help yourself to one. Rhonda and I will join you."

To get to the bathroom they passed through Joe Crust's bedroom. It looked like a movie set. The bed was huge and round, covered with a heavy black and white velvet spread. The carpet, fully three inches thick, was white and shaggy, nearly impossible to walk on in high heels. The ceiling was high, and the walls were covered with dozens of tastefully erotic pictures suggesting sexual intercourse. The shades were drawn and dim blue lights shed an ethereal glow over the whole scene.

"You seem to know the Japanese couple pretty well," Jody commented.

"Yoko was famous among the high American officers and government people. She had affairs with so many she began to think she was American. Joe used her to further his Japanese interests and introduced her to Arki. He arranged the marriage for business purposes; they see that Joe's goods are well represented in the U.S. PXs throughout Japan. As a swinging husband-and-wife team they are very popular with the Americans in Japan."

"When you look at Joe Crust it's hard to imagine he has all that money and power," Jody mused. "If he lay down with his eyes closed they'd bury him."

Marie chuckled. "Yes. And the booze gets him too. He has to go to a rest home in Taiwan every few months to dry out. He's a real bastard when he's on the wagon."

"Where is he from?" Jody asked.

"He was born in Shanghai, he claims, of American parents. His father's dead, but his mother lives in Hanoi. He's always been in the Orient, but for a while he was spending a lot of time in Germany, selling to the military market, particularly the PXs. In fact, I'm surprised that none of the Saigon PX wheels are here today. He usually has one or two of them running around."

Stepping through the bedroom door into daylight was like awakening from a strange dream. Besides the girls, the only other person swimming was Crust. The others sat at the side of the pool, sipping drinks.

After the swim, Jody, Marie, and Rhonda changed into their clothes again, and the party moved from the patio into the spacious Chinese-motif parlor. Stereophonic music provided a restful background for the conversation. Cocktails were being served when the buzzer indicated that someone was at the gate.

The front door was opened, and almost immediately everyone in the room was conscious of an overpowering scent of perfume permeating the house. The eyes of all the men were riveted on the hallway as an exotic Vietnamese woman swept into the room. She was wearing a dark-red, gold-trimmed *au dai*. Her long, black hair curled from the top of her head halfway to her waist. Two huge diamonds glittered from each hand, and diamond bracelets encircled both her wrists. Another multicaret diamond hung suspended from a frail platinum chain around her neck.

Jody whispered to Marie, "If those stones are real, she's wearing a quarter of a million dollars."

"They're real," Marie assured Jody. "Madame Sang owns a million dollars' worth of diamonds. They were given to her by her Chinese boyfriend, who's in business in Paris. Confidentially, he's one of the chief financiers of the Vietnamese Communists.

As Madame Sang advanced across the room, the men rose to their feet. "Look at that," Jody said softly. "They can't take their eyes off her. She reeks sensuality."

"And would you believe, she's fifty years old," Marie commented.

"She doesn't look a day over thirty," Jody marveled.

"Oh, she looks great," Marie conceded. "I don't want to be catty, but she never goes out with less than an inch of expertly applied makeup masking her face."

It was some minutes after Madame Sang's electrifying entrance before anyone noticed the two very young doll-pretty Vietnamese girls who had followed her into the room. General Hare immediately rushed to Madame Sang's side and gallantly offered her a cigarette, which she took with the grace of a queen accepting some trifle from an adoring subject. Joe Crust stumped up to Hare and Madame Sang. "Rabbit, this is the little lady I've been wanting you to meet. Madame Sang."

General Hare took the Oriental lady's right hand in his and bowed his head as he greeted her. "Later on," Crust continued, "I think you and Madame Sang will find many mutually interesting topics of discussion." Then, leaving them together, Crust approached the two young Vietnamese girls and began talking to them. He led them to a sofa and sat between them.

Marie took Jody over to Madame Sang and introduced her. Jody found it difficult not to stare at the near magic of her cosmetology. Joe Crust was so occupied with the two little Oriental toys Madame Sang had brought him that he was virtually incommunicado.

As the cocktail hour continued, Jody, Yoko, Marie, and Rhonda gossiped while Arki and Tony DeMarlo talked business. General Hare was completely absorbed in intimate conversation with Madame Sang.

After an hour of intense conversation, Joe Crust led the way into the dining room. As his guests laughed and chatted, the host seemed to be slipping into a stupor from which the two young Vietnamese girls on either side of him laughingly tried to jog him. Immediately after coffee was served, Rabbit Hare stood up. "Hate to eat and run, Joe, but I've got to get back to duty. I'll drive Madame Sang home." He and Madame Sang took their leave and walked arm in arm to the front door outside.

Joe Crust pushed himself to a standing position and, taking his cane in his right hand, beckoned to the two Vietnamese girls with his left. "Good night," he slurred, and the three of them left the dining room and disappeared into the bedroom.

"I don't believe it," Jody said. "He looks such a wreck I don't see what use he could have for one girl, much less two."

Marie stood up. "Well, the Great God of Saigon has dismissed us." She turned to Tony DeMarlo. "Shall we leave?"

After Rabbit Hare and Madame Sang left Joe Crust's villa, they decided to go somewhere for a quiet nightcap. Madame Sang sent her own car home and rode with the General. As they drove, Madame Sang offered to show Hare an interesting place where they could have a drink without being disturbed. She directed the driver to a dingy-looking two-story building on a back street. Rabbit helped her out of the car and followed her to a heavy door, which was opened for them by an old Vietnamese man. Madame Sang led Rabbit into a musty-smelling office. Filing cabinets, record books, and loose papers were strewn around the room. A sign on the wall read, TRAN-TAM IMPORTS, EXPORTS.

Rabbit was a little confused, but he followed the Dragon Lady through the office and up a rickety staircase. At the top of the stairs she unlocked a door and pushed it open.

Rabbit stepped in and pulled up short in surprise. The opulence before him was breathtaking. The entire room was bathed in a soft pink glow. The lighting, the carpets, the velvet chairs, all were a pastel pink. Huge mirrors covered the walls and a crystal chandelier hung from the ceiling. Even the minuscule bulbs in the chandelier sparkled with a pink light.

Madame Sang clapped her hands, and immediately two young Viet-namese girls glided into the room. They were wearing floor-length diaphan-ous pink gowns with nothing underneath.

The Dragon Lady put a drink into Rabbit's hand and said a few words to the girls in Vietnamese. One of them left the room; the other knelt down and removed Rabbit's shoes, took his feet in her lap, and began to massage them as Madame Sang talked.

"This place is only, how you say, a sideline for me," she began. "It is the salon for a steam bath and massage parlor. You will see the premises after we have talked. I have only a small, select clientele here. Mostly high Vietnamese government officials and generals. A handful of prominent Chi-nese and French patrons come to me, but you are the first American I have invited here."

With the girl caressing his feet and the exotic Madame Sang beside him, Rabbit began to get carried away. He reached out for Madame Sang; she merely took his hand, squeezed it, and continued working on him. "My friend Joe Crust tells me you are taking on a very big job at Long Binh. But he is afraid you may be lonely. I would like to help you enjoy life a little more."

"I think you could do that just fine," Rabbit responded, trying to get his arms around her. She pressed against him for a moment and then slipped away.

"One reason I wanted you to see this place," she said, beginning to sound businesslike, "is because I have a wonderful idea to help the poor American boys over here. If they had a chance to enjoy a nice steam bath and massage their morale would be greatly improved."

"There are a hundred steam baths here in Saigon the men can use," the general answered.

"Yes. But most of them are dirty and no good. Besides, most of the boys can't get out of Long Binh. My idea is a much better one. It would take your help and authority to make it work." She looked at him tauntingly. "There would be many rewards in it for you."

Rabbit bit on that line. "Let me hear what you have in mind," he asked eagerly.

"Well— I have a million dollars in piasters to invest. I asked Joe Crust if he had any suggestions. We talked for a long time, and we both decided that it would be very good if I were allowed to build a very big, modern steam bath inside the Long Binh post. I would put up a beautiful big building and hire maybe two hundred lovely young girls to give massages. It would be so wonderful for the poor boys who can't leave the post. All we need is for you to get us permission."

Rabbit sat back startled. He didn't want to lose Madame Sang before he even got her, so he tried to sound promising. "I wouldn't want to be accused of giving permission for prostitutes to come right on an American military installation," he hedged.

"Oh, no!" cried the Dragon Lady, highly offended. "I would pick all the girls myself. They would all be very high-class girls. They would receive training from our best masseuses. It isn't prostitution the way my girls would make the men feel happy and relaxed."

Madame Sang quickly decided that more persuasion was necessary. She stroked his neck with her long fingers, her nails scratching slightly. "We would be more or less partners," she said. "There would be no trouble."

Now Rabbit understood matters. "Well, maybe it could be worked at that," he said finally.

"Why don't you let my girls give you a steam bath and massage now while you think about it? Then we will talk again." Without waiting for his reply she clapped her hands, and the two young girls were at her side. She talked rapidly in Vietnamese, and they disappeared. Then she turned to Rabbit and started unbuttoning his shirt, her closeness and scent cutting off all objections. The girls reappeared, one carrying a robe, the other a large bath towel.

Rabbit surrendered. "Well," he said, "I suppose anything Joe Crust recommends should at least be thoroughly investigated." When they had him undressed and wrapped in the robe the two pretty girls led him away.

Half an hour later a smiling, satisfied, and slightly weary Rabbit Hare followed the two girls back to the pink salon where Madame Sang was waiting. He sat back in the chair beside her, and a snifter of cognac was placed in his hand. "Were my girls pleasing?" Madame Sang inquired.

"Very much so," he affirmed.

"Good. Then we can make a deal."

Rabbit sat upright. "Now wait a minute. Yes, your girls are great. But I can't allow them to be dressed like this and—ah—finish up their massage the way they do, on my post." He was grinning sheepishly.

"Oh, my dear, lovely general, it would be different out there. My girls were so anxious to please you tonight that they perhaps went beyond moral procedure, but my girls are trained to be discreet. We make one or two small changes for the Long Binh operation so there is no trouble."

"Well,"—Rabbit yawned and stretched sleepily,—"I think we will work something out." He covered a second yawn. "I have a hard day tomorrow, but perhaps tomorrow evening the two of us can discuss this further."

Her lips formed a self-satisfied, feline smile. "I will be happy to see you tomorrow, General," she said.

"Oh, don't be so formal." Hare chuckled. "We're practically partners. Call me Rabbit the way my friends do."

Madame Sang's laugh was like the tinkle of a crystal bell. "Yes, Rabbit. Tomorrow."

She watched the girls help him finish dressing, and then he walked out of the luxurious room, down the stairs, and through the musty office to the front door. The old Vietnamese unbolted it and let him out. He turned for a moment and looked back at the building, then stepped briskly into the staff car.

September, 1967

Madame Sang's brother stepped off the Air France 707 jet that had just flown him into Saigon from Paris. As soon as he had passed through customs and immigration they embraced and then hurried from the hot terminal to the large, white air-conditioned limousine.

The driver veered out into the traffic and started for downtown Saigon. Madame Sang turned anxiously to her brother. "How is my lover?" she asked.

"He is well. He said to tell you he wishes you could still be with him in Paris, but your work here is of great importance."

"I understand that," the Dragon Lady replied wistfully.

"I was with your lover, Siao, when he received your last letter about the steam bath in Long Binh. He is very pleased with your efforts."

"I'm so glad to see you back. I need your help badly. There's much more than I can do here. The contractors have already started building the steam bath, and they are working furiously to finish it in six weeks. The demand will be extreme. Oh, these dirty, thieving Vietnamese sons of dogs are robbing me cruelly."

"You shouldn't talk about your own people that way," the brother protested.

The Dragon Lady spat. "I am from the North, and so are you. Never forget it. These southern pigs are not my people."

"All right, all right," her brother said placatingly. "Now, speaking of the North, I have another message for you from Siao." He looked around cautiously. "Are you sure the driver can't hear us?"

"He can't hear through that glass divider."

"Good. Siao is worried about the money you will make from the steam bath. He has learned that the Americans will only pay Vietnamese nationals in piasters."

"I know that."

"Siao believes you will make the thirty thousand dollars a month you estimated, but he cannot purchase arms for the National Liberation Front and North Vietnamese with piasters. You must arrange to get U.S. dollars."

"That will be difficult."

"What about the French citizenship and French passport you obtained during the ten years you lived in Paris?"

"You mean I should claim to be French and not Vietnamese? A third-country national?"

"That's the only way you can receive the steam bath profits in dollars."

"But everyone knows I'm Vietnamese. That passport wouldn't fool anyone."

"What about this American general of yours? As long as you have a French passport wouldn't he go along with you? It sounds as though you have made some sort of a love slave of him."

"It's possible. As a matter of fact, it would save him a lot of trouble if I could give him his share directly in dollars." Her eyes lit up with excitement. "Siao will have his money in hard currency to help finance the war against these southern swine and their stupid American advisers."

Madame Sang's brother put his arm around her affectionately. "When we take over the government in the South your contribution will not be forgotten, Sister."

15

In the old De Soto Jody headed for Long Binh to keep the appointment she had made the previous day with Earl Picking. As always, the drive was nerve-racking and hot. She opened the windows a little to let in some air, being careful not to allow too much dust to blow in.

When Jody arrived, there were several salesmen sitting in Picking's outer office, waiting to see him. He waved her into the inner office. "Wait ten or fifteen minutes," he said, "and then we'll have us a cool drink."

Half an hour later, over two cold Cokes at the nearest club, he said, "The reason I asked you to come out here was to see if you'd like to manage a Vietnamese band that works for me. I know you have show-business experience, and I figured this might interest you."

Puzzled, Jody asked, "Why do they need a manager if they work for you?"

"The Army is starting a new system. No entertainer or group can work unless they have an agent. That way somebody is responsible for them if anything goes wrong." He took a long sip of his drink. "Special Services is registering agents now."

"Why doesn't one member of the band act as agent for the group?"

"Because Special Services won't accept Vietnamese agents. The clubs all pay by U.S. checks, and it's illegal to give a U.S. check to a Vietnamese national. But if the club pays an American or third-country national by check, the regulations say that's okay, providing the checks are mailed to your account out of the country and not cashed within Vietnam. Then you make a money exchange with the bank, and pay your people in piasters."

Jody began to feel a tingle of excitement at getting into a new and compatible enterprise. "When can I hear the band and talk to them?"

"This evening. They have a Vietnamese agent, but under the new rule this is the last day I can book them until they get a new agent."

Jody paused, then, concealing the wariness she felt, asked, "You could have gone to Ronnie Jasper. He's become the biggest agent out here, and I hear he makes it worthwhile for club sergeants to book his shows. Why are you helping me this way, Earl?"

"In the first place, I don't take no kickbacks. And I thought you had some help coming your way. You won't get anywhere selling furniture, and you know show business. I'd take the band on myself, but the new regulations say no military man can register as an agent."

Jody stayed down at Long Binh that evening and listened to the band. Their spokesman was the lead guitar player, Kim, who was about twenty years old, taller than average, with a mouth full of gold teeth and an irregular patch of bleached blond at the front of his wild head of hair. His shoes had no laces, and he wore no socks. The band's sound was passable, she thought, but she would have to do something about their appearance.

She worked out the financial arrangements with Kim. She would have to rent a microbus to transport the group, which included two girl singers, to and from their engagements. Still, she calculated that with a reasonably full booking schedule she could clear two to three thousand dollars a month. There were many more entertainers in Vietnam than when she had first arrived sixteen months earlier, Jody discovered. For the past six months they had been pouring in from Korea and the Philippines, but most of the talent was third-rate.

One week later she hired a microbus, signed contracts with the members of the band, and registered herself as a talent agent under the name Jody T. Promotions. The newly formed Commercial Entertainment Office of the Special Services was headed by a Lieutenant Pine, an artillery officer trying desperately to understand how he ended in show business. He handed Jody a list of regulations, and after reading them she began to understand the problems of doing business with a military bureaucracy. Among the rules was one that forbade agents and entertainers to possess MPC. Yet on the posts where they would be working, all food and drink was sold for MPC only. So it was either acquire and use MPC illegally or go hungry and thirsty. Most of the other regulations were equally absurd.

Apparently other entertainment bookers realized that Jody was potentially a formidable competitor. Only hours after she had registered at the CEO she received a call in her hotel room from Lieutenant Pine.

"Lieutenant Pine, here," the youthful voice said, trying to take on a stern sound. "After you left here this morning I had a visit from some of the other agents who said you are a striptease dancer."

She immediately suspected Ronnie Jasper. He was the most powerful and most ruthless of the agents and had never forgiven Jody for quitting his stable. "No, Lieutenant, I'm not a stripper. I used to be for a brief time, but I gave it up."

"I've already given you your papers, but if you continue to strip I will have to revoke them," Lieutenant Pine went on severely.

"Lieutenant Pine," Jody said patiently, "I've read the regulations, and as I said, I have no intention of stripping again."

"Okay," he said crisply. "But don't forget that, or you're finished." With this friendly conversation and with the good wishes of her colleagues so obviously expressed, Jody began her new career as a talent booker.

It particularly annoyed her to see some of the other people who were getting licenses to act as theatrical agents. Half of them were Filipino truck drivers and laborers working for General Crowninshed's Orient Architecture and Engineering. To them, becoming a talent agent seemed an easy way to make extra money. The fact that they were moonlighters who didn't know a guitar from an oboe meant nothing to the confused Lieutenant Pine and his staff, since they didn't know the difference themselves.

During the ensuing months, Jody's band was booked regularly at Long Binh, and Jody found herself an apartment in a new building on Plantation Road. She brought My Linh down from Nha Trang to assist her in the booking business, and before she knew it, she was experiencing her second Tet celebration, the treacherous Tet offensive of 1968. Although fighting was heavy at Tan Son Nhut, less than a mile from her brand-new apartment, and house-to-house fighting with the Vietcong raged in the streets, she woke up the morning of Tet unaware that a battle had erupted around her during the night. She had been to a party the night before and was suffering from a hangover. She had only moved into the apartment the day before and cursed the noise from the street, assuming it was the customary Tet firecrackers. For the past seven years she had lived through the Lunar New Year celebration in various countries throughout the Orient and always dreaded the event.

Her apartment was all but empty, with no radio, food supplies or even drinking water. Furthermore, being the first tenant to move in, she was all alone in the building. Jody had sent Tien and My Linh home for the three-day holiday, so, feeling hungry and thirsty, she set out on foot for the villa of some former Special Forces men, now working for the CIA's private airline, Air America. As she walked along the deserted streets she idly wondered where all the people were. Then, as she neared the villa of her friends, she heard a roaring noise. Several helicopters appeared overhead. She looked up into the sky at the gun ships and almost stumbled over a couple of ragged, black-clad bodies lying on the side of the road.

Shocked at what she thought was police negligence in leaving bodies lying about, she grumbled to herself the rest of the way to the villa. Her four friends were shocked to see Jody and stared at her as though she were some kind of apparition. Jody was somewhat shaken herself to learn that the war had moved into Saigon and that nobody was allowed in the street. Only her flowing blond hair, the men decided, had saved her from gun-ship fire. The pilots had orders to shoot anything in the streets that moved.

Jody spent the day at the villa, listening to reports of the fighting on the military radio. In spite of the protests made by the former Green Berets, she decided to return to her apartment for the night. "If I made it safely up, I'll make it safely back," she declared. "Besides, I have my trusty twenty-five-caliber pistol. That's all the protection I need."

Troops from the Twenty-fifth Division had been flown in from their base at Cu Chi, twenty-three miles west of Saigon, to drive out the VC who had penetrated Tan Son Nhut and the surrounding area all the way to Cholon. It was a noisy night: the sky was alight with illuminating flares, and few people tried to sleep.

Across the street from Jody's apartment was a USAID hotel building, which housed American male and female civilian personnel. During the entire period of the Tet offensive, from morning to night, they romped around the rooftop, drinking beer and enjoying an enforced holiday from the office. In fact, everywhere Jody looked, groups of people could be seen on the roofs of the taller buildings, drinking and enjoying the fun. For them, it was a carnival rather than a war.

These were the Saigon warriors (or Saigon queens, as the fighting men called them with contempt), military men who had cushy desk jobs in Saigon, lived in comfortable air-conditioned villas, worked in air-conditioned head-quarters offices, ate good food, and watched floor shows and movies every night. Under the latest regulations they even drew combat pay the same as the men out in the jungles who were fighting for their lives.

The civilians, men and women alike, enjoyed high-paying jobs, felt perfectly safe in Saigon, and avoided all likely danger spots. Long, leisurely lunches at the post Circle Sportif were the order of the day, and what was left of the afternoon was spent planning cocktail and dinner parties for the evenings. Having seen how the GIs lived out in the "boonies," Jody was disgusted by the attitudes and way of life of these people.

She wondered how the helicopter pilots felt up there in the sky, being shot at from the ground while looking down on a sea of grinning, drinking American faces. One pilot later told her, "Flying long hours over Saigon, constantly taking rounds in the fuselage and being badly in need of sleep, and then seeing those Americans partying on the rooftops gave me the greatest desire to let loose a couple of rockets into their cocktails instead of into the VC!"

Tet of 1968 marked a change in Jody's operations. For over a month after the offensive all floor shows were canceled at the camps. Naturally her musicians were happy, since they were on salary whether they worked or not, but Jody couldn't afford to pay them indefinitely, and her funds were being depleted at an alarming rate.

June, 1969

Although Rick Townsend and O'Neill were constantly interviewing people who could shed some new light on the operations of the Khaki Mafia, Sergeant Picking had proved to be their most knowledgeable and cooperative witness by far. O'Neill found that by taking testimony from Picking a little at a time, and checking it out afterwards, he could amass a sizable investigation file.

"I'm sorry to have to hold you in town like this, Picking," he said before their third interview," but I suppose things aren't too uncomfortable at that villa Joe Crust keeps at the club sergeants' disposal."

Picking grinned sheepishly but said nothing.

"Before we finish I'd like a complete rundown on what happens over there," Rick interposed.

"I'll be glad to tell you what I know," Picking replied. There was a look of concern on his face. "But people will be wondering what I'm doing so long in Saigon this trip."

"We're going to be very careful, Picking," O'Neill reassured the custodian. "Now let's hear more about Vamalot. How much money did they put up to get Vamalot going?"

"I never was involved in their company. I heard a lot about it, of course. They pulled off a lot of big deals; they still are."

"Did Cotsworth put up the original money?"

In spite of his anxiety Picking grinned and let out a chuckle. "I can tell you, it was something else the way they got the first twelve thousand in the kitty."

"Let's start this morning off with you telling us about it," O'Neill suggested.

"That was back the first of 1968. I was getting ready to turn my job over to Sergeant Elroy James. Red Fisher had just arrived at Long Binh and was waiting to go over to Di An and take over as custodian there. Red came up to my office looking for Jesse James, who was going through my files with me."

"Go on," Rick urged as Picking paused.

"Just trying to get things straight in my mind, sir. I didn't see everything that happened myself, but I sure heard about it."

"We're happy to have you give us hearsay testimony, Sergeant," O'Neill assured him. "It all helps the pieces fit together."

"Right, sir. I remember telling James and Fisher I was kind of sorry to be leaving with all the big projects underway. A Chinese restaurant was

111

just being finished, and a bunch of new clubs were being authorized. There was even a big steam bath under construction. I couldn't believe it when I heard that two hundred girls would be there to give the guys massages Saigon style— and on a military post!"

Picking grinned and shook his head. "Jesse told me to see Cotsworth when I hit the States. He said they needed experienced men who knew how to cooperate.

"Ole Jesse and Red were really pleased they was going to be custodians so close together. The First Division at Di An where Red was going is only fifteen miles from Long Binh. I remember Jesse didn't think much of the beat-up old jeep I drove when I was custodian. Before I was processed out of the Nam he had an air-conditioned station wagon with a radio. That's when I knew it was going to be Germany all over again, only on a bigger scale."

Picking glanced uneasily at Major Unger. The provost-marshal officer represented military discipline and retribution. He was leaning forward in his chair, his sharp features intent. O'Neill sensed Picking's uneasiness. Telling all to civilians was one thing, but confessing to an MP officer was something else.

"Please go on, Sergeant," O'Neill said quietly. "You have nothing to fear personally from this investigation."

Picking nodded dubiously. "Well, Red Fisher and Sergeant Munn, the bookkeeper at Di An, were two of a kind. And Red didn't waste any time making the first deal for Vamalot. He had Norman and Lavinia Ferris in his office his first day on the job and ordered a twenty-ton walk-in freezer from them. They took the order, acting as sales representatives for Snead Electronics, Joe Crust's company. And of course, Lavinia was sitting there in Red's office, crossing and uncrossing her legs and kind of promising him everything. The price of the freezer was nine thousand dollars. That included ten percent for Red and a commission for the Ferrises on top.

"And while Red was talking to the Ferrises, Jesse James was holding a meeting of the board of governors of the Long Binh open-mess system. These governors were all sergeants that Cotsworth had been putting in for several months.

"Jesse asked for more slot machines and a walk-in freezer that would cost twelve thousand dollars. Naturally, the board okays anything he wants. The officer adviser to the board goes along too. And Jesse gets approval to buy the freezer from a new sales company, Vamalot." Picking chuckled and looked over at O'Neill.

"I guess you can figure what happened. The freezer was delivered to First Division and paid for out of open-mess funds. But it never got off the truck. The truck leaves Di An that same night and hauls the freezer over to Long Binh, where Jesse James takes delivery and gets an invoice for twelve thousand dollars from Pancho O'Leary, who runs Vamalot in Saigon. He gives Pancho a check for the twelve on Long Binh open-mess funds, and that's how Vamalot got started."

Picking paused again, shaking his head. "Of course, Red got laid by Lavinia and eventually almost all of the custodians ended up doing business with her and her husband."

Picking paused at the end of his narration and looked questioningly at his inquisitors.

"That was most useful information, Picking," Rick said encouragingly.

"About one or two more sessions and we should be finished with you," O'Neill went on. "You are helping us greatly. We'll certainly do anything we can to help you in the future. We're going out to your division tomorrow morning and interview Sergeant Munn."

"Picking's jaw dropped, and a glint of fear showed in his eyes. "He won't tell you anything. Munn's an old hand. He's supposed to be working for me, but sometimes I think it's the other way around."

"Does he do a good job?" Rick asked.

"Right now he's pissed off good at me because I told him I wanted new food suppliers. Munn's married to a Viet girl, and her father has been selling the club system at the First Division everything from the printed chit books to vegetables, eggs, fruit, and poultry. His prices are too high, and his quality gets worse all the time. It's not fair to the guys when they come in from the field."

"Munn has been the bookkeeper out there for two years, hasn't he?" O'Neill asked.

"That's right. But he's one of them, the syndicate."

"What about the killing of the witness to the alleged beer stealing you and Munn were accused of?" Rick asked.

"I don't know anything about that. But I have my own ideas." Picking's voice quavered. "You won't tell him you've been talking to me, will you?"

"Of course not. Don't worry, Picking, we wouldn't want anything to happen to you."

"That Munn's a bad one, sir."

"That's why we want to talk to him, Picking. Come on by tomorrow afternoon about four and we'll try to finish up with you."

16

FEBRUARY, 1968

After Tet Jody drove out to Long Binh, where her band played most of their engagements. She found Sergeant Picking in his office.

"Well, you come just in time to say good-bye, Jody T.," Picking drawled a greeting. "I'm going home."

"I'm really sorry to see you go," Jody said.

"Be real nice to get back, but I'm kind of worried for you."

"Why, Earl?"

"Well ole Elroy James is coming in, taking my place. Back in Germany we called him Jesse James 'cause he's such a damn robber. I was wondering when Tiger Cotsworth would start moving his crowd in on Vietnam."

"Sergeant Major Cotsworth?" Jody asked, her face lighting up.

"That's right. He's soon going to be command sergeant major at MACV."

"That's wonderful. I met Sergeant Cotsworth at my club in Nha Trang. I hope I'll get to know him."

"You will, Jody. You sure will."

"Has Sergeant James come in yet?"

"He's here," Picking sighed. "You can look for plenty of changes."

"Maybe you could introduce me," Jody suggested.

"Sure, I'll do that." Picking seemed to want to tell her something, Jody sensed, but he couldn't get it out. He merely sat, looking pained. Then a fat, red-faced master sergeant with a bull neck and heavy jowls appeared in the office. His hair was gray and close-cropped. As he and Sergeant Picking talked, his words came out slowly, in a monotone. Picking introduced Jody to Jesse James, explaining that the Long Binh clubs had been using her band regularly.

"I am looking forward to keeping my bands busy out here now that all the Tet excitement is over and the clubs are running shows again," Jody said with a brightness she didn't feel as she looked into the sergeant's unresponsive, heavy features.

"I'm gonna have to look things over real careful," Jesse James replied in his grating voice. "Until I make my survey, don't send your band out here. I've got all I need."

Picking looked on helplessly and managed to say, "Jody's done a first-rate job for the clubs, James. She tells you she'll have a band at the club a certain time, it's going to be there."

Jesse James stared at the younger sergeant insolently. "I guess I know how to handle clubs, Picking." Then turning to Jody, "Don't count too heavy on Long Binh no more to book your band."

Later Picking took Jody to a club for a cold drink. "Sorry about that, Jody. Now you see why we call him Jesse James."

"Why doesn't he want to use my band?" Jody asked.

"He'll be making his own deals with his own people, I guess."

"I've heard a rumor at the I House that from now on there's going to be a lot of people asking for kickbacks."

Picking looked at her uncomfortably. "I don't know. I never went in for nothing like that."

"Of course not, Earl. But judging by Sergeant James's attitude, it doesn't look good for me at Long Binh anymore."

Picking nodded somberly. "Ole Jesse and his gang're soon going to be taking over here, I'm afraid."

Despondently Jody rode back to Saigon wondering what to do about her band. That evening she talked the problem over with My Linh, and early the next morning she had Tien drive her out to Cu Chi, the home of the Twenty-fifth Infantry Division, in the hope of getting her band booked steadily there.

The road to Cu Chi was a far cry from the four-lane highway to Long Binh. The convoys, their horns constantly shrieking, had the right of way on the pitted dirt road and stopped for nothing because of the frequent VC ambushes. The chief hazard of the trip was the nightly mining of the edges of the road by VC sympathizers. A prudent driver always tried to keep well in the center; it was like a game of Russian roulette when the convoys forced smaller vehicles onto the shoulders.

The color scheme of the drab camp, sitting like a scab in the earth, was black, brown, and gray. The smell was of grease, dust, sweat, and smoke. Unlike Long Binh, at Cu Chi one custodian did not control all the clubs in the area. There were about thirty-two NCO and enlisted men's clubs, and each one had an individual manager who did the buying for his own club. Each thousand-man battalion had three clubs—a large one for the EM, a smaller one for the NCOs and the smallest for the officers. With the clubs sprinkled all over the spreading camp, Jody felt like giving up and going back to Saigon; it seemed impossible to contact even a small percentage of the club managers. But a conversation with one of the club sergeants stopped her.

The club manager told her that the whole division was starved for entertainment—the camp took more mortar attacks than most of the others near Saigon, and the facilities were exceedingly primitive. Most shows, particularly those with Caucasian girls in them, avoided Cu Chi.

As she drove through the dust and heat from one battalion to another, Jody everywhere discovered a desire for a band and a floor show, even if the girls were Vietnamese. The problem was that the various battalions were mostly out in the field, and there was no way of knowing definitely when one or another would be in.

However, Jody sensed that a reasonable business could be done at Cu Chi and discussed it with the club manager at the Wolfhound battalion. After an hour or more of talk, Jody and the sergeant arrived at a deal. She would bring the band out to Cu Chi on a permanent basis, and it would play for whatever battalion was in from the field. The Wolfhounds would feed and sleep the band in return for which it would put on a free show whenever they were in from the field. Lieutenant Colonel Ed Carrera, CO of the Wolfhounds, would be in with his men in a week or two, and he would ratify the arrangement, or so the club sergeant hoped. Meanwhile he informed her that Jody and her troupe were welcome to take up residence.

The Vietnamese band settled in happily. All the musicians were draft dodgers, and there was always the chance that they would be picked up if they traveled around too much. Inside the camp they were safe from the Vietnamese police. Each of the girls in the show was the girl friend of one of the musicians, so they were all content and making money. But for Jody it was roughing it.

They all had to sleep in the club and had to wait until the last drinker left each night before they could go to bed. After the club was cleared there was still the task of setting up the folding canvas cots, which had dirty sheets but no pillows. With the Vietnamese musicians all around her, jabbering in their dissonant tones, she found it almost impossible to fall asleep.

After each uncomfortable night a shrill whistle blast awoke them all at six a.m. In her crumpled clothing, Jody staggered outside and passed the troops relieving themselves at the urinal tubes that protruded from the dirt, and walked to the nearest toilet, a hundred yards away. They all pretended not to see each other with the exception of an occasional extrovert who would bid Jody a bright, "Good morning," while shaking the dew from his lilly. After leaving the toilet, she lined up with her troupe at the water tank and waited her turn to wash and brush her teeth, all in full view of the troops. Then she borrowed the room of Sergeant Brown, the club manager, long enough to change her clothes.

116

Just as she had adjusted to these limited conditions, the VC began mortaring the camp continually in retaliation for the heavy toll the GIs of the Twenty-fifth were taking of the Communists. The NVA and VC averaged three attacks a night, at eleven p.m., one a.m., and five a.m. The bunker that was nearest to the NCO club where they were sleeping was seventy yards away, and when the incoming began Jody rolled her troupe out of bed, and herding them in front of her, made a dash for the bunker.

During the first attack Jody struggled for a few moments to get her feet in her combat boots and lace them up. Then, in disgust, she ran barefoot for safety, arriving at the bunker with bruised and cut feet. From then on she always kept a pair of rubber thong sandals beside her.

As the attacks kept up night after night, the musicians and the two girl singers, Mai and Ellen, already tired from an evening of performing, became more and more irritable. At the end of the second week, Mai sprained her ankle running for shelter, and for some days hobbled around on a bandaged foot. Soon everyone was so exhausted that it became increasingly difficult to awaken the band at night and make them run for the bunker. One night, during a particularly heavy attack, Jody put her arm around Ellen, trying to hurry her along as they ran for cover. Suddenly they were bracketed with mortar rounds in front and behind them. Jody shouted at Ellen to fall to the ground, but the terrified girl kept running. Jody grabbed her and threw her to the ground, falling on top of her and pinning her down. They both trembled as the rounds burst so close that acrid smoke tingled in their throats and made their eyes smart. Twigs and pebbles fell on their backs. When the attack was over, Jody discovered that a flying pebble had cut through Ellen's cheek. Her face was badly swollen, and it was obvious she would not be able to sing for a while. Because of Ellen's injury and the general state of exhaustion from which the entire troupe was suffering, Jody decided to take everyone back to Saigon for a few days of rest. She finally realized why it was they had the Cu Chi business all to themselves.

For some time Jody had wanted to import a show from the Philippines. The talent was better there, and the girls looked more Caucasian than the Vietnamese. However, the Vietnamese wanted to keep every piaster worth of U.S. military business to themselves, and made it virtually impossible for foreign entertainers to get visas. Finally, the GIs protested: Why would they want to see only Vietnamese entertainers who looked just like the people they had been out fighting all week? Jody realized that American diplomats would soon insist on bringing in better entertainment for their soldiers.

When Ellen and Mai had recovered and the musicians were rested, Jody took her troupe back to Cu Chi. On her first evening back she met Lieutenant Colonel Ed Carrera, the Wolfhounds' battalion commander. It was obvious he had just returned from the field. His muscular body was baked a deep brown from many months under the tropical sun. The grim lines of his tanned face relaxed when he broke into a smile, and his dark hair, although short, was long enough to form a tousled nest of locks that fell onto the high forehead.

Sergeant Brown came up to Jody and whispered that she was staring at Hounddog 6, the Wolfhounds' CO. The number 6 denotes command, the sergeant explained, and then he made the introductions. Carrera and Jody were immediately attracted to each other. She was impressed by the regard the troops had for their CO. He was reputed to be the division's most esteemed battalion commander. Carrera, in turn, was grateful for all the time she and her band had spent entertaining his enlisted men.

When Carrera found out Jody was living in the NCO club with her band, he insisted she move into his hooch when he returned to the field. The following day he ordered his executive officer to have a private shower and toilet built onto the hooch. Jody was grateful, though worried about how it would look to the men. The colonel was unruffled. He and his men had full confidence in each other.

A week after Houndog 6 went back to the field with his men, Jody decided it would be a good time to make a trip to the Philippines and bring back a second band. Foreign entertainers had been approved once more. Those that had remained during the ban paid off as much as a thousand dollars to Vietnamese immigration officials to have their visas renewed.

In Manila Jody picked up a lively, talented, very Americanized group of ten musicians who called themselves Mary Jane and the Mammals. After endless paperwork, she arranged for them to come to Saigon. Even with Jesse James blocking her in Long Binh, Jody found plenty of bookings for her second group. Meantime, Ed Carrera was writing to her often from the jungle battlefields where the Wolfhounds were fighting. The pride he expressed in his men, and the cutting sorrow he experienced each time the casualty reports reached him, made her eyes brim with tears.

17

Now that Jody was obliged to keep two shows booked, she was very busy. Much of her time was spent with the Vietnamese band at Cu Chi. Although My Linh could be relied upon to accompany the Filipino show to their nightly bookings, she was no saleswoman, and Jody had to spend her days flying and driving around Vietnam in quest of bookings for Mary Jane and the Mammals.

Losing the business at Long Binh had been a blow to her. Had she gotten the bookings at Long Binh, those, combined with the permanent employment at Cu Chi, would have made her life simple and profitable. For a few weeks the Filipino troupe was working in the Saigon area. But after they had played all the clubs in Saigon and Tan Son Nhut, Jody had to start looking elsewhere for bookings.

She decided to try the II Field Force and the 199th Infantry Brigade. Both camps were near the big Long Binh installation.

Jody's first stop was the 199th, where she found the custodian in his office talking with the brigade sergeant major. To her surprise, it took little persuading to get the custodian to agree to book her show. She was about to leave, thinking how the rumors she had heard at the I House about kickbacks were exaggerated, when the sergeant tapped her on the shoulder.

"Now look here, girl," he said gruffly, "what's in it for me?"

Jody gasped and didn't answer.

"Come on, you know the score," he continued.

Jody decided to test the situation. "How about fifty dollars a show?" she asked.

The sergeant looked her up and down lewdly, as though waiting for her to add another inducement. "If that's all you're handing out I guess it will have to do. Don't forget to bring the bread next time you come."

What surprised Jody was the presence of the sergeant major during the conversation. Angrily she spun around on her heel. "There won't be any next time. I'll book my group elsewhere." The startled expressions on the faces of the sergeants was some consolation.

Next she drove to the camp at II Field Forces. Once there, she went in search of the club where she was told the custodian could be found. She walked into the club and was pleasantly surprised to see her old friend Ned Andrews, an Australian cowboy who, with his pretty Japanese wife, used to put on a Wild West show. He was sitting at a table waiting impatiently for the custodian.

"Ned! It's terrific to see you again," she said, hurrying to him. "Are you trying to book your act here?"

"Yeah, kid. Been waiting an hour for the bastard. Strike the flamin' crows, he's a rude bugger. He knows I'm waiting out here, and he's probably in the back room screwing one of the gook hooch maids."

Jody ordered a beer and was lifting the can to her lips when the custodian entered. He was a weedy-looking man with greasy, lank hair and bad teeth.

"You two lookin' for me?" he asked sourly.

"Yeah," Ned grunted.

"Okay, I'm in a hurry. What are you peddling?"

Ned looked annoyed but unfolded his posters and went into his pitch. When he was finished the sergeant turned his back and said to Jody, "Are you both together?"

"No. I'm the agent for a Filipino show," Jody answered.

"Okay, hang in." He turned to Ned. "I don't need any of yours," he said, dismissing the cowboy with a wave of his hand. Then, taking a step toward Jody, he stabbed at her with a grimy finger. "Whatever you're selling, girl, I'll buy some of it. But first it will take you thirty minutes out the back in my office."

Jody couldn't believe she had heard him properly, but the leer on the sergeant's face gave her indisputable proof of his conditions for securing a booking. Suppressing her rage, Jody managed to control her voice. "I'm not interested in that kind of *quid pro quo*. Good day, Sergeant."

As she drove back to Saigon, Jody realized that the stories about the kickback system were true. With her Filipino show played out in Saigon, and no business for her at the three camps in the surrounding area, it was going to take more effort than ever to keep them working. Her anger at the two sergeants had not abated when she arrived back in Saigon, and taking Ned as her witness she reported the two incidents to the CID. She was worried now about keeping her Filipino band working.

It was a month after her two disastrous interviews when Ed Carrera returned from the field with his Wolfhounds. Jody knew Hounddog 6 was back when she returned to his hooch after two days in Saigon and found his gear strewn all about the place. It was another couple of hours before he could get away from the meetings and briefings. Finally, he appeared, a big, happy smile on his face, and gave Jody a rough bear hug. "Let's have us a nice cold beer, and you can tell me what's been happening while I was away."

They talked for a while, and then before she knew it, Jody had to supervise her band for the next show. She started to leave, and then turned back to Ed. "By the way, I'll move back into the NCO club tonight."

"You'll do no such damned thing," he retorted. "You stay right here. I'll sleep in my office."

"That won't look so good to the men," Jody said.

"They won't know. I don't see you enough. Wait a few minutes and I'll change into civilian clothes and come with you and the band."

When the regular show was finished that night, Jody brought her troupe back to the Wolfhound officers' club. The officers had found a handful of Red Cross girls and nurses, and a real party ensued.

Around midnight, Ed was dancing with Jody when he stopped in mid-step and snapped his fingers.

"Hell, Jody, I promised one of my sergeants I would introduce him to you, and I clean forgot all about it."

"What does he want to meet me for?"

"He wanted your permission to sit in with the band on a few numbers whenever he is in from the field. I've heard him, and he's a damn good guitar player. Good soldier, too. One of my best."

"Well let's find him if it's not too late," Jody replied. "He can play with them now if he wants to."

"Good. I'll send my duty officer to try and find him."

Twenty minutes later, the duty officer led a youthful-looking staff sergeant into the officers' club. Ed Carrera hurried forward to meet him and threw an arm over his shoulder. "Sorry I didn't get you earlier, Crawley. Here, meet Miss Neale. I told her you were the greatest guitar player in all of Vietnam." The fair-haired, freckle-faced boy, obviously embarrassed, extended his hand toward Jody.

"Just call me Jody, sergeant," she said, and put him at ease.

"Thank you, ma'am. My name is Bryan Crawley." He clasped her hand and looked at her from deep, green eyes.

"Thank you, Bryan. I told the band you might play a few numbers with them—whenever you're ready."

The sergeant's face lit up, and he hurried over to the group. After he had been on the stand a few minutes it was obvious he was as good as Carrera said he was.

It was almost two in the morning when Ed walked Jody back to the hooch. "You may as well come in for a nightcap," Jody suggested. "It's your place, after all." Ed followed her in and put the wire latch over the door.

The only drink in the place was room-temperature bourbon, which Jody hated. But they made the best of it, and sat on the bed to talk. Ed had a lot on his mind. As usual, he had seen a great deal of heavy fighting. He talked quietly, telling Jody of his anxieties, his pride in his men, and his anguish each time one of them was killed. "I feel as if a little bit of myself dies each time one of my young troopers gets killed," he said sadly. "But as bad as I feel, I can't allow myself to dwell on it too long. If I did, I wouldn't be able to keep my mind on my business, and I'd end up with even heavier casualties."

Carrera stretched, drained his glass, and set it on the floor beside the bed. He put an arm tenderly around Jody. "You must have been able to read between the lines in those letters I wrote to you. Sure, I needed someone to unburden myself to, but it was more than that."

"Yes, Ed. I think I know."

He stroked her hair, and then kissed her on the nose. "Do you mind if I put the light out?"

"No, Ed," she whispered. As he pulled the cord, plunging the room into darkness, Jody felt excitement course through her veins. A shadowy light from outside filtered through the bamboo curtains. Only the distant boom of outgoing artillery broke the stillness of the quiet room. Ed took her face in his hands and kissed her eyelids and then her neck. As he kissed her gently on the mouth, she ran her fingers over his suntanned cheek. His kisses became demanding, and as she responded, he gently eased her back onto the bed. Lying on top of her, he continued to kiss her violently. Her pulse raced as he pulled away in order to undress her.

While he removed her garments one by one, he covered her body with gentle, nuzzling kisses. He kissed her ears, and then, running his tongue down the nape of her neck, began caressing her throat with his lips and tongue. Her eyes closed; she abandoned herself to the complete enjoyment of him. His lips moved over her shoulder and continued on down to nibble softly on her nipples, which sprang up erect between his teeth. She writhed with pleasure. Wearing only her nylon bikini panties, she waited expectantly as he stood up and quickly pulled off his clothes. Then he was back on the bed, kissing her mouth, his hands exploring every part of her body. She shivered as she felt his hands remove her panties, as they came free she strained her body upwards, pushing against his flesh with all her strength. She loved the feel of his hard, firm form as she felt his hand probing between her thighs, his fingers lovingly running back and forth over her moist wellspring of desire. Quivering all over, she reached down and caressed his hard manhood. As she closed her hand over it, it swelled even more, pulsating with life and sending little electric currents through her fingers, up her arms, and throughout her body.

He moved forward over her and then firmly lowered himself, pushing as she guided him into her trembling body. As he entered, Jody cried out ecstatically and threw her thighs around his buttocks. They moved together frantically, uncontrollably, one hot, electric circuit tingling in the darkness—bouncing, straining, clinging, and biting. Then, with one last convulsive thrust, their passion exploded. Jody cried out, her leg muscles taut, as she held him tightly to her. Then, drained, they fell back limply on the bed, lying there panting, their eyes closed. After a few moments she stirred and opened her eyes. She noticed that some of the little black, curly hairs from his chest had been shed and were stuck in the sweat on her breasts. He leaned forward and gave her a soft little kiss on the lips, and as he did so more sweat from his brow fell into her eyes, stinging them. Then he lay back again and fumbled for a cigarette in the pocket of his pants, which were in a heap on the floor beside them. Jody shakily stood up and made for the shower, taking a brown Army towel with her. She dipped it in the cool water, wrung it out, and sprinkled it with cologne. She turned to Ed, knelt beside the bed, and gently toweled his body.

"I'm sorry I was so quick, darling," he said dreamily. "It's been a long, long time."

"I wasn't left behind, don't worry," she replied smiling.

It was five in the morning when Lieutenant Colonel Carrera crept back to his office. Jody lay on the bed, half asleep, a smile on her lips, hoping nobody saw him leave.

18

For the next few months Ed Carrera was back and forth from the heavy fighting. Jody never knew when she would see him, or even if she would see him again. But when he was in camp she dropped all her other work and devoted her time to him. When he was away, which was most of the time, she flew all over the country keeping her Filipino band booked. She was getting a fair amount of business from the Ninth Division at Dong Tam in the Mekong Delta but the telltale signs of the sergeants' kickback system were beginning to show everywhere, as the divisions consolidated their clubs into the open-mess system and appointed sergeant custodians.

During one of his trips in from the field Ed had introduced Jody to his Brigade CO and immediate boss, Colonel "Hard Bill" Lane: a rough, tough, gravelthroated officer who was known as "Barking Dog" his radio call sign. Lane was cool to Jody when she first met him and she suspected he knew of her romance with Ed Carrera. His only comment to her was a disapproving, "War zones are no place for a woman."

One day during a lull in the fighting Jody finally persuaded Ed to take her out to the field so she could try to raise the spirits of the men. While she was talking to them, a helicopter suddenly swooped in and landed beside Lieutenant Colonel Carrera's chopper. From the helicopter a man in the starched fatigues of a rear-echelon officer nimbly jumped to the ground and strode toward Jody. The men around her stiffened to attention.

"Lord, have mercy, it's General Springer," Carrera said. He snapped a salute as the general came up to him.

The general frowned at the sight of a girl out in the middle of a combat zone.

"General Springer is the division deputy commander," Carrera explained after making the introductions, pleased that the general made no comment about Jody's presence. The men also relaxed as Springer asked routine questions about the Wolfhounds' positions and possibilities of contact with the enemy.

Just before returning to his helicopter Springer smiled warmly at Jody and asked her to come pay a visit to him sometime when she was back in camp. Jody and Ed watched the general's chopper ascend into the sky. "He's pretty frustrated in his desk job," Carrera observed. "But he'll get his ass shot off paying calls like this."

On the way back to Cu Chi in Ed's command and control helicopter Jody felt the chopper change course abruptly.

"What is it?" asked Jody.

"One of my platoons has just been ambushed and is pinned down. The company commander wants to send in two more platoons as a relief column. That's the oldest trick in Charlie's bag. He'll end up with the whole company trapped."

"What are you going to do?"

"We're heading for the ambush area immediately. Sorry, Jody. No time to take you back to Cu Chi."

"Don't worry about me, Ed. Just take care of your men."

Jody took a headset and pulled it on over her ears, so she would have some idea of what was going on below. They were soon flying over the ambush area, but from the air she could see nothing of what was going on. Ed, however, was able to tell exactly what was happening between the communications with the platoon leader and what he could see. She gathered that two platoons were fast coming up on the pinned-down men and that Ed had spotted the enemy ambush awaiting the relief column. He was directing his men to fan out and come in behind the secondary ambush. It both amazed and frustrated Jody that Ed could see exactly what she saw on the ground and could know where everybody was and how to direct the battle. As they circled above the troops on the ground, the pilot skillfully dodged enemy ground fire with erratic maneuvers, while another helicopter came into sight and began circling around beside them. At the same time Jody heard a new rasping voice over her headset, alternately barking orders and obscenities.

"Son of a bitch!" Ed exclaimed in a quick aside to Jody. "That's Barking Dog beside us—Colonel Hard Bill Lane."

After an hour of fighting, ending with nightfall the platoon was relieved and the enemy driven off. All elements of the company were united and dug in for the night. Carrera called to the pilot to take them back to Cu Chi, where he would drop Jody off and then return to his battalion.

They dropped into the helipad at Cu Chi. As Jody prepared to scuttle out from under the rotor-prop blast, another chopper landed beside them, and the short, broad-shouldered, red-faced, angry-looking colonel jumped to the ground, emphasizing his bellowing with hand signals to indicate that he didn't want Ed's chopper to take off.

He motioned Ed to follow Jody as she climbed out. His face was compressed in lines of rage. Ed and Jody quickly ran out from under the swirling blades, and when they reached Barking Dog, Carrera snapped to attention.

"What in the hell are you trying to pull, Colonel?" Hard Bill Lane sputtered. "Taking a female in your C and C over a battle area." He spat the words, his eyes bulging. Ed's discomfort was obvious.

"Sir, have you met Miss Jody Neale?" he started.

Jody interrupted. "Ed, I think I can explain to the Colonel."

Barking Dog shot a withering look at her. "I wasn't speaking to you, ma'am." Then turning to Ed, "Don't you know a battlefield is no place for a goddamned woman. There is only one place for them, and you didn't waste any goddamned time finding it when this female came here."

Jody blushed with embarrassment.

Colonel Lane paused, breathing heavily. He lashed out at Ed once more. "Don't you know you could lose your command over a stupid stunt like this? Now get your ass back to your men. I'll talk to you later. I can guarantee you haven't heard the last of this caper, Colonel!"

Jody gave Ed a look of worried sympathy and then hurried off, her heart aching at the trouble she had caused her lover. It was clear that Ed was no longer the colonel's favorite battalion commander.

Fortunately, Barking Dog never followed up on his threat, and Hounddog 6 continued to lead his Wolfhounds into battle. Jody avoided the grouchy Hard Bill Lane from then on, though it was difficult, since he seemed to know of her comings and goings and often happened to be on the scene where she was.

Late one afternoon Colonel Lane's chopper had just landed at Cu Chi, carrying him in from the field for an evening meeting with the commanding general of the Twenty-fifth Division. Jody was returning from Saigon, and her chopper alighted at almost the same time as Hard Bill's. As a testimony to the enemy's excellent intelligence, a mortar attack was launched just as the colonel was stepping out of his helicopter. The dozen men who had been aboard the two helicopters immediately hit the ground. Jody, who was wearing a clean, new dress instead of her customary fatigues, cursed aloud at having to dirty it. She was about to throw herself on the ground with the others when she noticed Hard Bill striding unconcerned toward his waiting jeep. Without thinking, Jody strode off behind him. He did not speak a word to her, but she didn't miss the flicker of surprise and grudging admiration in his eyes as they reached the now driverless jeep, the unmistakable whine of shrapnel cutting the air.

The driver was lying under the jeep, shaking. At the colonel's command he emerged, staring at Jody sheepishly, and took his seat behind the wheel.

Hard Bill stepped into his jeep and, without a backward glance, drove off, leaving Jody to walk back to the Wolfhound battalion in the shrapnel storm.

Ed Carrera arrived back from the field three days before he was to leave the Wolfhounds to return to the States. Jody was desolate at seeing him go. She had known from the beginning that he was married and that it would be a brief romance. But Jody thought that unless a girl is hell-bent on finding a husband it doesn't matter whether a man is married or not in Vietnam. With wives and families so far away, each man is temporarily a bachelor. The best thing a girl could do was enjoy it while it lasted, but be prepared, when the time came, to say good-bye with a smile.

Mournfully, Jody watched him pack. The quarters that had become so familiar to her became more and more alien and bare, as his toothbrushes, uniforms, helmets, and other personal belongings were put into his footlocker for transport. They shared one last night in the hooch, drinking room-temperature bourbon in memory of their first night. The following morning he turned over his command to the incoming battalion commander.

The change of command ceremony was graced by bright sunlight. Lieutenant Colonel Carrera stood in front of the battalion formation, so dark from the sun he looked like one of the Montagnard natives. The new commander looked strangely white and fragile by comparison. Jody heard the enlisted men muttering the usual comments. "What the hell have they given us now? This mother looks like a god-rotting desk jockey," or "This jackass is going to lead us? Thank God I'm short." Such were the comments at every change of command ceremony from the beginning of time.

The commanding general came down to witness the ceremony, to make a speech about Lieutenant Colonel Carrera's leadership capabilities, and to pin on his chest the medals he had earned. General Springer was on hand to congratulate Ed on his successful tour. Then, aside to Jody, he said, "I'm sure you'll be lonely with Ed gone. Please call me soon. We'll have dinner together at the generals' mess."

After the ceremony Jody walked with Ed to the chopper pad from which he was to fly to Long Binh, the first stop on the way home. There were no other passengers, and after Ed had loaded his gear aboard he turned to Jody and kissed her. She held him tightly to her, dreading the moment she would have to let go of him forever. Suddenly, impetuously, Ed picked her up in his arms and loaded her aboard.

"Make the last flight with me?"

"I'd love to, Ed."

They strapped themselves into the seat, and Ed signaled the pilots. The lazily rotating blades started whirling at full power, taking a deep bite out of the air.

The doors had been taken off the chopper, and the wind was so strong it was impossible to talk. Although Jody shouted, the howling wind picked up the sound and hurled it back into her teeth. She gave up and leaned

127

back against Ed, her head resting up against him, the noise of the engine filling her ears, her clothes flapping. Jody put her arms around Ed's neck and held him. The heat from his body warmed her as they kissed. Her hair lashed their faces in the wind. Moving her hand playfully down his shirt-front and across his trousers, she stroked him lightly, and could see the outline rise against his tight pants. Smiling, she fumbled with the buttons of his pants and gradually got them all open, exposing his erect maleness. Then after kissing his lips a light farewell she buried her face in his lap. The cloth of his slacks rubbed against her cheeks as she gave herself up to the enjoyment of his taste, while the wind whistled around her head, and her eyes, closed tight, shut out the outside world.

She felt his hand stroking the back of her neck and lifting her up and off him. With a wide grin he pointed to the cockpit, indicating his fear that the pilots might look around and see. Jody shook her head and laughed. Then, pulling her panties off under her skirt and holding them in one hand, she climbed across his knees, the wind blowing her skirt above her bare behind. Jody's knees crossed his legs and rested, one on each side of him, on the canvas seat. She caressed his face with her lips, gradually raised herself, and then lowered herself right on mark. They began the long, slow, undulating road to ecstasy, the bumpy atmosphere through which the chopper was flying lending encouragement to the proceedings. The medals that had been pinned to his chest an hour earlier imprinted themselves into her breasts as she moved on him.

Ed had completely forgotten the pilots and unbuckled his own safety belt to make it possible for him to achieve the tightest possible contact with Jody. He held his hands behind her head, holding her face against his. As he began to move harder into her, he reached down and cupped her buttocks in his hands, guiding her movements to match his. His fingers dug into her flesh as he forced her to him, tighter and tighter, faster and faster, flying ever higher.

Slowly Ed's hands relaxed their hold as Jody opened her eyes. The daylight flooded back into her head as she smiled up at him and lifted herself from his lap, moving back onto the seat.

Finally the chopper landed at Long Binh, and they could talk. "For God's sake," Jody laughed, looking him up and down, "you've got a lousy-looking uniform to go home in."

Ed grinned and nodded. He stepped stiffly out on the pad and helped her out to stretch her legs before the return flight to Cu Chi. One of the pilots stepped out of the pilot seat and asked, seriously, "Was it rough riding back there without the doors, sir?"

"You bet, Lieutenant," Ed laughed.

128

19

JUNE, 1969

A helicopter was provided for O'Neill and Rick, accompanied by Major Unger, to make the twenty-mile trip out to Di An, home of the First Infantry Division. For security reasons they were not permitted to drive anywhere outside of Saigon.

O'Neill noticed with satisfaction that Major Unger was daily growing more interested in the investigation and more friendly to the investigators. "This could be a crucial interview," O'Neill said. "Sergeant Orville Munn has hung on at the First Division for three years as bookkeeper to the club system. He's had some expert guidance under Sergeants Red Fisher and Ben Bigley. Now he has Picking as custodian."

A jeep picked up Rick and O'Neill at the helipad, and a few minutes later they pulled up in front of the main NCO club. Rick, followed by O'Neill and Major Unger, mounted the plank steps to the club and entered the air-conditioned building. A few off-duty sergeants looked up as the two investigators and the MP major strode through the club to the offices of the custodian at the rear.

Sergeant Munn was waiting for them in the small auditor's office next to the larger office alloted to the custodian. "Since Sergeant Picking isn't here today, we might be more comfortable in his office," Munn suggested. O'Neill nodded, and they sat down.

"Now, what can I do for you, sir?" Munn asked when they were all seated and introductions were made.

"You've been the bookkeeper here for a long time, haven't you, Sergeant?" O'Neill asked.

"Almost three years, sir."

"Unusual, isn't it?"

"I suppose so, sir. But I married a Vietnamese girl, and so I keep extending. Nobody really wants to be a bookkeeper in Vietnam, so the division commander is always happy when I extend."

"What we're looking for, Sergeant, are the club records over the past three years. As you know by now, we're making a study of the open-mess system in Vietnam."

"Where do you and your wife live?" Rick took up from O'Neill.

"We have a home in Saigon, sir. I get in on weekends. I have a hooch out here too."

"Do you own your villa in Saigon?" O'Neill asked.

"No, sir."

"I suppose rentals are kind of high in Saigon," Rick remarked.

"They are that," Munn agreed.

"Do you share the villa with anyone?" O'Neill inquired.

"Yes, sir. With Hernandez O'Leary and his girl. She's also Vietnamese."

"Hernandez O'Leary, sales manager of Vamalot Company?"

"Yes, sir."

"I've talked to some of the Vamalot people. Are you paying a share of the rent?"

"Mr. O'Leary's girl is my wife's sister. They invited us to stay with them."

"And Mr. O'Leary does a large business with the military clubs in Vietnam, right?" Rick threw in.

"I suppose he does."

"And I suppose you're in a position to be helpful to him," O'Neill insinuated.

"Not really, sir. I'm not a custodian, just the bookkeeper out here."

"Isn't your wife on the payroll of First Division?" O'Neill asked.

"She's been a great help in buying from the local Vietnamese, hiring Vietnamese help like hooch maids and waitresses, and acting as an interpreter."

"And you are on the payroll of the club also, as well as drawing your Army pay?" O'Neill half stated, half asked.

"There's nothing unusual about that, sir," Munn replied.

"On the contrary," O'Neill pounced. "Although it's true that custodians and club managers are paid for overtime work, it is not usual for bookkeepers who are assigned this work to be drawing extra pay." He paused. "Your wife's father is in the wholesale grocery business, is he not?"

"Yes, sir."

"And the club system here has been buying about two thousand dollars' worth of produce and bread a month from your father-in-law?"

"His prices are the best, and his quality is good," Munn replied primly.

"How much money would you say you have saved in the three years you've been in Vietnam, Sergeant?" O'Neill pursued.

"Between my wife and I, living very frugally, we've managed to save about eight thousand dollars." He reflected on his statement a moment. "We hope to open a bar and restaurant in Hong Kong with some friends when my present tour of duty in Vietnam is up."

"I've heard, Sergeant, that your father-in-law charges higher prices than his competitors and his quality is all but unacceptable now," O'Neill pounded.

Munn looked at his interrogator in surprise, as though puzzled at his fund of information. "There have been some complaints," he finally admitted. "I think the custodian has been asked to try some new suppliers. But it is becoming harder and harder to get good local food."

"I suppose so," O'Neill acknowledged. "Now Sergeant Munn, Mr. Townsend and I would like to examine the records of the First Division club system for the past three years."

A crafty smile came to Munn's face. "I'll get you all the records we have, sir. They're in the closet." Munn stood up and walked across the room. Opening the closet door he walked inside and brought out a thin ledger book which he handed to O'Neill.

Startled, O'Neill looked down at the book. "These are the records? All the records you've kept since you've been here? Three years' worth of records?"

"Actually they are the records for the last two months of club operations."

"Where are the others?"

"Well, sir, as you can see we don't have much room here, and the records took up so much space I asked permission to destroy them. Permission was granted and I burned them."

"You burned them?" O'Neill sputtered. "On whose authority?"

"An auditor from the Internal Review Division of USARV, Captain Arthur Lineberger, audited the books to the end of March. I pointed out how much room they were taking up and asked him if I could get rid of them. After making his audit he checked with General Hare, who gave his permission, so I burned them." With more than a trace of sarcasm Munn added, "I didn't know you were coming or I would have waited."

"Sergeant Munn, do you have a Swiss bank account?"

"No, sir."

"You do not have a Swiss bank account in the neighborhood of two hundred thousand dollars?"

Munn shook his head slowly, as though in awe of the statement. "Sir, it scares me to hear you even talk about so much money."

"Who are you planning to go into business with when you leave the Army, Munn?" Rick shot at the sergeant.

"That's my own private concern, sir," Munn answered.

"Shortly before charges against you and Sergeant Picking were dropped, the CID's chief witness to your alleged stealing of fifty cases of beer was found dead, shot in the stomach and head at close range with a forty-five pistol. His name was Herrera. Specialist Pepe Antonio Herrera. Do you know anything about his death?"

"I don't even know Spec Four Herrera," Munn replied.

"Are you in partnership with former Master Sergeant Hernandez O'Leary in a restaurant in Bangkok and one in Saigon?"

"I have no connection with Mr. O'Leary, sir."

"They tell me the price of having an American murdered is fifty dollars over here. Do you know anything about that?" O'Neill went on relentlessly hammering away.

"Sir, I certainly wouldn't know about murder. Better check Special Forces. They're the experts on that sort of thing."

O'Neill switched back to questions on the destruction of the records, while Munn blandly denied all wrongdoing and claimed he had authority to burn the ledger books.

Unable to contain himself, Major Unger jumped to his feet and started toward Sergeant Munn, barely restraining himself from grabbing the tall, skinny sergeant by his thatch of black hair and hauling him to his feet. "He's a disgrace to the Army," Unger thundered. "He should be court-martialed and jailed, damn it. How come Picking didn't mention the books being burned?"

Suddenly Unger caught himself, but it was too late. He found himself staring into O'Neill's scowling face and angry blue eyes. He went back to his chair and sat down. O'Neill stared levelly at the MP major and said clearly to him, "Picking didn't even give us as much help as this one." But Unger had inadvertently betrayed Picking, and nothing he could say would alter that fact. The only course was to get as much out of Picking now as they could before he was threatened into silence.

"Sergeant Munn, have you ever been to Sergeant Major Cotsworth's villa in Saigon?"

"No, sir. I do not know the Sergeant Major."

"Munn, I think you've been lying to us." O'Neill fixed the sergeant with a hard stare.

"Sir," Munn replied in a clear, forthright voice, "I haven't been lying to the best of my ability." Rick found it difficult to repress a chuckle at the irony of Munn's twisted syntax. Even O'Neill smiled grimly.

"We'll be talking to you again, Munn," O'Neill said, standing up. "There are a lot of questions we need answers to from you."

Silently, the two investigators and Major Unger trooped out of the club and were driven to their waiting helicopter. Unger turned to O'Neill. "I'm damned sorry, sir. I just got so angry with that criminal, getting away with his thieving for three years, that I forgot myself."

"Let's just hope they don't take it out on Picking too badly," Rick said. "Though I guess if we have Major Unger with us instead of against us, we've made progress."

"I'm with you," Unger said. "In the provost marshal's office we don't much like seeing people from the outside coming in and doing our job, but I'm about ready to admit that somehow we just clean missed one hell of a mess right under our nose." They climbed into the helicopter and the rotor blades began turning.

20

Predictably, Jody lost her hooch when the new battalion commander replaced Ed Carrera. By now, however, she had befriended some of the Red Cross girls at Cu Chi, and they invited her to share their quarters until she could find another place to live. Donut Dolly 6, as the head girl was called, showed Jody to a small cubicle where she stored her belongings. There were about ten Donut Dollys at Cu Chi, and Jody thought they were a nice group of young girls. However, she had never lived with a group of women before, and the new life-style took some adjusting to on her part. There was little privacy, and standing under the showers with a number of naked young women made her feel more naked than she had ever felt on stage in front of the GIs.

Not unmindful of the influence a general could bring to bear on her behalf, Jody tried to get in touch with General Springer. The sergeant major at division headquarters informed her that the general would be at MACV headquarters in Saigon for two weeks, coordinating new planning for the division. Disappointed she returned to the Red Cross hut just in time to find Colonel Hard Bill Lane looking for her.

She had not seen Barking Dog since Ed's change of command ceremony. He was impatiently pacing the floor of the small living room of the Donut Dollys' Quonset hut when Jody walked in.

"Colonel Carrera mailed you a letter care of me," he said brusquely, thrusting a sealed envelope at her. He was looking hot and dusty.

"Thank you, Colonel," Jody replied. "Do you have time for a Coke before you leave?"

Hard Bill cleared his throat noisily and then said, "Guess I do. I'll have to make it snappy though."

Jody poured him a Coke, and he drank it quietly, seemingly at a loss for words. During the awkward silence Jody smiled to herself, thinking of the blustering, cocky little man she had seen swaggering around in front of his troops. She wondered if they would recognize him now, unable to find his voice, let alone his customary bark.

Putting his glass down he said, "Well, time to move out. How has everything been with you?"

"Fine, thank you, Colonel."

Abruptly he said, "Could your troupe get away from Cu Chi for a few days and come up to my camp? My troops will be in from the field for a rest."

"We'd love to. What day do you want us?"

"I'll send air transportation Tuesday morning." He pulled his helmet on and surprised Jody by saying, "Be sure and come with them."

Dau Tieng, Colonel Lane's brigade headquarters, was located about forty miles west of Cu Chi. Jody had heard it was one of the most beautiful as well as one of the most dangerous camps in South Vietnam. The area was on a rubber plantation known as Michelin. When the VC moved in, the military leased the plantation from its French owners for a considerable sum. The rubber planters climbed into their private planes and flew off to sit out the war in Saigon.

The rubber plantation was Hard Bill Lane's domain, although he spent most of his time flying in helicopters over his troops' positions. The entire area was surrounded by rubber trees, which sheltered the VC. The Twenty-fifth Division's commanding general issued an order that no Red Cross girls were allowed to stay there overnight when they made their weekly visits.

The following Tuesday Jody arrived at Dau Tieng with her group. It lived up to to her expectations. The camp contained beautiful flower gardens, trees, lawns, two swimming pools, and several luxurious villas in which the higher-ranking officers lived. Colonel Lane was away when she arrived. Jody was resting in her quarters at six p.m. when a captain told her the colonel had invited her to have cocktails with him and some of his officers at his villa.

Jody was pleasantly surprised by the invitation. Since arriving at Cu Chi she seldom wore anything but Army fatigues and boots, her hair either plaited or stuffed under her Army hat, but she decided to dress up for the colonel's cocktail party. Fortunately she had brought, of all things, a cocktail dress with her as well as nylon stockings and high-heeled shoes. Forty-five minutes later Jody was ready.

The captain drove her to a lovely white two-story stone villa, surrounded by pepper trees. Jody could see the officers sitting on the balcony. She walked up the stairs to where the colonel and six other officers were seated around a table, drinking martinis.

"Good evening, gentlemen," she said, waiting for the shock waves to crash over the officers.

The men turned and gaped at her. They all stood up, astonished, as Jody walked over to them.

Hard Bill was still staring at Jody. "I know I said come to cocktails, but I didn't know you were going to get all dressed up for the occasion."

"This is how a girl would dress for cocktails back in the States. So why not here? Besides, I'm tired of looking like a boy."

"You, ma'am, could never look like a boy," Hard Bill sputtered as he introduced Jody to his staff officers.

Hard Bill and his officers heartily enjoyed Jody's company at their all-male cocktail hour. After dinner they joined the men in the club where Jody's band was playing. Hard Bill was grinning from ear to ear.

A row of empty seats in the front was reserved for the colonel. As his party sat down, the band was playing a rock number, and the pretty Vietnamese go-go dancer was shimmying herself into a sweat, much to the delight of the officers and men, who were leering and whistling.

The band sounded better than usual, and looking closely at them, she was surprised to see that Bryan Crawley, the young sergeant she had previously met at the Wolfhounds', was playing his guitar, a big smile on his boyish face. She tugged Colonel Lane on the sleeve and pointed to the stage.

"How did Sergeant Crawley get up here? He was with the Wolfhounds at Cu Chi."

"You know him, do you?" chuckled the colonel. "He's a damn good musician. I've had him over to the villa a couple of times." His face became serious for a moment. "But what is more important, he's a fine soldier. One of my best young troops. He had not planned on staying in the Army, though he shows a remarkable talent for leadership. Lately he has been talking about going to OCS and making the Army his career. Naturally I said I would help him all I can."

As the colonel finished talking, Jody caught the young sergeant's eye and waved to him.

After the club closed, Colonel Lane and Jody wandered back to his villa for a nightcap.

"Jody," he said, "I don't think it's convenient for you to be housed with the Vietnamese. I left orders for you to be moved into an empty trailer we have. My men will take you to it first thing in the morning. Besides," he said with a grin, "it's closer to my villa."

For the remainder of the week Colonel Lane never allowed Jody out of his sight whenever he was in the camp. Every night they talked, ate, played dice, and drank together. The change in his character amused Jody. He no longer disapproved of her but rather admired her. Strangest of all, he began taking her everywhere in his helicopter. She couldn't help thinking about the chewing out he'd given Ed Carrera for doing the same thing.

136

"How come you've stopped growling that I have no place in a war zone?" Jody asked one night.

Hard Bill looked thoughtful a moment and then paid her what she felt was a supreme compliment. "Because you've earned it," he replied. "You don't lose your cool in a hassle, and you can understand the soldier. You think like a soldier, not like a woman."

The day arrived, all too soon, she thought, when Jody and her troupe had to leave Dau Tieng and return to their regular bookings at Cu Chi. Colonel Lane provided two choppers, and Jody supervised the loading of equipment.

Back at Cu Chi Jody had been living with the Red Cross girls in their Quonset for less than a week when Hard Bill Lane arrived.

"Pack up your gear," he ordered. "I'm taking you back to Dau Tieng with me."

Confused, Jody stammered, "You mean you want my show again already?"

"No, leave your show here. You can live at Dau Tieng. You'll be much more comfortable with me." He shrugged slowly. "No fun there anymore without you, Jody."

"But what about my band?" she asked. "How can I look after them if I'm at Dau Tieng and they're here?"

"Don't worry about that. You just tell me what time you need a chopper each day, and we'll see you get a ride down to Cu Chi. When you're ready to come back, give us a call and I'll send somebody down to meet you."

Jody agreed to go up to Dau Tieng the following morning, and that night she thanked the Donut Dollys for the past few weeks' hospitality.

Jody enjoyed living at the Michelin plantation. Her trailer was air-conditioned and sat in the middle of a wide expanse of lawn and flowering trees. It was near the officers' club and the large swimming pool. She spent most of her days at Cu Chi with the band, and in the evenings had cocktails with Hard Bill; sometimes his staff officers joined them. They sat around talking and playing poker dice until the colonel felt hungry, which was usually about nine o'clock. Then they would proceed to the club for dinner.

Jody had been at Dau Tieng about a week when the camp took a particularly heavy mortar attack at two o'clock in the morning. She wanted to get up and run for a bunker, but she knew there was none nearby. There was nothing but a three-quarter-inch plyboard wall between her and the hot steel, should any of it happen to be flying her way.

The following morning a truck pulled up beside her trailer, and a group of GIs jumped off. "The colonel sent us to sandbag this trailer," one of the soldiers told her "We'll be working here a few days."

That night during dinner Hard Bill said to Jody, "You'd better sleep in my villa until your place is sandbagged. I am told we can expect more of the same."

After dinner Jody moved into his villa and slept in a small bedroom adjoining his. Although they had become inseparable companions, they had not reached the stage of sharing a bedroom. At five the next morning Jody awoke to hear the colonel bustling around outside. She joined him just as his young driver came walking in with a big pot of coffee. They drank it together, and then, strapping on his pistol belt, Hard Bill said, "Back to the war."

An odd statement, Jody thought, because it was so true. He was living like a king in the evenings, but come morning, he strapped on his automatic, climbed aboard his chopper, and went to work. But his office was the battlefield. Such an unreal situation.

Ever since Jody had reported the two club custodians who had demanded kickbacks, she found it increasingly difficult to get bookings for her two bands outside of Cu Chi. It cost her dearly to have the Filipino band idle four and five nights a week, and she resolved, somehow, to stimulate bookings.

She arrived in Saigon just in time to make it to the I House for lunch and an earful of the latest gossip. She had just seated herself in the coffee shop when Ronnie Jasper approached her.

"Mind if I join you, Jody?" he asked.

"Go ahead."

He pulled up a chair, called the waiter over, and gave his order. "How's business?" he asked.

"Not so good," she replied straightforwardly. "My Vietnamese show keeps busy out at Cu Chi, but my Filipino group, which is really better, isn't even working half the time lately."

"I expected as much." He gave her a sympathetic smile. "It's your own fault, you know. The sergeants don't like you too well."

"I've done nothing to them," Jody protested.

"Oh, come on now. You reported two custodians. I thought you were a smarter girl than that."

"I didn't feel like paying them a kickback. What have they done to deserve it?"

"Now look, Jody," Ronnie said in serious tones, "someone had better straighten you out or you won't be in business much longer. The open-mess system will soon be adopted in every division in Vietnam, including the Twenty-fifth. If you don't pay kickbacks you'll never get your shows booked."

"Are you paying?" Jody asked.

"Of course. We all are."

"Who do you mean by 'we all'?"

138

"Well, maybe not all the other agents, but most of them for damn sure are."

The waiter brought their lunch, and Ronnie continued his conversation between mouthfuls. "Sure, Jody, you and some of the smaller agents are holding out. But all of you are feeling the pinch. All the bigger agencies are paying off. It's the only way."

"How many shows do you have in country now, Ronnie?" she asked.

"I've got fourteen. The Lem Brothers are bigger than me. They've got twenty shows working six and seven days a week."

Jody nodded, thinking of the enormous profit they were making. On her two shows she should be making two thousand dollars clear profit every week, but the profits of the Vietnamese at Cu Chi went to cover the losses of the Filipinos in Saigon.

"Lem Brothers and I have started importing Australian shows since you have been in Cu Chi," Jasper volunteered. "It was my idea in the first place, but as soon as I flew down and hired my first group, the Lem Brothers did the same. Non-Oriental groups are much more popular with the troops because there are so few of them here."

"Why don't you bring over some American shows?" Jody asked.

"Use your head. There's no profit there. It would cost us about ten thousand dollars to fly a group all the way over from the States, and then they would all want a high salary. No profit left for the agent. The Commercial Entertainment Office marks all show prices about the same, regardless of where they are from or how good they are. But we can get the Australians cheap, three hundred a month each. They cost no more than Filipinos.

"That's no bargain for them. They make that much at home, whereas the Filipinos only earn about fifty dollars a month in the Philippines if they are lucky enough to get work at all. I hope you prepared the Aussies, particularly the girls, for the rough living conditions."

"Are you out of your mind? We don't want to frighten them off. In fact, the only thing to do is relieve them of their passports and plane tickets when they arrive, so they can't leave before their contracts run out."

"Oh, that's nice," Jody said sarcastically. "My poor fellow countrymen."

"Your old friend Lee LaRue is making a fortune playing the game," Ronnie remarked.

Jody sighed. "I suppose if I don't want to go broke I'll have to start paying off myself."

"Now you're getting the idea," Ronnie approved. He finished his lunch, lit a cigarette, and ignoring the ash-tray, dropped the used match onto his plate. "Since we're old friends, Jody, let me give you a piece of advice. The word is that you take officer boyfriends. If you really want to make it over here, be friendlier with the custodians. Officers will get you nowhere."

"Are you saying I should sleep with the sergeants?"

"How do you think Lee LaRue makes out so good?" he said with a laugh. "She doesn't know anything about the business, but she does have one big advantage. I have to hire a hooker to go along with each show and take care of the sergeants."

"To hell with that," Jody retorted angrily. "It's bad enough to pay off, without going to bed with the slobs!"

Jasper sighed and picked up his check. "Don't say I didn't try to warn you. You've got two strikes against you already."

After Jasper left, Jody had another cup of coffee and thought about what he had said. Lee LaRue had four Filipino shows working for her, all of them busy every night.

Later that day Jody went to see My Linh and the Filipino band. She told My Linh that as of now they would be paying kickbacks. The Eurasian girl was vastly relieved, knowing this would mean an immediate rise in the number of bookings. Returning to Dau Tieng late in the afternoon, Jody felt relieved to get away from the phony Saigon scene. She hated the place more each time she visited there.

That night a sumptuous dinner was served in the villa for Hard Bill and his staff officers, and later the colonel suggested that they all climb into jeeps, take some champagne, and head for the swimming pool for a midnight swim.

Naturally, Victor Charlie decided to throw a few mortar rounds into the camp at two a.m., but everyone was feeling so happy that the rounds exploding only added to the excitement of the night. The relationship between Jody and the colonel had become more physical, and she sensed that that night it would be consummated. When the mortar attack tapered off, Jody, feeling drawn to Hard Bill, splashed up against him in the pool and kissed him. Her wet body pressed softly against his, and as their lips parted, she felt the warm breath from his mouth in hers. His taste was good, and Jody melted into him. After a few moments the colonel jumped from the water onto the side of the pool and pulled Jody out and onto her feet. To the others he called out, "I think it's time we called it a night, gentlemen."

Most of the officers had already left, but three or four remained, including the artillery commander, who was hurling himself inexhaustibly from the diving board, apparently trying to combat the effects of the cocktails, wine, and champagne.

"Come on, Whitey," the colonel called again. "You can have a nightcap at the villa, but that's it. Anyone else want to join us?" The others diplomatically declined, but Whitey jumped into the jeep with Jody and the colonel.

After the nightcap, the colonel lifted Whitey out of the chair in which he dozed and placed him in a jeep outside the villa, instructing the duty officer to take him to his quarters. When they were alone Jody asked the colonel, "Do you mind if I take a shower and get out of this wet swimsuit?"

"Just don't be too long," Hard Bill said, leaning back on the balcony daybed and smiling. After showering and drying herself, Jody wrapped one of the colonel's dressing gowns about herself and returned to the balcony. The long sleeves of his robe dangled over her hands, and as she sat down beside him she rolled the sleeves up.

"Why don't you let me give you a massage?" she asked.

He looked surprised but didn't object.

"Lie on your stomach," Jody ordered.

He was wearing only his blue swimming trunks. As he lay face down, Jody straddled his buttocks and began gently massaging his neck and shoulders. As she massaged she occasionally leaned forward and ran the tip of her tongue in and around his ears. Then, untying the sash around her waist and slipping out of the gown, she said softly, "Turn over. It's time for the other side."

When Hard Bill turned over, Jody was nude on top of him. She looked down at the swelling under his trunks and whispered, "Now I see where you get your nickname." The colonel laughed, and Jody lowered herself on top of him. They kissed so hard she tasted blood where his teeth had gashed her lip.

Soon Jody felt him pull his trunks off and kick them free. Then he lay on top of her, kissing her, as she reached down for him.

Somewhere in the vicinity, crumping explosions of mortar rounds blasted through the night, and Jody learned a secret about the colonel. As the shells exploded, his buttocks stiffened, his muscles tensed involuntarily. At that moment she discovered that even Hard Bill knew fear, no matter how expertly he concealed it. But not even the mortar attack could sway him from his course. They were out on the balcony, not protected by the heavy stone walls of the villa, and the rounds seemed to be inching toward them, but their passion blocked out all distractions. Jody cried out as he rode hard into her, gripping him with every muscle, every fiber, arching her body high off the bed to him. Low moans came from deep in her throat. Her arms clung to him as shells exploded not far off; then after one last shudder they lay back on the bed, drained, contented.

Then a truly close round resounded; shrapnel flew close by. "Let's go inside," the colonel said. "It wouldn't do to have the men come by and find us sleeping naked out here."

Jody nodded and followed Hard Bill into his room, where the bed was protected by the heavy masonry walls.

"You weren't scared, Jody?" the colonel asked.

"Why should I be?" Jody laughed "I was safe under you."

They fell asleep in each other's arms, and the next thing Jody knew she was aroused by Hard Bill shaking her gently.

"What's wrong?" she asked sleepily.

"Jones will be here soon with the coffee. You'd best finish sleeping in the other room." The colonel was dressed and looking as fresh as ever. "I've got to go to work. Lock the door and the housemaid won't disturb you. See you tonight."

"I can hardly wait."

Neither can I. Maybe we'll have dinner early."

21

Sergeant Major Cotsworth arrived in Vietnam to begin his MACV assignment at the time Jody was dividing her time between Dau Tieng, Cu Chi, and Saigon. Although Ronnie Jasper's warning to her about giving up the officers in favor of the club custodians had no effect on her relationship with Hard Bill, she did begin to wonder how she might improve her relations with the men who directly controlled her source of income.

One day at the I House, after listening to My Linh tell of her troubles with the underworked Filipino band, she met Tony DeMarlo, who suggested that she come with him for another visit to Joe Crust's villa the next day. Although she was of a mind to refuse and fly back to Colonel Lane's headquarters, she decided to stay over when DeMarlo mentioned that the new command sergeant major at MACV would be there. It looked like an opportunity to begin her campaign to ingratiate herself with the club sergeants.

The Sunday afternoon at Joe Crust's was much like her previous visit, and many of the same people were there. And poor Art the Cork was, as usual, out in the boonies. General Hare and Madame Sang were both present, and there was some talk about her new steam bath now operating very successfully at Long Binh.

Jody was delighted at the opportunity to renew her acquaintanceship with Tom Cotsworth. He looked like so much more of a gentleman than even General Hare, and the contrast between him and the custodians he controlled was so vast that she found it hard to believe the rumors about his illegal activities. She made up her mind not to believe anything bad about him unless it was conclusively proved.

Jody sat beside the pool and talked with Cotsworth. Tony DeMarlo joined them. Listening to the two men talk, Jody began to realize what an intelligent and well-informed conversationalist Cotsworth could be with anyone. Although he drank Scotch throughout the afternoon, in no way did he show any sign of inebriation.

He listened with interest as Jody told him how she had become a booking agent since closing The Waltzing Matilda, but he never once mentioned the club system or custodians.

By the time Jody left, she and Cotsworth had become friends; he invited her to have dinner at his villa two nights later. Jody accepted, a little worried at what Hard Bill would say about spending two nights in Saigon so close together. Tien was waiting outside Joe Crust's villa to drive Jody down to Tan Son Nhut where she took a military bus to Hotel 3, the helicopter landing zone where Colonel Lane promised to have a chopper meet her at six p.m.

Two evenings later, with Cotsworth's address scrawled on a piece of paper in front of him, Tien negotiated the streets of Saigon until, with a triumphant exclamation, he pulled up at a two-story villa.

"Is this it, Tien?" asked Jody, looking at the elegant building rising above the surrounding walls. She was surprised that a sergeant, even the sergeant major at MACV, would have such an elaborate villa.

"Numbah same-same paper, missie. Must be house."

"Good, Tien. You drive home, have dinner, then come back for me."

"Okay, missie." He grinned his gold-toothed smile at her.

Inside the gate, Jody saw several sedans and jeeps parked. As she walked up to the open door, an old Chinese looked out and asked, "You want Mistah Tom?"

"Yes, please."

"Okay, sir. Fallie me."

Jody followed him through a large dining room and on toward a living room from which emanated the drone of male voices.

As she walked in, Cotsworth was leaning on the bar, holding court with a group of sergeants and sergeant majors. He straightened up and walked across the room to her. "I am glad you could make it, Jody." Then he introduced her to the eight or nine noncoms and ex-sergeant salesmen present. His choice of companions left much to be desired. Bert Bannahan was there, and for the sake of appearances, grunted a greeting to her. General Crowninshed was also there, but he barely stopped talking with Red Fisher long enough to acknowledge her. Most of the custodians were at Cotsworth's villa that night. James, Bigley, Halaby were staying close to the bar; Pancho O'Leary was introduced as a salesman. For the first time Jody began to wonder whether there was some truth to the rumor she heard at I House— that Cotsworth was the kingpin of the whole custodian kickback network.

All the custodians were surprised to see Jody at Cotsworth's villa. The two men she had reported were not present, a fact that greatly relieved her.

144

Since this was the first time she had mingled socially with the club sergeants, she hoped to avoid all unpleasantness.

She followed Cotsworth through the rooms of the lower section of the villa, admiring the plaques and mementos of his past assignments. The villa was built to suit the tropical climate. High ceilings, white walls, and gleaming tile floors kept it cool. The furnishings were tasteful, and Cotsworth's many battle souvenirs gave it a handsomely masculine appeal.

After Jody had finished the grand tour, Cotsworth sat her down in his study adjoining the living room and began to talk to her earnestly. "Jody, I've heard many of the sergeants complaining about you, and I want to try and straighten things out.

"Yes?" she murmured noncommittally.

"You should never have reported those two sergeants. Nobody trusts you now, and it is difficult for me to help you."

"Why should you?" she asked.

"Because I like you. I know you are intelligent. If you would only listen to reason, you could do very well here. You are playing a very strong hand, you know. But even with the best hand you can lose the pot if you don't play it wisely. Women in business here have an edge over their male competitors. There are only a handful of women, and you are younger than the others. You could really make a fortune if you wanted to—others are." He gave her a smile. "Men here get lonesome for their wives and girl friends."

"They've got plenty of Vietnamese girls," Jody retorted.

"Yes. But after a while a man likes to have a woman he can talk to as well. You could be set for life if you cooperated. One or two years more, and you'd be richer than you ever dreamed of being."

"It's funny, I discussed this only recently with Ronnie Jasper."

"Well, Jody, what do you say? You won't survive more than another month or two the way you're going."

"I know." Her resignation showed on her face.

"Hey, Jody T.," he said sharply yet good-humoredly. "It isn't all that bad, this cooperating with the group."

"If you can put in a good word for me, I'd appreciate it, Tom. I'll follow the lead of the other booking agents and start making payments to the custodians."

Cotsworth beamed his approval. "That's straight thinking, girl."

"Just one thing, though," Jody said grimly "I'm not running a whorehouse. If that were part of the deal, I'd be better off taking a room in a hotel and not busting my tail running all around the countryside playing nursemaid to a bunch of temperamental musicians."

"Have it your own way in that respect, Jody. But you could be a little more friendly with the boys. Join them for a few drinks occasionally. They all think you're a snob."

Jody was about to reply when they were interrupted by loud horn-blowing and shouting outside. "Now what the devil is that?" Cotsworth exclaimed, hurrying to the window. "It's Ronnie Jasper with a truck. Let's go see what it's all about."

Jody followed him as he walked briskly from the room. Out in the courtyard Ronnie Jasper was pulling open the huge double gates and waving a truck through. The old truck, driven by a ragged Vietnamese, had four jabbering laborers standing in the back around a huge wooden crate. Closing the gates after the truck, Jasper looked back and saw Cotsworth. "Hey, Tiger. Just wait until you see what I brought you this time," he yelled out. The commotion had brought the rest of the guests out of the villa to see what was going on. They were all standing around watching, glasses in hands, as the truck came to a grinding halt.

The four Vietnamese were struggling to lower the heavy crate to the ground, the little men sweating and screeching at each other in Vietnamese. Ronnie was shouting instructions to them, even though they didn't understand a word of English. Suddenly, a terrifying roar came from the wooden cage, and the workmen jumped back in fright as the crate fell sharply to the ground.

"What the hell now?" Cotsworth bellowed as the other sergeants began pointing and laughing.

Visible to everyone was the wire-mesh front section of the crate. Looking out of the cage was an enraged vicious-looking Bengal tiger, clawing and roaring his rage.

Ben Bigley, drunker than the others, staggered toward the cage. "Here, kitty, kitty, kitty. Have a drink." With that he threw the contents of his glass through the wire into the tiger's face. The beast opened his huge mouth, and the concussion from his terrible roars could be felt by those close to the cage. The Vietnamese scattered to the far end of the yard. Most of the sergeants retreated, but not Bigley, who took the tiger's reaction to the drink as a personal affront.

"That fuckin', no-good, ungrateful cat, I'll fuckin' drown it!" he cried.

"Get out of the way and leave him alone, Bigley," Ronnie Jasper yelled. "Let my dinks move this box out of the driveway, will you?"

With the other hard-drinking sergeants egging him on, urging him to "get the fuckin' cat by the neck and teach him some manners," Bigley grabbed a fallen tree branch and started prodding the tiger, swearing back at the beast each time it let out a snarl or a roar.

Meanwhile, Ronnie Jasper was trying to round up the frightened Vietnamese, who refused to return to the cage. While Jasper shouted at the confused and terrified men, the rest of the sergeants formed a line and started dancing around the cage, sloshing their liquor through the mesh over the nose and open mouth of the fearsome animal. Bigley was giggling inanely and poking at the enraged beast. Jasper, unsuccessful with the Viets, lost his temper.

146

"You son of a bitch!" he hollered, striding up to Bigley and pushing him, "get away from there and let my gooks finish the job."

Bigley stopped giggling. "What's wrong, Ronnie? I'm just having a little fun with the kitty cat."

"You're buggering up the unloading is what you're doing. Now move."

"Watch your mouth when you're talking to me, mister," Bigley cried nastily.

Cotsworth, who stood silently with Crowninshed, finally shouted, "That's enough, men. Everybody back inside for a drink. Let the Viets take care of the tiger."

The response was instantaneous. Bigley stopped glaring, Ronnie Jasper stopped shouting, and the men, one by one, trooped back inside the villa. Jasper joined Jody, Cotsworth, and Crowninshed at the bar. With a puzzled look on his face, Cotsworth said, "I certainly appreciate the gift, Ronnie. But why a tiger?"

"Well, Tiger, I said to myself, what can I give a man who has everything? Then I said, what else? A tiger for Tiger." Jasper laughed uproariously at his own joke and slapped Cotsworth over the back, spilling his drink down his immaculate shirt and causing a frown to crease his forehead.

Outside, as darkness fell, the Vietnamese handlers screwed up their courage and finished moving the crate. The truck was just driving off when three young Vietnamese girls arrived. As they entered the living room the sergeants whispered among themselves in pleased anticipation. "Is that all's coming, Tiger?" someone called.

The drinking and conversation continued until dinner was announced. The meal was superb and well served, and an appropriate wine was poured with each course. Jody was seated between Cotsworth and Crowninshed, the only two sober men in the room.

"Pass me some more of the wine, Chinky," Red Fisher called to the Chinese servant. He held up his wineglass, and Bigley, beside him, did the same. The two of them made a toast, loudly clinking their glasses, red wine sloshing onto the white-linen tablecloth in a spreading splotch. Crowninshed, glancing around the table, frowned. Bannahan was sitting beside one of the Vietnamese girls, entertaining her by beating on her water glass with a fork. He punctuated the beats occasionally with loud belches, at which the girls giggled merrily. Another of the girls was feeding Pancho O'Leary with a spoon, much of the food trickling down his chin.

Finally, the meal came to an end, and Jody sighed in relief. She, Cotsworth, and Crowninshed had a nightcap in the living room before saying good-night. Cotsworth walked her to her car and, as she was getting in, said, "About our earlier conversation. I've already put the word out to the boys that you're working with the setup. You won't have any trouble keeping your shows booked anymore."

"Thank you, Tom. As long as the payoff is only in money we'll all get along fine."

"Just don't forget what I said about being more friendly," Cotsworth reminded her with a smile. "My boys are sensitive, you know."

The sensitive sergeants, she laughed bitterly to herself. She might have to drink with "the boys" but she vowed to avoid eating with them again.

22

Rick, O'Neill, and Major Unger arrived back at USAID Number One still in a state of frustration from the interview with Sergeant Munn. "Let's hope we get more out of Heffer," O'Neill remarked, glancing at his watch. "He should be here in a few minutes."

Unger was still annoyed at himself for revealing in front of Munn that Picking had cooperated with them. He sat silently, waiting for the next session.

Sergeant First Class Myles Heffer arrived precisely on schedule and was brought into the office. O'Neill began his interrogation with the usual polite acknowledgment of the time and inconvenience involved. The fact that through pressure brought to bear in Washington, D.C., he had been ordered to talk to the Senate investigator was glossed over.

Carefully, O'Neill worked into the sensitive areas he wanted to explore. "Am I correct in stating that prior to your present assignment as assistant to Sergeant Major Cotsworth you were in the NCO assignment division at the Pentagon."

"Yes, sir.

"In the Pentagon it was your job to make assignments of noncommissioned officers throughout the Army?"

"Yes, sir. Of course there was an officer over me."

"During most of the time you were at the NCO assignment office at the Pentagon was Cotsworth the Sergeant Major of the Army?"

"That's correct, sir."

"Did Cotsworth make recommendations about assignments of NCOs?"

"Yes, sir. That was part of his job."

"Who was in charge of your office, Sergeant Heffer?"

"Lieutenant Colonel Max Shroud most of the time."

"The same Colonel Shroud who is now assistant to General Hare at USARV?"

"That's right."

"Colonel Shroud was a great friend of Cotsworth back in Germany, wasn't he?" O'Neill probed.

"No, sir. I expect they might have known each other, but officers and NCOs don't become close friends."

"At any rate, you, Colonel Shroud, and Sergeant Major Cotsworth have been soldiering closely together for a number of years."

"Sir," Heffer spoke up, "I don't know what you are trying to lead up to. But if you are implying that the sergeant major ever used undue influence on Colonel Shroud, or for that matter on me, you're all wrong."

"Did you know personally such friends of Cotsworth as Willy Halaby, William Fisher, Ben Bigley, Hernandez O'Leary, and Elroy James?"

"Of course, I knew them all."

"Ben Bigley once said that each time he was sent back to the States he paid off a friend in the Pentagon four of five hundred dollars and he was transferred right back to Germany. That's how he stayed there for eleven years."

Heffer stared at O'Neill sullenly. "I don't know who you've been talking to, but I don't believe Master Sergeant Bigley said or did any such thing. I never heard of an assignments NCO taking a bribe."

"Cotsworth, I suppose, did tell you who to slip the club-custodian jobs around the world."

Vehemently, Heffer shouted, "No, sir! Cotsworth never made a recommendation relating to the assignment of a custodian."

"The job of club sergeant certainly isn't in a man's MOS, which is supposed to determine assignments. It's just coincidence, then, I suppose, that all Cotsworth's friends go from one club assignment to another."

"I wouldn't know about that, sir. Assignments to the open-mess system are handed out by the sergeant major at division level."

"I suppose the records in Washington would show how you decided upon which NCO would receive which assignment," Major Unger interjected, unable to sit quiety in the face of what he considered gross deception.

"Yes, they would," Heffer replied confidently.

"Except, as we discovered before coming over here," O'Neill said, a sarcastic ring to his voice now, "all the records of your tenure in the Pentagon have been destroyed."

Unger looked shocked, but Heffer went on blandly, "Yes, that's true, sir. According to new regulations, records relating to the assignment division are only kept for a year and then they're destroyed."

"How new is that regulation?" Major Unger asked.

"Came in early in sixty-eight, sir."

150

"Just before Cotsworth's tour as top sergeant of the Army was finished," O'Neill noted dryly.

"Sergeant?"—there was a look of incredulity on Major Unger's face—"How long were those records kept before this new regulation was adopted?"

"I believe they were kept indefinitely. Cotsworth has done a lot to streamline Army administrative work," he added brightly.

"Hasn't he," was O'Neill's ironic rejoinder. Then, after a pause, "Have you had any dealings with Vamalot? We know you are familiar with the company, Sergeant," O'Neill added sternly.

Heffer was unable to stop the look of surprise from flashing across his face, but he quickly recovered. "I have heard of it," he admitted.

"We have been told that Vamalot has had a man in the assignment branch at the Pentagon since the middle of 1967."

"I don't believe anything like that is true," Heffer said, affecting bluster.

"But you do know about Vamalot?" O'Neill probed.

"It's a sales company."

"And you know that Cotsworth is a stockholder?"

"I don't know anything about that," Heffer insisted.

"You get over to Hernandez O'Leary's villa quite often, don't you?"

"Now and then, I suppose."

"Once or twice a week?" O'Neill kept the pressure on.

"I guess so."

"And Cotsworth gets over there the same amount of time?"

"I wouldn't know the sergeant major's schedule."

"But you have seen him there."

"Yes."

"You see quite a few of the custodians gathered for drinks and conversation at O'Leary's, don't you?"

"I don't know who all the NCOs over there are."

"You see Sergeant Munn and his Vietnamese wife over there, don't you?"

"They show up sometimes."

"And Sergeant Fisher is over there, isn't he?"

"I've seen him."

"And Sergeant James?"

"Sometimes."

"And Bigley and Halaby?"

"Sure."

"And at these meetings, doesn't some talk of Vamalot business creep into the conversations?"

"They never talk business. I never heard any talk about Vamalot selling anything to the custodians." Heffer's tone reflected his growing irritability, but O'Neill continued to press him.

"The custodians know Cotsworth is interested in Vamalot, so they want him to know they're buying from the company, wouldn't you say?"

151

"The sergeants don't know that Cotsworth has an interest in Vamalot. Even I don't know."

"It happens that we know precisely the amount of the company he owns. It's a matter of legal record. Vamalot was formed in January of 1967 in Oakland, California."

"You know more than I do, sir," Heffer said stubbornly. "As far as I know none of the sergeants know that Cotsworth and O'Leary are in business together."

O'Neill stared his disbelief a moment and then continued his questioning. "Why couldn't Sergeant Major Cotsworth say to the custodians gathered at O'Leary's villa something like 'Vamalot is my company. We can sell you anything you want to buy'?" O'Neill looked up quizzically. "If there's nothing wrong with his interest in Vamalot, why wouldn't he tell the custodians about the company?"

"Why should he?" Heffer snapped.

"It would be to his benefit. He has a big interest in the company."

"Well, then you're going to start a scandal."

"Then you think it's wrong for Cotsworth to be part of the company?"

"That's not what I said. But if all the custodians knew that Cotsworth was interested in Vamalot, they'd start saying 'Good Lord, if I don't buy from this company, I won't get a reassignment to the club system.'"

"So as long as Cotsworth remains quiet about his interest, it is all right for him to own this company that sells to the military clubs."

"I repeat, the sergeant major is careful not to talk business with the custodians at O'Leary's villa."

"Because otherwise it would be a conflict of interest situation?"

"No, I don't think it would be a conflict of interest situation," Heffer retreated.

"Why couldn't it be?" O'Neill pursued.

"Because Cotsworth can't do anything about their reassignments in the first place. So how can there be a conflict of interest? If he had the power to make an assignment or change an assignment, then maybe it would be a conflict."

"In actual fact, Sergeant Heffer, as you and the other sergeants well know," O'Neill pounded away, "Cotsworth can and does make recommendations to the present Sergeant Major of the Army regarding assignments. We've examined some recent correspondence, and we know that Cotsworth's recommendations carry considerable weight and are invariably approved."

"So you've just said yourself then," Unger leaped into the discussion, "that Cotsworth is guilty of conflict of interest."

"Sir, you can't put your words in my mouth."

"It does seem to me," O'Neill commented, "that if this Vamalot was a legitimate business, Cotsworth would feel free to talk about it. And if it is not legitimate, why is he in it?"

152

You'll have to ask the sergeant major that question," Heffer replied weakly. "It goes beyond my area of information."

O'Neill decided to terminate the interview. "Thank you for coming in, Sergeant. You have been most helpful."

"I don't know how," Heffer blurted, an expression of alarm on his face. O'Neill walked to the door and opened it, giving Heffer a quick, tight smile as he left.

"You'll want to talk to Cotsworth directly, I suppose," Unger said. "By God, O'Neill, I'm shocked by this. I couldn't believe such a cancer could grow in the United States Army. It's an insult to every honest officer and enlisted man who is making the Army his career."

"That's right, Ed. As a matter of fact I want to talk to the commanding general while we're at it. I wonder how much he knows about what his sergeant major is doing. And what our friend General Rabbit Hare is up to, for that matter."

23

Jody's idyll at the Michelin plantation with Barking Dog had lasted about six weeks when news of the romantic attachment between the brigade commander and the blonde booking agent reached the ears of the division's deputy commanding general. Although Brigadier General Walt Springer was a rather docile man, he seemed almost as annoyed about his brigade commander dallying with the booking agent as Barking Dog had been when he discovered his favorite battalion commander, Ed Carrera, was maintaining a liaison with Jody T.

Here we go again, Jody thought, when she heard that General Springer had called Hard Bill into his office and questioned him about the affair. "They're not going to tell me how to run my life when I'm off duty," Hard Bill said belligerently. "Not as long as my field record is beyond criticism."

Jody was worried. "Does he write your efficiency report?"

"No. The CG himself does, and somehow I don't think Walt will say anything to him. We went to the War College together. He's only been a general six months, and we were colonels together for several years and have always been friends." Colonel Lane chuckled to himself. "You know, Springer is damned jealous that I have one of the best commands in the war and he's just the CG's errand boy. He'd do anything short of giving back that star to be a field commander."

Two more weeks passed, and although General Springer made several trips to Dau Tieng and talked to Jody a number of times both at Barking Dog's headquarters and Cu Chi, he never mentioned the involvement again. Then, unexpectedly, the CG of the Twenty-fifth told Hard Bill at one of the evening command meetings that he wanted to leave his executive officer in charge of the headquarters at Dau Tieng and set up a temporary tactical operations center at a location along the perimeter of Cu Chi itself.

The reason for this, Barking Dog explained to Jody later, was the stepped-up enemy activity in the immediate area surrounding Cu Chi. Charlie was putting the pressure on, Hard Bill conceded, but he couldn't help but wonder whether the deputy CG had made the suggestion of bringing him down from Dau Tieng to set up the TOC.

The designated area had once housed a battalion, but no troops had occupied the ramshackle collection of blasted buildings for several months. No repairs had been made, since mortar attacks immediately destroyed any improvements. The new camp was a far cry from the luxury of Dau Tieng, but Hard Bill was accustomed to living under all conditions, and he didn't seem to mind his primitive surroundings.

After preparations had been made, all the officers and men who were to move climbed into the helicopters and headed for Cu Chi. Jody, as usual, flew with Barking Dog in his C and C. When she arrived at the area, she surveyed the dismal scene before her. Hand Bill showed her a small eight-by-eight conex trailer that had been airlifted in by chinook. Small as it was, it was to be his home as long as he was there. Inside there was just enough room for a narrow bed, a thin wall locker, and a small desk. A telephone and an air-conditioning unit were being installed, and an enlisted man was busily painting Colonel Lane's code, Barking Dog, in big red letters across one of the exterior walls.

Jody sighed mournfully. "Looks like it's back to the Donut Dollys for me. I certainly can't stay with you in that little trailer. Not with your men so close all around."

The colonel roared a deafening "No! You will stay here. I'll have my men fix up one of the hooches for you." Dismally, Jody gave in.

The closest hooch to the colonel's trailer was set aside for Jody and the one beside it for the colonel's driver, young Sergeant Jones. After dinner in the mess hall each night, Jody and Hard Bill would talk with the men for a while before retiring to his small trailer. About four thirty each morning he would shake her awake, and she would wearily sneak back to her own hooch before the men got up.

It was difficult for her to fall asleep again in her own hooch because the mattress smelled foul from being rain-soaked frequently and then baked dry by the hot sun. Mildew and rot caused a stench that was almost unbearable, and the roof leaked. The top half of her walls were wire mesh and afforded no privacy; she had to dress and undress after dark with her lights off. Dust lay heavy over everything in the room, and she quickly abandoned the futile struggle to keep the place clean.

The men had built a small enclosed outdoor latrine for Barking Dog and also a makeshift shower beside his trailer. Jody used these facilities, but the shower was only enclosed from about the height of her hips up, so showers also became a nighttime activity.

Jody was sure, from his knowing smiles, that the colonel's driver heard her going back to her hooch each morning. Nevertheless, she had grown very fond of the young, towheaded Southerner and trusted his discretion.

During the afternoon heat on one particularly scorching day, Jody retreated to the cool of Barking Dog's trailer while he was out in the field. The paper work she was trying to get out of the way was interrupted when Sergeant Jones came bursting in.

"Quick," he said, "I've got to get you out of here. The division CG just flew in to see Barking Dog. They're on the way to the trailer now."

Jody and the sergeant raced out and ducked behind the trailer just as the general and his aide appeared. "The old man's chopper just landed. He called me on the radio and said to get you out of sight."

"Where are we going?" Jody asked. "All the hooches are open."

"We're going to drive around in Barking Dog's jeep until the general leaves again."

With all the clubs closed until five p.m. and the temperature at 110 degrees, there was nothing to do but climb into the open jeep and circle endlessly around the dusty camp. The sun beat down on them, and sweat trickled down Jody's face as the heavy military vehicles trundled by, enveloping them in clouds of clinging red dirt.

They were negotiating the perimeter road for the twentieth time when the all clear finally came over the radio. The wilted, grimy pair quickly returned to their camp.

Hard Bill couldn't restrain himself from laughing at Jody's expression when she returned. He suggested that she use his shower. She refused, unwilling to expose the men constantly walking by to the sight of her bare legs and buttocks below the shower stall wall.

The one and only advantage to being back in Cu Chi as far as Jody was concerned was that she could supervise her band during the evenings, a job she had neglected in recent weeks. When they performed in the NCO clubs, Jody always took Jones with her. But on the nights they were scheduled for the officers' clubs, Hard Bill always insisted on coming along.

Jody continued making her trips to Saigon to attend to the other group managed by Jody T. Promotions, but because of the number of damaged helicopters which were inoperable in Barking Dog's brigade, a sure sign of increased enemy activity, he was not always able to give her a chopper, and she had to find a ride as best she could.

On one of those days when no chopper was available, Jody was waiting up at "Hotel 3" in the hope of getting a flight back to Cu Chi when an Army staff car pulled up and General Springer jumped out.

"Are you on your way to Cu Chi, Jody?" he asked.

"Yes, and having a rough time finding a lift."

"Well, it so happens I'm on my way back right now. Why don't you join me?"

156

Jody thanked him and followed Springer to the chopper on the VIP pad. As they were buckling themselves in, Springer said, "We don't see too much of you lately. The Red Cross girls told me you moved out. Where are you staying?"

Somewhat embarrassed, Jody admitted to being in Barking Dog's area.

"Good God! The worst area in the entire perimeter. I can imagine what kind of a hooch you've got. What do you do for showers?"

"It's a bit rough," Jody admitted. "I usually come down and use the Red Cross girls' bathroom."

The chopper's rotors bit into the air, and they were airborne. Because of the engine noise and wind, they were incommunicado until they set down at the pad in Cu Chi. Springer jumped to the ground and then helped Jody out of the helicopter.

"Jody, how about coming over to the general-officers' mess some evening?"

"I'd like to, General Springer."

"Oh, don't be all that formal. Call me Walt."

"Okay, Walt. Sometime I'd like to come over to the general's mess." She waved and hurried off toward Barking Dog's area. Although General Springer had the reputation of being a straight arrow, Jody had not missed the appraising glances he had given her whenever they had met.

The following day the general came looking for Jody around six in the afternoon. He found her in her musty hooch and invited her to have a drink with him. Barking Dog was still out flying over his brigade's various operations in the field, so Jody left word that she had gone to the generals' mess. When she returned a couple of hours later, Hard Bill was in his trailer. He made no comment about where she had been, but Jody received the definite impression that he was jealous.

The following day, while Jody was sitting disconsolately in her hooch, swatting at flies and working on some invoices, General Springer's aide arrived.

"Miss Jody T. Neale?" he inquired.

She nodded listlessly.

"The general sent me to tell you to pack your things and come back with me. He says you can't live here. He has secured a trailer for you."

The thought of a real trailer sounded wonderful. She stuffed her things into her suitcase carelessly, and then it occurred to her that Barking Dog might be upset by her hasty move. She wasn't running out on him, she told herself. She would still come back at dinner time each evening. It was just that she wanted somewhere more comfortable to live, somewhere with a toilet and shower.

At seven she was sitting in the generals' mess having a drink with General Springer when Hard Bill came bustling in, looking like an angry thundercloud.

Springer saw him coming and called out, "Hey, Bill. Why don't you join us for a drink and dinner?"

Lane stared at his old friend as though he were an enemy. Sensing Barking Dog's annoyance, Jody clarified the situation. "Bill, I was just about to leave and come over to your place, but since you're here, why can't we all have a drink and some dinner together?"

The colonel, somewhat placated, smiled sourly. "I guess I can spare the time for a drink, but then I'll be getting back to my own area. Some other time for the troika, huh?"

Lane and Springer had a drink and attempted to be congenial, but the conversation between them was strained. The general didn't improve the atmosphere when he placed his hand possessively on Jody's knee. Barking Dog didn't miss the move. He immediately set his glass back on the table with a sharp click, stood up, and pulled Jody to her feet. "Thanks, General, but Jody and I have to be running along. My men are holding dinner for us." As Colonel Lane strode purposefully from the room, pulling Jody along behind him, the general called out, "If you feel like a nightcap when you come in tonight, Jody, just knock. I'm in the trailer on your right as you walk in your door."

"What's this about a trailer?" Hard Bill demanded when they were outside.

"General Springer has allowed me the use of a trailer," Jody replied. "It won't make any difference to us, I'll still see you just as much, but I will be more comfortable." True to form, Barking Dog exploded in his own inimitable way. The colonel's grumpy mood lasted most of the night. But Jody stayed with him until about four in the morning when she finally had to leave, and he was in a happier frame of mind.

Jody's quarters were small but neat, and General Springer had managed to find a bunch of flowers and a bowl of fruit for her. Jody figured he had appropriated them from the mess hall, but she appreciated the thought.

Very early the following morning a jeep pulled up outside Jody's trailer with a squeal of brakes and a cloud of dust. Jody looked out and saw Sergeant Jones walking up the path. She opened the door.

"Morning, Miss Neale. The colonel sent me to get you and your clothes and bring you home with us."

"I can't do that, Jones. There's nowhere up there private enough for a woman to live."

"Begging your pardon, ma'am. The colonel said I was not to take no for an answer. He's in a terrible bad mood. Never seen him so red-ass like this, forgive the word, Miss Neale. As to your living quarters, you will be living in his trailer, he's moving in to live with me. The shower is now completely private. And there's going to be hot water tonight."

"For God's sake!" Jody exclaimed in amazement. "What will the men think of me living in the commander's quarters and he living with his driver? Besides, there's no phone at your hooch."

"There is now. He had the signal officer moving at five this morning. As for what the men think, he's so red— mad," the sergeant corrected himself, "right now I don't think he cares about anything except getting you back." Jody couldn't help but be flattered to think Barking Dog would give up his own quarters to get her to return to camp. So once again she packed her bags.

When Barking Dog returned from the field that night he was delighted to find that Jody had returned. "Are you comfortable in the trailer?"

"Yes, but I feel pretty rotten about putting you out of your quarters," she answered.

"That's okay. I'm never in them anyway, and I'm not going to have that goddamn Springer cutting my time." He paused and put on a supercilious smile. "I'm in the trailer on your right if you want a nightcap," he mimicked.

The next few weeks went by smoothly for Jody, but General Springer didn't accept defeat easily. Jody had worked up a schedule which called for her band to play at the same officers' clubs three nights every week; the other four nights they played in enlisted men's clubs. Wherever her band was playing, Jody was most likely to be found. Thus it was easy for General Springer to pinpoint Jody's evening movements about Cu Chi. So whenever Barking Dog and Jody showed up at an officers' club to check on the band, General Springer was always there, waiting for them.

Since it was most unusual to find high-ranking officers in regular officers' clubs, the trio soon became a source of amusement to the junior officers. As a result, the young captains who ran the officers' clubs felt they could stand well with the deputy CG by giving Jody's band extra bookings. And so the circle went—more bookings, more evenings with Springer and Lane visiting the clubs. Since the colonel never went anywhere without one or two of his favorite staff officers, the entourage always took up an entire table.

The *ménage à trois* continued for a number of weeks, but as time went on Hard Bill became more and more angry and Springer more and more aggressive. Jody knew it couldn't go on much longer; she had to make a decision and make it fast.

After Barking Dog returned from the field a few weeks later, Jody made her decision. One night, after another disastrous dinner with Barking Dog and Springer, Jody made her move. When the threesome was about to leave, Jody asked Barking Dog to excuse her and wait for a few minutes. She and Springer walked together to a table at the back of the club.

After a short, painful silence, Jody began. "You know I like you Walt, but this intrusion of yours can't go on any longer. After all, I am Barking Dog's girl, and you do keep hanging around me and trying his patience."

"Sure, but I knew you before he did. I waited until Carrera went home thinking I'd have my chance with you." The general smiled reminiscently. "The first time I saw you, you were out in the field with the men, wearing fatigues and boots and a bush hat, and you looked dirty. You shouldn't have been there, and I was going to chew out Hound Dog six, but then I saw how you were making those troops laugh and I decided to say nothing." He shook his head ruefully. "I had to go to MACV for a couple of weeks, and when I came back Lane had policed you up. You'll never know how happy I was when he got orders to move down here."

Jody was silent for a while. Then she said, "I understand, Walt, but I am going with Bill now, and I don't intend to change that." She paused. "I know this sounds horrible, but Bill is going home in about two months. If you're still of the same mind then, we'll see what happens after that. Meantime, let's be friends, and don't you bug him any more."

The general thought a few moments. "I hate to wait another two months," he said. "But I guess I don't have much choice. Promise me one thing, though. Have dinner with me one night a week at the generals' mess until then."

"It's a deal, Walt," she said and kissed him lightly on the mouth.

24

My Linh accompanied the Filipino show on many of its bookings. It was her responsibility to see that the musicians started on time and that things ran smoothly while they were in a camp. Managing the Filipinos was not nearly as arduous a task as keeping the Vietnamese band straight. The Filipinos were more responsible people, and not only took pride in their performance but enjoyed their work. With the Vietnamese band, however, either Jody or My Linh constantly had to watch over their work, making sure they gave the best possible performance.

Since Jody T. had spent an evening with Cotsworth, the custodians were grudgingly giving Jody T. Promotions some business. Even Jesse James at Long Binh had relented and given the Filipino show a two-week contract each month. Of course, Jody was now paying off.

One afternoon Tien picked up the Filipino performers at the villa Jody rented for them and, with My Linh sitting up front, started out for Long Binh. As they made their way through the Saigon traffic, Tien and My Linh talked in Vietnamese. Tien was glad Jody T. wasn't with them these days when he made this drive. When the Vietnamese motorcycle riders—and there were thousands of them—saw a white woman sitting beside him his troubles began. They deliberately drove their Hondas against the bus, going slowly enough to do no damage to themselves or the Hondas, but falling over onto the road. When Jody stopped the vehicle, the Vietnamese refused to get out of her way, loudly claiming damage to their bikes and themselves. They continued to make an angry scene until the embarrassed victim finally paid for the alleged damages and was allowed to pass. The same ruse was extensively practiced against the Americans. The going rate for a normal spill was five hundred piasters, and a few scratches would bring more. Some of the Honda riders earned quite a good living in this fashion. Tien did not agree with all the practices of his countrymen. After all, he was an ex-soldier and now an honest workingman. But his children could not afford a Honda as so many other children could.

As Tien drove along toward Long Binh, My Linh checked the seven hundred dollars in MPC folded and held together with an elastic band. Jody had flown in with it that morning from Cu Chi. My Linh was to make the payoff to Sergeant James for the present contract. Business was good again, My Linh thought. She never could understand why Jody hadn't started paying off sooner. Jody was her friend, but sometimes My Linh could not understand her methods.

As they drove through the gates of Long Binh, Tien flashed the pass Sergeant James had given him. My Linh marveled at the steady improvements taking place in the drab camp. They had started when Jody's friend General Hare had taken over as personnel officer. He seemed to have lots of rich business friends—Chinese, Vietnamese, Americans, Koreans—and with their help he was changing the face of the camp.

The general had given a contract to a Korean, who had quickly started building swimming pools all over the post. He had also given a contract to an American to install gift shops, so the troops could buy anything from diamonds to Chinese-made wigs. The general had given a concession to a furrier; in the 100-degree heat the troops were buying fur coats for their women at home. Another of the general's friends had a concession to put a fleet of ice-cream trucks on the post. Some wealthy Chinese brothers the general was said to have known in Germany had built a Chinese restaurant.

A little further along was Madame Sang's steam bath establishment. It was the fanciest building of all, with its statues of nude women guarding the entrances. Long Binh was certainly one of Vietnam's biggest industries. Thousands of Vietnamese lined up every day for work, swarming into the camp by bus, truck, Lambretta, Honda, or on foot. They cleaned the barracks, polished the officers' boots, washed their clothes, cooked their food, operated their telephones, served their drinks, drove their vehicles, sold them merchandise, and gave them massages.

My Linh thought of all the stealing these people must do. One day she had seen a woman stopped by the MPs for an inspection. Under her *au dai* she had two steaks taped to each leg. But how could you blame these poor people for stealing? she thought. After all, wasn't everyone?

The clanging bell of a passing ice-cream truck interrupted her thoughts. She told Tien to stop and called out to the Vietnamese ice-cream vendor.

"Give me twelve cones. Different flavors." They exchanged a few words in Vietnamese, and he gave her the cones, which she handed to the band members. Then she paid him in MPC. My Linh knew that she would be in trouble if the military police ever caught her, a Vietnamese, with military scrip, but she felt safe enough. All the Vietnamese used MPC and the military police, knowing there was no way to stop them, seldom made trouble. Sometimes the new MPs, fresh from the States, would try to do their duty and search the Viets, looking for the illegal currency. But after a few months they too would change.

Tien pulled up in front of the NCO club the group was working at that night. My Linh supervised the unloading of the instruments and then told the band to change for the show. She climbed back into the van and asked Tien to drive her over to Sergeant Jesse James's office.

By the time she arrived, Sergeant James had left his office for the day, but a Vietnamese office worker gave her directions to his quarters. She and Tien quickly drove over. The luxurious building was screened by a high fence, providing privacy from the curious eyes of passing grunts. Inside the fence was a well-kept lawn, an outdoor barbecue, and a cement path leading up to the new timber villa.

My Linh knocked on the door. Although she heard considerable noises inside, nobody answered. She knocked again and waited. Still nobody answered. Then she turned the knob and peeked in.

A group of five men were sitting around drinking. Then a squealing Vietnamese girl ran through the room, a naked man in hot pursuit. My Linh was about to close the door and leave when one of the men noticed her.

"What are you doing here, girl?" he bellowed. She recognized him as Sergeant James.

"Very sorry to interrupt, Sergeant. I was sent by Jody T. to see you, but I can come back tomorrow."

"Don't be bashful, come in," James urged. The girl and the naked man had left the room, so she ventured in.

"You've got something for me?" asked James expectantly.

"Yes." She looked at the others hesitantly.

"We're all friends here," he chuckled coarsely. "What have you got?"

My Linh took out the roll of MPC and handed it to him. He took it disdainfully and counted it before saying, "What's the idea of that stupid broad sending MPC. I wanted green. Doesn't she know I've got to lose money on the exchange?"

"I'm sorry, sir," My Linh replied. "Jody T. said she has no contacts for getting green. She only has MPC or else her personal check."

"A check," he growled. "What are you, crazy? Leave myself open to be caught like that?"

"No. That why she sent MPC."

"Okay, okay. Only next time try to bring green. Anyway, now you're here, meet the boys and have a drink."

My Linh didn't want to stay, but she remembered what Jody told her Cotsworth had said about having a few drinks with the sergeants. She allowed James to introduce her to the USARV sergeant major, the post sergeant major, Red Fisher, the custodian from Di An, and two assistant custodians. My Linh greeted the men and then asked for a Coke.

"We don't keep no Cokes here," James guffawed. "Have a Scotch."

Reluctantly, she accepted the Scotch and sipped at it while the men's eyes undressed her. "We've been hearing about your boss," said a sergeant major. The broad with the big boobs. Why isn't she here herself?"

"She's with another group at Cu Chi," My Linh answered uncomfortably.

"She thinks she's too good for us," continued the sergeant major petulantly. "She'll damned soon find out who runs this show if she doesn't get with the program."

My Linh sipped her drink and didn't reply. She looked around the room, surprised by the luxury of it. The walls and ceiling were soundproofed, and an expensive speaker system piped music throughout the villa. Two air-conditioning units kept the place cool and smoke free. The furniture was elegant; rare Oriental artifacts were scattered around haphazardly.

The front door was kicked open, and a mess sergeant staggered in carrying a tray piled high with steaks. "Shall I put this in the freezer, Sergeant Major?" he asked.

"Sure thing," one of the sergeant majors replied.

My Linh watched as the mess sergeant passed through into the stainless-steel kitchen and transferred the steaks to the freezer. "Excuse me," My Linh said to the sergeant beside her, "could you show me the bathroom, please?"

He stood up grinning and led her down a passageway, passing two air-conditioned bedrooms and one closed door, which she assumed led into a third bedroom. When she returned to the living room she asked the sergeant, "How many people live here?"

"Three," he replied. "Sergeant James and the two sergeant majors."

"This is a lovely place," My Linh continued innocently. "Do all American sergeant majors live like this?"

The sergeant roared with laughter. "Hell no, girl. Norm and Lavinia Ferris built this place for the custodian and the two sergeant majors."

"Why did they do that?" My Linh asked.

"Because this post has been good to them, that's why. We paid them a hell of a lot of money to build and decorate some new clubs for us. They just happened to have surplus materials and used them to put up this place." The sergeant put his hand on My Linh's thigh and grinned at her lecherously. "My name is Willy Halaby. Sergeant James will be finishing up his tour and then I'll be the custodian and live here. I hope you'll see much more of this place then."

My Linh gulped the rest of her Scotch down and stood up. "If you'll excuse me, I have to be getting back."

164

James overheard her and went over to them. "Don't be in a hurry, My Linh. "I'm going back to my office with the mess sergeant. Hang around awhile and talk to the boys. I'll look up my schedule and maybe I can extend your group another two weeks. I'll tell you when I get back."

"Oh, that would be good," My Linh said eagerly, returning to the sofa and gingerly accepting another Scotch.

Shortly after James left, the two sergeant majors stood up, saying they wanted to have a look at a new show appearing in one of the clubs. My Linh was left with Red Fisher and his assistant, Sergeant Halaby. Hillbilly music from the stereo filled the room. My Linh sat silently as the sergeants had made a few derogatory remarks about Jody T. Once again the naked man chased the Vietnamese girl into the room. This time the girl was also naked. She fled, giggling and squealing, from his clutches.

"That's Kin, one of hooch maids," Halaby informed the embarrassed My Linh.

The girl, her small breasts bobbing, ran playfully behind the chairs, darting from place to place and avoiding the man's grasp until, with one wild lunge, he caught her around the ankle and threw her onto the rug in the center of the room. They rolled together on the rug until he maneuvered the slender girl onto her back and pinned her down by straddling her hips. Her long dark hair covering her face, she was still giggling as he slowly entered her. As he pushed further in, her giggling modulated into soft moans. The others in the room watched the tableau intently. My Linh, frightened now, jumped to her feet and ran toward the door. Halaby darted ahead of her and turned the key.

"What your hurry, girl?" he drawled. "Come and watch the action."

"I've got to get back to my band. They'll be getting ready to go on soon." Her words came breathlessly, her hands trembling. The sergeant gripped her arm and dragged her back to the sofa.

"The band can take care of itself," he rasped.

My Linh, her mind racing, sat shaking on the sofa. She tried not to look at the writhing, moaning Vietnamese girl on the floor in front of her with the big white man atop.

It occurred to her that there must be a back entrance, and she leaped up again and ran down the hallway past the bathroom, her heart pounding. She reached the back door and frantically pulled the knob, but it was locked. Terrified she checked all the bedrooms, but could find no way out. Before she knew it, Red Fisher had picked her up in his arms and carried her back to the living room. She kicked and scratched and screamed, but the sergeant held her tightly.

Dropping her onto the sofa Fisher said to the others, "Hold this little bitch down, and be careful she doesn't scratch you." They pinned her arms to her sides and she sat slumped, unable to get away.

The naked man on the rug groaned aloud as he erupted into the hooch

165

maid, then slowly, breathing heavily, he stood up and helped her to her feet.

"You give us all hards now," Fisher said to the hooch maid. "How about you give us frenchie. We know you like frenchie." As he spoke, he began to unbuckle his belt and pull down his trousers.

The girl giggled. "Okay. I do for you."

Wearing only his shirt Fisher stood in the middle of the room as the frail Vietnamese girl knelt down and took his engorged organ in her hands, playing with it, moving her lips tantalizingly over the tip until he thrust his fingers into her hair and forced himself all the way into her mouth.

My Linh closed her eyes. Halaby, sitting next to her said huskily. "Open your eyes and look, honey. It's your turn next. All the agents provide girls for us. It's about time Jody T. did the same."

My Linh closed her eyes tight and suddenly felt a stinging blow on the face as the sergeant slapped her, saying, "Look at them, I said. I want you to get turned on too."

A second blow, harder than the first, forced her eyes open. Her face was smarting, and a tear trickled down her cheek. Silently, she watched the scene in front of her, thinking how she hated these American men. First Talltree and now these sergeants. She thought of screaming, but she knew it would be no use.

The half-naked sergeant cried out coarsely. "Here it is, baby! Keep sucking." He held the small girl's head firmly.

My Linh trembled, knowing it would soon be her turn to appease the lust of the men. As the hooch maid stood up again one of the sergeants holding My Linh said, "You know what I'd like to watch? Kin going down on My Linh here."

"Yeah," chorused the others. "How about it Kin?"

Kin wrinkled her nose. "I no like eat pussy. Maybe you pay me ten dollars I do."

One of the men wordlessly pulled two five-dollar MPC notes from his pocket and handed it to her.

My Linh cried and began to struggle, but the two sergeants pulled her roughly to her feet as the other two ripped at her clothes, tearing them off her.

Sobbing, she stood with her arms held behind her until they had her naked, her torn garments lying on the floor. "Not too bad," said one of the sergeants, eyeing her lasciviously.

They lifted her up and lowered her on the rug, two men holding her legs apart and one more holding her arms. Firmly pinned, she cried and beat her head on the floor as Kin crawled between her legs, which were held apart in a wide V.

Terror-stricken as she was, My Linh began to enjoy the sensation in

166

spite of herself and stopped beating her head. Her heart was pounding and the adrenalin raced through her veins from fear, but the expertise of the young hooch maid soon had her moaning quietly as the beady-eyed sergeants devoured the scene. Kin went about her art zealously, driving My Linh to a frenzy of delight which disgusted her and made her even more afraid.

Suddenly Halaby and Red Fisher tore their clothes off. Kin got up and helped herself to a drink while the two naked sergeants pulled the sobbing, struggling My Linh to her feet.

"Why she fight so much? Better she like," the hooch maid commented with a shrill laugh.

With My Linh standing, Fisher forced his entrance from the front. When My Linh began to scream, the sergeant hit her across the face, cutting her mouth and making it bleed. Halaby had been standing anointing himself with baby oil, which he had earlier taken from one of the bathrooms. Now he stepped up behind My Linh and tried to force his way in from the rear. My Linh screamed in pain and bit Halaby on the shoulder. He cursed and hit her hard—bright lights and pain seared through her head. She gasped and then went limp, giving up the struggle, tears streaming down her face, blood trickling from her mouth. Holding her small, shaking body between them they grunted greedily as they pushed and strained into her.

Fisher finished first with a cry and withdrew. Halaby forced the unresisting, sobbing girl into a bent position over the arm of an overstuffed chair and renewed his ramming action from the rear.

As Halaby pushed on, there was a sudden loud knocking at the door. With one last thrust Halaby ejaculated and pushed on My Linh's buttocks, separating himself from her, and fell back exhausted on the sofa.

"Let me in!" yelled Sergeant James. "What the hell's going on in there?"

Someone opened the door wide enough for James to get in and then closed it quickly behind him. The first thing that greeted the custodian's eye was the crumpled form of My Linh over the chair. "What the hell have you fuckin' crazy-ass bastards been doing?" he roared.

"Just a little fun, Jesse. Nothing to get mad about," Fisher said soothingly, standing naked with a drink in his hand.

James strode over to the girl and tried to lift her to her feet, but she slumped to the floor. He picked her up and put her into the chair. "She's hurt, you goddamned idiots! Don't you know better than this? You may end up doing a lot of explaining to the CID."

"Aw, come on, Jesse," Halaby said. "The CID is ours."

"They can protect us on most everything else, but rape,"—he shook his head, a shocked expression still on his face—"I don't know about that. Now get your clothes on, all of you. Halaby, I would have thought you at least would know better."

The men began dressing, and the little Vietnamese hooch maid ran from the room. My Linh lay exhausted on the chair over which she had been raped. James picked up her torn garments and looked at them, throwing them aside in disgust. He went back to his room and returned with a robe.

"Here, girl, put this on." His tone was quiet and kindly. He helped the dazed My Linh into the robe. She sat motionless, her eyes glazed, as James tied the garment around her waist and dabbed at her mouth with a wet towel.

"Get out of here, every one of you!" he shouted in rage. "Get out, you goddamned animals." Quickly the sergeants slunk out of the house. Finally, Sergeant James was alone with My Linh.

"I'm real sorry about this, My Linh," he said, a worried look on his face. "I hope you won't talk about it to anyone. I'm sure the boys didn't mean any real harm."

James poured some brandy and held it to My Linh's lips. She shuddered and sputtered at the strong liquor and then spoke for the first time.

"Can I use your phone, Sergeant?" she said brokenly. "I want to call Jody T. at Cu Chi."

"To tell her about this?"

"Yes."

"I don't know," he said hesitatingly. "You must understand something. What happened was wrong, and I'm sorry. I don't hold with rape. But if you tell Jody T. and she reports it to the CID, that will be the end of Jody T. Promotions. I'll take care of the boys who did this, and it will never happen again. But," he added in matter-of-fact tones that gave his words shattering impact, "if you want to stay in business let me handle everything."

My Linh took another sip of the soothing liquor. "Maybe I'd better not tell her until she comes to Saigon. On the phone is not good, she has a very bad temper."

"All right. But give her my message."

My Linh nodded, holding the cold, wet towel he had given her against the swelling at the side of her head. "I see your driver is out in front," James continued. "I'll send him away. He can take your show back to Saigon tonight, and I'll drive you up now. I don't want anyone seeing you like this." He went outside and was soon back.

"All set. Let's go."

My Linh took a last sip of the brandy, put the glass down, and docilely followed Master Sergeant James from the house to the station wagon. They made the trip in silence, but before she stepped out at the apartment building he leaned to her and said, "Tell Jody T. that if you will both forget

168

about tonight, there will be lots of business for you at Long Binh. You'll need another band to take care of it."

Numbly, My Linh nodded and then let herself into the apartment as James drove off.

25

The same day that My Linh had taken the kickback money to Sergeant James, Jody was returning to Colonel Lane's campsite after visiting her Vietnamese group over in the Wolfhound area. It was late afternoon as she walked by the heavily sandbagged building that was the brigade TOC, and she was surprised to see the operations officer hurry to the doorway and beckon her in. The TOC was definitely an off-limits area to all except those who officially worked there. Security was tight because the building housed the powerful radio-monitoring and transmitting system that kept brigade headquarters in communication with every battalion in the Third Brigade.

The operations officer spent most of his waking hours in the TOC, keeping records of all operations and planning future attacks. The aviation officer was equally busy controlling and coordinating the use of all aircraft at the disposal of the Brigade.

As Jody followed the major into the top-security structure she glanced around curiously at the map-covered walls and the handful of sergeants who were monitoring the reports which were pouring in over the various radios around the room. Wondering why she had been brought in, she stopped in front of one of the radios. At first it was difficult for her to understand the words coming from the radio, but she concentrated as hard as she could.

"It's Barking Dog, Jody," the major said, answering her unspoken question. "He's at Hoc Man."

The Wolfhound battalion had been ordered to sweep through the village of Hoc Man on its way to carrying out a search-and-destroy operation on a suspected North Vietnam Army headquarters five miles west of the village. Although it was known that Hoc Man was a village of VC sym-

170

pathizers, the policy in the area had been to spare it from complete destruction, hoping that if the main force of the enemy could be separated from the village, the rural pacification program might be successful in winning the villagers over to the side of the government.

Barking Dog in his C and C was hovering over the approaches to Hoc Man as the First Platoon of Alpha Company, the Wolfhound battalion, led the way into the village. It had been Colonel Lane's inclination to level the village with artillery fire before sending his men in, but at division level he was refused permission on the grounds that intelligence had positive information that no VC soldiers had been in the village for two weeks.

"It's not the uniformed enemy I'm worried about," Lane had argued with the division commander. "It's women who are sniping at us, knocking off my point men and platoon leaders. It's the little boys who come running out calling 'okay' and smiling. In their hands they're carrying a paper bag with a grenade or time explosive which kills or maims my men. It's the women and children who are planting the claymores and land mines."

"Look, Bill," the general had said. "We can't go around blasting villages off the face of the map. You know how many newspaper correspondents have become famous by reporting our alleged atrocities? I don't care if every woman and child is a Communist in Hoc Man, this is a political war and we don't kill them. Now if we had hard intelligence that there were NVA hiding in the village that would be something else."

"Then why not go around the village to reach our objective?" Hard Bill asked. "I don't want to take chances with my men. A lot of them came over here at the same time I did, and they're getting ready to go home. I don't want to see them killed by the civilians we can't touch."

"Policy is to go through the villages and let the people see we're here and mean business."

"If we wiped Hoc Man out with artillery, they'd damned soon see we mean business," Barking Dog growled.

"Top policy is to destroy the Communist infrastructure. The experts, ours and Vietnamese, will take care of Hoc Man. Our job is to cut it off from the enemy main force by pushing Charlie back and holding him back. Between our Phoenix operation and the Viets' counterterror groups, they'll neutralize the infrastructure."

Barking Dog thought of this conversation as he anxiously watched the Wolfhounds approaching Hoc Man. The Wolfhounds' battalion commander was flying over one of his other companies, two miles away, which had made contact with enemy troops. Colonel Lane's instinct told him that what happened at Hoc Man was crucial to the brigade's entire method of operating and, for that matter, would give another clue to the police and strategy of the overall war plan in Vietnam.

The platoon was just crossing the fields surrounding the village. Hard Bill thought of young Sergeant Bryan Crawley. He had only two weeks to go before going back to Fort Benning and entering officer candidate school. Just that morning the colonel had put out an order that all men with two weeks or less left in country would be taken off combat status. Over his mouthpiece Barking Dog kept talking to the company commander to find out what was happening with the two platoons about to move through the village. Then, crackling across the radio, he heard the message relayed in from the First Platoon radio operator. The lead element had just suffered multiple casualties from claymore mines. Barking Dog immediately ordered his pilot to circle the village. Then he called to the company commander over the radio, "This is Barking Dog. I'm going to try and spot the VC detonating those mines."

For a few minutes Barking Dog tried to spot suspicious-looking villagers, but they were all in their houses or otherwise concealed. The village appeared to be deserted, and he ordered the pilot to set down near the casualties.

"Barking Dog coming down," Hard Bill said with finality. As they descended, the colonel could see the twisted bodies near the village. He was out of his helicopter and running toward the remnants of the platoon before the skids had settled into the earth. A lieutenant hastened up to him.

"Sir, it isn't safe here. Those VC villagers may set off more claymores, and there are probably land mines all over the place."

The colonel studied the situation. Hoc Man was a typical village, actually a complex of hamlets with a population of two thousand people. The houses were arrayed in neat rows behind mud walls. There were eight American bodies lying in the field about fifty yards from the entrance to the village. The C and C had landed as close to the casualties as seemed safe.

Each body was badly torn by the bits of shrapnel that cut a lethal scythe from the concave-faced surface mines that were usually detonated electrically by an observer. Heads, arms, and legs were so torn and shattered that the bodies would be almost impossible to collect and send back.

Colonel Lane cursed the civilians, the old men and the women and children who had placed these mines. There was only one way to handle a village like this, and the pacification program of economic and agricultural assistance wouldn't do the job.

"Sir, there are more mines in the ground around them," an officer said. Lane nodded and started to back away when he saw one of the bodies move slightly. He stared at a shattered human form, about twenty yards from where he was standing, and his eyes narrowed.

"One of them seems to be alive," he observed. "His head moved." He looked again. "Isn't that Sergeant Crawley?"

The lieutenant looked surprised. "You know him, sir?"

Barking Dog nodded, and suddenly, before the lieutenant could utter a word or move, Hard Bill charged across the field to the sergeant who had shown some sign of life. As the startled platoon members watched, the colonel reached down and picked the man up. It was all the lieutenant could do not to avert his eyes. The colonel was carrying what was left of Sergeant Crawley toward them. The remains of both legs hung stringily from him; there was no left arm, just a few bloody shreds of cloth.

As they watched, horror-stricken, there was a splitting explosion from behind Barking Dog, and he pitched to his knees, still holding tightly to the sergeant, whose eyes they could see were both open, though his body was gushing blood. Hard Bill staggered back to his feet and continued toward his helicopter.

"Thank God that last claymore wasn't aimed directly at him," the lieutenant whispered to the men around him. "I hope he lets us go in there and kill everything that moves."

The machine gunner beside him had his weapon trained on the entrance of the village. "Just let me so much as see one fuckin' dink and I'll let him have it."

Barking Dog reached the lieutenant and the remainder of his platoon. "I'll get this man back to the hospital."

He looked hopelessly at the sergeant, miraculously still alive. He wasn't even unconscious. "Thank you, sir," Crawley managed to croak.

"Sir, you're hit in the back," the lieutenant exclaimed.

"I'm walking, aren't I? Can't be too bad."

"Can I help you, sir? Let me carry Crawley."

Barking Dog shook his head, his mouth contorted in pain. "I'm managing, Lieutenant. Stay in communication with the company commander."

The colonel kept walking to his C and C, and his door gunner jumped out and helped him aboard with his burden. "Sir," the crewman said, "he'll never make it."

"I'll make it. I refuse to die," came the dry, hoarse voice of Sergeant Crawley.

In the TOC, the operations officer was telling Jody what had happened. "Barking Dog landed his C and C and went into a minefield to save a sergeant. The colonel was wounded by a mine himself."

Straining her ears, Jody anxiously strained to catch every word. Then Barking Dog's own voice crackled loudly across the wires, and Jody sighed with relief.

"This is Barking Dog. Tell the evac hospital to have a stretcher ready at the pad. ASAP. This man's losing a lot of blood."

For another five minutes Jody listened. Then she ran out of the TOC, looking for Sergeant Jones. She found him in the colonel's trailer, cleaning Hard Bill's boots. Panting, she told him what had happened. Jones imme-

173

diately dropped the boot and hurried with Jody out to the jeep. They leaped into the vehicle and, after a quick ride, reached the pad beside the hospital just as the colonel's C and C settled in.

Jody watched as two hospital attendants lifted Sergeant Crawley out of the chopper. Jody recognized the white-faced sergeant instantly and then, suddenly, realized what else she saw. Blood was still seeping from the mess of skin, cartilage, and shattered bone—all that was left of his left arm. She clapped her hands to her face when she saw that both legs were gone, right up into his lower abdomen. Barking Dog and his crew had applied pressure bandages as best they could, but the wounds were too massive for them to be effective. The corpsmen laid Crawley on the stretcher and quickly carried him, still conscious, into the operating theater, where two surgeons were waiting.

Barking Dog looked after the stretcher and, as it passed Jody, she tore her hands from her eyes and looked down at Crawley, desperately fighting the convulsions she felt in her stomach. "Have strength, Bryan," she said. "We will all be praying for you."

"I won't die, Jody, I just won't." His voice was a faint, dry wheeze.

The stretcher disappeared, and Jody turned from the hospital, her face buried in her hands. She felt two arms on hers and slowly looked up. It was Sergeant Jones. "The colonel has to go into hospital now. His back is pretty badly cut up."

Jody nodded and managed to get control of herself. She went to Hard Bill and reached out for him in spite of the other officers and men around. He put a hand on her shoulder. "They say I've got to go in for a while, Jody. It can't be too bad."

"Can I come with you, Bill?" Jody said.

Despite the pain in his back, Hard Bill smiled. "I'd like that, Jody. But the staff and the other patients might not understand."

Jody looked at the back of the colonel's fatigue jacket. It was sliced open in ugly streaks where the shrapnel had grazed him, and blood was seeping from his wounds. "I'm the luckiest dog in Vietnam," he said. "The claymore wasn't aimed at me, and I just caught the edge of the blast."

"Thank God it was no worse." There was a prayer of thanks in Jody's voice.

"I was lucky." He shook his head, his eyes misting. "Crawley. The Army is losing a fine young soldier." The colonel's voice noticeably quivered. "Goddamned Vietnamese. I didn't know how bad he was until I picked him. He shouldn't be alive. No arm, no legs—" He turned his back as the tears overflowed and trickled down his seamed cheeks.

Jody, unable to fight back her tears, took hold of the wounded colonel's hand.

"I must be getting too old for this," he said. "Commanders don't cry."

174

The chief surgeon, a colonel, came out of the hospital. Colonel Lane straightened up and composed himself before turning to meet him.

"Come on, Bill," the hospital commander said, "Let us take a look at you. We're doing the best we can for the sergeant."

"When can I come in to see him?" Jody asked anxiously.

"Better wait a day or two, Jody."

Hard Bill leaned over and kissed her and then allowed himself to be led into the hospital. This was the first in a long time that Jody could remember allowing herself the feminine luxury of bursting into tears. Sergeant Jones led her to the jeep and drove her back to the colonel's trailer.

For the next three days Jody accompanied the chaplain to the hospital every morning and afternoon. For the first few days Jody couldn't face seeing the horribly wounded sergeant. Instead, she sat at Hard Bill's bedside, talking to him for hours on end, trying to bolster his spirits. It was a difficult task, since the commanding general of the division, after lightly admonishing him for putting himself in such danger, told him that it had been decided that he would be evacuated to a hospital in Japan, where he would receive expert medical attention. Then he would be returned for duty to the United States. Hard Bill's wounds were more serious than he had realized. Shrapnel particles were embedded close to his spinal column.

The day Colonel Lane was to be evacuated to Japan, he and Jody went to say good-bye to Sergeant Crawley. Jody steeled herself for the sight as they walked into the amputee ward. So many young men missing arms and legs, she thought. And for what? To keep the war going so the back-bar bunch at the I House could get richer?

The sergeant was lying in a pool of blood on a plastic sheet, a bottle of blood plasma hanging above him with a tube running down into a needle inserted into a vein in his arm. His body was at last beginning to retain the blood that was constantly flowing into him, although now, four days after he had been so critically wounded, a certain amount of the blood constantly flowing into his veins was still seeping out. The doctor had told Jody and Hard Bill that never in his career had he administered so much blood to a man. It was only sheer will that had kept him alive.

When Crawley looked up at Colonel Lane and Jody, a wan smile came to his face. Jody was too choked up to speak at first. Sensing her loss of words, the sergeant said, "I still have a good right arm, sir. Maybe there's a desk job in the Army I could handle."

"I'll look into it, Crawley," Lane said huskily.

"I promise I'll be in to see you every day, Bryan," Jody managed.

"That would sure be nice."

The hospital commander came over to them. "Time for you to go, Bill."

"Sir." Crawley's voice was strong. "I want you to know that it was an honor serving under you. I'm sorry I'll never get to OCS and maybe be a company commander in a division of yours some day."

175

Colonel Lane didn't try to form an answer; he nodded and covered Crawley's hand with his own before turning and walking out of the ward and back to his hospital room. Waiting for him was Sergeant Jones. To the commemorative plaques and other gifts that Barking Dog's staff officers had been bringing to him, Jones added his offering. He unfurled a black velvet scroll on which a Vietnamese artist had skillfully painted a dog, mouth open and fangs showing. On it, in fancy lettering, was written, THIRD BRIGADE, 25TH DIVISION. Barking Dog smiled faintly and shook hands warmly with his driver.

"Sir, I sure am going to miss you," Jones said in a choked voice.

"I might say the same, Jones. You've been a loyal man. And by the way, anything you can do to help Jody T. will be much appreciated."

With the help of Jones, the colonel finished packing the mementos and clothing he had in his hospital room. While the driver was taking them out to the big hospital plane, Jody and Hard Bill had a few moments alone together.

"I had hoped we might have a more exciting good-bye, Jody." His voice was gruff. "Perhaps even a night on the town in Saigon. It's damned frustrating to leave you this way."

"Maybe someday I'll get to the States," Jody said and then almost bit her tongue, realizing that there was a Mrs. Lane and three teen-agers. The colonel was not disturbed.

"If you ever do, let me know and we'll get together. But what I'm going to work on is getting assigned back here. And when I do, the first thing on my mind will be to find you."

"I guess I'll be around. Business is good. I might even pick up a third band." Then the shadow of a frown passed across her face as she thought of Sergeant Crawley and the custodians. To think that they both wore an American uniform!

After Barking Dog was put on the plane, Jody asked Sergeant Jones to try and find a helicopter ride into Saigon for her. Somehow she couldn't face the Donut Dollies now that Hard Bill had gone. She had moved out of Barking Dog's trailer an hour after he had gone into the hospital, knowing that the executive officer would be moving in to take over right away until a new commander was assigned to the brigade. And she was not ready to begin a new liaison with Springer so soon after Hard Bill's evacuation.

Within hours of the time the hospital plane took off, Jody was climbing out of a chopper at Hotel 3, wondering how My Linh was doing with the Filipino show. She had been out of contact since the day Barking Dog was wounded. She went straight to her apartment on Plantation Road.

In her office she found My Linh sitting at the desk. Her eye was swollen and purple discoloration stained the skin on her cheek.

"What on earth has happened to you?" Jody asked.

"Some sergeants at Long Binh did it last week," My Linh replied matter-of-factly.

Jody cried out in anger. "You mean James? Tell me who did it. They'll be damned sorry."

As My Linh related the story, Jody's fury increased. "Those sons of bitches!" she exploded. "What kind of bastards are we dealing with? I pay up and they rape my staff. It doesn't stop. Next they'll rape my Filipino girls—Rosemarie is only sixteen. I'm sick of the whole stinking business. Get me Alvin Bruce on the phone. This has got to stop."

Jody stalked to the phone angrily. As she lifted the receiver, My Linh put on a restraining hand. "Listen to me Jody. Do not do it. It is good to know you care so much about me, but the trouble is done. Sergeant James say if you report it we be out of business. That bad. I have no more job. No money for little Andre."

Jody hesitated, but only for seconds. "Trust me, My Linh. Even if they blacklist me, we will keeping working somehow. There is still Cu Chi. Maybe I can keep both bands working there."

My Linh sighed deeply as her hot-headed boss picked up the phone and dialed the CID number. She doubted that there was enough work at Cu Chi for both bands.

After Jody spoke to Alvin Bruce, My Linh turned to her, puzzled. "Never can I understand you, Jody T. You have two sides. In Nha Trang when you need money for the club and again when you need liquor, you do those strip shows. Then I see you come to Saigon and have two boy friends at Cu Chi. Why you don't take a sergeant boy friend? That way you make a good business."

"If a man is a real soldier, I don't mean because he is wearing a uniform, but a real man with courage and decency, I can respect him and care about him. It makes no difference what age he is or whether he is handsome. If he becomes my man, even for a short time, I am proud. After so many real men I have known, after the number of decent boys I've seen dead or wounded—" The image of Sergeant Crawley's maimed body flashed before her eyes. "Those slobs, these stinking carrion, these, these—" She sputtered in anger. "These filthy parasites make me sick. I can hardly be pleasant to them, let alone spend my nights in bed with them."

My Linh was thoughtful. "I see. I try to understand, but I think you let heart rule head. It make very bad business."

Thirty minutes later Alvin Bruce arrived, accompanied by another CID man. They entered the office and prepared to type up the statement that Jody forced the unwilling My Linh to relate for them. As the CID agents pried the details from My Linh, Jody sat listening, her anger rising.

Certainly she had been making plenty of money over the last couple of months, but it hadn't brought her the happiness she had expected. Visiting the custodians on her sales trips, she had to learn to bite her tongue, suffer their snide remarks, and parry their clumsy advances. Many times she had wanted to confide in Hard Bill about the Khaki Mafia. However, he had more than enough problems of his own, and as a field commander, he was in no position to do anything about this administrative problem anyway.

Alvin Bruce and his partner stayed for two hours, working on the statement. As they left, Bruce took Jody aside. "I don't know what will happen, Jody. So far anything that concerns club custodians, or for that matter military personnel involved in PX management, seems to get mousetrapped somewhere above my level. I'll follow this matter up as far as I can, though. I promise you."

For a week after making the report Jody left her Vietnamese group unattended in Cu Chi and accompanied My Linh and the Filipino group to Long Binh every night. They managed to avoid the sergeants, and Jody somehow controlled her temper. She was sorry that she couldn't be at Cu Chi to visit Sergeant Crawley, but her major concern now was that word of her latest report to the CID would leak out. Once it did, Jody T. Promotions was through.

Stopping at the I House for lunch during the week, Jody was joined by Saigon's chief gossip forwarder, Marie Monahan. Jody never ceased to be amazed at how much information Marie managed to pick up in her daily routine.

Marie sat down, uninvited, at Jody's table. "Haven't seen you lately," Marie observed after beckoning over a waiter and asking him to have her drink sent in from the bar.

"I'm back for a while, taking my Filipino group to Long Binh every night," Jody replied.

"Mmmm," Marie mused. "You won't be getting any more business there after this month."

Jody's heart skipped a beat. Was she blacklisted already? "How's that?" she asked.

"Why, Lee LaRue is taking over a monopoly on the place. Didn't you know?"

Jody shook her head.

"Oh she and Jesse James made a lulu of a deal. I don't know how they think they're going to get away with it, but James must have protection at the top. For the next six months James is hiring all his bands from Lee. He just extended his tour another six months." A smug look settled over her at the news gem she had dropped.

"But that's against all regulations," Jody cried. "CEO regulations say a custodian can only book one month in advance."

Marie laughed harshly. "Who cares about regs? Nine bands every day

178

of the month. At two thousand dollars each, that's a total of eighteen thousand."

"But Lee has only four groups," Jody answered.

"She's leaving today for Manila to pick up another five."

"It doesn't make sense," Jody argued. "We all pay James and the others. Why should he drop all the agents and give Lee exclusive bookings?"

"I'll tell you why, if you keep it confidential." Marie glanced around to see that no one was listening. "James and Lee have become partners. She is splitting fifty-fifty with him on all profits. Eight thou apiece."

"But that's so illegal it defies description!" Jody exclaimed.

"Wait." Marie held up a hand. "You haven't heard it all. On top of everything else, he is purchasing nine Volkswagen buses with open-mess funds to be used by the bands."

Jody was stunned. Each agent had to hire a bus and driver for their groups. Since a bus cost around four hundred dollars a month, the free use of nine of them would be an additional thirty-six-hundred-dollar profit a month for Jesse James and Lee LaRue.

"I don't know why I'm so surprised," Jody said after a few moments. "The things that go on over here get more unbelievable every day. It seems the rich get richer and the poor die."

Marie gave Jody a sharp look. "Why so gloomy?"

"I don't know. It's just that I see both sides. You only see the Saigon side. People getting rich, Americans and Vietnamese alike, everyone having a ball. But don't forget, I spend most of my time out in the boonies. No one is getting rich out there, but a damned lot of them are getting killed or maimed. What for? To keep the war going so the carpetbaggers can keep making money?"

Marie looked at Jody strangely. "Well, aren't we all here for money? Your attitude is damned odd. Come to think of it, I hear you're always driving around insecure roads. They say even your Viet driver refuses to take you some places and you ride in those crappy little Viet buses. Are you trying to play some kind of Vietnamese roulette?"

"Maybe. But I like to see what's going on. And something is very wrong about this war. The same village peasants I saw two years ago are still poor and living in their miserable huts. All the money the Yanks are pouring into this place"—she laughed bitterly—"to win the hearts and minds of the Vietnamese is benefiting all the wrong people. I only pray these Paris peace talks they're holding will be successful and all the troops can go home."

Marie stared at Jody in disbelief. "You are crazy. You're the first person I ever heard say they wanted the talks to succeed. We don't want our beautiful bubble to burst." Marie looked at Jody almost angrily and stood up. "If you'll excuse me, I'm going back to my friends at the bar."

One week later, when Jody was back at Cu Chi, trying to undo the sloppy habits the Vietnamese band had picked up in the seven days she had been away, My Linh telephoned her at the Red Cross Quonset hut. Jody T. Promotions had been blacklisted. The night before, when My Linh and the Filipino group had showed up for their engagement, Sergeant James turned them away and said that the contract was finished. Harshly he told My Linh that Jody might as well forget trying to get work with any custodian in country. She was through.

When she hung up the phone, Jody vowed she would fight this injustice to the end. Leaving the Red Cross girls' quarters, she hurried out toward the main headquarters building of the division in search of General Springer.

When she had finished her story he said calmly, "I've been in the Army for over twenty-five years, Jody, and I don't see how it is possible for a group of military men the size you are speaking of to wield the kind of power and influence you describe. Maybe your informants have exaggerated. You'll need hard proof to back up such accusations." He smiled condescendingly. "Now let's forget all these problems. How about a cocktail before dinner?"

Jody acquiesced. He didn't believe her. All she had left now was Cu Chi, and she at least wanted to hold on here.

26

JUNE, 1969

Late in the afternoon of the day they had interviewed Sergeant Munn at Di An and then Sergeant Heffer at the office, O'Neill, Rick, and Major Unger sat waiting for Sergeant Picking. This, his fourth interview with them, would conclude their day's work.

"When you have finished interviewing the people on your list, I have some ideas of new men to talk to," Unger volunteered.

O'Neill looked up quizzically. "Who, Ed?"

"I contacted a provost marshal major who worked closely with General Hare earlier this year. He's ready to talk about how Hare pulled a raid on the only real competitor Joe Crust had over here and put him out of business. After the raid, this fellow claims, all the independent salesmen threw in with Crust."

"Why is he willing to talk?" O'Neill asked.

"Major General Walter just announced he will retire next month. He's a lame-duck top cop now."

O'Neill nodded. "Should be a number of provost-marshal and CID types that wouldn't be afraid to talk."

"Before we're through I'll get as many as I can to come in and give you depositions," Unger promised. He glanced at his watch. "Picking should be outside now. I'll take a look."

"Thanks. I think we can finish with him this session," O'Neill said. "He's been the best informant we've had. He should make a convincing witness at the hearings."

"Picking," O'Neill began when the sergeant had seated himself, "earlier this afternoon we talked to Sergeant Myles Heffer. You know him?"

"Sure. He's been a big buddy of Cotsworth since Germany." Picking chuckled. "I'll bet he wasn't much help to you."

"He wasn't," O'Neill replied dryly. "I'd like to hear your version of how a man gets himself assigned as a club custodian."

"Well, sir, the way things are working today the first thing he does is go to Cotsworth."

"What are the mechanics?" Rick asked. "I mean if the operations were working legally, the way they were designed."

"All assignments clear through OPO in the Pentagon. That's Office of Personnel Operations," Picking explained. "OPO assigns the men to theater of operations or country. In Vietnam USARV assigns them to divisions."

"So how did Sergeant Major Cotsworth get his gang, en masse, so to speak, moved in on the clubs in Vietnam?"

"At APO there's a Lieutenant Colonel in charge who used to be in the Twenty-seventh Division in Germany. He made a lot of money with Cotsworth. And Heffer, until he came over here, was top NCO at OPO. Tiger gets OPO to assign his men to Vietnam. General Hare is head of personnel at USARV and makes sure they get to the right division. Then Tiger calls the division sergeant major, who assigns the guys to the open-mess system."

"Is that how you got back a second time?"

"Yes, sir."

"It must have taken a lot of planning and groundwork to set up this machine."

"It sure did, sir. But there was no special influence got me the job my first tour. It just happened because Cotsworth was working so hard to get his people all into Fort Benning from Germany that he forgot about me. Like I said, I was never really part of that bunch until this assignment."

O'Neill smiled benignly. "And fortunately, Picking, I came along in time to extricate you before you got in too deep. They aren't going to get away with it this time."

"No, sir," Picking agreed dubiously.

"It was shortly after your second tour in Vietnam began that the entire U.S. Army in Vietnam was ordered to go onto the open-mess system, was it not, Picking?" O'Neill asked.

"Yes, sir. I can tell you something about that too."

"We're listening," Rick prodded.

"While I was waiting to be assigned I dropped in on Sergeant Major Cotsworth's villa to get some idea of where they were going to send me. Tiger treated me real great, offered me a drink, and told me how glad he was to have a man of my experience back in the group. He started to give me his cooperation lecture, and then a car drove up. Through the window I could see it was a staff car. Tiger told me to go into the next room and look at TV until a meeting he had called was over.

"So I went into the den and nothing was on TV, so I looked at some magazines and I couldn't help hearing the conversation in the next room. It was General Hare himself come to see Tiger." Picking paused as though regrouping his thoughts.

"What did they talk about?" Rick asked, leaning forward eagerly.

"The general couldn't wait to tell Tiger there would soon be an order from General Flint to all division commanders that beginning the first of the month they would go on the open-mess system. Well I never saw a happier tiger in my life than ole Cotsworth after the general left. We had a real celebration that night."

"That was something to celebrate, all right," O'Neill remarked.

"Sure," Picking continued. "In the open-mess system the individual club managers had no purchasing power. And every morning they had to turn their take over to the custodian. You can imagine what pours into a custodian's office from thirty or forty clubs. And of course the biggest cash item was the slot-machine skimming. We learned in Germany how to put a small wire bug on the wheels to make them pay off lower than they're set. And of course when the agent of Joe Crust's Snead Electronics, which owns all the slot machines in country, comes around every day or so with the custodian, he splits a big piece of the take with him. Half of this money goes up the line to Cotsworth and the higher-ups who provide protection and the other half is for the custodian and his boys.

O'Neill worried Picking's statement around in his mind. "It's incredible. In the course of our investigation it appears that an annual turnover of seven hundred and fifty million dollars in military clubs around the world is legitimately recorded. Think of all the illegitimate money that is never reported. The clubs are at least a billion-dollar-a-year industry. And the major portion of all this money is handled by a bunch of sergeants with no qualifications and no prior business experience. Most of them are high-school dropouts, as a matter of fact. I can't understand how the Department of Defense has let this go on for so long. Can you imagine the credentials a civilian would need to manage a business of equal size?"

Major Unger, who had been listening quietly, shook his head in disbelief. Once more O'Neill turned to Picking. "I don't mean to appear unappreciative of your assistance, Sergeant, but I am curious about another thing." The sergeant returned the investigator's steady gaze.

"If you were so honest the first time you were a custodian here, what caused you to return after less than a year and join up with Cotsworth? By your own admission you already knew what was going on."

Sergeant Picking's face flushed, but he didn't flinch. "Sir, I hope to retire in a year or two. Without any money I don't have much future outside the Army. You see, I am one of those high-school dropouts you just spoke about. I am divorced now, and my alimony and support payments to my wife and three kids keep me broke all the time. She gets most of my paycheck. I figured one year as a Cotsworth boy would get me started in

Japan when I retire. Trouble was, I didn't know exactly what I was letting myself in for. That business with Spec Four Herrera getting shot shook me up. I've got no proof, mind you, but I've got my suspicions, and I don't hold with murder. I don't know what happened when you talked to Munn today, but he's been over here three years, and he thinks more like a gook than he does like us." Picking's mind seemed to come back to more pleasant things, and he smiled self-consciously. "Once I got to Japan I even had plans of looking for a Japanese wife."

"I see," O'Neill responded, flashing a brief smile of sympathy at the confused sergeant before him. "Well, I hope everything works out well for you now that this is over."

"Tell me one more thing, Picking," Rick broke in. "We heard you did a big favor for Joe Crust a few weeks ago. Want to tell us about it?"

Picking looked down at the floor for a moment. "You mean the gift-shop thing?"

"That's right," O'Neill confirmed.

"Well, that wasn't my doing. I just obeyed orders. Crust had me over to his villa one day and offered to sell the inventory of his gift-shop concessions at First Division to the club system. I knew he'd already tried to peddle it to the VRE, that's the Vietnam Regional Exchange." O'Neill nodded and motioned Picking to go on.

"The civilian buyer didn't want to take it. Crust was losing a hell of a lot of money on the shops and maybe had a hundred thousand dollars tied up in inventory. Junk it was mostly." Picking laughed aloud. "You heard what happened to that PX civilian, didn't you?"

Rick and O'Neill shook their heads.

"Well he was living with the other PX officials in one of Crust's villas in Saigon. They paid about a hundred a month rent for the place each and had girls, a swimming pool, a chef and servants. Old Cockeye got so mad when this independent swinging dick wouldn't buy the stuff he turned the guy in. Crust reported up the line that this buyer was living it up in Saigon while American boys were dying out in the boonies. You can bet he was fired. But now Crust didn't want to push his luck at the PX system, so he started in on me, being club custodian out at the First."

Picking shook his head wonderingly. "They're sharks, that Crust gang. They not only wanted out of the concession, they wanted to get out at a profit. Well, I wasn't going to pay them one hundred grand for their crap that the guys wouldn't buy and then try and make the boys buy the stuff. Even Cotsworth told me I could do what I wanted in this case."

He paused and looked up at his interrogators as though asking for understanding and sympathy. "My unappropriated funds belonged to the men really. Some of the money, at least, should have been used to make the clubs nicer for them, give them a free beer party, give them better entertainment. So I told Crust the day he called me over to his villa, I told him 'Hell, no!' In a nice way of course," Picking added.

"The next thing I know direct orders come down from General Hare that I have to buy the stuff, one hundred twenty thousand dollars."

Rick let out a low whistle and then asked, "General Hare gave orders at the Division?"

"Well, sir, it didn't work exactly that way. Cotsworth came to me and said things had changed. He wanted me to buy the junk. When I argued he said it came directly from Hare and had been cleared with the commanding general of the division. You have to remember that mentioning General Hare is like mentioning the Supreme Being. He controls all personnel assignments in Vietnam, and that gives him more muscle in our racket than anyone else in country."

"Did you get a commission on the sale?"

Picking's Adam's apple bobbed, and he nodded. "Ten percent. Twelve thousand dollars. Half went on up to Cotsworth, the other half I kept— toward the Japan fund."

"So you have saved a little something along the way," O'Neill said sarcastically.

"Something. Yes, sir."

The tight smile twitched briefly across O'Neill's face. "I guess we're about through with you, Picking. I'll have your statement typed up. By the way, where can I reach you?"

"I'm at the custodian's villa."

"The one where Lavinia Ferris plays housemother?"

"She's there a lot," Picking concurred. "I just hope to hell she's not getting suspicious. I've been around longer than usual so I could talk to you."

"We'll be ready for you to sign your testimony in a couple of days. Then you're on your way."

"Thank you, sir. The sooner I get out of Vietnam and out of the Army now, the better."

"We all agree," O'Neill said, thinking of Ed Unger's slip that morning during the Munn interview. He walked to the door with Picking and shook his hand as he left.

27

During the early weeks of 1969 Jody began having dinner with General Springer every night. Once again she packed her things and said good-bye to the bemused Donut Dollies and moved into the trailer next to Walt's.

Walt Springer's driver was waiting for her at the helipad when she came in after a day of scratching for bookings for the Filipino group. Only the few units that the syndicate had as yet been unable to control were available to Jody T. Promotions, and Jody visited them all.

Jody had the driver stop at the hospital and wait while she visited with Sergeant Crawley. Then she went to the general's trailer and sat down to wait for him. She sat browsing through the *Army Times,* the only periodical Springer seemed to read.

Twice in the past week she had shared Springer's bed, making the predawn scuttle back to her own quarters. Both nights had been frustrating for them. His never-ceasing worry about the entire division and the lives of its fighting men, and the constant ringing of the emergency telephone beside his bed had rendered Walt all but impotent. He was embarrassed and miserable at his poor performance.

Jody had been sitting, thinking about her situation for half an hour when the door to the trailer was kicked open and Walt came bustling in.

"Jody," he said happily, taking her in his arms. "Sorry to keep you waiting, darling." He kissed her passionately.

She broke away from him and said, "Had a hard day?"

"As usual. Haven't stopped since six this morning. But today I managed to get out and take a look at some of our fire-support bases. It beat hell out of that damned desk work."

Jody smiled. Hard Bill had been right when he said Walt's trouble was feeling thwarted at not having a field command. "You relax while I make you a drink," she said.

Later, over a second cocktail, trying to sound casual, he said, "Oh, Jody, I may have a bit of bad news for you. General Flint in Saigon put out an order that the division must go on the open-mess system by January first. The CG can't buck it any longer. We're one of the last holdouts."

Jody groaned aloud.

"Don't worry," Walt said, trying to reassure her. "If those stories you told me are true, it won't happen here. I plan to keep a close watch over whoever we appoint as custodian." Jody just looked at him skeptically. The news depressed her.

One Sunday late in January General Springer told Jody they had a sergeant arriving to take over as custodian of the division's open-mess system.

"Why didn't you appoint someone from the division?" Jody asked apprehensively.

"None of our club managers had the experience. I told you I would get a man with the best credentials, and I have. This sergeant comes to us directly from the States, and he has excellent references."

"Is that so?" said Jody. "Who is he?"

"A Sergeant First Class Anthony Gambino."

"Oh, no!" Jody shrieked. "Not Tony."

"You know him?" asked Walt in surprise.

"I sure do, and if he is not one of Cotsworth's men, my name is not Jody T. Neale."

The general frowned. "Well, as I said, I will keep a close watch."

Two days after Gambino arrived, Jody paid him a visit.

"Jody!" he cried in surprise. He seemed pleased to see her. "This is like old times. I never thought I'd see you in Cu Chi."

"It's partly your fault," she retorted. "After your trouble in Nha Trang they tried to say I was in with you. The CID harassed me so much it was easier to close down."

"Hell. I'm sorry to hear that."

"But what about you? I thought you'd end up in jail."

Gambino let out a hearty laugh. "Not a chance. Cotsworth takes care of his people. Anyway, Jody ole girl, I'm going to be running the club at this dump now. I sure didn't know what I was letting myself in for though. What a hole. Maybe you can make it a little more enjoyable for me. You were always too busy to be friendly when you had the old Waltzing Matilda." He leered at her.

Same old Tony, she thought. Same black, greasy hair, too long for a soldier and parted in the middle. The same cunning look in his eyes. His paunch had increased in size since she had last seen him.

"What are you doing these days?" he asked.

"Booking a couple of shows. Got one here now and one in Saigon. I was kind of hoping you could use them both."

He shrugged. "I dunno. Got my orders already. Supposed to use Ronnie Jasper's shows. But who knows, I might be able to help you out for old times' sake. Come back and see me Monday."

Later that night Jody once again tried to tell Springer about the Cotsworth gang but still with little effect.

On Sunday morning following Jody's chat with Gambino, Walt surprised her by saying that he had to go into Saigon for a Monday meeting at MACV and suggested they go in together, so she could give him a guided tour of Saigon that afternoon.

At Tan Son Nhut a staff car picked them up. As they stepped into it, Jody asked, "Do you want to go to my apartment first or would you rather go downtown and see Saigon?"

Walt understood her meaningful look. "How about your place for starters."

Jody gave the sergeant at the wheel her address. When they arrived at her apartment, Walt looked around appreciatively. "What a lovely place, Jody. Just what I expected. It really is you."

"Thank you, Walt," she said, pleased. She made him a drink and put a tape on the player. With soft music filling the room she pulled the drapes, closing out the direct sunlight.

"It just so happens that I have a bottle of champagne in the fridge. Are you sure you don't want to see Saigon?" she asked mischievously.

"I'd rather just relax here with you, Jody."

"Good. I'm so happy we're away from those damned hot lines."

Walt smiled down at her. "So am I. Can we go inside?"

"Let's," Jody said, leading the way to the bedroom. While he sat on the bed taking off his boots Jody pulled the Venetian blinds closed and then began undressing. As Walt stood up to remove his uniform, she handed him a hanger and then pulled back the cover on the bed and lay down on the satin sheets to wait for him.

Naked, he joined her on the bed, took her in his arms and kissed her passionately. Jody responded instantly and pulled his body closer to hers. As they kissed, his tongue beat against hers, and he rolled on top of her. Jody's limbs stirred as her fingernails scratched lightly on his shoulders.

She reached down and took him in her hand, making him shiver with pleasure, and he moaned into her open mouth as his body moved, ready to plunge into her. But even as he moved, and she guided him with her fingers, she felt him stiffen on top of her and ejaculate stickily over her belly, then collapse with a curse onto her. With another curse he moved away and thumped the pillow in rage.

"Hey, that's enough," she said sharply. "Now that you've got that one out of your system, maybe we can take a rest and then start again. This time you can take your time and we'll enjoy it."

Surprised, he looked at her.

"Well, you didn't plan on stopping there, did you?"

As Jody swung her feet onto the floor and started for the bathroom, she turned and saw him smiling. She let him rest for half an hour, and then, running hot water into the sunken tub, she sprinkled some detergent powder into the tub to simulate a bubble bath. It foamed up quickly and gave the water a pleasant smell. When the bath was ready, she called to Walt. "Come on in."

"What's this?" he asked, plodding into the bathroom.

"Climb in while I go and get you a drink," she ordered.

In the kitchen she popped the cork of the chilled champagne bottle, took two long-stemmed glasses, and returned to the bathroom. Pouring the bubbly wine into the glasses she set them on the edge of the tub and climbed in beside the luxuriating general.

"You're not on duty now," she said, handing him one of the glasses.

He breathed a deep sigh of pure pleasure and sank deeper into the bubble bath. Holding his glass up to her he said, "This is the first time in a rather active life that I've ever had a bubble bath with a lovely girl and a bottle of champagne." He grinned contentedly and took a long sip.

They stayed in the bath until the water turned cold, then climbed out, and, still wet, ran laughing back to the bed.

Finally, with no problems of any kind, Jody and Walt enjoyed a frenzy of lovemaking. Hours later she lay happily with Walt curled up beside her, sleeping peacefully. Quietly she slid from the bed, put on a Chinese silk dressing gown, and went out into the living room.

About an hour later, with the smell of ham and scrambled eggs in the air, Walt woke up and came looking for her.

"Are you hungry?" she asked.

"Now that I smell it, I sure am." He came up behind her and slipped his hand under her dressing gown.

"Hey!" she protested. "Don't do that or I'll burn the toast."

On Monday afternoon Walt and Jody flew back to Cu Chi together. He was definitely a far more exuberant and youthful general than he had been when they left for Saigon the day before. The general's driver was waiting for them at the landing pad, and after leaving the general at head-quarters, he drove Jody to the office of the new custodian of the Twenty-fifth Division open-mess system.

It was a totally different Sergeant Gambino who received her this time. Gone were all the pleasantries. "Get your band out of here tomorrow, Jody," he snapped. "I've hired all I need. Can't give you any more business."

Instantly Jody understood. He must have been at Saigon over the weekend. One of the syndicate sergeants had talked to him.

"This is a fast change of heart, Tony," Jody said coolly. "I think you owe me a favor or two from Nha Trang. Why don't you level with me?"

"Why not?" he asked moodily. "I don't reckon you need any explanations, really. You've changed, Jody. I thought you were smart once."

"I haven't changed, Tony. You just never knew me."

"Maybe you're right. Anyway, I can't do a damn thing for you now. The syndicate has blacklisted you."

"Tell me about this high and mighty syndicate, Tony," Jody cried angrily. "Just who are all these people who have the right to say who does and who does not do business with the Americans in Vietnam?"

"I'm telling you nothing. You got a big mouth. You're finished in country. You may as well pack up and leave. Jesse James and Red Fisher are pretty goddamned mad."

Alvin was right, Jody thought. Her reports only did her grievous harm; no action was being taken against the syndicate. "You can all go to hell, you bastards. But don't think you've heard the last of Jody T. Neale. I'll find someone in the United States Army who can and will get you all." She turned on her heels and was opening the door when Gambino shouted after her.

"Now hold on, Jody. Don't be so hasty. Maybe I was getting too rough just then. Let's look at a few facts. Okay?" His friendly smile and his attempt at placating her were dismal failures, but Jody paused in the doorway anyway.

"They gave me the worst custodian job in the Nam here. You think I'm happy about spending a year at Cu Chi?" He shook his head. "The troops here are always out fighting, so these clubs can't make the kind of money the other open-mess systems are taking in. Besides that, the camp itself is a mess. Now if you'd stay here with me I'd keep both your bands working all the time. I could be passing the same money on up the ladder, it wouldn't cost you any more, and you and me could have us a real nice year together."

"Forget it," Jody spat. "I've heard that story before." She walked out, slamming the door behind her.

She went straight from the custodian's office to division headquarters and in minutes was sitting across the desk from General Springer.

"Sorry to bother you, Walt," she said apologetically. "I know you're busy."

"Never too busy to see you, Jody."

"Thanks. I thought I'd drop by and tell you that your competent custodian has fired my band. No more business at Cu Chi, he said. That syndicate you think I made up has blacklisted me. I'll be leaving Cu Chi with my group in the morning."

190

General Springer looked startled. "When did this happen?"

"About ten minutes ago."

"What's his reason?"

"Nothing he could ever tell you. I told you, I've been blacklisted by the syndicate. From now on he's going to hire groups from a competitor of mine, Ronnie Jasper. Jasper charges almost twice as much as I do for the same-size band."

"If that's the case, I'll look into it personally. If I find he is firing one group to give another equal group the work for twice the price, or even one dollar over the price he's been paying, I'll order him to put your people back on."

"Well thanks for trying to help." Jody felt justifiably vexed. "I'll see you later."

True to her prediction, when the deputy commanding general called the custodian into his office the following morning, demanding to know what his plans were for entertaining the troops when they came in from the field, Gambino was obliged to deliver a lame defense of his plans to pay from one hundred and fifty to two hundred dollars more per show for a new band. Unmercifully the general interrogated Gambino, attacking his arguments for changing the band. Finally, he issued a direct order to use Jody T. Promotions' group for the next month, at which time they would review the situation.

When Jody walked back into Tony Gambino's office, she found him literally twitching with rage. He could neither sit nor stand; he simply banged about his office in impotent fury. "How do you fucking dare to get a general to pressure me," he raved. "Officers got no right interfering with the sergeants' clubs. I'll report this to Army headquarters in Saigon!"

"Oh shut up, Tony. He had a legitimate reason to turn you off for a month and you know it. Just give me the contract and let's sign it."

His eyes glinted angrily, and his face was flushed.

She took the contract that he had scrawled his signature on and perused it. "Sign it, you conniving bitch," he hissed. "But let me tell you something. He can't order me to book you every month. As soon as this contract is done, you're out of here. Get me?" His eyes were bright with rage, and veins stood out at his temples. "You're out! Out! Out!"

Jody signed the contracts and handed one copy back to Gambino. "So long, Tony. Try to keep your blood pressure down."

A week later, with the Vietnamese band safely booked, Jody took another trip to Saigon. In the office she found My Linh alone, her head buried in her arms on top of the desk. The girl's shoulders were shaking as she silently sobbed. Jody put a hand on her shoulder. "My Linh. What's the matter?" she asked.

My Linh straightened up and looked at her through eyes bloodshot from crying. She reached for a handkerchief and wiped her tear-stained cheeks. Jody had never seen her so upset before, and it affected her.

"I sorry, Jody. I not expecting anyone."

"What's the trouble, My Linh?"

"I hear all Army on open-mess now, so you must send band home and I have no job, no money." She sobbed again for a few moments, and Jody tried to comfort her.

"I have American baby," My Linh tried to explain. "So I all time worry. If South don't win the war I think the Communists kill all American baby. That why I need money. Take my son to another country. Now I have no money to escape."

"The Communists won't win the war, My Linh," Jody said firmly.

"How you know? They much smarter, better fighter than the South. American send much men, much money here for five years, but they no win."

Jody sat down and let out a deep sigh. Maybe she had not been facing facts. By standing on her principles she would be putting half or all her employees out of work. Didn't she owe them something? It was obvious that Cotsworth and his syndicate had the upper hand. In another few weeks they would control all the Army clubs in Vietnam, and Jody would have to leave the country with two wasted years behind her. They had given her one chance; she wouldn't get another.

She made her mind up suddenly, suppressing the feeling of revulsion that gripped her. "Don't worry, My Linh. Jody T. Promotions is not going out of business."

My Linh looked up inquiringly. Jody put her hand on the girl's shoulder. "You remember Sergeant Gambino from Nha Trang? He's back. I'll make a deal with him."

28

Tony Gambino welcomed Jody to his bed, board, and business with open arms. He determined to keep this arrangement secret from Cotsworth, who would not approve, he knew. Since it was easy to get from Cu Chi to Saigon, Tony suggested that Jody stay at her own apartment. He would see that her two bands were looked after. He also didn't want Jody around Cu Chi where she could continue to see the general. Gambino spent three or four nights a week in Saigon.

Jody quietly acquiesced to the custodian's wishes. Not having much work to do, she remained in her apartment a great deal and frequently lay awake nights, wondering about Walt Springer. She had walked out on him suddenly, without explanation, and he had tried for two weeks to get her on the phone. My Linh needed no urging to short-circuit all his attempts to talk to Jody. To My Linh's way of thinking, Jody had finally come to her senses by taking one of the sergeants for a boyfriend. She had no desire once again to jeopardize the security of their business.

Jody had even given up going to the I House, since she did not wish to see any of the custodians, particularly Sergeant James and Red Fisher. As she stayed in Saigon, her guilt over Walt growing each day, she vowed to expose Cotsworth and his men. She was determined to gather the hard evidence Walt said would be necessary if any action were to be taken.

As Jody became more and more listless, My Linh's spirits soared. She was deftly handling what few business details remained, and her generous salary was secure. One evening Gambino phoned Jody from Cu Chi. He would be coming to Saigon the next day. "I've set up a meeting with Bert Bannahan," he said. "Could we use your apartment for an hour, Jody? We need complete privacy."

"Of course, Tony," Jody answered. "What's mine is yours."

"There's my girl," Gambino said, missing the irony in her tone.

"My Linh and I will go for a walk and leave you two alone."

After she had hung up, she called My Linh into her apartment from the office. Jody's listless manner and dull expression had suddenly changed. She seemed alive and excited. "What you want, Jody?" My Linh asked, showing surprise at her employer's sudden change of attitude.

"The chance I've been waiting for has come. Tony is having a private meeting here tomorrow afternoon with Bert Bannahan. "I'll get that hard evidence on them."

"Oh, Jody! My Linh nearly wept with apprehension. "After all the trouble, everything is good now. Sergeant Gambino treat you pretty good."

"I may get proof that will help break up the whole syndicate. Tony may not be as bad as some of them, but I don't like being blackmailed."

Despite My Linh's distress, Jody tested the small high-power tape recorder she had hidden under the bar the following day. It was working perfectly and could make a ninety-minute tape when set at its slowest speed.

Gambino arrived at seven p.m. Jody made him a drink and then put a tape on the large stereo player on top of the bar. With the volume turned up, the music blasted out. Jody took her own drink and sat on Gambino's knee.

It wasn't long before there was a knock on the door, and Bert Bannahan entered. He and Gambino exchanged greetings and Jody told My Linh to get Bert a drink. "You're not going to discuss our business in front of this broad, are you?" Bannahan asked roughly, nodding at Jody.

"Oh, Jody T.'s all right, Bert. You just don't know her like I do."

"Don't trouble yourself, Mr. Bannahan," Jody interrupted, "My Linh and I have better things to do than sit here with you." She turned to My Linh. "Come on, we'll leave them." As she reached the door and opened it she said sweetly to Gambino, "We'll be home in an hour, darling. You can turn the music off if it's too loud. There's plenty to drink in the kitchen."

Out in the street, Jody and My Linh walked to a nearby coffee shop. When they were seated My Linh asked, "Why did you turn that loud music on? It will ruin what the other recorder picks up."

Jody smiled slyly. "They won't be able to hear themselves talk with that music going, and I fixed the machine so it can only play at full volume. They'll turn it off. Bannahan doesn't trust me, but seeing that I'm gone he won't be suspicious that I am doing what I'm doing."

By the time My Linh and Jody returned, Bannahan had already left the apartment. In his wake were squashed-out cigar butts; heavy acrid smoke hung in the air. Jody opened the windows to air the place out, and at her bidding, My Linh emptied the ashtrays.

"I'm sorry he had to smell up your place with his cigars," Gambino apologized.

194

"I don't mind if it helps you do some business."

"Ah, you're a great girl, Jody," Gambino said expansively, gulping down a drink. "Real understanding."

Since he would have to get up early in the morning to get back to Cu Chi they went to bed. Jody had a strong drink and steeled herself to endure Gambino's lustful use of her body. By seven the following morning he was on his way out to Hotel 3 to hop a ride back to the post. Hardly had he left the apartment than Jody locked the door and raced over to the bar to get the small tape recorder. My Linh sat beside her as they placed the recorder on the coffee table and switched it on.

At first they heard nothing as they anxiously bent forward to hear what had been recorded. There were a few unidentifiable sounds and then, to their delight, the voice of Bannahan came through the music, "For Chrissake, Tony, will you turn that fuckin' noise off!"

"This is it," Jody whispered excitedly, as though her voice could be heard by the two men.

"All right." They heard Gambino's voice clearly. 'For twelve months I'd need four hundred and eighty thousand dollars' worth. I've got the exact quantities written on this paper. Mostly mixed nuts, peanuts, chips, pretzels, and Polish sausage. Each month I will need forty thousand dollars' worth delivered to Cu Chi.

"Got it, Tony," Bannahan's deeper voice said jovially. "We'll send it to you in twelve separate loads the first of each month."

"Just be goddamned careful nobody knows I signed this purchase order for a year's supply in advance or all hell will break loose. General Springer, the deputy CG, is after my ass already. I think he suspects I got his girl away from him."

A pained expression came over Jody's face as she listened. Poor Walt. She wished there were some way she could tell him everything. Well when she had the hard evidence she would, but not before.

"Don't sweat it, Tony, I'll take care of you. Don't I always? Just give me the signed purchase order today, and I'll see the company has your check mailed to your Swiss bank account next week."

"Yeah, hurry it along, Bert. I wouldn't make a deal like this with anyone I didn't trust. You gotta be damned certain you never mention it to any of the boys. I've gotta keep this little packet all to myself. Tiger and them would be pretty pissed at me if they found out."

"Shit, Tony, I wouldn't want this to get out no more than you. This was a hard one for me to swing, you know. The big boss don't like paying your ten percent in advance. That's like lending money without interest. And there's always the chance if you got transferred they wouldn't honor the order you signed. The boss was real worried about that."

"They gotta honor the signature of the custodian, even if a new one should come in. So don't you worry. I'll help push future sales for Far Eastern Trading. And the general isn't going to get me out either. We go higher than him. Matter of fact, there's a big meeting three weeks from tonight at the Tiger's villa on expanding the operation and protection."

"Yeah?" Bannahan said. "I heard something about it."

"Just custodians going to be there. And Pancho, of course."

"That Vamalot really moved in on us," Bannahan growled. "Doing a lot of selling we used to do."

"There's plenty of business for everybody. Haven't you been making more since things was organized, even with Vamalot in the picture?"

"Yeah, sure," Bannahan conceded. "The way things are I guess I don't have to worry none you'll talk about your advance commission. The boys ever find out, they'd all want it."

"My lips gonna be closed tighter than a Viet virgin's cunt," Gambino assured the salesman. Bannahan's course laughter cackled over the tape.

"My wife's really gonna be happy with this money. There's a house she's been on my back to get her in Hawaii. Right near a beach. We gotta put down one third of the money this month."

"You'll have it. Just be fuckin' sure we get ours."

"You can pick up your check from my office each month as we take delivery," Gambino replied. "Sorry I can't make a better arrangement, but our open-mess system got nothing like half a million bucks lying around."

Bannahan's gravel-throated laugh came over the tape recorder again, and the girls heard the rustle of paper. "Not a bad order for one day," the salesman gloated. "Almost half a million bucks for peanuts!"

The tape continued playing as the two conspirators talked of inconsequentials, then Bannahan took his leave. Smiling with satisfaction, Jody said, "First step of my plan completed. Now if the second phase three weeks from tonight works out as well, I'll have that hard evidence."

"I do not like, Jody T." My Linh's eyes were wide with worry. "If they catch you do something funny they beat you up, maybe worse. Maybe even send Apache to get you!"

"What are you talking about?" Jody shot at the girl. "What is Apache?"

In an involuntary gesture My Linh clapped a hand over her mouth. Jody gave her a hard stare. "Is there something I don't know about?"

The Eurasian girl shook her head, wide-eyed.

Jody took My Linh forcefully by both shoulders. "Now I want you to tell me anything I should know and don't. Start with Apache."

Reluctantly the words came out. "Apache name of Americans who live in Cholon."

"The deserters?" Jody asked.

My Linh nodded. "They very bad, Apache. They kill for money."

"Apache?" Jody said to herself. "That's an American Indian." Suddenly she shook My Linh. "You've been seeing Talltree? He's an Indian."

196

My Linh nodded. "He say I don't see him sometime he find Andre, take him to Cholon."

"That's a lot of bloody nonsense. I'll talk to Alvin Bruce. I wish the Sheriff was still in Vietnam. I'd make you take him to Talltree."

My Linh looked frightened. "They kill anyone. You get caught by the sergeants they get the Apache kill you."

"Then I won't get caught."

My Linh shook her head hopelessly. She would never learn to understand her blond boss if the worked for her the rest of her life.

"If you not go against the sergeants in the first place," My Linh pointed out, "you be making eight thousand dollars a month all the time instead of losing money."

"If my plan works," Jody retorted, "these sergeants will be finished and we'll have honest sergeants back, the way it was before Cotsworth came. I'll be making plenty again, and making it legitimately."

"We hope." My Linh's skepticism was unmistakable. "Better you forget about this crazy plan. You make more and quicker with Tony."

"You know what makes me sorry, My Linh?" Jody asked rhetorically, ignoring her last comment.

"Having no money," My Linh said flatly.

"No." She shook her head thoughtfully. "Having to ruin Cotsworth. I like him, you know. And crooked as he is, you almost have to admire the way he set this thing up. That's what I call thinking big."

"Very big," My Linh agreed.

29

FROM: Rick Townsend
TO: Subcommittee Investigating Staff
DATE: June 30, 1969

O'Neill and I have almost completed our investigation. With the cooperation of a few provost marshal officers and CID agents, suddenly feeling free to talk as a result of the recent retirement of Major General Walter, the Army's top cop, we have been able to fill in many of the gaps in our investigation.

We have one more key witness to interview, an Australian girl named Jody T. Neale. She seems to have been intimately involved in the activities of the Khaki Mafia. We believe she will be coming through Saigon on her way to Hong Kong within the next week or two and we will make every effort to interview her. According to one of the CID agents we are working with, she actually has proof of some of the activities we know are going on but cannot substantiate sufficiently to bring out in the hearings. We may even try to persuade her to be a witness at the hearings. From all accounts she would be sensational.

As you have gathered from our previous reports, the big power here is Joseph Crust, known as "The Mint of Vietnam." He has refused to talk to us. Even the Commanding General seems to be afraid to put pressure on him to see us. Crust sells everything to the Army that isn't government manufactured. His only competition is Vamalot, which is owned by the club sergeants, but even Vamalot works closely with Crust. Wherever we find Crust we invariably find Brigadier General Robert Hare, better known as "Rabbit," somehow involved. Our efforts to question Hare have been futile, and although we did have what was termed a "limited interview" with Sergeant Major Cotsworth, it was most unsatisfactory. We had to submit the questions we wanted to ask in advance, and half of them were disallowed.

General Hare is the most powerful military man in Vietnam from a commercial point of view. He is Chairman of the Policy Board of the PX system and is also the final authority on matters relating to the club system at Long Binh. The Post Commander has been relegated to the role of janitor. His biggest triumph was to make Madame Sang take away the nude statues in front of her steam bath on post. He also won the undying sympathy of the men by having the doors taken off the two hundred massage cubicles, thereby curtailing the activity most interesting to Madame Sang's GI clients.

Our biggest coup to date was locating Arthur "Art the Cork" Line, until a few months ago Joe Crust's closest associate. Mr. Line felt he was being deliberately kept away from the center of activity by Crust and thus not getting his fair share of the loot. He attempted to go into business for himself, but Crust successfully stifled his efforts. We are fortunate that Line's resentment has reached such a point that he is willing to come to Washington and testify at the hearings in the fall.

Here are some actions concerning our "Rabbit" and old Walleye that occurred early this year which we recently learned about. We are trying to get the kind of proof that will give the Justice Department a case to prosecute Brigadier General Hare. More to follow.

(Signed) Richard Townsend

Sergeant Elroy James drove up to Joe Crust's villa in his air-conditioned station wagon and was soon in the presence of the money king of Vietnam. With Crust was his associate Art Line. They glanced with some interest at the black satchel James was carrying.

Joe Crust poured himself a Scotch. "Dou you want a drink, Jesse?" he asked.

The sergeant shook his head. "Little early for me, Mr. Crust. Besides, I've got a lot of figuring to do."

"You been down to Customs yet?"

"No. I wanted to talk to you first here."

"Okay. But there are thirty-four Datsun sedans from Japan I want to get into circulation as soon as possible. I'm getting so many orders for cars I can hardly keep them filled."

"I'll go down and claim them for the NCO club system by noon," James promised.

"Okay," Art agreed. "Now what's on your mind, Jesse. Don't keep us in suspense."

Sergeant James placed his satchel on a table, opened it, and poured the contents out. "I'm being rotated back to the States in another week or two. They won't let me extend no more," he added sorrowfully. "This here is what I've got to show for my tour besides what I was already able to salt away. I got me here about two hundred thousand dollars in negotiable instruments: checks, bank drafts, MPC, piasters, whatever. What do I do with it? How do I get it into dollars? How do I keep it?"

Crust limped over to the table, his good eye fixed on the paper. Art the Cork was also staring at James's accumulated wealth. "You did all right, Jesse," Art said, stirring the checks and currency around with his index finger. "Considering you had to throw half of everything came through your hands on up to Cotsworth and the syndicate, I'd say Long Binh is the most lucrative custodianship in the world."

"We'll set up a Swiss bank account for you," Crust said decisively. "You've cooperated with us, and we show our appreciation. Art will be making a trip to Switzerland for me in the next couple of weeks anyway."

"I will?" Art asked, surprise and a trace of hostility in his tone.

Crust ignored the query and continued talking to James. "What we'll do is convert all this into a dollar check through Bank of Commercial Trading in Hong Kong. Whatever the face value of what's here, we'll discount twenty-five percent for services and fees for conversion to dollars. If, as you say, there's two hundred thousand in paper, we'll put one hundred and fifty thousand into a Swiss numbered account for you. Is that right with you?"

"Yes, sir. I sure as hell can't do it."

"Then we're in business. Now, my Jap, Arki, will be here in a minute. I want you two to go down to the pier and get those cars out of Customs and safely stored in the VRE lot General Hare set aside for me at Long Binh."

"Right, sir. By the way, there's a couple of big problems I want you to know about."

"Go ahead, Jesse," Crust encouraged.

"First place, we have a new major, Carton's his name, as officer adviser to the NCO club system."

"I know about Major Carton," Crust replied grimly.

"Did you know that he gave orders just yesterday to split the slot machine business at Long Binh between your Snead Electronics and Pacific Vendors?" James asked.

Crust let out a wounded growl and poured another slug of Scotch into his glass. "He won't get away with it."

"Major Carton is also aware that we are storing your merchandise at Long Binh, so the Vietnamese Customs can't pull a raid on the stuff you brought in duty free on NCO-club purchase orders. He's planning to expose it."

"Goddamnit, I'm going to call Rabbit. I run the club system at Long Binh and nobody else."

"While you're at it, ask him how he expects to have Sergeant Halaby replace me. Major Carton is trying to put in Lalley from the 90th Replacement Battalion, and he's straighter than a crease in the general's fatigues."

At that moment the smiling, diminutive Japanese executive Arki, came

200

into the room. Crust wasted no time in preliminaries. "Arki, go down to Customs with Sergeant James and get those thirty-four Datsuns out on the duty-free NCO-club forms." Arki nodded and briskly headed for the door. James turned and gave an anxious look at the satchel and the pile of paper on the table.

"Don't worry about it, James," Art said with a confident smile. "We'll have you set up with that account in a couple of weeks."

After Arki and James left, Art Line turned to Joe Crust seriously. "What about this trip to Switzerland? I thought I was supposed to be here in Saigon. You've got enough minions who can visit all the posts in Vietnam. I want to be here in Saigon where I can watch things."

"Watch things, Art?" Crust's voice was low. "What things?"

"I'm supposed to be in for a percentage of the total action. How can I tell what the total action is if I'm not here where it's at?"

"If you don't trust me, you can always study the books," Crust said and took a long pull on his drink.

Art laughed bitterly and loud. "Books? Records? You're telling me I can check books? You know goddamned well I had four shredding machines sent over for our regional offices. We don't keep books and records. We shred them."

"Art, I wouldn't cheat you," Crust said placatingly.

"You wouldn't if I was here and could see what was going on every day," Art retorted. "I'm getting tired of all this travel. Every time I run across something interesting, a deal or a girl, I have to go on to the next place and someone else follows up. I could have had a nice thing going with that Jody if I could have stayed in one place long enough to move in."

"Now, my boy, what you need is a vacation," Crust soothed. "A couple of weeks in Switzerland with nothing to think of but pleasure. Get away from this Oriental atmosphere for a while."

"And find I've had my back slashed while I'm away?"

"Art, this whole line of discussion is unwarranted. Now I've got to get Rabbit on the phone right away and see what can be done about Phil Kester's Pacific Vendors horning in on our business. I warned him that he either worked with me or he didn't sell over here. We'll get to your problem later. Hare is costing me a thousand dollars a month on top of his commissions. Today he's going to earn it."

Hare sat in his office at Long Binh, drumming his fingers on the desk, fighting the urge to have a cigarette. He had always known they might give him cancer, but when he had been unequivocally convinced that cigarettes cut the sexual prowess of a man his age in half, he had given up smoking. There was a knock on his door and the provost marshal came in. "I came as soon as I received your message, sir."

"Thank you, Colonel, sit down." Hare flipped a piece of paper across his desk at the colonel. "There is the address of Pacific Vendors' warehouse in Saigon. I have reason to believe that Mr. Phil Kester, who owns the company, has been bringing in merchandise duty free, using fraudulent NCO-club purchase orders. I want him raided."

"Well, sir, we can't really initiate such action. The Vietnamese Repressment Squad has to do that."

"Colonel,"—Hare's voice took on a dangerous edge—"I know that. But you know how to get the Viets to initiate such a raid."

"They do what they want to do, sir. For all I know Mr. Kester has the squad paid off."

"General Walter would be very unhappy to hear that his provost marshal in Vietnam can't stop an obvious smuggling operation," Hare fumed. "He hasn't retired yet, you know."

The provost marshal got the point. "I'll do my best, sir. But you've got to realize all these Viets around customs are paid off."

"Bring the dink in charge to me as soon as you can," Hare commanded. "I'll talk to him personally."

"Yes, sir. I'll try to get him out here this afternoon."

The phone rang and Hare picked it up. "Mr. Crust calling you again, sir," a sergeant's voice said over the line.

"Put him on," Hare snapped. Then looking up at the provost marshal he waved him off. "Let me know when you can get our man in here."

"Yes, sir." The provost marshal hurriedly left the office.

"Rabbit?" There was a ring of annoyance in Crust's authoritarian tone. "You've got to do something about this new major. Either get Carton transferred or I'll take care of it my way."

"What's the matter, Joe?" Rabbit asked solicitously.

"My cars! Major Carton and some punk-kid lieutenant at customs are accusing us of using fraudulent NCO purchase orders to bring the cars in duty free."

"Where are you now?" Hare asked.

"My office at the villa. I sent Art Line down to find out what the hell is going on. He just came back. If Vietnamese customs gets on this we won't get those cars out without paying a hundred and fifty percent duty."

"Do you know where Major Carton is now?"

"Last I heard he was at customs, examining the purchase orders on each car."

"I'll try and get him on the phone and see what we can do."

"You do that. And by the way, Rabbit, I hear Major Carton is trying to keep James from being replaced by Cotsworth's man Halaby. Are you on top of that?"

"Of course I am, Joe. Carton's got two other qualified sergeants he wants to put in, men who aren't with the program. The post commander is with Carton. But I'll take care of it."

"I'll be right here waiting to hear from you, Rabbit," Crust said, his tone unmistakably threatening.

It took General Hare only a few minutes to reach Major Carton at the U.S. Army advisers' office at Vietnamese customs.

"Major," he began sternly, "you are interfering with a carefully worked out plan at USARV. You're new here and I'd advise you not to create unnecessary problems."

"But General Hare," the major protested, "there is every reason to believe that these cars are being smuggled into the country on illegal NCO-club purchase orders."

"Forget it, Major," Hare snapped. "You don't know what you're doing. These Viets are very hard to work with as it is. Are they complaining?"

"No, sir. But as adviser to the NCO-club system it's my duty to—"

"It's your duty to get out of that office, come back to Long Binh, and be in my office before the end of the day. I want those cars released now!"

There was a long hesitation on the other end of the line. Finally the major replied, "Yes, sir," and hung up.

Hare immediately called Joe Crust back. "Okay, Joe," he said, "tell your men they can get the cars out of customs."

"Ah, Rabbit," Crust boomed back exuberantly, "you really know how to handle things. Now one other thing. Can I send the cars out to Long Binh to be stored? When that raid ruins Kester he'll be trying to do the same to me."

"Sure, bring them out. They can go into the extra VRE storage lot. I'll put a twenty-four-hour guard on them."

"Number one, Rabbit. By the way, when are you going to be up in Hong Kong again. Your place is waiting for you at Conrad's, the Conrad Hilton hotel, you know, and there's something for you to pick up at Commercial."

"As soon as the raid's over, and Halaby is picked as replacement for James, I guess a few days in Hong Kong would be in order."

The following morning the provost marshal appeared in Hare's office with Colonel Vo, head of the Vietnamese Fraud Repression Squad. After the usual amenities Hare got down to business.

"Colonel Vo, I am very worried. Much smuggling is going on. I have learned that Pacific Vendors company has been bringing in slot machines, air conditioners, freezers, refrigerators, kitchen equipment, even automobiles and trucks, using fraudulent duty-free NCO purchase orders to get them past customs."

"I have not heard about this," Vo said. He assumed a pained look. "This is very bad."

"Very," Hare agreed. "How can we fight a war and keep Vietnamese currency stable if we let all this smuggling go on.'

Vo nodded, his frown deepening. "Very bad."

"We must do something to stop this. Find the guilty people."

Again Vo nodded solemnly. "Yes. We must stop this."

Hare handed Colonel Vo a white card. "Here is the address of Mr. Philip Kester's warehouse and office in Saigon. You make a raid and check the papers on all the things he is storing. If any of our club purchase orders are on the things, you arrest everybody, confiscate everything."

"I must seek permission from Vietnamese customs," Vo replied.

"That isn't necessary," Hare shot back. "Maybe someone in customs tells Kester and he moves his things."

"Vietnamese customs very honest," Vo protested.

"Oh, of course," Hare agreed. "Now I know this raid may be dangerous," he went on, taking another tack. "I know we would not want you to take any chances without being paid." Hare pushed a large manila envelope across the table. "This will compensate you for extra time and danger in this special mission."

Vo took the envelope, glanced at the stacks of piasters and MPC inside, and smiled. "This smuggle very bad. Must stop."

"Now you've got the idea," Hare said, pleased. "You go in tonight? Very secret?"

"Tonight. Very secret," Vo agreed. "Go now and get ready."

"Fine. I will have one American adviser from the provost marshal's office go with you."

After Vo and the provost marshal left the office, General Hare's sergeant major appeared in the door. "Sergeant Major Cotsworth is waiting to see you. Shall I send him in, sir?"

Hare nodded and Cotsworth came through the door. "Sorry to summon you this way, Tom, but we're having a problem, and maybe you can help. The post commander and Major Carton are trying to block the appointment of Halaby to succeed Sergeant James as custodian at Long Binh. They're having a meeting today with the Board of Governors."

"We've got to get Halaby in," Cotsworth said emphatically. "All our planning depends upon it. What's the matter with this Major Carton. Doesn't he know officers aren't supposed to interfere in the administration of the enlisted men's clubs?"

"He's some kind of a zealot."

"Well I'll talk to the NCOs on the Board of Governors."

"And I'll put the pressure on Carton and the post commander."

"I'll get out and see my people right now, sir. Anything else?"

Hare shook his head. "By and large I'd say all systems are go. We should be able to take care of the Major Cartons when they surface. I'm expecting him in my office any time now."

Cotsworth left General Hare's office, walked through the row of officers, sergeants, Vietnamese secretaries and interpreters and out of the USARV G-1 office and almost into the arms of Major Carton. Carton was smaller and far less imposing than the command sergeant major. Cotsworth paused and looked down at the officer who was causing so much trouble. The major stepped back as though expecting a salute. Cotsworth shook his head at him.

"Major, you could get hurt the way you're going over here," he said laconically.

Major Carton glared back at Cotsworth. "A major outranks a sergeant, Sergeant. I think you're forgetting yourself."

Again Cotsworth shook his head sadly. "Major, you just don't understand this war at all." And with that he walked off, a righteously angered Major Carton looking after him.

One week later General Hare and Joe Crust were having cocktails in one of the lavish suites of the Hong Kong Hilton Hotel. Each was accompanied by a gorgeous Eurasian girl.

"I'm proud of you, Rabbit," Crust said, holding his glass up. "Kester is out of business; fined forty-five thousand dollars, told to get his body out of Vietnam, and had all his inventory confiscated. That has effectively ended all of Snead Electronics competition."

"And we got Halaby in as custodian and Major Carton transferred to a job in Da Nang where he can't do any harm." Hare swallowed his drink, squeezing one of his companion's breasts. She giggled excitedly.

"Crust finished his drink and stood up, leaning on his cane. "We'll leave you two alone, I'm sure you have your own plans for the rest of the night. Don't forget to drop in at Commercial Traders Bank tomorrow. All arrangements have been made for the transfer to Zurich."

Rabbit Hare grinned broadly. "This is really a very beautiful young lady, Joe. I may have to stay a few extra days here on business."

30

Jody had been thinking about the summit meeting of custodians and Vam-alot personnel since the first time she played back the tape of Gambino and Bannahan's plotting. Sergeant majors and club sergeants were flying in from everywhere—Pleiku, Chu Lai, Phu Bai, Dong Tam, Di An—from all points of the map.

Jody had thoroughly tested her powerful little tape recorder and had put new batteries in it. An hour before Cotsworth would be back home from his office, she slung the leather case containing the recorder and the microphones over her shoulder and left her apartment to find Tien. The old De Soto was waiting at the curb.

"Tien, I want you to take me to Sergeant Major Cotsworth's villa."

"Okay, missie. We go." He smiled broadly, his gold tooth gleaming.

As Tien approached Cotsworth's villa, Jody stopped him. "See this small alley, Tien?" She pointed out the window. "I want you to come back here after you let me off and wait for me. Keep out of sight."

Tien, never surprised at Jody T.'s requests, nodded. She left the car, walked up to the gate leading into the front lawn of Cotsworth's villa and let herself into the yard. Her watch said five fifteen. He never arrived home before six o'clock. The old Chinese servant answered the door.

"Hello," said Jody T. "I came to see Sergeant Major Cotsworth."

"He not home yet," replied the old man.

"Then I will sit and wait for him," said Jody.

The old man frowned and looked at her intently. He seemed to remember her and nodded for her to enter. He led her to the living room, where she waited until the servant had brought her a drink and disappeared into the back of the house.

She quickly took two small microphones out of the leather case and walked around the room, studying it. At one end of the room she noticed two large armchairs, each placed in front of huge windows running from floor to ceiling. The chairs, separated by a third French window, seemed like the perfect place. She approached the chairs and, taking a role of electrician's tape from her case, secured the microphones to the top of one of the back legs on each chair. Then she raised the heavy window, first behind one chair and then behind the other, and slid the cords from the microphones out the windows. When she pulled the windows down again, it was impossible without a thorough inspection, to see the cords or the microphones.

Jody began to tremble as the full impact of what she was doing dawned on her. The house was air-conditioned, but if by some chance someone decided to open one of the windows to let out the cigar smoke they would see the cords. She didn't let herself think of what would happen to her.

With her apparatus in place, she went back to the kitchen where the old man was and said, "I'm sorry but I can't wait any longer. I'll come back later." She saw he was in the middle of stuffing a chicken. "Don't interrupt your work, I can let myself out."

The Chinese nodded gratefully. "What name I say you are?" he asked.

"Lee LaRue," Jody promptly replied. The servant repeated the name with difficulty. Jody stepped outside and walked to the gate. Then, looking over her shoulder to see that no one was watching, she quickly turned and darted around the side of the house where the two black cords dangled from the windows. There was a three-foot-wide stretch of ground between the side of the house and a high wall which had three strands of barbed wire strung along the top of it. There was no way she could climb over it. She would have to leave through the front gate as she had entered. Her fingers shook as she gathered up the ends of the two cords and plugged them into the recorder. Then she crouched low and waited.

Before long she heard the sounds of vehicles arriving. Then she heard Cotsworth, his voice booming, enter the front door with a group of men.

Unconsciously she crossed her fingers. It would be impossible to pull the little microphones out when it was time to leave. They would have to remain there and eventually be discovered. But by then it wouldn't matter. She would have the hard evidence General Springer needed, and they couldn't touch her.

As soon as everybody was inside she started the tape. It was getting dark. She had ninety minutes of tape, and there was nothing to do but wait. Surely in an hour and a half they would have enough evidence to incriminate them all.

The minutes ticked by slowly, and every minute she was sure she would be discovered either by the Chinese servant or by one of the sergeants. At the end of half an hour her nerve ends were tingling, but she stuck it out and watched the last of the tape roll off the feed spool. Deftly she opened the cassette recorder and turned the tape over. Another forty-five minutes to go. Ten minutes later she heard the front door open. Someone walked out and, a moment later, began relieving his bladder. She wondered why whoever it was hadn't used the toilet. Thinking that the meeting was probably over, she decided to leave. Jody clicked off the tape recorder, unplugged the microphone cords, closed the case, and slung it over her shoulder. She waited indecisively around the corner of the house for the man who had left the meeting either to drive away or go back inside. After a few moments she heard him return to the house.

The front yard was dark except for the street light outside the gate. The only thing to do was to check that the yard was clear, calmly walk to the gate, let herself out, and head for her car down the street. Bending low to the ground, she crawled past the windows to the front of the house and then, peeping around to make sure the lawn was empty, straightened up and walked quickly toward the gate. She was breathing a sigh of relief as she reached the gate when she was frozen by an angry shout. Spinning around she saw Sergeant Fisher hurrying toward her from the kitchen.

"What the hell do you think you're doing here?" he yelled.

"I came to see Sergeant Major Cotsworth," she replied in quiet, confident tones, her heart pounding. "But as he seems to be busy, I decided not to disturb him."

"What's that hanging over your shoulder?" he asked suspiciously, increasing his pace and reaching out toward the tape recorder. "Let me take a look."

"It's nothing," she murmured nervously slipping through the gate.

"Come back here!" he shouted, running to the gate, which Jody had slammed shut. As he struggled with the latch, Jody ran down the sidewalk, her heart thumping in her breast.

She could hear Red Fisher pursuing her down the street. She glanced over her shoulder as she ran and saw that he was gaining on her. Jody ran faster, her lungs feeling as though they would burst.

"Tien, Tien!" she shouted, her throat aching, a sharp pain below her collarbone searing her. She was nearing the lane in which her car was parked. The sergeant was only ten yards behind her now.

"Tien!" she screamed. And again, with her last reserve of strength, "Tien!" Then, as though in answer to her prayers, the green De Soto came edging out of the lane. Tien looked out the window and took in the situation. He quickly opened the back door and revved the engine.

Jody threw herself into the back of the car as Fisher made a lunging dive for her. He snatched at her foot with both hands, but she slipped out of her shoe and pulled her leg in, slamming the door closed. Tien shot off in a spray of gravel. Jody, gasping for breath, looked out the window to see

Fisher pick himself up, her shoe still in one of his hands, and run back toward the villa.

"Good man, Tien," she gasped. "Quickly now, the apartment. Go fast!" She sat gasping as the normally careful Tien sped through the streets, forcing Hondas onto the sidewalk and sending chickens flying out of their way. When they arrived at her apartment building she called, "Be ready to leave again, quickly!" She dashed up the stairs and let herself into the apartment, calling out, "My Linh. We've got to go. They saw me."

My Linh stared at Jody in surprise and fear. "Grab the tape of Gambino and Bannahan. Now!"

Jody ran into her bedroom and snatched up the handbag with her money and slipped her feet into a new pair of shoes while My Linh went looking for the tape. They hurried down the stairs and leaped into the car. Tien gunned the engine and took off just as an army station wagon careened around the corner.

"Can you lose them?" Jody asked.

My Linh repeated the question to Tien, who answered in Vietnamese, a big grin splitting his brown face. "He say don't worry. He know Saigon street and alley much better than they. They never catch us."

For half an hour they raced through narrow, winding streets and back alleys until, finally, Tien looked back with a grin and said, "No more follow. Where go now?"

"Good question." Jody looked questioningly at My Linh. "They're sure to have someone watching the apartment, we can't go there. I must get in touch with Alvin Bruce, but meantime where will we sleep."

"Hotel is too dangerous," My Linh said after deliberation. "Maybe they check all hotels. I have some Chinese friends in Cholon. We could stay there for a while. Nobody find us there, but house is very bad. I think you don't like to stay at very poor house."

"I don't care what the house is like as long as they don't find us." Jody looked at My Linh sharply. "We're not going to Talltree, the Apaches?"

My Linh shook her head. "They would kill you. All work for Cotsworth." She gave directions to Tien as Jody opened her purse. She had about fifteen hundred dollars in MPC that Gambino had given her in advance against that month's bookings. She took two hundred dollars out and leaned forward, handing it to Tien.

"You know where to change MPC for piaster?" she asked.

Tien nodded. "Good," Jody said. "You change this and take your pay for this month and bring what's left back to me." My Linh, ready to translate, listened carefully to the instructions. "I want you to take this car back. It's paid up to date and it's no good to us anymore. Too many people know it. I want you to use a cab or a bus and come every day to see My Linh and me in case I have any errands for you. Don't tell anyone where we are."

As My Linh translated Tien nodded his understanding. Jody pulled her Browning twenty-five-caliber automatic pistol out of her bag and checked to see if there was a round in the chamber. My Linh was watching, her face wrinkled with lines of worry.

"You never know when I might be forced to use this," Jody said. "Thank God those Green Berets taught me to be a pretty fair marksman while I was in Nha Trang."

My Linh shivered. She hated guns and doubted she would ever be able to use one even to save her life. "I don't suppose they have a phone at this house?" Jody asked.

"They have the local phone, PTT."

"Damn local lines. If we start a call tonight, maybe tomorrow we'll get through." They turned into an even narrower back alley and finally came to a halt in front of a forbidding brick wall and a padlocked gate.

"Wait here," said My Linh, getting out. She pressed a button in the wall, and an old Chinese man with a long, silky gray beard hurried out. He bowed in greeting to My Linh and unlocked the gate. My Linh looked back and waved to Jody to follow her in.

"Tien," Jody said before she climbed out, "leave the car behind when you come back with the money. Very, very important."

Tien nodded again and drove off. Inside the small, four-room house Jody was introduced to the Chinese man and his elderly wife.

The house, though small and old, appeared spotlessly clean. It was gloomy inside, and the smell of incense drifted from a vase on an altar set up before a statue of Buddha and permeated the house.

The old man led the two girls to a corner of the room where a curtain could be drawn along a rod, screening off the low wooden table which was a bed.

"Looks as though we bunk together tonight," Jody observed.

The old lady shuffled toward them with a tray on which sat a couple of small Chinese cups and a pot of steaming green tea. My Linh took the tray and thanked her. After the two of them talked for a few moments My Linh turned back to Jody and said, "Drink the tea and then we start trying to make the telephone call."

As they sipped the tea My Linh asked, "What our future be now, Jody? What you think will happen?"

"Well, first let's hear a sampling of what we have?" She reached for the tape recorder, turning the cartridges over, and pressed the rewind button. In minutes the tape was close to the beginning, and she started it. Jody and My Linh listened intently for ten minutes, a wide, happy smile of triumph spreading across Jody's face. Then she switched it off.

"I've got the bastards," Jody cried jubilantly. "I don't have to hear any more now. Let's try to get through on the PTT to the Tiger line and talk to Alvin Bruce."

210

For two hours Jody struggled with the local Saigon telephone service in an effort to be connected to the military circuit. Finally she succeeded. Although it was after eight o'clock Alvin Bruce was still in his office.

"Alvin, it's me," she said. "Is there any chance someone could have our phone bugged?"

"It's possible."

"I've got to see you right now, urgently."

"Where do you want me to meet you?"

"Go to La Cave restaurant. Someone will bring you to me."

"I'll be there, Jody."

"Thank you, Alvin. I knew I could count on you."

After she had hung up, she turned to My Linh. "Take a taxi to La Cave restaurant and bring Alvin Bruce here. You remember him from Nha Trang?"

"Sure, I not forget him."

"Make sure you are not followed on the way back. Alvin's office is full of Cotsworth's people."

One hour later Alvin Bruce and My Linh were admitted through the wall by Jody's Chinese host. "I hope nobody followed you here," Jody said.

Bruce shook his head. "I was careful. My Linh gave me some inkling of the problem."

Jody was about to explain everything when the bell at the gate tinkled again, and My Linh went to investigate. She returned with Tien.

"I get only one eighty piaster for a dollar," he said apologetically, handing Jody a roll of piasters.

"Are you changing money on the black market?" Alvin queried sharply.

"Oh, stop being such a cop and sit down, Alvin," Jody said irritably. "Don't bother me with trivialities." Jody counted the money and returned all but twelve thousand piasters to Tien.

"Here's your salary plus an extra two thousand piasters for bus and cab fares." My Linh translated as Jody talked to make certain that there was no chance of a costly misunderstanding. "Now, Tien," Jody continued. "You have an extra twelve thousand piasters. I want you to buy food with all of that tomorrow and take it to the villa of the Filipino band."

Tien looked puzzled, but he pocketed the money. "Why are you doing that, Jody?" My Linh said.

"Because after tonight the first thing Gambino will do when he gets back to Cu Chi is fire my bands." She turned back to Tien. "Have one of your children watch the villa, and you come here and tell me when the band gets back." Tien gave Jody a sloppy salute and left.

"Now," Bruce said impatiently, "would you mind telling me what this is all about?"

"All right, Alvin. Earlier this evening I got caught bugging Cotsworth's villa. But I got away with the tape of a meeting he held. The sergeants chased me to my apartment, but Tien lost them and brought me here."

"Christ! They'll really be after you now. How good is the stuff you got on the tape?"

"The ten minutes I listened to is dynamite. Even General Crowninshed was there."

"Let's hear it, right now," Bruce said jumping up eagerly.

"Why not," Jody replied. She picked up the recorder, turned the tape back to start, and began. Parts of it were indistinct, but fortunately Cotsworth and Crowninshed had been sitting near one microphone, and there was enough of the meeting clearly recorded to indicate plainly the enormity of the syndicate, as well as the staggering amounts of money that were being gleaned every week all over Vietnam in kickbacks, slot-machine skimming, Vamalot sales, and, especially, in money changing. When the tape ran out, Alvin Bruce jigged about the room and clasped and hugged Jody.

"You're a living doll, Jody T. A police doll. Now if I can only get this into the right hands, we've got that group at last. So Crowninshed is the big American in currency. After five years of frustration in Germany and Fort Benning, we've got them. Manipulations! I never would have guessed. We've got them here. Give me that tape!"

"Not on your life," Jody replied. "You come around tomorrow with the equipment and I'll let you make a copy."

Alvin gave her a hurt look. "Don't you trust me?"

"Sure I trust you. But look what always happens when I give you statements. You've said yourself that your department is compromised, so I'm certainly not giving you the one and only tape."

Bruce nodded. "I see your point. Okay. I'll bring another tape recorder around tomorrow. Ten a.m. all right?"

"That's fine. See you then."

After Bruce left, My Linh and Jody lay down fully clothed on their hard bed. Jody slept fitfully, waking at every outside noise and feeling for her Browning automatic on the floor beside her.

31

Alvin Bruce arrived at Jody's hideout on schedule the following morning carrying a tape recorder. Without wasting any time he began making a duplicate of the incriminating tape. As the conversation was retaped, the CID man discussed his plans with Jody.

"There is obviously a spy, and probably several, in the Saigon CID and provost marshal's office," Bruce confessed. "I've decided to tell nobody about this tape. I'll take a few days off and catch a military flight back to the States. Then I'm going straight to the Pentagon and put the tape and my conclusions directly in the hands of General Trenton Walter."

"Who's he?" Jody asked.

"He's the boss of all military police and CID worldwide. The Army's top cop you might say."

"Now that's what I call doing it right," Jody exclaimed approvingly.

"That's what I thought." He bent over the tape recorder and tested the duplicate. It had reproduced the original in its entirety.

"Alvin, there's something I want you to do for me," Jody said, as the CID man slipped the tape he had copied into his pocket.

"What Jody? You know I'll always do my best to help you."

"I want you to get me a chopper ride up to Cu Chi around seven this evening. I don't want anyone to see me, so pick me up here and get me to Hotel Three."

"Don't you think it's dangerous to be going out?"

"This is something I have to do. If you have any trouble getting a helicopter, call Cu Chi and ask for General Springer. Tell him you are with CID, and a friend of mine. Tell him I need to see him on urgent business, and ask him to send a chopper for me."

"All right," Bruce said dubiously, "but I'd better go with you."

"I'd appreciate that," she replied. "I'd also like it if you'd leave your tape recorder here until you come back to get me."

"Sure. No problem, Jody." My Linh saw the CID agent out, and Jody began to make another duplicate of her original tape.

It was almost three in the afternoon when Jody finished the last tape and My Linh came in with a bowl of food. "You didn't have any lunch, Jody. Eat this." The bowl contained a mixture of chopped beef and vegetables poured over rice.

Jody took the bowl. "It looks good, but I'm sure going to get fat if we stay here too long, eating rice three times a day."

After eating, Jody put the duplicate tape she had made in her handbag and handed the original to My Linh. "Take this and hide it. It may be an insurance policy of sorts."

Jody slept for an hour and was awakened at five o'clock by My Linh. Tien had arrived. He entered the room and squatted down on his haunches beside Jody. In his rough English he told Jody that both her apartment and the band's villa were being watched by Americans. As Jody had expected, the band had returned that day from Cu Chi. She gave Tien three hundred dollars in MPC and told him to change it into piasters and give it, with a note she handed him, to the Filipinos.

Tien left to do his errands. Shortly afterward, Alvin Bruce arrived to take Jody to Tan Son Nhut. It was dark when they ventured out into the car Bruce had borrowed.

"The general will have a chopper meeting us," Bruce said. "I'm leaving at noon tomorrow for Washington. I got myself manifested on an R and R flight to Hawaii, and I'll change flights there."

"How long will I have to hide out?" Jody asked.

"I should be back in four or five days. Don't leave your safe house again in that time."

"I won't have to. My band is back in Saigon, and I wrote them to sit tight for a week or two and not to worry, they'll soon be working again."

On the way to Tan Son Nhut Jody noticed that Alvin Bruce was constantly checking his rearview mirror, and twice actually turned in his seat to look out the rear of the car.

"Do you think we might be followed?" she asked.

"It's always a possibility. I tried to be careful on the way over to you this evening, and I'm reasonably certain I wasn't tailed, but it pays to be alert. This syndicate employs some nasty enforcers."

Jody shuddered. "I heard about the Apaches. Well, I'm glad you're going straight to the top in Washington."

The chopper was waiting for them at Hotel 3, and when they reached Cu Chi General Springer and his driver, Sergeant Jones, were waiting for them. As Jody alighted she couldn't miss the look of eagerness that crossed the general's face and then was quickly replaced with an expression of reproach. Alvin Bruce saluted and said, "Good evening, sir. Chief Warrant Officer Bruce, CID."

The general returned his salute smartly. "Hullo, Walt," Jody said. "Thank you for meeting us."

"It was nothing, ma'am," Springer said briskly. They all climbed into the jeep and headed for division headquarters. As they entered his austere office, General Springer asked them if they would like some coffee. Jody, who had been drinking nothing but Chinese tea the past twenty-four hours, nodded eagerly. Jones went to get the coffee for them.

"I take it you're here on business," the general opened coldly.

"Yes, Walt. I've brought you a little present. Proof of what I have been trying to tell you, and proof that your own division is involved." Jody reached into her handbag, pulled out the two tapes she had copied, and handed them to Springer. "The top one concerns this division. Do you have a tape recorder?"

Sergeant Jones entered the room with the coffee. "Jones, do you think you could get the tape recorder from my trailer and bring it here?"

"Yes, sir." Jones handed out the coffee cups and left.

"Sir," Alvin Bruce said, "Miss Neale here has put herself in very great personal danger by making these tapes. Unfortunately, she was seen by some of those she was attempting to get evidence on. They are looking for her now. She is in hiding and only ventured out to talk to you."

For a moment the general lost his cold aloofness. "Is that right, Jody?" he asked reaching for her hand.

"Mr. Bruce may be exaggerating a little," she replied feebly. Jones reentered the room and set up the tape recorder; they all sat silently, listening to the conversation between Sergeant Gambino and Bert Bannahan. General Springer's agitation grew as the deal between the two unfolded. By the time the tape was finished, he was pacing the room angrily.

"Bring us some more coffee, Jones," Springer said as Bruce put the second tape on the player. It was after ten o'clock by the time the last tape ran through. They sat in silence for a while, and then the general spoke up, softly at first, trying to mute his rage.

"I'm sick. Sick to my soul." He shook his head and looked almost beseechingly at Jody. "And to think you kept trying to tell me. In all of my twenty-five years in the service I've never encountered anything like this."

Jody glanced at Bruce. "Would you mind waiting in the other room for a while, Alvin? There is something I'd like to talk to the general about in private."

"Certainly," the CID man said, rising and leaving the office. Jody and the general looked at each other silently for a moment, and then Springer took her hand.

"Is that why you left me, Jody? Because I didn't believe you?"

"It would be so easy for me to say yes to that question, Walt. But I'd

215

be lying, and I've always tried to be truthful. But no," she said, removing her hand from his gently. "The real reason is unpleasant, and you won't like it. But it will explain how I was able to get the tapes you heard. The first one was made at my apartment."

Jody hesitated and took a deep breath before continuing. "I was very happy with you, Walt, and I hated more than anything to hurt you, but I couldn't help it."

"It's not too late," Walt said, looking at her tenderly. "We can pick up where we left off."

"I wish we could," she replied sadly. "But I'm afraid it is too late; too many things have happened. You see, to save my business I made a deal with Sergeant Gambino. Part of that deal meant I could never see you again." Jody averted her eyes. "I became Gambino's girl friend."

A look of pain crossed General Springer's face, and he turned away.

Quietly Jody said, "I'm sorry, Walt. It hurt me too."

"Does money mean that much to you?" he asked bitingly, turning back to her.

"You've never been utterly without security of any sort, Walt. You can't put yourself in my place."

"I guess it is too late," he said sorrowfully. "You'd better call Mr. Bruce back in."

Jody went to the door and motioned Alvin to rejoin them.

"Mr. Bruce, I want to thank you for escorting Miss Neale up here tonight," General Springer said. "It may seem to you like a case of very tardily locking the stable door, but Sergeant Gambino will be relieved of his duties in the morning, pending an investigation by the division CID. I'll try to keep him confined, so he can't add to Jody's troubles. As for the staggering implications of the other tape, that is a matter which goes way beyond the jurisdiction of the command of this division. But I'm sure you know what to do."

Bruce nodded. "Yes, sir. I do."

As though a thought just struck him, Springer glanced at his watch. "I'm sorry. I became so involved in these tapes I lost track of the time. It's after curfew in Saigon. I'm afraid you'll both have to stay here tonight. You'll be safer, anyway. We'll see that you're comfortable. I'll have a chopper standing by to take you back in the morning." He looked longingly at Jody, whose sad expression mirrored the general's regret at the unbridgeable gulf that had split their once joyous relationship.

"I'll call the duty officer and have him find quarters for you," Springer said.

At nine thirty the following morning Jody and Alvin Bruce entered General Springer's office to say good-bye.

Jody and Alvin were about to leave when the division commanding general burst into the room.

216

"Walt, what the hell's going on out there?" he shouted, pointing to the window. They all looked out and saw a convoy of mammoth trucks churning up the dust as they lumbered through the camp. So astonished was the CG that he completely ignored Jody, whom he had known for almost a year, and Bruce, whom he had never seen before. Jody counted seven semi-trailers, all with the words SEA-LAND painted in big red and black letters on their sides.

Springer shook his head. "I don't know, General, but I'll sure find out." He picked up the phone and dialed the MP office.

"It's a damned bad show when a commander isn't informed what's going on in his own command," the CG blustered irritably. The convoy had pulled up out front, blocking all other traffic, and a growing knot of jeeps and trucks were honking their horns to pass. The driver of the first truck climbed out of the cab and seemed to be looking for someone to give him directions. Suddenly, a jeepload of MPs screamed up to the lead driver and stopped.

As the two generals watched from Springer's office, an MP vaulted from his jeep and started speaking to the driver while several other MPs ran up behind the trucks and opened the doors. To the utter amazement of everyone, the MPs were almost deluged in a sea of peanuts that came cascading out of the trucks making knee-high mounds on the dusty road. Pieces of the torn bags that had contained them attested to the rough journey the peanuts had endured from their point of shipment.

"What the devil now!" the CG cried. "Is that peanuts? I'm going out there myself!"

"Shall we go watch the fun, Alvin?" Jody suggested. "Somebody in Bannahan's little group must have goofed."

By the time Alvin and Jody reached the trucks, a crowd of GIs had gathered and were looking at the deluge of peanuts. The first truck driver was trying to explain to the CG. "We were delivering these to the custodian, a Sergeant Gambino, sir." He was trembling under a withering blast of invective. "I'm only a civilian driver, I don't know any more. I've got the invoice here. You can have it." He reached into his breast pocket and pulled out a blue paper.

The CG practically snatched it from him and scanned it. A roar that might have come from a wounded tiger burst from him, causing the startled GIs to leap into the air, some of them backing off to escape the general's ire.

"Half a million dollars!" he yelled. "Is this some kind of a sick joke? Half a million dollars' worth of peanuts?" General Springer was standing beside his commander, a stunned look on his face, as the realization hit him.

"What are we supposed to be here," the CG continued to roar, "an army of goddamned monkeys?"

Some of the troops began to titter. "MPs, goddamnit," he hollered, "disperse this crowd. Get these trucks off this road and bring the custodian to my office immediately. And I mean immediately!" As he turned and stalked off, General Springer paced beside him. "I think I can tell you what happened if you will come into my office."

"Alvin, I think we would be well advised to get to the chopper and get out of here," Jody suggested.

"I agree, Jody T." They headed off on foot for the helicopter pad. "What do you think happened?" Alvin asked.

"Obviously Bannahan's company sent the whole year's supply of peanuts all at once." Jody could hardly walk she was shaking so with laughter. "They could barely store a month's supply of cocktail snacks. God knows where they will put a year's supply."

The CID man permitted himself a grim smile. "Wouldn't matter if they did. Those nuts can't last long in this hot, humid weather. How many nuts can a GI eat in a week?"

Six days later, Alvin Bruce was back from his hurried trip to Washington and called on Jody at Cholon. "Mission accomplished," he said triumphantly. I put the tapes personally into the hands of General Walter. We should see action any day now. You'll be able to come out of hiding and go back to work."

"Thank God," Jody sighed. "I've got a stiff back, and I'm becoming allergic to rice and tea. I can't wait to go home and sleep in a bed for a change."

"Brought you a present," he said with a laugh, handing her a copy of the *Overseas Weekly*. Jody took the tabloid and scanned the front page. Suddenly she burst into laughter. There, staring out at her from the front page, was a photograph of Sergeant Gambino and another of the division CG. The headline read, "CONVOY OF PEANUTS." My Linh was reading over her shoulder.

"What about that?" Jody giggled. "The division not only didn't have storage space, but it hadn't the money to pay for them. The general had to assign officers to go around to the other divisions and sell them. Now they're calling the Twenty-fifth Division the peanut vendors."

"I love the *Overseas Weekly*," Jody went on. "It's the only paper that tells it like it is and tells it with humor. No wonder so many generals object to it being sold on their posts."

"Hey," My Linh said. "We celebrate. Drink beer, no more tea. Soon go home, Do big business again."

"When will it be safe to go back to the apartment, Alvin?" Jody asked.

"Soon, but not tonight. I'm afraid the syndicate has men out looking for you still. We'll have to wait until I get the all clear from Washington. With what I gave General Walter they ought to get Cotsworth out of here

218

very suddenly. General Walter's about to retire, so I know he'll want to take care of this situation quickly."

"We'll take your advice," Jody said. "I can hardly wait to get back into business with all those crooks out of here."

"That's fine, Jody, but don't get overanxious. They still control this town, and you are their number-one target." He smiled warmly at her. "It won't be long."

But five more days passed before Alvin Bruce returned to Jody's hide-out. The sergeants' syndicate was still flourishing, and a watch was still on Jody's apartment and the Filipinos' villa. Jody was to wait until Alvin got back. Bored to desperation, she slept half the days away, playing cards with My Linh the rest of the time. They were in the middle of a game when Alvin Bruce arrived again.

Jody was shocked at the CID agent's appearance. His eyes were bright pinpoints of rage and frustration, his face was pale, and he looked more harassed than any CID victim she had ever seen.

"What is it, Alvin?" she cried out in alarm. "Are you sick?"

"Worse than that. This has been the worst day in my entire Army career. This morning I was called into the office of the provost marshal. The head of the CID in Vietnam was with him."

"What happened, Alvin?"

"I've never been so abused and reamed out before. I was threatened with everything from a transfer to a dishonorable discharge."

"My God, why?" Jody cried.

"I was accused of going over the heads of my bosses here, making an unauthorized trip to the United States, breaking lines of communications by trying to see Major General Trenton Walter." He paused and took several deep breaths. "You name it and they threw it at me."

Jody was speechless. Finally, after a minute or two of silence, Jody asked, incredulous, "Does that mean what I think it means?" She paused again as though unable to say what was on her mind. "That this general you went to see in Washington, the top man in the Army police force, is protecting Cotsworth?"

Alvin Bruce nodded slowly. "It's gotta be that way."

Jody sat down on the edge of her bed. "Oh, my God. What a mess. What can we do now?"

"I don't know about you, but I'm so disgusted I'm getting out of the service. As soon as my tour is up here I'll have twenty years. If I want to get out honorably with my pension, I've been told to stop trying to deliberately embarrass high command."

"My God," Jody said, "I'd better get out on the first plane for home. There's nothing more I can do here." She looked at My Linh's crestfallen face. "How would you like to leave Vietnam, My Linh?"

The lovely Eurasian girl's face brightened. "For many years now I want to leave."

"How would Hong Kong suit you?" Jody asked.

"Oh, yes. Oh, yes." My Linh clapped her hands excitedly.

"Well, you wait at the apartment until I send for you. I should be able to sell my jewelry for about forty thousand dollars. I've been investing in my collection for seven years. With the money we'll open up another Waltzing Matilda. Once I get out of Saigon, the pressure will be off and you can come and go as you like."

"What about Andre, can I bring him too?"

"Of course." Jody turned to Alvin Bruce. "If I give you the money, would you buy me a Pan Am ticket for Sydney? I'll leave the day after tomorrow."

"Be glad to do it for you, Jody."

She gave a wicked smile as she pushed the currency at him. "Have you any connections for changing MPC?"

For a moment he was all cop again. "Now damn it, Jody T., you know better than to ask me." He cut himself off with a bitter laugh. "Sure I'll change it for you, at the best rate you ever got. What the hell is the use anyway? What the hell is the use?"

From her bag she took out her passport and five thousand piasters and handed them to My Linh. "Tomorrow you go to immigration and get my exit visa. You'll have to take care of shipping the Filipinos home. Stay at the apartment until you hear from me."

"Yes, Jody. I take care of everything."

Two days later, Jody walked up the boarding steps to the plane that was to take her home. She turned at the top and waved to Alvin and My Linh before disappearing out of sight. She belted herself into her seat and looked out the window at the drab terminal. What a fiasco, she thought. When she arrived in Vietnam well over two years ago she already owned the jewelry, and now she was leaving after all that period of hard work with nothing but her jewelry left in a bank in Sydney and the little money she had managed to get out of Vietnam. She hoped she would never see this corrupt and dirty country again.

As the plane taxied down the runway she settled back and sighed with relief. She glanced at her watch. It was six in the evening. Well at least she had escaped unharmed.

The same evening, as Jody was not to learn until it was too late, Ronnie Jasper climbed out of his car on the grounds of Cotsworth's villa and strode up to the front door. He was admitted to the house and found Cotsworth relaxing before the TV set in his study.

"Hi, Tiger," he said jovially, "What be you wanting me for this evening?"

"Hello, Jasper. Make yourself a drink."

Jasper went over to the bar and sloshed a heavy slug of whiskey into a glass, poured some water over it, dropped in a couple of ice cubes, and sat down next to the sergeant major. "To get straight to the point," Cotsworth said, "I hear you're doing some business in Australia now. Have you any good contacts in Sydney?"

"Some," Jasper replied cautiously. "Why?"

"Jody T. Neale. She tried to hurt the syndicate. I want to make an example of her, so no one else ever tries the same stunt."

"Isn't she still in Saigon?"

"We haven't been able to locate her. Anyway, she's all washed up here, and she knows it by now. She'll have to go home if she hasn't already. We know she's about broke, but she's got an expensive collection of jewelry in Sydney, and my sources tell me it is uninsured." Cotsworth smiled briefly. "If she is broke she'll probably try to sell that jewelry to get another stake."

"What's all this got to do with me?" Jasper asked.

"I don't want her to get a stake. I want her on the balls of her ass. Busted. If you can arrange to have someone relieve her of her jewelry, I'll be mighty grateful. And I always find some tangible way to express my gratitude."

"That's right, Tiger," Jasper agreed.

Cotsworth handed him a slip of paper. "Here's her address and the name of her bank in Sydney. Have someone watch the bank until she goes to her safe-deposit box and gets her jewelry out. They'll know what to do after that."

"It's as good as done, Tiger. By the way, what's going to happen out at Cu Chi?"

Cotsworth made a wry face. "Don't ruin my evening talking about it. I'll have another custodian there in a month. That Gambino was a bad boy —making that deal with Bannahan without letting the syndicate know. And Bannahan, I don't know whether it was an honest mistake or the greedy bastard thought he would somehow make the division pay for a year's supply all at once. Well, there's nothing I could or would do for Gambino now. He was going to keep the whole forty-eight thousand for himself. The greedy, stupid son of a bitch."

Cotsworth flashed a knowing grin at Jasper. "If everybody cooperates and works together, things go smoothly and everybody profits. But let one man get out of line—or one female—and he's got to suffer bad."

PART TWO

1

JULY, 1969

It was with trepidation that Jody T. Neale stepped off the flight from Hong Kong at Saigon's Tan Son Nhut Airport on the first day of July of 1969. No one was expecting her, so she had to try and hitch a ride out to the main gate of the airport where she could find a taxi cab to take her to her apartment on Plantation Road. Before she had always been met at the airport, but this time she wanted to get into Saigon city without attracting much attention. She knew she had two days at best to negotiate her business and get out. Vietnam was no longer the hospitable country it once had been to her. She felt a sense of danger as she cleared through customs and immigration.

One thing hadn't changed. A pretty, blonde, well-proportioned Caucasian girl did not go unnoticed. The Americans and Vietnamese alike gaped at her. As she finished clearing customs an American sergeant wearing a green beret came up to her and offered to carry her bags. Seeing he was a Special Forces man, she gratefully accepted his offer of help. To her relief, the sergeant had a jeep and promised to drop her off at her apartment. Once in the vehicle, he introduced himself to her as Master Sergeant Billy Wall of the Fifth Special Forces Group. When Jody told him who she was, he immediately knew all about her, and they talked excitedly as they drove off.

Wall accepted with alacrity Jody's invitation to come up to her apartment for a drink. My Linh was waiting in the apartment. Billy Wall took her hand and smiled appreciatively at the lovely half-French, half-Vietnamese girl as Jody explained that she would only be in Vietnam long enough to get a loan from an old friend, so that she could go to Hong Kong and open up a bar.

"Why not stay in country where we can all help you?" Billy suggested hopefully.

"You don't know how bad it is for her in Saigon," My Linh said quickly.

"And you don't know how the club custodians work," Jody added tartly.

"I've got an idea," Wall replied. "But you must have done pretty good when you were here before."

"Sure. And I put all my money into jewelry, which was stolen in Sydney. But that's another story."

"Gee, Jody, I'm real sorry to hear that," the Green Beret sergeant commiserated with her.

"Yes. And I know who was in on the stealing, but of course I can't prove anything. So,"—she attempted a bright smile—"I'm going to borrow from an old friend here in Saigon what I need to get started again. I already have my place in Hong Kong picked out and ready to be redecorated."

"Well, as long as you're in Saigon, Jody, let me drive you over to the Special Forces Command Liaison Detachment on Pasteur," Billy pursued. "You'll find some friends at the CLD, not to be confused with the CID," he grinned, "who'd like to see you."

"That sounds like a good idea. Just let me make a couple of phone calls, and I'll be ready."

It was late in the afternoon when Jody and Billy Wall left her apartment and stepped into the jeep. He unlocked the chain around the steering wheel, and they drove off to the Command Liaison Detachment where the Special Forces kept one of the most exclusive off-duty clubs in Vietnam. Only Green Berets and their friends were allowed.

As they drove through the center of Saigon Jody couldn't resist smiling and waving to the whistling GIs. Then she heard a sharp, authoritative shout directed at Billy Wall. They looked over at the sidewalk and saw a tall man wearing blue slacks, a white shirt, and a narrow black tie. Billy pulled up quickly.

"CID," he muttered. "What does the goddamned cop want?"

Staring at the man on the sidewalk, Jody suddenly recognized him. "Alvin," she called out. "I thought you would be back in the States."

"You know him?" Billy asked incredulously.

"He's one of the good ones," she answered.

The CID agent walked up to the jeep. "Sorry to stop you, Sergeant, but I had to talk to Jody T."

"Alvin Bruce, Billy Wall," she introduced them. "What's happened, Al?"

"I just finished telling a couple of guys from Washington, D.C., how to locate you in Australia. One of them was going to fly down there in a few days to find you."

"I don't know anyone from Washington. What do they want me for?" she asked, puzzled.

226

"They're Senate investigators. They read your statement in our files and want to talk to you about it."

Jody laughed. "They must be the first people to have read it who can do anything about it. As far as I can see, the CID spends most of its time protecting those crooks I informed on."

Al Bruce nodded, his face tightening into a grim note. "Maybe, Jody. But a lot of us in CID are hoping the whole story comes out." Suddenly a look of surprise came over his face. "Hey! What the hell are you doing here in Saigon anyway. And riding around in an open jeep. Sergeant, don't you know this young lady's life is in danger?"

Wall looked distressed. "No, sir. No, I sure didn't. But if that's a fact she's going to be with the right people."

"Jody T., why did you come back?" the CID agent asked beseechingly.

"I had some business to take care of, Al."

"Well, as long as you're here, you might as well talk to these guys from Washington. They're at the USAID office right now."

"I'll be at the Special Forces CLD for a while. They can reach me there."

"The office is only a couple of blocks from here on LeVan Duyet," Alvin Bruce pursued. "I could take you over to the CLD right after you see them. They could do more than anyone in this part of the world to get the truth exposed."

Seeing that Jody was weakening, Billy Wall said, "I'll wait for her outside the USAID office." He gestured toward the back seat. "Get in. I'll take you both over."

Rick Townsend stared at the striking blonde girl who walked into his office with the CID agent. "It was an extraordinary stroke of luck that you happened by, Miss Neale," he said.

"I hear I saved you a flight to Australia. I'm sure you would have enjoyed it, though," she replied. "But what could you possibly want of me?"

"Mr. O'Neill here," Rick said, gesturing at his associate, "and I were very interested in the statement you made some months ago to the CID, and we want to discuss it with you. Is now a good time?"

"Well, if it's going to take long I'd rather come back tomorrow. I have a friend waiting outside."

"How about ten o'clock tomorrow morning, right here?" O'Neill asked. "We'll be waiting for you, Miss Neale."

"I won't hold you up. I need to get out of Saigon as soon as I can complete my business here." She nodded pleasantly at O'Neill and started for the door.

Outside the USAID building Jody climbed into the jeep with Billy Wall and they drove down Rue Pasteur, Saigon's most elegant residential street, and pulled up in front of a gate. The high-fenced villa before them looked no different from the outside than any other except for the Chinese Nung guards on duty. One guard, leaning on his rifle, stared at the jeep and then, recognizing Billy Wall, came to attention and opened the gate, beckoning the jeep through. They crunched over the gravel driveway, past well-tended gardens and a front villa which was used as quarters for transient Green Beret field commanders.

When they pulled up in front of the larger building at the back, Billy Wall helped Jody out of the jeep. They entered the four-story building which housed the approximately thirty men assigned to the CLD which coördinated Special Forces operating with MACV.

Pushing open a door on the ground floor they found themselves in a different world. Jody, her damp dress clinging to her back, was grateful for the cool air-conditioning which enveloped them.

"Nobody can say the Green Berets don't go first class all the way," she laughed. The scene before them could have been any intimate night-club back in the States—plush furnishings, soft lights, tinkling music, and the inevitable paintings of nude women hanging behind the bar.

Coming into the club at the CLD was like old times for Jody. Billy Wall, somewhat of a legend among the old-timers of the Green Berets, was a hero once again for bringing Jody around. Officers and sergeants mingled and socialized freely as in no other club in Saigon. All men who wore the Green Beret were comrades, regardless of rank. Lieutenant Colonel Pat Vreeman pulled up a chair and sat himself down beside Jody, who was surrounded by sergeants.

"Hello again, Jody, remember me? Nha Trang two years ago?"

"Of course, Pat. Congratulations. You were a major then."

"What a memory," Vreeman remarked, pleased.

"I couldn't forget you. Two of your sergeants ate up all my flowers one night," she laughed. "Every time they have too much to drink they try to live up to being called 'snake eaters.'"

"You had no pretzels, and they wanted a snack," Vreeman answered in defense of his men.

"Yes. I can still see the dopes, pulling every flower out of the vases, dipping them in their beer, and eating them. Flowers are expensive. I had to charge them two dollars apiece for supper."

"That wasn't so bad, but I didn't get any work out of them for the next two days. They spent all their time running to the latrine." Vreeman chuckled at the memory. "Seriously Jody, why don't you come down to the Delta for a visit? I've got the 'B' team at Cao Lam now."

"That's what I've been trying to tell her, sir,' Billy Wall chimed in.

"We could keep you booked, you'd make money with us," urged Vreeman. "And you know that with the green hats there's no dicking around. Everything is straight."

"I wished I'd thought of that when I was here before. But I've got to get out of Vietnam. When I get my bar going in Hong Kong you come up on R and R and we'll do the town."

"R and R? What's that?" Vreeman asked with a harsh laugh. "Just getting up here to Saigon is the biggest break I've had in three months. Charlie's keeping the pressure right on us." He reached for Jody's hand. "Not that you wouldn't be reasonably safe," he added.

"It's not Charlie I'm afraid of," she replied grimly. Then she laughed. "How does a girl get a drink here?" she asked.

2

Early the next morning Major Edwin Unger opened the door to the office in which Rick and O'Neill were discussing the final stages of their investigation.

"Miss Jody T. Neale is waiting," he announced.

"Send her in, Ed," O'Neill said. "By the way, I think this first time we talk to her she might be easier if just Rick and I talked to her. From what Mr. Bruce says she's had bad luck with MPs and CID agents."

"I understand. No problem, O'Neill."

Unger stepped back into the corridor and returned almost immediately with Jody.

"Miss Neale," Rick said in his most cordial tones, "we thank you for coming over. You can be a big help to us if you want to."

Jody shrugged. "Every time I cooperate with the so-called authorities I get into trouble." There was a bitter tone in her voice. "But as I expect to be out of Vietnam tomorrow, and I'd still like to see those crooks get what's coming to them, I'll tell you whatever I can that might help you."

"We want to hear everything you know about the corruption over here. Anything you might have observed. Things have a way of fitting together when you gather enough facts."

"Do I get any kind of immunity?" Jody chuckled. "I wasn't always so legal myself. But then the way your regulations are written for Vietnam, and the way the Army sometimes lets things happen over here, nobody could stay legal and survive."

"We can't promise anything," O'Neill replied. "But your help will be greatly appreciated, and we will show our appreciation in every way we can?" A fleeting smile crossed O'Neill's face.

230

"I tried to tell the CID what I knew last year, but all they did was ignore my statement and tell the interested parties that I had informed on them. And as a matter of fact, since the CID knows I am here today talking to you, I'm in trouble already."

Rick placed his hand on Jody's arm. "We are aware that the CID is infiltrated by people benefiting by the corrupt practices we are trying to investigate." He led Jody to a chair. "We have a great deal of faith in you, Miss Neale."

"Miss Neale, do you mind if we tape your statements?" O'Neill asked pleasantly.

"Not at all. I have nothing to hide." She watched as Rick set up the tape recorder, tested it, and set the microphone in front of her.

"Why don't we start with your first trip to Vietnam," Rick suggested. "According to the CID records, you started out in business with a salesman who was recently involved in paying off a club custodian. His name is Bert Bannahan."

Jody sighed. "Yes, it was Bert who first inveigled me into coming to Saigon." She began to tell her story.

By the time she had finished telling about her visit to Binh Duc and General Rabbit Hare, both O'Neill and Rick were leaning toward her, listening intently. Jody paused in her narrative at the point where she reached Nha Trang. Looking at her watch, she said, "It's almost time for lunch. My Linh, my assistant, will be waiting."

"Will you come back after lunch?" Rick asked.

"I have a better idea. Let me use your phone and I'll ask My Linh to fix lunch for four. She's a very good cook."

"You have a Tiger line in your apartment?" Rick asked incredulously.

"Of course."

"But I thought—" Rick began and shut himself off.

"It was illegal for unofficial civilians to be on the military telephone system?" she asked with a laugh. "By now you must realize that almost everything that goes on over here is illegal, including the fact that you Americans are here with over half a million men." Neither Rick nor O'Neill replied. Jody pointed to the phone. "May I?"

"I won't be able to join you, thanks just the same," O'Neill said. "I have to finish processing the testimony of one of the custodians."

"Anyone I know?" Jody asked.

"Sergeant Picking," O'Neill answered.

"Oh, yes, I know Earl. He was one of the honest ones. As a matter of fact, he really put me into business."

"You like him, I take it."

"Yes. He never did me any harm, even when he came back a full member of the syndicate."

O'Neill nodded. "Make your call. I'm sure Rick would enjoy having lunch with you, and he can continue the interview at your own place."

Jody telephoned My Linh, and then Rick took her arm and led her from the office.

Out on the sidewalk the sedan and the Vietnamese driver assigned to them were waiting. The driver took them to Jody's address on Plantation Road.

"How long have you had this place?" Rick asked as they entered her apartment building.

"A year or so. After the CID and local police harassed me out of Nha Trang where I had my club I came to Saigon. That was late in sixty-seven."

Rick helped Jody out of the car, and they were walking across the sidewalk toward the entrance to the apartment house when a youthful-looking American in slacks and a sport shirt came up to her.

"Miss Jody T. Neale, ma'am?" he asked.

"That's me. What do you want?"

"I have a letter for you, ma'am." He held out an envelope.

Jody took it and asked, "Who's is it from?"

"I guess it will say inside, ma'am." With that the youth turned and darted into the crowded street. Puzzled, they watched him disappear into the crowd, then Rick gave the driver instructions and they entered the building.

Inside the apartment Rick looked about, impressed at its size and tasteful Oriental decor. My Linh entered the living room, and Jody introduced Rick to the lovely Eurasian girl. "Sit down while I read this letter, Rick. My Linh will get you a drink."

"I'll wait for lunch, Jody. Take your time."

My Linh watched her mistress as she ripped open the letter, pulled the piece of notepaper out, and started to unfold it. A small feather fell out of the note. My Linh, her eyes suddenly almost round, stared at it fluttering to the floor. Jody inadvertently gasped. "The bloody Apaches. How did they find out I was back?"

"You should never come back here!" There was a tremor of fear in My Linh's voice.

"Let's see what the rotten bastards have to say for themselves." Jody unfolded the letter and began to read.

"What's all this about, Jody?" Rick asked.

"The Apaches, as they call themselves, are the most powerful of the American-deserter gangs in Vietnam," Jody explained. "There are hundreds, maybe over a thousand Americans, either AWOL or out and out deserters, hiding in Cholon, the Chinese area of Saigon. There were only a hundred or less when I first came here."

"Yes, I've heard about them," Rick acknowledged.

"For self-protection they divide up into gangs, each gang with a strong leader," Jody went on. "One of these leaders is part red Indian, and his

232

gang is called the Apaches. It happens that My Linh knew the leader of the Apaches, a sergeant named Jack Talltree."

"What is he writing to you about?" Rick said.

"Everyone knows I'm back. There's been a price put on my head, and the Apaches want to collect it."

"You haven't told us enough to warrant a price on your pretty neck," Rick protested.

"I haven't told you anything yet. And for that matter, I'm not sure just how much I will tell you." She looked over at the frightened My Linh. "Don't just stand there staring at me. I'm sure Mr. Townsend will have a drink now if you'll fix it for him. I'll have a gin and tonic."

Jody finished reading the letter and turned to Rick. "Yes. The Apaches are watching me all the time. If I talk to the men from Washington they'll kill me. Now how do you suppose," her tone was mocking, "they know so much so soon? You wonder why we don't like to talk and don't trust anyone?"

"The American deserters will kill for money?" Rick asked incredulously.

"Oh, of course," Jody snapped in vexation at this Senate investigator's naïveté. "It costs the deserters about fifty dollars a day to pay for their food, rooms, girl friends, marihuana, and protection from the Saigon police and the MPs. They do all sorts of odd jobs, from smuggling and selling dope to buying or stealing PX goods to sell on the black market. Many of them could be caught and returned to their posts, but they are so valuable to certain people as they are that they are allowed to roam free."

"That sounds like a situation we should investigate," Rick declared.

"Lots of luck," Jody said ironically. "If you try it, be careful. They are desperate men. They have nowhere to go, nobody to turn to, and no way to get home to America. They're cornered rats, fighting to survive, and most of them are dope addicts." Jody handed Rick the drink My Linh brought on a tray. "Mr. Investigator, you have a lot to learn about this city. A lot you won't like and the American people won't want to hear."

"What about you, Jody?" Rick asked. "We'd better get you some protection."

Jody laughed. "There's no protection in Saigon. Maybe I can negotiate." She handed the letter to My Linh, who read it quickly. "Do you think Jack would really kill me or let his gang do it?" Jody asked.

"Maybe if I would go see him he would tell me," My Linh suggested.

"Well, I can't outbid Sergeant Major Cotsworth's gang. They've already ruined me financially."

"I will go see Jack," My Linh avowed. "Right after lunch."

My Linh finished cooking lunch while Jody and Rick sipped their drinks and chatted about Saigon, the Apaches, and the corruption.

Rick found it difficult to discipline his thoughts. Jody was certainly a most desirable girl, and he wanted nothing more than to touch her, run his hands through her hair, along her breasts—enough! That was all the anti-investigation camp would need, some proof that Rick was having an affair with a potential witness. My Linh hovered around, cleaning up the last of the luncheon dishes. She was a beauty herself, Rick thought. Maybe that was the direction to look for romance. He was conscious of Jody looking at him, an amused smile on her face. She was obviously reading his mind, he thought.

"That sure was a delicious lunch," he complimented My Linh. "The kind of light midday meal that doesn't bog you down," he said, struggling along as My Linh smiled warmly at him and then turned to Jody.

"I go see Jack now. This is a good time."

"Be careful," Jody cautioned.

"I know what to do." Purposefully My Linh walked to the door, opened it, and left. Rick swallowed the remainder of his green tea and began setting up his tape recorder and positioning the microphone in front of Jody.

It was five o'clock when three sharp raps at the door brought Jody and Rick abruptly out of the past and back into the present.

"I wonder who that could be?" she asked, a tremor in her voice. "My Linh has her own key and I'm not expecting anyone else."

Rick walked to the door silently and stood to one side of it. "Who's there?" he asked hoarsely.

"O'Neill."

Relieved, Rick opened the door and O'Neill walked in. "Nice pad," he remarked as he entered, looking around.

"How did you find it?" Rick asked.

"I'm an investigator, remember?" He gave his hostess a twitch of a smile. "Good afternoon, Jody. How's everything?"

"Okay, Mr. O'Neill. I guess."

"You can drop the mister. O'Neill is good enough."

"She's just had her life threatened if she talks to us," Rick said.

For once O'Neill showed surprise and concern. "By whom?"

Rick and Jody explained about the Apaches and My Linh's mission. "We're waiting for her now," Rick said, glancing at his watch.

"I hope she'll be all right." Worry wrinkles creased Jody's forehead. "I hated to let her go to the deserter colony.'

"Did you notice any American types around this building when you came in?" Rick asked.

O'Neill thought for a few moments. "Now that you mention it there was a big black boy on the corner, just standing there."

"Probably an Apache," Rick said. "There isn't much we can do until My Linh comes back and tells us what's going to happen."

"Well I can tell you what's going to happen tomorrow," Jody said positively. "I'm calling Tony DeMarlo, getting a loan, and taking the next plane for Hong Kong."

234

"But there is so much more you could tell us that would aid our investigation," Rick protested.

"Can't we finish it all now?" Jody asked.

"Not really. After I have your interview transcribed new questions will come to mind. And there is so much from the other testimony we have taken that we'd like to cross-check with you."

"Well, why don't we see how much we can do now?" Jody suggested.

"All right, Jody," O'Neill said. "Wherever we turn, the name of General Robert Hare seems to crop up. What can you tell us about him?"

"Let me see. I've just told Rick about Binh Doc. The time I saw a lot of Rabbit was when I was friendly with Joe Crust."

"That's what we want to hear," O'Neill said eagerly. He pointed at the microphone, "Give, Jody."

It was getting close to the curfew hour when Jody paused in her testimony. The sound of a key in the lock alerted Rick and O'Neill. The door opened and My Linh walked in. She was disheveled, her hair, which was usually pulled back from her forehead, was now loose and hanging stringily, so that it partially covered her face. There was a hurt look in her eyes; the usually bright smile was replaced by a slack-mouthed, expressionless attitude. Jody took a long look at her, then she went to the girl and led her to a chair.

"What happened, My Linh?" Jody asked anxiously.

"I saw Jack," the Eurasian girl answered. "I talk to him and then—" She bit her lip and lapsed into silence.

"Let me get you some hot coffee." Jody hurried out and soon returned with the coffee.

"You were right," My Linh said after a few sips of the beverage. "Cotsworth men pay Apaches five thousand dollars, in green, not even MPC, to kill Jody."

"They must figure she knows a hell of a lot more than she's told us for that kind of money," O'Neill remarked.

"Or else somebody knows the value of a dramatic witness to us," Rick added.

"Normally the syndicate wouldn't take the risk or spend the money to have Jody killed," Rick argued. "It's been investigated for ten years and never suffered. Cotsworth, with a criminal record, became Sergeant Major of the U.S. Army. You think he's worried about Jody enough to have her killed?"

O'Neill shrugged. "He might. In the first place, it's no big risk to knock someone off over here."

Jody and My Linh nodded emphatically at this.

"And this is the first Senate investigation of their activities."

"Jody will be okay until tomorrow night," My Linh declared. "Jack Talltree promise me she not be killed for one day."

"You think he'll keep his promise?" Rick asked.

"As you Americans say, we sealed the deal," My Linh replied bitterly. "Twenty-four hours. She got to get out tomorrow night."

"My Linh," O'Neill asked. "How does this Jack communicate with the sergeants? Isn't he afraid of being arrested?"

My Linh laughed tauntingly. "Cotsworth men go to Cholon. They eat and drink with Jack. They make love to girls he gives them. The Chinese, Vietnamese black-market operators need Americans like Jack." Again she chuckled bitterly.

"Jack could go home. He has tickets and ID. But he make too much money. He live like prince. But the young boys desperate. They need gang like Apaches to stay alive, not go to jail. They live in fear like rats."

"Have you ever been on an investigation like this one?" Rick asked his partner.

O'Neill shook his head. "Never. And we're twelve thousand miles from the States on top of it all." He looked at his watch nervously. "Hey, it's damned near curfew." He flashed his tight-lipped smile and stood up.

Reluctantly Rick followed O'Neill's example. "You both feel safe to-night?" he asked solicitously.

"Yes," Jody replied. "I'll take the five p.m. flight tomorrow for Hong Kong."

"I'll come around at noontime with your statement all typed up," Rick said. "We'll take it over to the Embassy where you can sign it and swear to it before the consul. That makes it a legal document we can use at the hearings. Of course, if you wanted to come and be a witness that would be the greatest."

"I don't even want to give a statement," Jody said. "But I will."

"Good girl. See you at noon."

"I'll be waiting. And don't be late. I'm on a tight schedule." She tried to smile.

"I'll be here, Jody."

3

Rick found O'Neill at seven a.m., having breakfast in the dining room of the USAID quarters assigned to them. O'Neill saluted him with his quick, tight twitch of a smile. "You look tired, my boy."

"I went to sleep over my typewriter at three. I'll have to work like hell to get Jody's statement finished by noon."

"Did you get a lot of good stuff?" O'Neill asked.

"Plenty. I just wish she were staying longer. I could spend a few days going over some of her stories in depth."

"Al Bruce, the CID man, sure thinks she has the hard facts we need. What about those tapes?"

"She has them in a vault in a Hong Kong bank. And like she says, maybe she'll let us have them, maybe she won't. You can't really blame her. When she let Bruce take them to General Walter that was the signal for her execution."

When they had finished breakfast, Rick asked O'Neill if he wanted to go to Jody's at noon with him. O'Neill shook his head. "You go on over. I have several interviews this morning." A semblance of a grin crossed the investigator's face. "I suppose My Linh will stay on at Jody's place after our girl leaves for Hong Kong."

"I'd be a liar if I said I wouldn't like to be caught alone up there with My Linh by the curfew for the next few nights."

"Just use Jody's Tiger line if you do. Keep me informed. This isn't like a Stateside investigation." He paused, his voice heavy with irony. "Those VC terrorists are everywhere."

Rick stood up. "Back to the typewriter. I used to think I wanted to be a writer. Now I'm not so sure."

"Have a last shot at persuading Jody to consider being a witness in

Washington. We need one like her to really grab the public's attention."

"I'll try, O'Neill." He put his hands together and bobbed his head. *"Chow ow."*

Jody woke up in her apartment and felt the knot of anxiety in her stomach. This afternoon, she told herself, she would be getting out of here once and for all. Even if Tony DeMarlo didn't make the loan she would leave and start over again in Hong Kong or Manila.

She looked at her clock. Eight a.m. pulling on her wrap she walked into the kitchen and began making her morning coffee. Impatiently she waited until eight thirty when she knew Tony DeMarlo would be in his office, then put the call through. Tony answered himself.

He understood immediately why she didn't want to get out in the streets and come over to his office and promised to be at her apartment as fast as possible.

While she was waiting for DeMarlo at arrive, she thought more about Rick and O'Neill. She liked them, but she had reached the stage of trusting no one. From past experience she had learned that most people's promises of help amount to nothing. If she gave them the tapes she had stashed away in Hong Kong it would really help them. But what she had to do now was concentrate on getting the loan and getting away. Later, if she decided to help the investigators further, she would write them from Hong Kong and they could stop by on their way to the States.

Her thoughts were interrupted by a knock. Jody hurried to the door and called, "Tony?"

"It's me, Jody."

She threw open the door. "Come on in." Tony kissed her on the cheek.

"I heard you were back through the jungle telegraph," he said, "but I didn't believe it."

"I got in two days ago, and I'm on my way out this afternoon," she replied. "The only reason I risked coming back was to see you."

"You never told me how much you cared." Tony smiled. "Think of the time we wasted."

"Have you had breakfast, Tony?"

"Could use a cup of coffee. But first tell me what this is all about."

Jody looked at Tony's gray hair and ruddy complexion, remembering how genial he was and how much she enjoyed being in his company.

"I'll have us each a cup of coffee in a minute. Sit down and I'll be right back."

Jody returned from the kitchen a few minutes later with two cups of coffee. She put them down on the coffee table and sat beside him on the sofa. "Tony," she began, "I need your help."

Tony raised his eyebrows but said nothing. "You know the mess I'm in here. I could never go into business in Saigon again. And now I've got no money to start in again back home."

Tony nodded his understanding. "During the three years I've known you, your misadventures have read like the Perils of Pauline. First Bannahan, then the sergeants. All your friends should have gotten together before it was too late and put together a Saigon survival kit for you. The most important piece of equipment being a rag to stuff in your mouth when you feel like talking."

"Okay, Tony," Jody cut in impatiently. "I didn't come to Saigon so you could preach me a sermon. What I need is enough money to get started in a small bar I've found in Kowloon. I figure six thousand dollars will be enough to get the place started, and I'll split fifty-fifty with you on the profits. You know I'm good in that kind of business. That is, providing I'm in a law-abiding community."

"Joe Crust and a few others I can think of wouldn't like me lending you a stake," Tony replied seriously.

"They wouldn't know. I wouldn't tell anyone. And you know it would be a good investment. I'd make money for you, for both of us."

"I don't doubt that Jody T., you're a natural. But could I trust you to keep my name out of it. You know who would be making it tough for me if it got out I helped you."

"I promise you, Tony. I've never hurt you, and I never will. We've always been friends."

"You're right, kid. I guess your only mistake was coming to Vietnam. You're not quite tough enough to make it here—no matter how tough you think you are."

"You'll do it?" she asked hopefully.

"Sure. You go on back to Hong Kong, and I'll join you there next week and make all the arrangements."

Jody laughed tensely. "If I'd known you were going to Hong Kong, I wouldn't have had to come back here. I tried to phone you for a week, but you know Vietnam communications."

"How are you for money right now?"

"I've got enough to get back to Hong Kong and wait for you. I'll stay at the Ambassador."

"Okay, Jody. The Ambassador, next week. Have everything set up, so I can look it over. I'll be damned busy. And don't ever forget," he said with a cautioning look, "I'm strictly the silent partner."

"I promise. And Tony, thank you. You'll never be sorry."

"I don't think so, Jody." He stood up. "I have to leave now. See you in Hong Kong."

Tony DeMarlo had been gone over an hour when Rick showed up at the apartment. He had typed out all the pertinent information she had given him the previous day and handed it to her to read.

"I'm sure there is a lot more you could tell us, Jody," Rick said, though

239

there was no hint of reproach in his manner. "We realize that you've had nothing but trouble when you've told about the things that happened to you, but at the same time we hope that Senator Rothmann's committee can put an end to the grafting and corruption that have become the rule rather than the exception over here."

"Maybe when I'm settled in Hong Kong you could stop and see me on the way back and I could finish my story."

"Would you?" Rick asked eagerly.

"I think so."

"What about those tapes you mentioned. I've tried not to push you, but we want everything we can get."

"In Hong Kong I'll give you the tapes," Jody said decisively. She was so relieved to be leaving Saigon with the promise of assistance from Tony DeMarlo that her whole outlook had changed. "Let me finish getting packed up, and then I'll be glad to sign my statement."

My Linh was bending over an open suitcase which she was vainly trying to close.

"Here, I'll do that," Rick offered. He managed to get the suitcase closed and the catches locked. "I'm sorry we didn't have a chance to discuss the possibilities of you coming to Washington as a witness."

"I have to go on living and working somewhere in the Orient," Jody replied. "Even a statement is risky enough."

Rick did not press his point. "We're going to the Embassy to get you to swear to this document, and then I'll drive you out to Tan Son Nhut. You'll make your flight to Hong Kong easily."

"I'm ready." Jody turned to My Linh. "Write me in Hong Kong. Let me know when you get the furniture sold. I'll need every bit of money I can get." Jody embraced My Linh and said good-bye, giving her a quick peck on the cheek.

As Rick and Jody emerged from the apartment building Rick looked about the street furtively. The Vietnamese driver of the black U.S. Government sedan opened the door at the curb, and Rick helped Jody into the back.

"Embassy first stop, then Tan Son Nhut," he told the driver. When they arrived at the Embassy, Rick led Jody into the vice consul's office on the ground floor. The vice consul watched her sign the statement that Rick had prepared, stamped the document, signed it, and they were on their way to Tan Son Nhut.

Outside the protective gates of the Embassy, the car was once more caught up in the traffic-clogged streets as the driver worked his way toward the airport. Finally, they broke out of the worst of the downtown traffic, making better time as they approached Tan Son Nhut. Then, not too far away, they heard a series of crunching explosions. Rick looked at Jody questioningly.

240

"That was a string of mortars," she declared. "I ought to know. I stopped counting how many times I've been in mortar attacks."

"Mortars falling inside Saigon?" Rick asked.

There was another series of explosions, closer this time. Rick looked around for shelter.

"Don't worry, they're not falling close to us," Jody said judiciously. "It sounds as though the airport is getting it."

"How can the enemy get close enough to the airport to drop mortars onto it?"

"They even manage to attack it with troops now and again."

From the direction of the airport came the wail of sirens. Moments later two MP jeeps coming from Tan Son Nhut began stopping traffic. Rick and Jody watched staff cars and jeeps ahead of them make U-turns and start back downtown. The MPs came abreast of Rick's car.

"Sir, turn around and head away from Tan Son Nhut," the driver of the MP jeep called. "Airport's under attack."

"We've got to make a plane," Rick called. "Urgent. U.S. Senate business." He started to reach for his identification.

"The airport is closed," the MP called out. "No planes coming in or out for the rest of the day. We don't know how long the attack will keep up."

"But this is a matter of life or death!"

The MP stared at Rick whose head was out of the window now. "Look here, mister," the MP began, "them mortars are falling all over the air base. You want to get killed just keep going straight ahead, and you'll soon be under them. But no planes, civilian or military, except gun ships, are taking off."

Rick withdrew his head and looked helplessly at Jody. "I don't know what else we can do except go back." He shook his head. "I'll see to it that the provost marshal assigns round-the-clock protection for you until we can get you out." He told the river to turn around. "Shall we go to your apartment?"

Jody sat in silence, thinking, as the car made its U-turn and began creeping along with the city-bound traffic. Rick said nothing until the driver turned and asked where they wanted to go.

"Special Forces CLD on Pasteur Street," Jody said with sudden decisiveness. "That's one place I'll be safe."

"Will they let you stay there?" Rick asked.

"I think so. They're my friends."

It took almost an hour for them to fight their way through the terrible traffic. The Nung guards came to attention as the car pulled up at the driveway of the Special Forces CLD. Jody and Rick got out, and the guards, recognizing Jody, waved her through. "We'll go in and talk to Jerry Danton. He's the commander of the CLD."

Rick followed Jody into the office building and stood behind her as she told the sergeant major on duty that she wanted to see Lientenant Colonel Danton. "I know he's going to want to see you, Jody," the sergeant major boomed, a welcoming grin on his face, "and he isn't too busy." He pointed toward the closed door. "Just walk in and surprise him."

Jody opened the door and stepped into the commander's office. Danton looked up, surprised indeed to see the blonde girl standing there in front of him. "Jody!" he exclaimed. "What fortune of war brings you to the CLD?"

"A mortar attack on Tan Son Nhut."

"Yes, we received the report a short while ago."

Rick followed Jody into the office and was introduced to the CLD commander. They sat down, exchanged pleasantries, and Jody explained her predicament. Danton listened intently.

"To put it mildly, Jody, you are making an unusual request." He rubbed his chin wryly. "But it so happens the VIP villa is empty." He turned to Rick. "Perhaps we could let her stay there a day or so until she can get out to Hong Kong."

"We certainly would appreciate it if you could do that for her, Colonel," Rick said, relieved.

"You can be sure she'll be safe while she's with us," Danton declared.

"Oh, thank you, Jerry.

"We'll love having you, Jody. Just don't flaunt the fact that you're staying here." He paused grinning broadly at her. "Though it certainly would be impossible for you to walk around without being noticed."

"I'll maintain a low profile."

Danton laughed heartily. "Some low profile."

"Maybe we can finish your story and have you sign it before you leave," Rick suggested eagerly.

"I'll go on with it until the planes are flying again," Jody replied.

Jody's suitcases were brought to the VIP villa, and she was ensconced in the suite ordinarily occupied by the Special Forces highest-ranking officer. Danton, who had accompanied them to the suite, looked around. "Everything seems to be in order." He turned to Rick. "You can interview Jody here. If you need anything, a typewriter, pads, refreshments, just let me know. I might add, I think your investigation is important. I wish it had started years ago."

"Thank you, Colonel." Rick smiled wanly. "Your minority position is appreciated."

Danton nodded and left them alone. Rick placed the microphone stand on the table in front of Jody. "By the way, Jody," Rick opened casually, "how did you find out that Cotsworth and Jasper were behind your jewelry being stolen?"

"Marie Monahan found out; she knows everything. The one decent thing she ever did in her life was to write and warn me. She didn't dare send me a cable, they're all read by U.S. and Vietnamese authorities. Marie's letter reached me two days after my jewelry was taken from me, right in the street, a few blocks from the bank, when I was on my way to the jeweler who promised to buy it from me."

"That was a miserable break," Rick said sympathetically. "Let's talk a little more about the I House."

Still looking out over the gravel area, she saw Colonel Danton suddenly appear from around the corner and stride to the front door of the VIP villa. She turned from the window. "Colonel Danton is coming."

As the CLD commander walked into the room, his face presaged bad news. His lips were tight, his chin thrust forward. "What is it, Jerry?" she asked. He took her arm, led her to a sofa, and sat down with her, nodding briefly to Rick.

"I'm sorry to have to tell you this, Jody. We lost our fifth general killed in action last night. Brigadier General Springer."

Jody gasped, both fists going to her mouth. "Not Walt?"

Danton nodded sadly. "His chopper was shot down. He was flying over a battle with a battalion commander. Apparently he was getting out into the field a hell of a lot more than a deputy should."

"Yes, he hated that desk." Jody regarded Danton stoically, trying to keep the tears from coming to her eyes. "Do they know for sure he was killed when his chopper went down?"

Danton nodded. "They located the crash site and brought back the bodies this morning."

Jody shook her head as memories raced through her mind. The fight Walt had waged over her with Barking Dog, the bubble bath, how hurt he had been when she confessed her affair with Gambino to save her business. It was impossible for her to think of him dead.

"I'm sorry, Jody. But I knew you would want to know."

"Yes. Thank you, Jerry." She was silent a few moments. "I wish there was something I could do, some way of paying my respects."

Jody looked at Jerry Danton and then across at Rick. She stood up in sudden determination. "I've changed my mind. I'm going to testify in person at the hearings if you want me, Rick. From what you tell me, that should be more effective than sworn statements."

Rick stared at her. "You are?"

Jody nodded. "If Walt could give his life in this stinking war, I guess I can take a chance too. Whenever you want me I'll come along to Washington."

"Jody, I'd be a liar if I didn't give a loud cheer," Rick replied happily. "We'll contact you in Hong Kong."

Jody shook her head. "Forget Hong Kong. I'm through out here anyway. When will all the hearings take place?"

"In September, we expect."

243

"Well I have an idea," Jody said. "I'll go down to the Delta and sweat it out with the Special Forces there. I'll be safe as it's possible to be, and maybe I can do something for morale."

"Goddamn, old Pat Vreeman will be happy," Colonel Danton chuckled. "I envy him. If Jody doesn't shake up the Delta, nobody can."

"Rick, you and O'Neill can check things out with me any time you need to through the CLD. Jerry will always know where I am."

Rick glanced at the colonel, who nodded. "I appreciate that, Colonel. Well, she's in your hands."

"I'll call Pat Vreeman today and try to get out tomorrow," Jody said.

"Jody, you numbah one!" Rick said, mimicking the Vietnamese. "I've got to catch up with O'Neill now, but I'll see you here tomorrow before you head for the Delta."

"Would you go to my apartment and ask My Linh to give you my fatigues and combat boots? I'll be needing them," she said, and added, "I guess this is my way of paying my respects to Walt."

"I'll be seeing My Linh for dinner tonight and collect your gear then. See you in the morning."

He left the room as Jerry Danton was saying, "So, at last the Special Forces inherit Jody T. Neale. It's about time."

244

4

O'Neill permitted himself one of his rare shows of jubilance when Rick reported Jody's willingness to personally testify at the hearings. "Just what we need to breathe a little excitement into the proceedings," he said happily.

Rick frowned. "I want to hear those tapes. I wish she hadn't stashed them in Hong Kong."

"It's the safest place for them. She did the right thing," O'Neill said.

Major Unger, who was sitting in the investigators' office in USAID #1, asked Rick, "How about you joining O'Neill and me for a drink? We'll dig up old Alvin Bruce and celebrate our progress."

"Sorry, Ed," Rick replied, smiling happily. "I'm taking a beautiful lady to dinner at the Guillaume Tell and then back to her apartment. If I'm lucky, we'll get curfew bound."

"But you have a curfew pass, Rick," Unger pointed out.

"Sure, but she doesn't know that."

"Just to be safe, you'd better tell us where you'll be at all times." O'Neill said, giving the younger man a sour look. "Not that I want to interfere with your social life, but Senator Rothmann wouldn't like it if his special assistant disappeared. I'd be the one stuck with answering the questions."

"All right, O'Neill, if you must know, I'm taking My Linh out, and we'll be going to Jody's apartment for a nightcap afterwards."

"She has a military telephone line there," Unger said. "If you even think there might be trouble, call my emergency number. You still have it?"

"Engraved in my brain. But there won't be any trouble. My Linh and I have a message for each other."

"Don't you think of anything but broads when you're not working?" O'Neill said, and shook his head.

"Even when I am working," Rick confessed in mock remorse. "So long, fellows."

Outside, the staff car and Vietnamese driver assigned to the investigators were waiting. Being in Saigon with the civilian rank equal to general officer was not an unpleasant experience. Rick gave the driver Jody's Plantation Road address and sat back to contemplate the evening ahead with My Linh. While by and large he found the Vietnamese women skinny and brittle, when they were half French they came out gorgeous. He would have been proud to take My Linh to the most exclusive parties in Washington, he thought.

My Linh greeted Rick warmly when he arrived, pressing herself to him, raising her lips to be kissed. "I get you a drink," she said, slipping out of his embrace. "You like bourbon?"

"You remember," Rick said, pleased.

When Rick had finished his drink they left the apartment and drove off in the staff car. My Linh was impressed, although Rick downgraded his importance. With the exotic-looking girl sitting beside him in the restaurant Rick couldn't help feeling smug at the envious stares directed his way by the Americans who filled the prestigious restaurant.

As they dined and sipped the wine he had ordered his hand frequently went to hers and she returned the gesture with little squeezes. My Linh told him about Talltree and about her son. When Rick asked her where little Andre was, My Linh said that the boy was with her mother in Nha Trang. My Linh was afraid to bring him to Saigon for fear Jack Talltree would try to see him, perhaps even kidnap him and make her and the child live with him in the Cholon deserter colony. After a brandy and coffee, Rick escorted her back to Jody's apartment.

"I guess I'll have to let the car go. It's overdue at the motor pool now," he said as he helped her to the sidewalk.

"Maybe you go home while you have the car," My Linh said without enthusiasm.

"I can always get a taxi or a cycle," Rick countered.

"Not much time to curfew," My Linh dutifully pointed out.

"You let me worry about that." He handed a hundred piaster tip to the driver, who grinned his thanks and drove off. Taking My Linh's hand, Rick guided her into the building and up the stairs to Jody's apartment.

"You want a nightcap, Rick?" she asked when they were inside. He nodded. "Okay, I make for us both."

"Just a minute," he said. She turned and he reached out and pulled her to him. There was no coyness now. She melted to him, her lips meeting his eagerly. When he dance-walked her to the sofa and they fell onto it together, however, My Linh pulled herself away from Rick and stood up.

"Are you ready for that nightcap I promised?"

246

Looking up at her he grinned. "Sure. Let's have one."

Rick watched as My Linh walked into the kitchen. He listened to her open the refrigerator door, take out an ice tray, and break out the cubes, which she brought back into the sitting room. She made building the two drinks into a ritual. She came back to the sofa on which he was now in a sitting position, and kneeling she proffered one of the drinks to him. He took it, and together they sipped their highballs. Then, placing her glass on the floor, she took off his shoes and socks and massaged his bare feet. Rick leaned back and sighed contentedly. Later My Linh, sitting on the floor, her legs drawn up under her, her left arm resting across his thighs, leaned her head against his knees.

"What will you do without Jody?" he asked, deciding against telling her right away that Jody was remaining in country. "Have you thought of going back to Nha Trang?"

"I go meet Jody in Hong Kong soon," she replied. "Someday maybe I go to America."

"If there's any way I can help you, I will," Rick replied, his fingers in her long black hair. "I'm sure we could find an interesting job for you in Washington." He thought of what an enchanting figure she would be about Washington. He could have a lot of fun introducing her around. She would make a beautiful and exciting mistress for a while.

She lifted her head, turning her face to his. "Could you, Rick?" She thought a few moments. "I hear in America the pay is highest in the world."

"And so is the cost of living." He took a long swallow of his drink and put it down on the side table. Then he reached both hands out for her, pulling her to him. She put her glass on the floor and allowed herself to be pulled onto the sofa and over him as he lay back full length. Her face was over his now, and he marveled at the soft, exotic beauty of her almond eyes and pert Oriental features. Her hair hung straight down and around his face, so that the two of them were enclosed in a shimmering tent of raven tresses. Rick could not remember a moment as exquisite as when My Linh slowly lowered her face and pressed her parted lips to his.

Time became compressed as they lay together on the sofa. Later Rick was uncomfortably aware of the constrainment of his pants. Gently he worked his legs out from under her, swung his feet to the floor, and stood up, holding her in his arms. Submissively she put her arms around his neck, laid her head on his shoulder, and allowed herself to be carried into the bedroom. He placed her on top of the wide bed, and standing over her, unbuckled his belt, opened his slacks, and let them drop to the floor. Then he pulled off his shirt. My Linh lay on her back, her eyes closed. Rick sat beside her and began fumbling with the unfamiliar *au dai* she wore. In spite of herself, My Linh giggled.

"I will have to help, Rick. The *au dai* does not come off like the western dress." He helped her up to a sitting position and she reached her long fingers inside the high neck and unhooked a catch. The top of the garment came apart, revealing her tawny upper bosom. "Now I must stand up."

He helped her to her feet, and as she reached behind her to unbutton the blouse portion of her *au dai*, she gave him a shy smile. "Why don't you go out in the living room and turn off the lights. You can bring in your drink."

"I'll turn out the lights, but you're all the nightcap I need," Rick whispered and kissed her on the nose. Going into the next room, he examined the lock on the door. It seemed to be well bolted. Then he turned off all the lights. It was dark in the bedroom when he returned, but he could see that My Linh was lying in the bed, a sheet drawn over her. With trembling hands he managed to divest himself of his shorts. Then he felt for the upper hem of the top sheet, pulled it down, and climbed into the bed beside her. Instantly they were in a tight embrace, and he slid one hand over a firm breast, the face of his thumb caressing the nipple. She sighed happily as he kissed her.

Never could he remember a more sensuous, totally complete reward to his youth and virility than the love climaxes that imploded within his being, fission feeding on My Linh's avowal of her love for him and the intensity of her desire for him and the ecstatic pleasure with which she gave of herself to him. Finally, convinced he was in love with her, he fell into a deep, surfeited sleep, My Linh's slender body and long legs entwined with his.

The sudden shock of the pounding at the door was like an electric prod to his vitals. He sat bolt upright, sudden fear and total confusion gripping him. The abrupt movement had awakened My Linh, who sat up beside him, her breasts standing out full and firm. My Linh stared at him, terror in her eyes.

"Stay in here, honey," he said. "I'll see who it is."

"Don't let anyone in," she begged.

"I won't." He stepped to the floor and pulled on his shorts and slacks, then slipped on his sport shirt. He walked to the door, which was trembling under the blows.

"Who's there?" he called.

"Military Police!" a harsh voice came back through the door.

"What do you want?" Rick asked.

"Open the door or we'll break it down," the voice retorted.

"I'll open up if you'll tell me your business."

"We're looking for deserters."

No good! he thought. The MPs wouldn't be looking in Jody Neale's apartment for deserters.

"All right, take it easy," Rick called through the door. "I'll open up in a minute. Just let me get dressed."

"You've got one minute before the door goes down," came the gravel-voiced shout.

As silently as he could, Rick grabbed for a heavy, wooden straight-back chair, wedged it under the door knob, and ran back to the bedroom, where the telephone on the military Tiger line was located. He picked it up, listened for the dial tone, and then dialed the emergency number Major Unger had given him.

The ringing began. He glanced at My Linh, who was hurriedly pulling on her *au dai*. He tried to give her a reassuring smile. The number still wasn't answering, and thirty seconds was almost gone. The short, fast buzzes continued. Desperately Rick wondered if he should hang up and dial again or let the number keep ringing. Could he have dialed wrong. He banged down the phone and then picked it up. Again the tone signal. This time, with great care, he dialed the numbers, one by one.

Once more the sequence of double buzzes sounded in the receiver. At the same moment the banging on the door began again. My Linh huddled against him now, shivering in fear. The rings kept coming, and the men outside began to throw their shoulders against the front door. Then, over the phone, came a sleepy voice.

"Provost marshal, Major Unger's office."

"This is an emergency!" Rick barked. "Richard Townsend, staff of the United States Senate here. Send a patrol immediately to two twenty-nine Plantation Road. Apartment three D, Jody T. Neale's place. Someone is breaking in. Notify Major Unger instantly at his quarters."

"Yes sir," the voice came back. "Who is this did you say?"

"Townsend, Rick Townsend, U.S. Senate!" he shouted into the phone. "Hurry. Send a patrol and call Major Unger. Got it?"

"Yes, sir! Right now."

"Extremely urgent!" Rick shouted. He slammed down the phone and, with his arm around My Linh, walked her into the living room. "Let them knock it down. We're stalling for time now."

The battering at the door continued. In moments the hinges burst and the door flew off into the room. Four men in khaki uniforms with white belts and caps strode into the darkened room, peering about in the gloom. One of them reached for the light switch by the door and snapped on the overhead lamp. They seemed very young and thin, almost emaciated. The pupils of their eyes were contracted to small gleaming points, a sure sign they were on drugs of some sort. Their uniforms were loose and ill fitting.

"Where is Jody T. Neale?" the tallest of the four asked in a raspy voice.

"She's not here," Rick answered.

"Okay, gang, shake the joint down," the hoarse-voiced one ordered. As the other three spread out through the apartment and My Linh clung to him, Rick demanded, "Show me your identification."

The tall young man laughed and patted the forty-five-caliber automatic at his belt. "There's my identification, wise guy."

"You're not military police," Rick stated.

"That's right. And we don't worry about no Senate people, because we got much bigger problems. So if you dont want to get hurt, you and your girl friend better be quiet."

"They're Apaches." My Linh's voice quavered.

"That's right, sweet lips. You must be the girl we gotta bring back with Jody T."

"I'm not going anywhere," My Linh said defiantly.

The tall one let out a shrill, reedy laugh. "The chief won't be so happy to hear he's going in on a wet deck tonight." He leered at My Linh.

One by one the others returned to the living room. "We looked everywhere, she ain't here."

The leader clapped a threatening hand on the butt of his pistol. "Where is she?"

"I told you, she isn't here," Rick replied in loud tones. "She's left Vietnam."

"The hell she has," the leader shouted. "She couldn't leave, because Tan Son Nhut was closed until this afternoon, and we were out there looking for her. She's here in Saigon someplace."

"If you know so much, why do you ask us?" Rick cried.

"Look, Buster, we're taking this girl with us anyway. When we find Jody, we'll let her go." He smirked evilly. "If you want your girl friend back in good shape, you better let us know where Jody T. is real damned quick."

"Hey, Cochise," one of the other three called to the leader. "There's a Tiger line in the bedroom."

The leader looked surprised. "The chief didn't tell us that." He took a step toward Rick, drawing his forty-five. "You make any phone calls?"

"That's right. I called the provost marshal. The real MPs will be all over here in the next couple of minutes."

One of the intruders panicked. "Let's get out of here," he said. "I'm looking at twenty years if they get me."

The other two looked equally frightened now. The leader raised the pistol and pointed it at Rick's head. "Maybe you called, maybe you didn't. But if the MPs come, they gonna find you dead."

"Hey, Cochise," another deserter in MP uniform called. "Let's don't take a murder rap."

Rick looked from the narcotic bright eyes of the Apache into the ugly black barrel of the automatic and began to talk fast. "Look, feller, there's still a chance you might be able to return home one day. This war is becoming very unpopular in the States. But if you have a murder rap hanging over your head, you haven't got a chance." He stared at the leader, who was called Cochise by his companions. "You take my advice and get out of here now. The MPs will be around any minute."

Cochise laughed nastily. "You yella-bellied jerk. We're taking the girl and getting out."

"Your only chance is to get out now and run." Rick said, addressing himself to the other three deserters. "I promise you that if you leave now, without trying to take the girl, I will cover for you with the MPs and tell them it was the Vietnamese who broke in. I will also try to help you get back to the world without going to jail."

"I say *di di we*, Cochise," one of the Apaches cried urgently.

"Yeah, let's get out of here before we get caught," another seconded. "Fuck the girl."

"That's what the chief has in mind," Cochise chuckled, but the sound of sirens in the distance wiped the lewd grin from his face.

"You see, goddamn it!" the third cried in panic. "You don't lead me no more." He ran for the door and started down the stairs. The other two watched a moment and then turned, scurried out the door, and rushed down three flights of stairs. Cochise turned toward the door, gripped the banister with one hand, and rushed down the staircase.

Rick and My Linh quickly went out on the terrace and looked down into the street below. A jeep with four MPs followed by a staff car screamed up in front of the door just as one of the deserters ran out the front of the building.

Seeing the genuine MPs, one of the Apaches turned and ran back into the building, two MPs after him, their guns drawn. A sharp fusillade of shots echoed up the staircase. Rick ran back into the apartment and out onto the landing.

At the bottom of the circular stairwell Rick saw one of the deserters lying on his face on the cement floor. Two others were standing near him, their hands held high. He could hear the MPs shouting to each other as they pursued the fourth Apache, who had disappeared out the back door into an alley. A series of shots reverberated from behind the building. Rick held My Linh close to him as they walked back into the apartment and sat down, waiting for the MPs to come upstairs. He prayed that Major Unger would arrive in time to prevent his name from being involved in the fracas.

Although Rick was a proponent of free speech and at times a bitterly outspoken critic of the way U.S. high command in Saigon hushed up potentially embarrassing stories about the military, he suddenly experienced a one-hundred-and-eighty-degree turn in his thinking. The thought of Senator Mike Rothmann reading about his special assistant being in the center of a beautiful Eurasian girl's near kidnaping after having spent half the night with her made him shudder.

As though reading his thoughts, My Linh wept, trembling in his arms, "Oh, Rick, will all this make it so we not see each other anymore?"

"Nobody is going to keep me away from you, angel. I promise." And he knew he meant it. "Just let us handle everything, do all the talking, and everything will be all right."

5

It was eight thirty in the morning, and SPC Earl Picking felt a sense of relief, of having atoned for his sins, as he walked through Saigon's teeming streets toward USAID #1. Once he had signed the deposition that O'Neill had written up, it would be like paying all the bills and starting off clean.

Picking was thirty-eight years old and due to retire in another year. He looked forward to retiring in Japan and taking a Japanese wife who wouldn't drain his modest resources as his first wife had. Japanese girls definitely made the best wives, he thought. They lived to please their man, and never demanded to see the pink pay slip their husbands brought home from work. They were ideal until contaminated by the American wives.

He was nearing the old opera house, now the Vietnamese House of Congress, when, from the corner of his eye, he saw a motorcycle veer out of the main stream of traffic and start toward him. The cycle looked as though it were going to climb right up on the crowded sidewalk. His head swiveled as he looked around desperately for some niche into which he could flatten himself, but there wasn't even a doorway into which he could retreat. His eyes scoured the street for help, but there wasn't an American in sight.

Now Picking knew what was coming. In a way he had half expected it. After all, hadn't he found out about Sergeant Munn's decision to have the only witness to their pilferage put away? But here in Saigon, in broad daylight, would they try to get him? He started to run and tripped over a sidewalk soup kitchen, spilling rice and soup all over its squatting owner and falling flat on his face. He quickly scrambled to his feet and began running again—dodging the men, women, and street urchins—as the cycle relentlessly pursued him.

Suddenly, the open front end of the cycle lurched up onto the sidewalk. He looked over his shoulder for a fleeting moment and saw a Vietnamese wearing a white sport shirt and khaki slacks leveling a short-barreled, folding-stock carbine at him from the front seat. The weapon wasn't much longer than a handgun. Picking continued to run through the street people, crouching low to the sidewalk. Then the weapon chattered sharply—he realized it was on full automatic—and a barrage of thirty-caliber slugs tore through the crowd. He felt the searing pain in his side as he was hit. Another round ripped through his back, then another and another as he fell to the sidewalk, fingers of blood reaching out from him, pointing toward the gutter.

Rick Townsend returned to USAID #1 at nine thirty in the morning and found O'Neill and Major Unger literally ripping the office apart. Composition-board panels had been torn out of the walls and ceilings, the telephones were ripped down to bare circuits, lamps had been unscrewed from base stands, even the air-conditioning unit had been pulled apart.

"What the hell is happening?" he asked.

"We figured the office has to be bugged," Unger replied. "But damned if we can find where."

"Why are you so sure?" Rick asked.

O'Neill looked up from a sofa cushion he was inspecting. "Sergeant Picking was the victim"—his tone was heavily tinged with irony—"of what was reported as a terrorist attack. He was shot dead on his way here to sign his deposition. Three other people were killed and five wounded. They called it VC terrorism."

Shaken, Rick said, "Then they must know Jody is still around too. They would have heard me tell you yesterday evening that she was staying in country."

"That's the picture," O'Neill acknowledged. He kicked the pillow in disgust and scrutinized the room for other possible places of concealment.

"After what happened at her apartment last night, that was our conclusion also," Unger said. He grinned wryly. "Did you get back to sleep all right?"

"My Linh was afraid to be alone," he replied. "I had better get over and warn Jody T. right now. It may be—"

O'Neill cut him off with a sharp look, pointing around the room. Rick nodded. "I'm going out. I'll see you later."

Jody awoke at eight thirty in the morning. She had tossed and turned most of the night, dreaming of Walt Springer and Sergeant Crawley.

She dragged herself from the bed, and after a long shower, felt revived and refreshed. She pulled on a pair of tailored slacks and a shirt, then

254

plaited her blonde hair in preparation for the windy chopper ride down to Cao Lam. With her bags packed and ready to go, she went off to the mess hall to have a cup of coffee and a chat with the mess sergeant while she awaited the arrival of Pat Vreeman.

Vreeman arrived on time, accompanied by the ever-present Billy Wall, while Jody was in the mess hall. Vreeman and Danton took the opportunity to brief each other on the latest development in the field while Billy loaded Jody's luggage into the jeep they had borrowed from the CLD. For added protection, Danton sent two well-armed Chinese Nungs out to the jeep to accompany Jody and her party to the airport.

"Damn it," Jody said, turning to Pat as they were about to climb into the jeep. "I asked Rick Townsend to come by with my fatigues and boots, and he hasn't shown up yet. I suppose he stayed up all night and now he's overslept." She shrugged her shoulders.

"Forget it," Vreeman replied. "We'll have some new ones fitted for you. Are you ready to go?"

"I suppose so." Jody climbed into the back of the jeep between the two grinning Nungs and was waving to Jerry Danton when the motor pool car assigned to Rick turned into the drive. Rick jumped out and hurried over to them, carrying one of Jody's overnight bags.

"Here's your gear," he said, tossing it into the jeep. "Thank the Lord I got here before you left."

"Is something wrong?" Jody asked, realizing Rick was distressed about something.

"Plenty. What a morning this has been. First the trouble at your apartment last night"—he held up his hand at her expression of concern—"I'll tell you about it in a minute. But much worse, Sergeant Picking was murdered this morning. O'Neill and I are seriously worried for your safety. These people really mean business. On top of everything else, O'Neill is convinced that our office has been bugged. That means they know you are going to testify and give us those incriminating tapes."

"Poor Picking," Jody lamented, forgetting her own jeopardy. "He was never really one of the syndicate at heart."

"We feel the same way," Rick agreed. "But look, Jody, if you want to get that plane to Hong Kong this afternoon we'll understand. We don't want anything happening to you."

"Nothing's going to happen to Jody while she's with us," Vreeman boomed forth, alarmed that she might change her plans.

"I'm not backing down," Jody said grimly. "Earl's murder only makes me more determined than ever to testify. How is My Linh?" Jody asked anxiously.

"She's a bit shaken up, but she'll be okay. It's you the Apaches are being paid to get. She was worried this morning when I had to tell her you were staying in country." He smiled to himself. "Anyway, right now she's having a new and stronger door put in and planning to stay on at your place until she gets further word from you."

"I guess I've got the message, all the messages." She sighed deeply. "Let's get going, Pat. It will be good to get into the field again." Then, as an afterthought, she turned back to Rick. "I almost forgot. Would you have this letter delivered to Tony DeMarlo's office? I thanked him for his offer to back me in Hong Kong and told him I had decided to go home to Australia instead."

Rick took the letter and nodded. O'Neill and I will fly down to Cao Lam to see you before we return to Washington. We'll give you your tickets then."

"I'll be there," Jody said, and climbed back into the jeep. She sat between Billy Wall and Colonel Vreeman in the back. The two Nung guards sat up front with the driver, their carbines held in a ready position for immediate action. With a farewell wave to Rick and Jerry Danton, they were off.

6

As Rick Townsend stared at the decrepit buildings the car was passing he wondered for perhaps the hundredth time why he was allowing himself to be driven deep into the mysterious interior of Cholon. It certainly wasn't because of any assurance he might have given the Apache called Cochise, he told himself.

The Vietnamese driver provided by the motor pool with the sedan pulled the car to a halt. This was it, obviously. One of Talltree's men would be waiting to guide him to the leader of the Apaches. He thought of how My Linh had received the message from the GI deserter who had been known to him as Cochise. It had been handed to her on the street to pass on to him, a chilling reminder that the Apaches knew where she was at all times.

Apparently Cochise had passed on Rick's promise of help to Talltree and requested that the chief give the Senate investigator a chance to tell the deserters how they could get back to the world again without going to jail for long terms. Rick's main objective was to get further information on Cotsworth and his methods of operation. If at the same time he could find some solution to the hopeless existence of the young Americans who had deserted, some method of turning them back into effective citizens, it would be worth whatever risk there was involved in making this visit to the lair of the Apaches and their chief.

"You know where to find me later?" Rick asked the driver, who nodded and held up a piece of paper.

Rick took a deep breath, opened the door, and stepped out of the car onto the sidewalk. He looked about him at the swirling mass of Oriental humanity and immediately felt a hand on his shoulder. He turned and saw a tall, cadaverous young Caucasian man standing beside him. "Just follow me, sir," the youth instructed.

"You're from Talltree?" Rick asked.

"Right, sir. Let's go."

Rick followed his guide through a door and down a long, dark, evil-smelling corridor with doors on each side. At the end of the hallway, they mounted a flight of stairs; on the second floor they came to a large open window. The deserter stepped through the window and took a long stride, swinging through the frame and disappearing from sight. Rick stepped through the window and saw the window of the structure opposite, a long step away. The Apache guide was standing just inside the window, beckoning Rick to follow. Rick stepped out over the shoulder-width alley between the two buildings and, ignoring the Apache's outstretched hand, pushed off with his rear foot and stepped through the second window inside onto the floor.

For several minutes Rick followed the guide through hot, airless corridors, into rooms, out of windows and through other windows, across a rooftop, and, finally, into a large, interior air-conditioned room. Rick was sweating profusely, and the coolness was refreshing. There were perhaps two dozen young men standing about the room or sitting at a long table. All were wearing khaki slacks and drab sport shirts. Although he had never met Jack Talltree, Rick immediately recognized him from My Linh's description. His slightly puffy face was sallow from living in hiding and out of the sun. His black eyes glinted above the high cheekbones. Beside Talltree sat the deserter named Cochise. Rick nodded to him solemnly; Cochise nodded back.

There was no mistaking the heavy aroma of marihuana smoke. Many of the deserters were passing rolled cigarettes back and forth to each other, drawing deeply on them, their unnaturally bright eyes fixed on Rick. Talltree motioned to an empty chair at the end of the table opposite him. Rick walked to it and sat down.

"I see our messages have reached each other," Talltree said. Then a sardonic tone crept into his voice. "We are all grateful that you want to help us. Cochise here was the only man to get away from Jody's apartment that night. Somehow you convinced him you could really help him. You must be a very fast talker." He grinned at the tall, blue-eyed blond man beside him. "Cochise is one of my best hoods. He kills first and evaluates the situation later."

"I merely told him the truth, Talltree," Rick spoke up. "I said that if I could help you get fair treatment in return for turning yourselves over to the Army, I most certainly would.

"Well, I gave all my Apaches the word to come here and listen," Talltree said. "Some of them have been bugging me to follow up what you told Cochise about getting them back to the world again. They can listen to you and make up their own minds. I don't force any of them to stay with me, but as long as they are Apaches, they obey me without question." Talltree's voice and eyes became hard. "What's your deal, Townsend?"

"No deal as such," Rick replied. "Maybe if the U.S. Senate understood the plight of these men," he said, looking about the room, "something could be done to help them, perhaps by drawing public attention to them and their problem."

"Attention is the one thing we don't want," Talltree snarled. "The less said about us the better—for us and for our families back in the world."

"Don't you men want to see your families, your girls, your home towns again?" The hunger for home, the sadness, was clearly written on almost every face. "Men, I promise you that I will personally follow up on the case of every man who turns himself in. I will do everything in my power, both as a staff member of the U.S. Senate and as private citizen, to see that you receive a fair hearing and just treatment. Who wants to go home?"

Talltree, his voice laced with sarcasm, called out, "Like I told you men before Mr. Townsend came here, anyone who wants to go back to the provost marshal is welcome to get his ass to hell out of here right now. Personally, if the President of the United States was standing here and promising none of us would get a year in jail I wouldn't believe him. The Army's going to burn you. Bad! Hear? There's not a man in this room could hope for less than five years, and there's a few gonna get the rope even if they give themselves up. So, anyone who wants to see firsthand what U.S. Army justice is like, can go out of here with Mr. Townsend."

Rick watched as those who looked as though they might leave heeded their leader's words, their faces hardening. Talltree emitted a mirthless chuckle as he turned from his men back to Townsend. "Sorry about that, Mr. Townsend. You see, you just don't understand." Talltree stood up and prowled about the room gesturing toward the men as he spoke. "Almost every one of these men has run away from charges. With some maybe it's just AWOL to avoid combat. Others are charged with disobeying an order. Some of the boys are running from dope charges, not just using it but selling it. I guess you know why they want me. Killing an MP. There's no way I can ever go back, and my men know it. That's why they follow me. Nobody has more to lose than me. When a man deserts and comes here, whatever he's charged with is magnified day by day, week by week. No way any of these men ever going to get a fair trial. This life is better than an Army prison, right men?"

The deserters nodded and mumbled affirmatively. "Mr. Townsend, let me show you some of the benefits these men enjoy as members of my Apache gang. Just follow me." Talltree walked to one end of the room and opened a door to a hallway; Rick stood up and followed him. They walked together down the dank hallway until Talltree stopped and opened a door. "Take a look."

Rick stepped into the room and looked at a wide bed made up with yellow silk sheets. A beautiful, very young Vietnamese girl was sitting nude, her nubile breasts tilted upward. Between her legs lay a young man face up, his eyes glazed, smoking marihuana from a neatly rolled cigarette. The girl, with her long, delicate fingers, was rolling another.

"That's old Andy. He's mean as a krait, and that's the meanest snake in Vietnam. There's a murder charge against him, so he didn't even bother to come to hear what you had to say." Talltree backed out of the room and closed the door. He opened the next door and a gorgeous Eurasian girl looked up from the lurid magazine she was reading and giggled. "That's Yvette, she's one of mine. She's worth a hundred bucks a night. I let her keep ten, plow her myself once in a while, and she's happy as a pig in shit. Each of my men has two or three girls in his stable, bringing him in his bread." Talltree waved. "See you soon, Yvette." He closed the door and they kept walking. At the end of the hallway he opened another door.

"This is our club," he announced proudly. "Beats anything the officers or NCOs got." Two bare-bosomed girls stood behind a bar playing cards with each other. Gatefold pictures of nudes adorned the walls of the air-conditioned room. A young man was sitting naked on a sofa, a naked girl on his lap. Both were drinking beer from a can. "That's Abe. He's just coming down off his shot of H. He brings us in a lot of loot, selling heroin as far up as Cam Ranh Bay. I tell my men not to go beyond pot, but some of them get so depressed that grass doesn't do it for them anymore."

The club was small and intimate with a little stage at one end. The leather chairs looked like they came out of a big-city men's club. At one end of the club was a poolroom where two men were playing. "You should see the shows we have here," Talltree boasted. "Some of the top NCOs in the Nam, even some officers, come here whenever they get to Saigon. My Apaches have everything they want—girls, hash, pot, H, beer, booze—hardly any of my guys like hard liquor, that's mostly for our visitors. You wonder why they don't want to go to an Army jail?"

Rick shook his head. "No, but in the long run most of them, probably even you, would be better off facing up to the charges and getting home."

"Look, Mr. Townsend, whatever they might of done before they came here, they've done a hell of a lot worse to get their daily bread. We receive and resell heroin all over the Nam. Abe and a lot like him travel all over with good ID cards and travel orders, all the forms correct and signed by the right people. We have plenty of muscle at MACV. My boys have un-limited PX privileges; they buy everything they want and sell it on the black market. After a man has been with me awhile, he goes on a team that works with PX officers and top civilian businessmen to steal large shipments straight from the States and put them on the black market."

One of the girls behind the bar looked up alluringly. "You want drink?" she called to him.

Rick shook his head.

"You want me?" She laughed musically. "Shakee up good Yankee."

Talltree chuckled. "She isn't kidding either. She's a human vibrator. There's a PX major comes in here, two, three times a week, for that treatment. Take a little time, Townsend. Not many get to this place." Rick again shook his head. "How about a cold beer?"

Rick's throat was dry, but he had resolved not to drink anything.

"Sorry you won't join me." Talltree went over to a bottle cooler and took a beer can from it, opened it, and drank. "Well there's plenty more I could show you, but you get the idea." Talltree led Rick out of the club and back down the hall to the room in which they had first met.

Rick noticed that the number of men had dwindled in their absence to five or six. Talltree stared at them a moment, then said, "Are you guys going to go back and turn yourselves in?"

All of them shook their heads emphatically.

"Then get out and get up your bread. It's almost noon." He watched the last of his men leave and then turned to Rick. "I'm sorry you wasted your time, Townsend."

"It was an experience. Why did you let me come here, see all this, discover where you are? I'm on the other side, you know."

"There's nothing you can do against us, and I need my men to know that they're free to go their own way anytime they want." Talltree laughed loudly. "Cochise really thought you could get him back to the world. Had some of the others believing it too. I wanted them to see how things really are." Talltree finished the last of the beer, belched, crushed the can in one hand and threw it into the corner of the room. Then he sat down at the table and motioned to the chair beside him. Rick took a seat.

"Okay, now I'll tell you why I let you come here. First place, you could never find it again. In the second place, no MPs gonna come in here anyway. They leave that up to the National Police, and we take care of them. So let's get down to business. You're My Linh's boyfriend now," he stated matter-of-factly.

Rick was so taken aback he couldn't answer. Finally, he managed, "Just because I happened to be at Jody T.'s apartment when your hoods broke in doesn't mean there's a relationship between My Linh and me."

Talltree gave Rick a long, bleak look. "Let's save time. You know that My Linh's little boy is mine."

"Yes."

"You might not believe it, but My Linh and Andre mean more to me than anything else in my life right now." Talltree's statement left Rick unsure as to how to answer, so he remained silent. "I know you must be interested in her, considering the number of nights you stayed with her." Talltree held up a hand as Rick started to protest. "We watch that apartment twenty-four hours. What you and My Linh do is none of my business now. I just want to know that you will do what's right for her and Andre."

Rick felt a dull, metallic ache in his stomach. He had compromised himself so far that this gang leader had the right to question whether he did the right thing for My Linh. He quietly said, "Of course I plan to do what I can for My Linh's welfare. I promised Jody I would take care of her." He noticed Talltree's eyes narrow as he mentioned Jody.

"Talltree," Rick said, throwing the burden back onto Talltree's shoulders, "promise me that you will leave Jody alone, and I'll promise you that My Linh and Andre will be well taken care of for life."

Talltree stared at Rick silently, his eyes narrowed to slits. "There's nothing I can do for Jody T., but you owe My Linh all the help you can give her."

"That's pretty one-sided bargaining," Rick said forcefully. "There's nothing to stop you from calling your gang off Jody. That way you'll have two people looking after My Linh and Andre."

"There's a five-thousand-dollar order out on Jody Neale." Talltree's voice was low but menacing. "All of my Apaches know it and are counting on the bounty—half to the men who actually get her, the other half to be divided among all of us. Even if I ordered them not to get her, they wouldn't obey me. The two best hit men in our bunch are down in the Delta now. They'll get her in another two or three days. What you don't understand, Townsend, is that if I had refused the order, I'd no longer have been the chief of the Apaches. Our muscle and protection at MACV would have turned on me, we might even have gotten policed up, and Jody would be just as dead because one of the other deserter gangs would get her. Five thousand in green is very important to a gang like us."

Talltree's matter-of-fact manner and deadly logic made Rick shudder. "So Jody becomes the victim of a terrorist attack the way Picking was," Rick said bitterly. Maybe, he thought, he could at least get some information.

"They'll frag her," Talltree said with a grim look. "Like a rattler, the most I can do is give you a warning. But that's worth something. Now you do everything you can for My Linh. I'll see to it she has a few hundred dollars from me at the right time."

"Jody T.'s blood money? She wouldn't want it."

Talltree ignored the remark. "All of us are lost men. None of us is going to be taken. It's only a matter of time before we're killed one by one by the MPs. At least my son can have a chance if some American helps My Linh get out of the Nam with him. You owe it to her Townsend. She's been giving you some nice times. Just don't try to leave the Nam without taking care of her." Talltree fixed Rick's eyes with his own. "Hear?"

Rick stared back at the Apache gang leader. "I don't need to be threatened to do what's right. Now, if it's all the same to you, I'd like to go."

"No sweat." Talltree cupped his hands around his mouth and shouted a name. Almost instantly the guide who had brought Rick to Talltree appeared. "Take him out to the street." Then he said to Rick, "I hope you learned something from this visit."

"It was instructive," Rick replied dryly.

"Tell My Linh that, in my own way, I loved her," Talltree replied.

Rick followed his escort out of the air-conditioned meeting room and into a fetid corridor. Ten minutes later, hopelessly confused by the twisting hallways and tunnels, he was back on the street. His car was parked across the street. The Apache guide disappeared as Rick stepped into the sunlight and made for the car.

7

Jody's weeks with Lieutenant Colonel Pat Vreeman's Special Forces B Team at Cao Lam had been her happiest in Vietnam. The headquarters supported eight A Teams of twelve men each at various remote locations in the Delta. After a week at Cao Lam, Pat Vreeman started sending Jody out on overnight visits to the A Teams. These men lead a lonely life patrolling their area and training Vietnamese civilians to fight the Vietcong. It was a welcome change for them to see a visitor, especially a female round-eye visitor.

The men at these small, primitive camps told Jody she was the only woman they had entertained except for Maggie. Maggie, of course, was Martha Ray, an honorary colonel in the Green Berets, who devoted a great part of her life to visiting the troops in Vietnam.

There was nothing much to do on these overnight trips except talk, have a few drinks, and shoot craps. But just having a new face in the camp greatly cheered the men.

Most of the A teams in the Delta are located on canals. Since Pat Vreeman could not get a chopper without making a special request, they usually traveled by Boston Whaler.

One morning Jody was standing with Billy Wall and Pat Vreeman outside his B Team HQ building at Cao Lam, waiting for a helicopter to land. Jody was heading for an A Team on the Cambodian border that was too dangerous to approach by Boston Whaler; the VC frequently darted out of their Cambodian sanctuaries to shoot up American boats coming along the canals to resupply the camp.

Before the helicopter arrived, a jeep drove up to the headquarters building and two young sergeants, wearing the MACV patch at their shoulders and equipped with combat packs and carbines, stepped out. One of the sergeants walked over to Colonel Vreeman, saluted, and handed him a copy of his orders. Vreeman read them and passed them to Billy Wall. "Civic-action team," he explained, as Wall stared at the orders. "They seem to be the advance men of a larger pacification team coming in here."

Wall nodded and looked at the newcomers. "Only one kind of pacification program works out here." He patted the M-16 rifle slung over his shoulder. "If you think you're gonna get somewhere giving out shirts the color of the Vietnam flag and all that kind of good shit, you're wrong." He turned to Vreeman. "When in hell they gonna learn back at MACV these pacification programs don't work?"

Vreeman shrugged and grinned. "Well, if they want to give away two leg sergeants to the Cong, that's up to them." He turned to the newcomers. "We could use a couple of extra U.S. combat men here. Why don't you forget the civic action and add a couple of extra guns to one of our A Teams."

"Our orders, sir, are to make an assessment of civic-action programs that could be put into effect in your area," the sergeant said. "I'm Stennert, this here is Sergeant Markey."

"Well at least you're carrying weapons," Colonel Vreeman said approvingly. "Even grenades."

"We're prepared to fight if we have to, Colonel," Markey said confidently. He stared at Jody. "We sure never expected to see a pretty lady like you out here." He seemed unable to contain his surprise.

"Are either of you medics?" Jody asked.

"No, ma'am, but there'll be some on the team that follows us in," Sergeant Stennert replied. He wore his sandy hair longer than usual, she noticed, and there was something faintly unmilitary about both of their bearings. Perhaps the civic-action teams were more like civilians than soldiers, she thought.

"Ma'am, are you going to visit any villages today?" Markey asked. "Maybe we could come along."

"I'm going out to an A Team and put on a show for the fellows tonight," Jody replied. "If we get a chopper in time, I'll probably go down to the nearest village and see the people."

"Maybe we could go along with you," Stennert suggested. "Both Markey and I are new to this civic action."

"You'll get yourself greased if you go into any of those villages out where she's going," Billy Wall cut in. "I'd sure hate for this B Team to get the first pacification team we've had out here KIA."

"We'll take a chance. We gotta get out somewhere in the boondocks so we can make a report."

"Sir," Wall said to Vreeman, "I think it'd be a mistake to send them two out with Jody to Captain Horner's team. He's got all the damned problems he needs without a civic-action team stirring up the dinks in town."

Vreeman looked down at the orders in his hand. "Their papers are signed by a Brigadier General Hare, personnel officer at USARV. They say to let them go where they want and see what they need to see to make their evaluation."

"Anything that Rabbit Hare has anything to do with is crooked," Jody said vehemently.

The two sergeants gave her hurt looks. "We don't know nothing about that. The head of our team is Major Mason. We can't help who signed the orders."

Jody felt a tinge of remorse. "I didn't mean to say anything against these two sergeants, Pat. If they want to come out with me when that chopper arrives, I don't mind."

"I guess we have to let these men do their job," Vreeman said hesitantly, as he stared at the orders again. "I wish to hell Saigon would let me know when they're sending people out to me," the colonel grumbled.

"Sorry, sir," Sergeant Stennert said. "We'll try not to get in your way none. And we're both good in a fire fight if you need us."

"That's the kind of civic-action people we need. When the chopper comes you can go out with Jody."

"I think I'll ride out with them too, sir," Wall said, regarding the two sergeants suspiciously.

"Just make sure you come back," Vreeman cautioned his sergeant. "I need you here."

As was usually the case, the helicopter was late arriving at Cao Lam. It was mid-afternoon when Jody, the two civic-action sergeants, and Billy Wall took off. It was a short flight straight across the rice paddies, jungle, canals, and reed-filled swamps to the A Team. Less than twenty minutes later the chopper sat down, and Captain Horner and two of his sergeants ran out to the landing zone to meet them. They were expecting Jody. Horner, a short, stocky red-headed officer, wearing a broad smile that split his round face, ran up under the revolving rotors to help her out of the chopper. He seemed taken aback when Billy Wall and the two sergeants jumped out after her.

In the A Team mess hooch, Wall explained to Captain Horner the mission of the two civic-action sergeants. Although Horner grumbled about civic-action programs in an area where everyone outside the barbed wire was a potential VC, he was pleased to have two more American guns in his camp, which was probed every few nights. After Billy Wall left, promising that a helicopter would be in the next day to pick up Jody, Stennert and Markey were given quarters. Then, on Jody's request, an inspection party was formed to visit the nearby village built along the side of the canal. One of the civic-action sergeants accompanied them; the other elected to stay in the camp and get acquainted with the area. Jody had picked up enough Vietnamese to ask a few rudimentary questions and understand the answers.

"If they'd let us go over the border and get the sons of bitches where they think they're safe, maybe we could pacify the village," the usually genial Captain Horner growled. "Some night I'm going to sneak over with two companies of my strikers and wipe out the goddamned VC company over there."

"And spend the next twenty years in Leavenworth," his executive officer added dourly.

When, late in the afternoon, they returned to the A Team, the communications sergeant met them at the gate. "Sir," he addressed Captain Horner, "something's wrong with the generator."

"Can you fix it?" Horner asked.

"I can't figure out what happened inside it."

"That means no lights tonight," Horner groaned. "How is Jody going to put on her show if there's no lights?"

"Without the generator we've also lost the single sideband. I was just talking to the B Teams, something urgent, when it went. I can't get back to Cao Lam on any of the hand generator equipment.

Horner looked apologetically at Jody. "I'm sorry about those lights."

"Why don't you police up all the candles in the camp, and maybe there's some in the village," Jody suggested. "I promised you a show, and a show you'll have."

A wide grin returned to Horner's freckled face. He turned to his exec. "You heard the lady," Then to the communications sergeant he said, "Let's both have a look at the generator."

It was four in the afternoon when Billy Wall returned aboard the chopper, waved it off, and went to find Vreeman. The colonel was in the communications room, anxiously talking to the CLD in Saigon. He turned to Billy when he walked in.

"That guy from the Senate committee, Rick Townsend, just got through to me from the CLD. He said there are two guys down here in the Delta from the syndicate with orders to kill Jody."

Billy Wall let out a string of oaths. "I thought there was something wrong with those two civic-action sergeants."

"That was the first thing I thought of. I've got the CLD checking on them now. So far, they haven't found anything."

"Let me get Captain Horner on the sideband right now." The sergeant started for the radio.

"No good. Their sideband cut out while we were talking. I've had commo trying to get back to them for the last ten minutes. Besides, we don't know that these sergeants," he stared down at the copy of their orders, "Stennert and Markey, are not just what these orders say."

"Sir," Billy Wall said earnestly, "I *know* those two are wrong. I could feel it all along. We'd best get us a chopper and get back to Horner's camp if we can't get through by radio."

Now it was Vreeman's turn to swear. "I should have had someone hold on to the chopper that brought you back. I was so busy trying to get Horner back and get through to the CLD I didn't think of it."

"I'll get over to operations and see what I can do, sir," Wall offered.

"Right. Tell them it's an emergency. We still may not get any air. Us headquarters Berets are about the lowest down on priorities."

One hour later Colonel Vreemon, Bill Wall, and two heavily armed American sergeants piled into the sturdy Boston Whaler and set off down the canal for Captain Horner's A Team.

"There's no other way to get to Jody, sir." Billy took his position behind the light machine gun mounted on the bow of the boat. The other two sergeants sat back to back, their submachine guns trained on the banks of the canal. The colonel took the helm. All four men were wearing armored vests and helmets.

"The good Lord willing and the Cong don't rise, we should be able to make it in a couple of hours," Vreeman said with a grim smile. "We'll be getting there after dark. I just hope commo gets through to the gun ships and tells them not to fire on us after the sun sets.

In half an hour the B Team's speedy boat had left the murky brown waters of the main canal and was skimming over the green waters of a side canal. They were now in VC territory. The Vietnamese didn't use the canal, because the Communists stopped them and made them pay taxes; for that reason, the water was clear. Unlike the banks of the main canal, there wasn't a soul in sight on this one—an ominous stillness pervaded the atmosphere.

Water lilies and weeds had grown all over the unused canal and kept choking up the propeller, smothering the engine into silence. Each time this happened, the two flank sergeants had to lean out into the water and chop the tangled vines from the propeller with knives as the boat drifted perilously close to the bank.

At the A Team camp, Jody was sitting at the head of the mess table surrounded by Captain Horner's men; the two civic-action sergeants sat opposite her. Darkness was falling.

"Sorry about that generator, Jody," Captain Horner apologized. "Damndest thing I ever saw how it went out, almost as if someone did something to it."

"We found plenty of candles, sir," the executive officer said. "Soon's we finish chow we can set up the show in here."

"Right. Now, men," Captain Horner said, standing up, "as you know, two Americans have to be on guard with the strikers. Be just like Charlie to probe us during Jody's act. That means that two men are going to miss it." There were groans and moans from the men. "You can relax." Horner grinned and ran the fingers of his right hand through his close-cropped red hair. "Our civic-action sergeants have volunteered to pull guard duty during Jody's show. They're both fresh from Saigon, and they don't mind so much missing it." There were approving shouts from the A Team; the men nearest Stennert and Markey shook their hands.

"So," Horner went on, "I suggest we get the show started."

The team sergeant took the two volunteers out to show them the key positions on the camp's perimeter where they would stand guard. Meanwhile, the rest of the team set up the candles in a wide circle within which Jody would perform her famous strip show. Jody no longer had the taped music she had used two years before and had to rely on whatever records or tapes the camps possessed. She also no longer owned any stage costumes and had to strip off her regular clothing. However, the lack of props didn't diminish the interest of her audience.

It was dusk when the Boston Whaler emerged from the weed-clogged canal and moved into a wider river. Then, without warning, bullets ripped through the boat as machine-gun fire shattered the stillness from the shore. Vreeman pushed the engine to high speed as Billy Wall raked the shore from the bow with his mounted machine gun; the two other sergeants let go with their automatic weapons. The colonel guided the boat at full speed around a bend, all guns firing, and the attack from the shore stopped as abruptly as it had begun.

"I've been hit, sir," Billy shouted. His leg was dripping blood into the bottom of the boat. Vreeman turned the outboard engine over to one of the sergeants and went forward, opening his first-aid kit as he moved.

For the first time during this tour of duty, Captain Horner was able to extend an exceptionally magnanimous gesture to his Vietnamese Special Forces counterpart, Captain Buu. Horner and Buu sat on chairs beside each other, facing the ring of flickering candles. Buu's team of officers and sergeants mingled with their American counterparts, eagerly awaiting the start of Jody's show. The platoon leaders and company commanders of the five-hundred-man civilian strike force had also been invited to witness this extraordinary event. Jody's performance would mark the highpoint of the cordial relations between the Vietnamese and American allies at the lonely camp.

One of the Americans had produced a battery-powered record player and a stack of records. At her sign a young Beret turned on the record player and Jody walked bare-legged out into the circle of candles in the dark mess hooch and began her show.

After she was a few minutes into her performance she realized that the batteries in the record player were nearly exhausted. The music droned out of the machine in a slow, mournful tempo. To make matters worse, Jody burned her toes each time she inadvertently kicked over a few candles. But the Americans and Vietnamese loved it.

Out on the perimeter, the two civic-action sergeants slowly walked toward each other. When they met, they turned from the barbed wire and headed toward the center of the camp. The off-tempo music and laughter became louder as they neared the American compound. Soon they came upon a knot of Vietnamese strike-force troops peering through the screen doors into the mess hooch, trying to catch a glimpse of Jody in action.

The two Americans silently sent the diminutive Vietnamese troopers away and stood outside the door, watching Jody's show. The attention of every man in the room was glued on Jody. Markey slowly, carefully reached for the door handle and quietly pulled it open, then let it close again. Stennert nodded and cautiously pulled a hand grenade from his combat harness; Markey did the same.

Jody had stripped down to her bra and half slip. The men cheered as each article of clothing was tossed out, beyond the ring of candles. Jody stepped out of her slip and shimmied seductively in her bra and brief panties.

Markey reached with his left hand to pull the pin. Five seconds after it was pulled it would scythe the area around it with a spray of lethal fragments of steel.

By now Jody had unhooked her bra in the rear; only her large, firm breasts held the intimate underthing to her. Stennert gulped and held up a restraining hand. Markey shrugged and kept his hand on the pin as he watched the show. Both of them stared transported, as Jody approached the climax of her act.

Markey was unaware of the grenade in his hand as he watched the show, and neither of the assassins heard the put-putting of an outboard motor on the canal. Like stone statues they watched as, with a quick motion, Jody pulled her panties down her legs and wiggled her bottom, knees together. The men let out a lusty roar.

Markey pulled open the screen door, held it open with his foot, and reached for the pin on his grenade. Stennert, following his lead, moved into tossing range.

Markey had just pinched the pin when a burst of fire from an automatic weapon spun him around and slammed him to the ground. Another burst stitched through Stennert, who fell on top of Markey. The still-safe grenades rolled from their hands. Lieutenant Colonel Vreeman, followed by two of his men, burst into the open as the Americans and Vietnamese, reaching for their weapons, pushed out of the mess hooch and stood staring at the sergeants lying on the ground, red splotches spreading over their fatigues, the American B Team commander standing over them.

Jody hastily dressed and followed her audience outside. She took in the scene, and then went to Vreeman, who placed an arm around her. "Were they going to frag all of us just to get me?" she asked, her voice trembling.

Vreeman nodded. "I'm shocked that I could have been so taken in. Fortunately, Townsend warned us that two men were somewhere down here to get you." Vreeman turned on Horner. "Captain, why didn't you get your sideband working. You could have saved us a boat trip and Sergeant Wall a nasty wound."

Jody caught her breath. "Billy? What happened?"

"Charlie ambushed us, of course. Wall's in the boat."

Jody went down to see what she could do for Billy as Vreeman berated the A Team commander for not getting his generator working, so he could call in a medical evacuation for the sergeant.

"Furthermore," she heard Vreeman finish, "this is the last piece of entertainment that I ever let get into any of my A camps."

Vreeman was obviously in a state of shock himself over the catastrophe that had almost occurred. When Jody turned to the mess hooch with Billy Wall, one sergeant under each arm carrying him along, the two bodies had already disappeared. Later Pat Vreeman told her he had ordered them buried immediately. No report would be made. The longer it was before the syndicate learned their men had failed to assassinate Jody, the safer she would be.

Pat Vreeman had an earnest conversation with Jody while the communications sergeant labored over the generator and the team medic cleaned Billy Wall's wound and rebandaged it.

"Jody, until just now I figured we could keep you safe from anything while you were with us." He shook his head sadly. "Now I don't know. When we have to worry about Americans with legitimate orders right from MACV coming down here to get you I can't be responsible."

"I guess there's no way of getting away from Cotsworth's syndicate," Jody agreed.

"It cuts hell out of me to say it, Jody, but I think you'd best get to the States as soon as you can. I know these Senate investigators wouldn't want to lose their star witness."

"I'll miss all the men, Pat." She put her hand on his arm for a moment. "Especially you."

"I'm short anyway," he said. "Two months and I'll be back at Bragg. Maybe you can come down and see me. I didn't tell you, but the old lady is divorcing me. Too much Vietnam time I didn't have to do."

"I'll get down there if I make it to the States, Pat." She paused and swallowed. "Let's go into the dispensary and see how Billy's doing."

They found Sergeant Wall in good spirits, and a few minutes later, Captain Horner came into the dispensary to tell Vreeman that the generator was fixed and the sideband working.

"Get a medivac chopper in here right away," Vreeman ordered. "He can pick us all up."

"Yes, sir," Horner answered.

Jody was surprised and impressed at the speed with which the medical evacuation helicopter arrived, and she said so to Horner.

"Yes," the captain replied, as the chopper settled onto the landing zone, "We send out quite a few really bad cases, so they always give us priority." He glanced over at Billy, who had been rebandaged by the unit medic and was sitting up on a stretcher, puffing contentedly on a cigarette.

"Good Christ! If they see him looking that good they won't come so quickly next time." Striding over to Billy he said, "Throw that cigarette away and make like you're hurt bad. "Can't you groan some?"

As the two litter bearers picked up the stretcher, Billy threw away his cigarette, and Jody, Vreeman, and the two sergeants followed after the bearers, who jogged with their load toward the chopper. Running alongside them Captain Horner was anxiously calling to Billy, "Louder, groan louder! Cry out in pain, goddam it!"

8

A small Otter aircraft was standing on the ramp at Can Tho where Pat Vreeman had come to see Jody off to Saigon. "As soon as you're airborne I'll notify the CLD of your arrival time, Jody," he said as she stepped up into the plane. "You'll be safe with our people. But get out of Nam as quickly as possible."

"I will, Pat." She leaned out the door and kissed him good-bye. "I'll wait in Washington for you to get home," she added.

The pilot came aft, closed the door, buckled Jody into a seat, and then went forward to the cockpit. It was a comfortable trip to Tan Son Nhut. Looking down on the crisscrossing ribbons that were the canals and the flooded rice paddies, she wondered if she would ever see this country again after she left for America the next day.

A jeep with three Green Berets was waiting for her at Tan Son Nhut. Jerry Danton greeted her warmly and threw her pack over his own back. They drove to the CLD and Danton escorted her to the same room in the VIP villa she had occupied the last time she had stayed there.

"We planned a little party for you tonight, a farewell party," Danton confided. "Your friend My Linh will also be coming. She says she has very important things to tell you."

"I hope no more problems," Jody replied.

"No security problems." Danton looked about the room. "The hooch maid is around if you need her." He walked to a closet and opened the door. "My Linh left your clothes here."

"I'm glad. I was just wondering about what I'd wear tonight."

"You'll look good to us in your fatigues, Jody."

"I think I can do better than that for my last night in country," she said, looking at her dresses hanging in the closet. "I'll take a long bath and be with you in about an hour. Okay?"

"Of course. You and My Linh will join my table." Danton smiled, and left Jody alone.

Jody enjoyed the dinner and the party. Despite the eagerness of the Special Forces men to keep the girls occupied, Jody and My Linh did have a few moments to exchange news at the villa.

"I got your letters," Jody said to My Linh. "So you really expect to go to America with little Andre?"

"Rick is trying to arrange a good job for me at the language school. I might even become an American citizen."

"I'm so happy for you," Jody said sincerely. "It's too bad we can't leave together tomorrow."

"I wish we could," My Linh sighed. "But I must be patient. I know it will not be easy for Rick to do these things for me."

"Did you fall in love with him?" Jody asked.

"Yes. He's young, he's rich, he takes me to America. But I do not think he will ever marry me. I am happy though. I will work hard and be very busy and be nice to Rick as long as he wants me."

"What more could a man ask for?"

"You won't let him forget me, Jody?"

"Of course not. Are you still at my apartment?"

My Linh nodded. "It is very nice. I will miss it."

"So will I," Jody agreed. "But I've got nothing left to stay for."

"Yes, you must leave. The sergeants know you have not yet left the country, and they know that their assassins did not kill you. They still want you dead." She shook her head emphatically. "Three times some of your old 'friends' come to the door and ask where you are. It is good we both go."

"Do you think the Apaches are following you?"

"Yes, all the time."

"Then they know you're here. They'll suspect you came to see me."

"I come here quite often, both with Rick and after he go back home."

"Talltree hasn't bothered you?"

"He send me messages come see him. But I never go." They finished freshening themselves and then started back to the club.

The following morning Jody sat in the back seat of a small sedan that belonged to the CLD. Danton sat on one side of her and an intelligence officer on the other. An armed sergeant sat in the front seat beside the driver, and a jeepload of sergeants followed the car to Tan Son Nhut.

Surrounded by her watchful escort detail, Jody was lead directly to the immigration officials at the airport. Soon, surrounded by Special Forces men, she was seated in the passengers' waiting room. She was surprised to see My Linh enter and come over to her.

When My Linh reached them, Jerry Danton frowned. "Why did you come here, My Linh?" he asked. "You might have been followed."

274

"No. I look, but no see someone follow. I bring Jody money." She turned to Jody. "I know you not have much money, so this morning I sell some of your furniture and get five hundred dollar for you. Here," she said, thrusting an envelope at Jody. "I sell a bit cheap, but get green dollar."

Jody was touched, but apprehensive. "Thank you, My Linh. Maybe you should have mailed it instead of coming here though."

The airport police in their white uniforms walked through the waiting room and demanded that everyone not actually boarding the plane go outside the terminal and remain in an area reserved for the guests of passengers. Colonel Danton quickly convinced the White Mice that he and the other military men were on an official mission, but My Linh had to leave. "I stay outside, watch you go Jody," she called as she left.

The room was rapidly filling up with boarding passengers, and Danton and his men looked over every person who entered. "We'll take her out to the plane now, before the departure announcement," Danton said tensely. "Let's go."

The colonel took one arm and a sergeant the other as they walked to the gate beyond which the big Pan American jet clipper was waiting. Jody showed her tickets and travel documents to the attendant who let her through. As her three-man escort started to follow her, however, they were halted by the Vietnamese gate official, who told them that only actual passengers could go further. Danton shouted forcefully in English and broken Vietnamese that this was an emergency. A team of White Mice and U.S. MPs quickly arrived on the scene. Finally, the MPs were forced to back up the Vietnamese officials.

"I'll be all right from here, Jerry," Jody said. "Nothing can happen now."

Reluctantly, Danton stepped away from the gate, and the other passengers began boarding. He watched as Jody walked toward the steps to the plane, stopped, turned, and waved.

As Jody waved she noticed a group of Vietnamese police rushing toward the outside compound where My Linh had gone. There was great confusion at the scene as the crowd pushed and shouted to the police.

Jody stared at the scene in terror and desperately tried to find My Linh among the crowd. Then she saw a girl, My Linh, she thought, suddenly collapse and fall to the pavement, holding on to the man next to her as she slid down. She could hear screams all the way across the apron. The man My Linh had been clutching seemed to be under attack; My Linh herself was lying on the ground, people milling around her. Out of the corner of her eye, Jody could see Colonel Danton frantically motioning toward the compound. Then she started back across the ramp herself.

By the time Jody reached the wire-mesh fence, two Special Forces men were bending over My Linh. Colonel Danton had raced across to the compound and forced the gate open. When he saw Jody coming, he rushed to her and tried to walk her back to the plane. Jody, pulled her arm from his grasp and pushed her way through the crowd to where My Linh was lying.

There was Jack Talltree, his chest heaving, being held by one of Jody's escort Special Forces sergeants and two MPs. At his feet lay what looked like an exceptionally long-barreled pistol: It was a modified M-16 rifle equipped with a silencer and used as a handgun, the same model she had seen used by Vietnamese government assassination teams in the Delta.

"It was a mistake," Talltree was sobbing. "Not My Linh. I couldn't help it. She was all over me."

Jody, kneeling beside My Linh, looked up questioningly at the Green Beret sergeant. "It happened so fast," he tried to explain. "She must of seen this bastard with the weapon or recognized him or something. First thing I know she's on him." My Linh's face was frighteningly white; the large red strain on the bosom of her *au dai* was steadily spreading. Another Special Forces man took off his fatigue jacket and, quickly folding it, placed it under My Linh's head. "My Linh," Jody cried. "My Linh, can you hear me?"

The girl's eyes fluttered. She moved her lips, but no sound came. "Listen to me, My Linh," Jody was crying. "No matter what happens, I will take care of little Andre. Do you hear? I will get him to America and see that he is taken care of."

Jody thought she saw the trace of a smile spread across My Linh's lips. Danton put an arm around Jody's shoulders. "There's nothing you can do for her now, Jody," he said softly.

She looked up and saw the anguished look on Talltree's face as he stared down at the mother of his son. Grief stricken and horrified, she stared him straight in the eyes.

"Get on that plane, Jody T.," Talltree rasped. "I'm not the only one out here."

"Come on, Jody." Danton shouted.

Jody nodded automatically and allowed herself to be led away toward the plane, tears running down her face. "Jerry," she said, struggling to keep the sobs from her voice, "will you ask them to check on her baby in Nha Trang? Then write to me about him. I'll get him to the States and see that he's taken care of somehow."

"Certainly, Jody. Now come on and get on that plane." Danton's voice was tense with urgency. "You heard what that murdering bastard said."

The rear steps to the plane had already been rolled away, and a stewardess was anxiously waiting at the bottom of the first-class section for Jody to come aboard. The pilot had already started the far outboard engine as an emergency measure.

"They'll be rolling down the runway before they even get the door shut," Danton exclaimed, hustling Jody up the stairs. "Tell the pilot there is no enemy action. Just an accident," he shouted to the stewardess.

"I'll tell the pilot," the hostess said, relieved. "The control tower didn't

276

know what happened." She disappeared into the pilot's cabin as Danton stood just inside the plane for a moment with Jody.

He kissed her lightly. "Stay easy, Jody. We'll take care of everything. I'll write you at Townsend's office."

"Thank you, Jerry. Thank everyone for me again. Do what you can for My Linh. Her mother's address in Nha Trang will be in her purse."

"Don't worry. Everything will be taken care of." Colonel Danton turned and started down the steps to the ramp. The door was closed behind him.

9

The subcommittee in its present form was twenty-one years old, Senator Michael Rothmann mused to himself as he sat in his office, reading over the witness sheets his special assistant had given him to review before the day's hearings began to unfold.

He was inclined to view as irresponsible at best the conduct of some of his predecessors on this subcommittee. In his own case, he found it distasteful to preside over a body that had left strewn in its wake the shattered careers of so many men obliged to appear before it. That they were guilty to a greater or lesser extent of wrongdoing, did not ease Senator Rothmann's concern for the havoc wreaked in their lives by the subcommittee.

The senator reflected on some of the more notable accomplishments, if they could be called that, of this committee. There was the raucous romp (when the subcommittee was only two or three years old) through the manufacturing concerns doing business with the Administration. He recalled the parties, improper gifts, and alleged payoffs that were unearthed in the probe on influence in government procurement. During those hearings, the subcommittee popularized the term "five percenters," referring to persons who used influence to secure government contracts for others and received five percent of the value of the contract for their efforts in cash.

Mike Rothmann thought of some of those leaders who had played important, truly useful roles in the activities of the committee. In the days before the subcommittee had been cast in its present form and was still known as the Special Committee to Investigate the National Defense Program (the so-called War Investigating Committee) Senator Harry S. Truman had been its chairman.

Others who served prominently on the committee were Richard Nixon and John F. Kennedy. Robert Kennedy had been General Counsel of the committee as had William Rogers. But the abuses of his most flamboyant predecessor, Senator Joe McCarthy, made Rothmann resolve that he and the sincere chairman of the subcommittee would do everything possible to guard against the kind of witch-hunting that had been the keynote of the McCarthy investigations.

Later, during the "hound's-tooth clean" Eisenhower Administration, the committee made it known to the world that the most elegant people wore vicuña coats. Still in the fifties the committee was being used more for political retribution than for its real purpose. In establishing the Permanent Subcommittee on Investigations, the Senate had sought to keep itself informed concerning the efficiency and economy of the operations and agencies in the executive branch of the government.

As the subcommittee grew from its rambunctious childhood to its more thoughtful youth, it held hearings into labor racketeering which led to important legislation, as well as many conflict-of-interest cases against high administration officials. It was the subcommittee that made known to America a new phase: *La Cosa Nostra*. And now, thought Rothmann, the Permanent Subcommittee on Investigations, under its dedicated leadership, had reached maturity.

At this point in the subcommittee's history, Rothmann was acting chairman for the latest and strangest investigative hearings over which he had ever presided.

Wryly Mike Rothmann looked at the newspaper clippings spread out before him. The American Civil Liberties Union was attacking him for making these hearings public. Why, the ACLU asked, couldn't Rothmann and his subcommittee take their case secretly to the Department of the Army or Justice and ask them to clean up their own house?

Through an intermediary, Rothmann had answered the ACLU. The executive branch has had the past four or five years to clean its own house, he explained. As a matter of fact, much of the evidence and information the subcommittee staff had assembled came right from executive-branch records. It was also true, he said, that many concerned persons in the Army and the government had assisted, indeed encouraged, the subcommittee to go ahead. They were convinced that only in this way, through public hearings held by the Congress, could the conspiracy be cracked. The ACLU letter attacking the senator had been released to the press twenty-four hours before the original had come across his desk.

What stung him most about this ACLU attack was that Senator Rothmann's record throughout twenty-five years of public service clearly showed his interests were in the field of individual liberties, health, welfare, decent housing for the poor, and saving the cities.

The senator sighed deeply as he sat at his desk, reading over the witness sheets. They plainly indicated the full scope of the hearings. Men once considered outstanding officers and NCOs would be incriminated. Civilian entrepreneurs would be vulnerable to indictments and Internal Revenue Service scrutiny. Clearly, the investigation was a bombshell that could implicate a large segment of the Army's Vietnam bureaucracy.

As Rothmann pondered over the documents, Rick Townsend came into his office. He glanced down at the Senator's desk, noticed the ACLU attack clippings, and frowned. Then, looking up, a more cheerful expression came to his face. "We have Jody T. Neale coming on next, sir. She should spark things up a bit."

Rothmann nodded. "Fine. Fine." He followed Rick out of the office and into the corridor of the old Senate Office Building. A few minutes later they were in the subcommittee room, located behind the hearing room.

"The television cameras will be running most of the time this witness is on, sir," Rick said. "I had thought they'd just grab a few minutes and then switch off their lights."

"I understand, Rick. They're primed for an unusual witness. Well that's journalism. I guess you can't blame them."

A few minutes later Jody T. Neale entered the hearing room. For the only time since she knew O'Neill, Jody saw him actually smile. It was a warm, appreciative smile, and his eyes had a happy twinkle to them. Senator Michael Rothmann also gave her an encouraging look, and she took her seat. Rick Townsend stared at her from his seat behind the subcommittee table with undisguised pride and admiration. The television cameras in the hearing room had not stopped whirring since Jody was called to the stand. The press noted her every word as she answered the questions put to her by the senators who sat on the subcommittee.

At the start of her testimony, she deviated from the carefully prepared statements Rick had worked up for her. Rick looked deeply disturbed; O'Neill was frowning ominously. But her manner of telling her story of corruption and fraud soon captivated the two hundred or so journalists and spectators in the hearing room.

"I will probably never be able to work in Asia again, certainly not in Vietnam," Jody said. "Having to close my business because I would not cooperate with certain military personnel who demanded sexual favors and kickbacks was a personal tragedy. I am faced with an uncertain future at best. But there is a far greater tragedy in this situation than losing my business. That tragedy is the terrible disservice being done to America's GIs in Vietnam. They risk and give their lives in a massive military effort and they ask very little in return. Yet they are exploited by a widespread syndicate of cynical men who are making millions of dollars at their expense."

For two hours Jody electrified the spectators in the hearing room as she freely told of her three years in Vietnam. She left out no names. Occasionally she met the eyes of Sergeant Major Cotsworth, who sat ramrod stiff in one of the front rows as he and Sergeants Elroy "Jesse" James, William

"Red" Fisher, Ben Bigley, and Willy Halaby listened stony-faced to Jody's account, their lawyers beside them.

The senators, shocked and indignant, made outraged comments as Jody's well-documented testimony continued. After complimenting Jody on her statement, one of the senators went on to say, "During World War II I proudly wore the shoulder patch of the Ninth Infantry Division." His eyes met Jody's as he went on. "I'm appalled at the statements you have made about the deterioration of the activities of some of the enlisted men.

"Now General Westmoreland," the senator's voice began to rise, "he too wore that shoulder patch of the Ninth Infantry Division. I will call and ask General Westmoreland to investigate this thing and have the officers of the Army who are responsible brought to justice. Many of us in the Ninth Infantry Division, and I know in the Twenty-fifth, were interested mostly, as you suggest, Miss Neale, in combat and not very much concerned with clubs and so forth."

The senator's voice vibrated with wrath as he glared out at Cotsworth and the other sergeants. "But the officers, enlisted men, and others who are responsible for this deterioration of a proud division should be brought to justice and properly punished." He glanced back at Jody. "Thank you, Miss Neale for bringing this to our attention at great personal cost."

Jody then answered questions concerning slot-machine operations and civilian involvement, with special emphasis on Joe Crust and his Snead Electronics Company. She revealed General Hare's connection with Joe Crust and, finally, she told what she knew and had observed of General Crowninshed's activities. The committee staff wanted to implicate Crowninshed, so that they could continue investigating him in connection with currency manipulations.

Finally, after a grueling two hours, she had told her story. The reporters were jerking their pencils across their notebook pages with excitement as they wrote. "Miss Neale," Senator Rothmann summarized, "you testified that on more than one occasion at the International House people said they hoped the war would not end, so the bubble would not burst. We recall other wars in which the United States has been involved. There was austerity at home, and there was austerity where the war was being fought. Not only is there corruption in the club system, but, in the next phase of our investigation, into the black market in currency, we again see corruption to a staggering degree. It is one of the great tragedies of the Vietnam war that the men who are out in the field, being shot at, wounded, and killed are the only ones who are really making a sacrifice. We want to thank you, Miss Neale, for coming here. We are most appreciative."

Jody stood up and headed for the door at the rear of the room. The press however had many more questions to ask her; they were waiting in the hall outside the hearing room. Rick, who had followed her out, stood apart watching her field the questions of the journalists.

She spotted Rick and went toward him, taking his arm, relieved. He began to usher her away from the press. "Come on, Jody, let me get you out of here. You've given them enough excitement for one day."

"When are the sergeants going on the stand?" she asked.

"Tomorrow morning. But you don't want to sit in, do you?"

"I'd like to hear how they answer the questions put to them."

"The newspapers will carry it. And we're getting General Walter tomorrow also. I'll tell you all about it."

"Okay. Take me back to my hotel. I could use a rest. Pat Vreeman is coming up from Fort Bragg tonight."

"Wherever you go, you'll be the big celebrity," Rick said.

"Maybe we'll just stay in my room. I didn't know it was going to be like this."

"Wait'll you see the TV and newspapers."

As they walked out of the Senate Building to the street, more flashbulbs popped. They ignored the photographers and strode down to the parking lot where Rick had his car parked.

When Sergeant Major Tom Cotsworth took the Fifth Amendment on the advice of his lawyers, the hard-line senators settled down grimly to ask questions they wanted included in the record.

"Were you a frequent guest at the villa of Joseph Crust?"

"Did you ever hold a meeting in the home of Master Sergeant Elroy James at Fort Benning to discuss strategy for currency manipulation and capturing control of the NCO club system in Vietnam?"

"Have you ever discussed currency manipulation with Major General Arjay Crowninshed, Retired?"

The senators ran through all the facts that their investigators had uncovered. Sergeant Major Cotsworth answered each question with the same monotonous line: "Under the rights granted me by the Fifth Amendment of the Constitution of the United States I refuse to answer that question on the grounds that my answer might tend to incriminate me."

Finally, an angry senator snapped, "Wouldn't you say, Sergeant Major Cotsworth, that you are a disgrace to your rank and to the United States Army and the uniform and decorations you are wearing?"

"I refuse to answer . . ."

"Isn't it a fact that you have committed treason against your government and deserve to be prosecuted, found guilty, and appropriately punished?"

"I refuse to answer . . ."

After a severe tongue lashing from the senators, witnessed by the people of America on television, the subcommittee let Cotsworth off the stand with recommendations that the Judge Advocate General and the Justice Department immediately take steps toward criminal prosecution.

Elroy James followed Cotsworth's lead and received the same verbal

282

punishment. Then came Willy Halaby, Red Fisher, and the rest of the club custodians. Sergeant Anthony Gambino, who had already been destroyed by Jody's testimony, came up last.

Jody almost began to feel sorry for him. He had already lost his family and all the money he had diverted to his own account. It was only a matter of the number of years he would serve in an Army prison.

General Crowninshed had refused to testify, and since he was a civilian and living in Vietnam, the committee was unable to subpoena him or Joseph Crust. Norman and Lavinia Ferris made the mistake of coming back to the United States for a visit and were subpoenaed.

Lavinia, her fleshy body barely contained in a tight, shiny black dress and wearing a large, feathery hat, looked exactly like what she was—an ex-patriate floozy of highly questionable morals. She denied all charges of paying kickbacks and denied knowing Cotsworth or any of the custodians other than casually. She testified to receiving an income of thirty thousand dollars a year. The senators referred her case to the IRS for prosecution on income-tax evasion and to the Justice Department on charges of perjury.

Brigadier General Robert Hare did not take the Fifth Amendment. Instead he lied. The senators accused him of perjury and recommended that the Justice Department prosecute him.

But all the testimony that came after Jody's dramatic appearance was anticlimactic. Even Arthur Line's factual account of Joseph Crust's dealings with Brigadier General Robert Hare could not compete with the effect of Jody's story. It was her indictment of the corrupt sergeants and generals, mentioning Hare and even General Walter by name, that made it necessary for the Justice Department and the Army to start cleaning house.

A week after the end of the hearings, Rick and O'Neill were hosting their two star witnesses, Jody T., and Art the Cork, at the Rotunda Restaurant, just a few blocks from the Capitol.

"Well, our Rabbit has been demoted to the rank of colonel, retired, and had his Distinguished Service Medal taken away," Rick said, exultant. "He's going to be up for court-martial next."

"Along with General Walter," O'Neill added. "They can get him for fraudulently acquiring guns for his personal use and not reporting his profit to IRS on their sale. I can prove he sold guns to a revolutionary group in Florida for the purpose of launching a revolution in Haiti."

"What about Cotsworth and his gang?" Jody asked. "They're the one's who tried to kill me."

"Every one of them will be court-martialed and jailed. Oh, the Army will stall it off because too many high-ranking officers were directly involved. I expect that if it was pushed we could show that the Chief of Staff was somehow implicated. Anyway, Senator Rothmann won't let the Army get away with putting off a final day of reckoning for Cotsworth and the others indefinitely."

Do you guys think you'll ever get Crowninshed on currency manipulation?" Art asked. "He was the biggest."

O'Neill nodded. "I'm quietly digging away. Probably between your testimony and what the Justice Department can get out of Cotsworth by making some kind of a deal with him, we'll catch up with Crowninshed."

"So what do I do now?" Jody asked. "I'm broke, and on top of everything else, I've got to find a home for little Andre."

"I think we've done that, Jody," Rick answered. "And anything within our power we can do to help you we will."

"Well, I'm sure as hell never going to get rich and open my club in Sydney now," Jody lamented.

"I'll find some dodge we can get into together, Jody," Art offered.

"Thanks Art, but I'm not looking for a dodge anymore." Jody smiled bravely. "I've taken care of myself this long, I guess I still can." Even O'Neill seemed to have a slightly guilty look on his face.

"I'm going down to Fort Bragg for a while," Jody went on. "Being around those guys will help me find where my head is. I know one thing, I'll never go back to the Orient again while Joe Crust is alive. He's got a permanent order out on me."

"Yeah," Art the Cork mused. "Joe Crust goes ever onward and upward."

"Isn't that always the way?" Rick asked rhetorically. "The master planner, the head of the octopus, remains free to continue corrupting those he can use. He did it in Germany with the occupation troops, he did it in Korea, he did it in Vietnam, and he'll do it again wherever the next buildup occurs."

"Amen," Art said. "Joe Crust's favorite saying was that every man, from four- or five-star general down to private, has his price and can be bought. Joe will always be right there buying them."

"And I have ten or fifteen years left in me to continue investigating and exposing them!" O'Neill lifted his glass to the self-proposed toast and drank deeply.

284